Again, but Better

Again, but Better

CHRISTINE RICCIO

WEDNESDAY BOOKS
NEW YORK

For my parents. I love yous.

AGAIN, BUT BETTER. Copyright © 2019 by Christine Riccio. All rights reserved. Printed in the United States of America. For information, address St. Martin's Press, 175 Fifth Avenue, New York, N.Y. 10010.

www.wednesdaybooks.com
www.stmartins.com

Designed by Anna Gorovoy

Library of Congress Cataloging-in-Publication Data

Names: Riccio, Christine, 1990– author.
Title: Again, but better / Christine Riccio.
Description: New York : Wednesday Books, [2019]
Identifiers: LCCN 2019002944 | ISBN 9781250299253 (hardcover) |
    ISBN 9781250299277 (ebook)
Classification: LCC PS3618.I279 A74 2019 | DDC 813/.6—dc23
LC record available at https://lccn.loc.gov/2019002944

Our books may be purchased in bulk for promotional, educational,
or business use. Please contact your local bookseller or the Macmillan Corporate
and Premium Sales Department at 1-800-221-7945, extension 5442, or
by email at MacmillanSpecialMarkets@macmillan.com.

First Edition: May 2019

10 9 8 7 6 5 4 3 2 1

Author's Note

Dear Reader,

This book you've picked up is the one I needed to read in college. Putting yourself out there to have experiences and meet people—"doing college," if you will—can be really difficult. Freshman through junior year I ended up spending almost all of my free time in the dorm with my books. I buried myself in novel after novel, finding solace in the adventures of other girls. But in the end they did little to ease my growing anxieties about impending adulthood.

The young women in all the YA books I loved were high-school age. By eighteen, the majority of them had saved the world, not to mention: kissed people, traveled, been in a relationship, had sex. At twenty I felt like a pathetic, unaccomplished, uncultured, virgin grandma. It sounds like a joke now, but at the time, around all these people my age casually discussing all of the above, I felt so small.

I, so badly, wanted to read a coming-of-age story about someone who was twenty—someone who was still finding themselves and struggling with becoming an adult even after they hit the double-decade mark. I needed to know there was at least one other twenty-plus person out there feeling as alone and lost as I was. At the time I couldn't find one.

This is for all the teens/young adults/adults who feel like they've been left behind. You're not behind. You have time to find yourself and love and adventure. It's all out there, and when you're ready to push yourself out of your comfort zone and look for it, you'll find it.

Again, but Better is fiction, but inspired by my own experiences. Thank you so much for picking it up. I hope you enjoy. ♥

xo, lovely day, sincerely, best,
Christine Riccio

Part 1

2011

1. Take a Chance

I'm leaving the country because I have no friends.

That's what it comes down to. People can continue along most paths, however unpleasant, if they have at least one good friend with them. Not having one has forced me to consider my path-changing options. Now, I'm thousands of miles over the Atlantic in a giant hollowed-out pen with wings, on my way to a study abroad program that's irrelevant to my major.

My parents don't know about the irrelevant part. Every time I think about it, my hands start shaking.

I grip the armrest nearest to the window. *No second-guessing.* I fold forward, trying not to bang my head on the seat in front to me, and extract the pen and notebook from my book bag on the floor—writing usually helps. I find it cathartic to pour out my soul via pen and paper. These days all my notebooks are Horcruxes, so I've started titling them accordingly; Horcrux notebooks one through eight are piled up in a Rubbermaid under my bed back in New York.

This new notebook makes a satisfying noise as I pull back the cover and flip it around to view my first entry.

1/1/11

COLLEGE, TAKE TWO: STUDY ABROAD GOALS
1) Kick ass at internship—turn it into a paid summer job.
2) Make friends you like to hang out with and who like to
hang out with you.

I'm going to make friends. I *am*. I'm going to talk to people I don't know like I already know them—that's the secret. I've watched my cousin Leo do it in school for years, and I'm ready. These friendless times call for extreme outgoing measures.

I click the pen and scribble down four more goals.

3) Kiss a boy you like. Stop kiss-blocking self.
4) Have adventures in the city you're in. You've done nothing
in New York City during the 2.5 years you've been there,
you idiot.
5) Maybe try getting a little bit drunk. Don't black out or
anything, but find out what it's like in a controlled, self-
aware environment. You're legally allowed to in the UK!
6) Start your great American novel. You've spent an absurd
amount of time trying to think of the perfect first sentence.
Stop it. Just write.

"What's that?"

I startle, my arm flying up instinctively to cover the page. The woman next to me—a slim forty-something-year-old with a pile of bright red hair on her head—eyes me impatiently.

"What?" I sputter.

"How in the world does one kiss-block themselves?" she asks in an irritated British voice.

My eyes bulge. "I—"

"How old are you?" she presses.

I'm silent for a beat before mumbling, "Twenty."

The left side of this woman's lip curls up in alarm. "Are you saying you're twenty years old and you've never kissed anyone?"

Leave it to me to get heckled by a stranger on a plane. I look away pointedly, unwilling to confirm or deny. This is never worth discussing. People can't handle it. They get condescending, like you've suddenly morphed back into a ten-year-old. General PSA: Kissing people doesn't make you better than non-kissed people. *Sit down.* And self-kiss-blocking is a real thing. I've experienced it. I've gotten close a few times, with random dancing frat dudes at parties my roommates dragged me to. When the time came, I turned away out of pure terror. I believe my exact thoughts were: *Demon, demon! Too close to my face!*

"How interesting. Am I to assume you're friendless as well?" Red-haired woman brings me back to the plane.

I shake my head in disbelief, glancing down at my list, and back up at her. "Oh my god."

"Why don't you have friends?" She cocks her head to the side.

I exhale a flustered breath. "I . . . I have friends at home, just not at college, because I did it wrong."

Not a lie. They're just not close friends. More like acquaintances I met through Leo back before puberty. Nowadays, Leo and I don't talk anymore, so, by proxy, Leo's friends and I don't talk either.

Did Leo ever even count as a real friend? Do cousins count as friends?

"I didn't know you could *do college* wrong." The woman rolls her eyes.

I hold back a scoff, thinking back to the list I jotted down in Horcrux Eight last month:

HOW TO DO COLLEGE WRONG:

1) Don't make friends outside your dorm room.

2) Don't get involved in extracurriculars you might enjoy.

3) Don't talk to people in your classes.

4) Stay in bingeing every show the internet has to offer.

5) Pick a super-hard major to please your parents.

"Well, you can." I add in calmer tone, "I'm going to London to fix it."

"London's going to give you friends?" She sounds way too amused.

"It's a fresh start!" My voice tightens.

She raises an eyebrow. I bob my chin up and down, more for myself than the lady, before turning back toward the window.

"Well, it's a doable list. I believe in you," she finishes.

Her unexpected encouragement strikes a chord in my chest. I glare out into the darkness with glassy eyes. Fear roils around in my stomach, making me all twitchy and uncomfortable.

When I first saw the Literature and Creative Writing program on the YU London study abroad site, my heart left my body, got in a plane, and scribbled out *YES* in giant, building-sized letters across the sky. The idea of leaving my current life behind: bio, chemistry, physics, the MCATs, even my family, and starting over with a clean slate—it was *everything*.

Last week, it was all that got me through vacation. This past Sunday, the fam and I were in Florida, fresh outta church (to quote my father: *Just because we're on vacation doesn't mean we skimp on church—we're good Catholics*), Dad caught me alone, reading in a little cove away from the hubbub of everyone else. To my horror, he snatched the book out of my hands. "What are you doing? Get in the water! Talk to us! Spend time with your cousins!"

I scurried over to sit on the edge of the pool where the cousins were socializing. My ten cousins are boys ranging from age eleven to nineteen. Joining them by the pool at any given time means subjecting oneself to verbal assault.

Maybe *verbal assault* is dramatic; more like volunteering as a human joke target.

It wasn't always like this, especially with the oldest, Leo. But it's like this now. They'll start talking about drinking: *Shane, do you even go to parties? Why the fuck do you come home every other weekend?* Roaring laughter. *Antisocial!* They start talking about relationships: *Shane, do you ever talk to people other than your parents? Why don't you ever have a boyfriend?* Sometimes I try to chuckle along with them. I'll treat them to endless eye rolls, cheeks burning, lips sealed in a tight line. But I keep quiet because I'm outnumbered. Super-fun times.

I close my new notebook. I take a second to admire the *See You in Another Life* word art I doodled across the front of it earlier while I was waiting to board, before shoving it back into my book bag. I pop the buds dangling around my neck back into my ears and set the Beatles to play on my iPod. My parents have been playing them for as long as I can remember, and their songs have become sort of a default calming mechanism. Four hours left. Four hours till new first impressions. New classes. New surroundings. New country. Try to find sleep, Shane.

2. Make a Change

I didn't find sleep, but I did find the taxi line outside the airport, so here's to that. Now, London hurtles by my window as we barrel down the wrong side of the road en route to my new home, the Karlston.

According to the *So You're Going to Study Abroad* pamphlet I reread five hundred times: Once off the plane, I was to collect my bag from baggage claim, find a buddy from my flight who's also headed to the Karlston, and share a taxi with them. Unfortunately, I'm allergic to *finding a buddy*. I've failed this task on countless occasions. At the baggage carousel, I determinedly positioned myself close to a college-age girl in a blue peacoat—and then stood there for five minutes trying to stifle the current of self-doubt cycling through me as I mentally rehearsed what I would say. Some variation of: *Hi! Are you headed to the Karlston? Hi! I'm headed to the Karlston. Hi! Me, you, Karlston?* Before I worked up the nerve to open my mouth, her suitcase came out onto the conveyor belt. I watched as she tracked it around the carousel with her eyes. And I watched in silence as she pulled it off and wandered away.

So, I'm alone in this taxi with no one to split the fifty-pound fee. I'm going to count that as my outgoing dress rehearsal. Once I get to the Karlston, I'm talking to new people. I'm starting conversations.

Outside the window, we're passing store after store that I've never heard of. Different. Already everything's so different, and I can't help but feel the distance. I'm 3,450 miles away from everyone I know.

Yesterday, my parents watched with solemn expressions as I walked away from them toward airport security. It made me feel like I was going away to war or something.

Out of habit, I reach into my bag and grab my cell to check for messages. It's dead. I let it fall back in. It was doomed to become a useless brick while in England anyway. My LG Voyager isn't new enough to support international calling. According to *So You're Going to Study Abroad*, I'm to buy a cheap plastic one like the fugitives do on TV.

The taxi rolls to a stop on a street lined on both sides with pretty, white, sophisticated-looking buildings with columns. Fancy. I drag my bags up four steps and into the one labeled THE KARLSTON.

Inside is a quaint lobby with burgundy carpeting. To the left is a typical curved lobby-style desk, and to the right is a little table with two people sitting behind it: a pale blond woman in her thirties and a balding black man in his fifties. They introduce themselves as the London program heads, Agatha and William. Agatha gives me my apartment keys. I'm in Flat Three, Room C. William directs me to a door on the left, past the desk, so that's what I waddle toward with my luggage.

I pull open said door to find stairs. I'm at the top of a carpeted stairway leading into the basement. Am I going to live in the basement? I heave in a breath.

This is fine. You're doing it. College, take two. Don't blow it.

I have three bags: a book bag, a carry-on, and a giant black suitcase. I secure the book bag high on my shoulder, grasp the carry-on in my front hand, and prepare to drag the giant suitcase behind me.

I take a single step down before something snags behind me. I fly forward.

"Shit!" I sacrifice the carry-on and lunge for the handrail, holding on for dear life as my bag continues on without me. It comes to a thundering stop at the bottom of the twenty or so steps. After a moment, I push against the wooden beam, back into an upright position.

I turn to see my puffy winter jacket snagged on rail at the top of the staircase. Way to almost die before you've even made it to the room. Leo's voice echoes in my head: *Can you do anything without causing a scene?*

With a huff, I pry myself free and slowly thump the rest of the way down with my remaining luggage. I sidestep the fallen carry-on and assess the area at the foot of the stairs. There's a hallway to my right, to my left, and behind me, parallel to the staircase.

"Are you okay?" a voice calls from above. I spin to find a curvy girl with dark skin and bright hazel-brown eyes standing in a bold green peacoat at the top of the landing.

Why does everyone have fashionable coats? Are peacoats a thing? She's wearing a white beret over her shoulder-length dark hair that flips out at the ends like a girl from the sixties. She looks so put together and sophisticated, and not at all like she just got off a plane.

I feel the sleep deprivation as I struggle for a moment to answer her. "Um, yeah, I'm fine."

Beret Girl starts down the staircase with her giant red piece of luggage.

"I just . . . I tripped, and my carry-on fell . . ." I mumble. *Don't mumble.*

"I thought maybe you had fallen. The noises were epic!"

My cheeks get hot. I clear my throat. "Cool . . . um, I'm fine, though. No worries!" I pick the carry-on up off the floor and start down the hallway parallel to the staircase.

"Where are you headed?" the girl asks, now dismounting from the last step. I turn around again.

"I'm in Flat Three, Room C. I'm taking a wild guess that it's this way, maybe?"

"Oh my goodness, no way, me too!" She shoots me a giant grin. I feel my own smile perk up.

At the end of the hall, we find ourselves between two light wooden doors: 3B is to our left and 3C is to our right.

I twist my key in the 3C lock. With a bit of pressure, it swings open, thumping lightly against the wall. My eyes dart around, surveying the space. We're on the long wall of a rectangular room with gray carpeting. There are three windowless walls, two of which have bunk beds pushed up against them. There's a bunk bed directly across from where I'm standing and another to the left of the doorway. Four portable, light brown, cupboard-like closets have been smooshed against the walls wherever space allows. The third wall is outfitted with a full-length mirror and a door to the bathroom. The fourth wall is a window. Well, it's not a full-on glass wall. It's about 40 percent wall and 60 percent giant window. The blinds are currently closed and a kitchen-sized table sits in front of it. We drag our things in and let the door click shut behind us.

"I love it," Beret Girl exclaims, forgetting her bags by the door and moving past me toward the lower bunk. "My name's on this one!" She holds up a blue folder she swiped off the bed.

I move my bags against the wall and walk over to look at the folder on the other bottom bunk. Not me. I hop up on the ladder to look at the folder on the top bunk. No name up here. I must be the bed above Beret Girl. *Exchange names, Shane.*

I turn from my perch on the ladder of the second bunk. "Hey, I'm Shane, by the way!"

The girl looks up from the floor where she's already unloading clothes into one of the two giant drawers under the first bunk. "I'm Babe!"

"Babe like the pig in that movie with the talking farm animals?"

Babe looks up, still smiling. "I love that pig."

I jump off the second bunk and climb to the top of the first. This blue folder has a little name tag that reads: SHANE PRIMAVERI. The bed's already made up with sheets and a plain black comforter. Enticing. Too bad it's only 11:00 a.m.

I hop off the ladder. I guess I should unpack. I grab my book bag from the floor and fish out my laptop, setting it up on the table near the window.

"Babe?" I ask hesitantly. My MacBook emits a *whoosh* as it powers up.

"Yeah?" She glances up from her suitcase.

"Do you mind if I put some music on in the background while we unpack, the Beatles or something?"

"Oh my goodness, I love the Beatles. Yes, please!" she gushes, slapping her hands against her lap for emphasis.

"Awesome." I turn back to my computer, pulling up iTunes. "A Hard Day's Night" seeps from my computer speakers. I close my eyes for a second. *I'm in England!* I do a little chassé-spin dance step toward my suitcase.

I'm working on the last bits of my closet. Roommate #3 has arrived, and she's intimidatingly tall. We're thinking there is no Roommate #4 because that bed's lacking a blue folder. The empty bunk's about to become a storage area for our many pieces of luggage. Babe's finished unpacking. She's lounging with her laptop. The wall near her bed is now decorated with various Mickey Mouse–related snippets and pictures, including a magazine cut out of the phrase THE HAPPIEST PLACE ON EARTH written in the flouncy Disney font.

Roommate #3, Sahra—pronounced Say-ruh—is still unpacking. She has these big dark eyes and tanned skin. Every time she looks over at Babe and me, her straight, shoulder-length, dark brown locks swish out around her face like she's in a hair commercial. I'm already kind of jealous of her effortlessly cool style. She's currently sporting fashion-y heeled booties with gray skinny jeans and a stylish, oversize cream sweater.

Sahra is prelaw, and hoping to Skype her boyfriend before bed later. There's already a picture of the two of them tacked up on her wall. After initial introductions and a brief conversation, the three of us fell into a comfortable silence as we emptied our belongings into the provided cupboards.

I hang my last sweater in my now-crowded closet and close the door. We're expected to be upstairs for orientation at 12:30, which is in approximately thirty minutes. I change into a cute white shirt and black jeans, walk through a perfume mist, brush my teeth, revitalize my curly, wave-ridden blond hair, and spruce up the makeup I did yesterday morning, East Coast time. I'm too tired to calculate how many hours ago that was. I pull the thick rubber bracelet I got for Christmas from my toiletry bag and tug it onto my wrist. I've worn it everywhere since, and I felt a little naked without it on the plane. It's black with neon-green numbers (*4 8 15 16 23 42*) etched into it. It's a *Lost* thing. *Lost* is the best TV show of all time. Carrying a physical piece of it on my wrist gives me a weird thrill. I want people in the world to ask me about it, so I can spread the *Lost* love to all the unknowing noobs. I took it off for the flight because it felt taboo to wear it up in the air, since the whole show revolves around a plane crash.

I step in front of the full-length mirror one last time to inspect my appearance. My sometimes-blue eyes flash ice gray today, and my hair hangs in a poofy blob to my mid-back. I was a vampire shade of gray while unpacking, but a light dusting of bronzer has brought me back to a living human skin tone.

My laptop (he goes by Sawyer) is still on the table, playing music. The blinds are shut tight across the giant window. I stride across the room and turn to look at Sahra as my fingers close around the skinny, plastic blind-opener stick. She's cramming what appears to be her five hundredth black dress into her closet. *Talk to them like you're already friends.*

I speak a little louder than necessary to ensure that both girls hear. "Guys, I wonder what our view is like in the basement. What even is this window?"

Babe leans out of the bunk to smile at me. "Right? Probably to give the illusion that we don't live in a dungeon."

Sahra shoves her closet closed and drops onto her bed. "Open it," she demands with a conservative smile.

"Okay." I twist the plastic thingy. The blinds open to reveal a courtyard. Well, courtyard is a generous word. A laugh bubbles out of me.

"Ha." Sahra grins for a moment before opening her laptop.

Outside the window is about ten feet of concrete sidewalk and then there's another wall with a giant window. The second window provides an incredibly clear view into a kitchen. Maybe that's our kitchen. This apartment—flat, British people call apartments *flats*—is supposed to have a shared kitchen. It would appear the kitchen has a window that peers right into our bedroom.

We have these blinds here for privacy, though, so I guess this is pretty cool. It's kind of like we have a spy window into the kitchen. What a weird architectural decision. Who puts a giant window wall in a basement flat that looks into the shared kitchen—

A boy.

There's a boy in the kitchen. A boy right up at the window facing me. How did I not see him immediately? He's washing dishes with a big, fluffy, yellow sponge. The sink must be right there up against the window.

He's a cute boy. A cute boy doing dishes. Is there anything more attractive than a boy doing dishes? I'm totally staring, and after a few moments, he looks up. We make eye contact through the kitchen window across the ten feet of concrete and back through my window, and he smiles at me. I explode.

Not literally. But you know that feeling like light being circulated through your veins when you see someone cute, and all of a sudden you explode all over with the thrill of said cute person noticing and acknowledging your existence as a human with whom they could potentially fall into a relationship?

I can't help it. My brain jumps right to:

GOAL 3) Kiss a boy you like.

I smile back at him and then look away so as not to appear to be a weird statue that stares at him. How do I meet this boy? Instinct says to retreat to my computer and hope I run into him later today.

I steal another glance his way. There's a dark-haired boy I can't see very well in there with him, sitting on a black leather couch on the other side of the room.

Maybe I can play it like I'm going to check out the kitchen? But I don't want to go over there alone. I might forget words and need someone to fill the empty air. I think my heart is palpitating. I turn back to Sahra and Babe, and sag a bit in an attempt to look chill.

"Hey, guys, anyone want to go check out the kitchen?" I ask quickly.

The last time I actively put *the moves* on a cute boy was in eighth grade. It's what first opened the rift between the cousins and me. Before that we were pals, especially Leo and me—we're so close in age and his family lives right

14

down the street. He used to come over and hide in my room whenever he did something to upset Uncle Dan (which was a lot).

When I was thirteen, I worked up the courage to instant message Louis Watson. We ended up IMing on a Sunday during one of the weekly Primaveri family BBQs. I was inside on Uncle Dan's PC while everyone else was outside in the pool. Twelve-year-old Leo wandered inside, saw me, and told the entire family I was in love with Louis Watson. I was roasted for the rest of the afternoon. It started with Leo, then the rest of the boys, then my uncles, and finally my dad. By the end of the night, I was nothing but a hot, sweaty puddle of embarrassment. That was the last time I spoke to Louis Watson. Today there are no family members here to judge me. *I will talk to the cute boy.*

Babe joins me on my kitchen quest. Together, we backtrack down the hall and take a left when we reach the staircase. *Be outgoing, be outgoing, whatever you do, be outgoing.*

We come to a stop outside the kitchen door. There's a keypad. Apparently, we need a code to get in.

"Did they tell us about a code?" I ask Babe.

"Maybe it's on the information in those blue folders they left on our beds?" she speculates.

Luckily, there are thin vertical windows on both sides of the kitchen door, so the boys inside can see us. A tall Asian boy with close-cropped hair and warm brown eyes pulls the door open. He's the guy I noticed on the couch.

"Hi!" he exclaims with a big dorky smile. He's lanky and sporting an oversize, black long-sleeve shirt with loose-fitting jeans. "Welcome to the kitchen! I'm Atticus."

"Hi," Babe and I chorus.

"I'm Babe," she continues.

"I'm Shane," I add.

The boy who smiled at me through the window is facing us, still by the sink. He meets my gaze and smiles again. Not a giant toothy smile, but a cool, chill half smile. He's holding a dish towel and leaning against the counter, wearing a long-sleeved plaid shirt and jeans. His light brown hair is haphazardly ruffled. He's fair (but nowhere near the ghost level I'm at); his skin is rosy with what looks like a fresh sunburn. He's all cool and leaning . . . and looking cool. What am I doing? Awkwardly standing in the middle of the room next to Babe. I reflexively put my hand on my hip. And drop it because it feels forced. And then I put it back up. And drop it. Oh god.

"Hey, I'm Pilot," he says.

Be outgoing. "Pilot, like a pilot?" The words escape my mouth before I can think them through.

What?

"Yes?" he answers, looking mildly confused.

"Like the first episode of a show!" I continue. *Stop talking.*

"Yes, exactly like that!" Atticus chuckles as he flops onto the black leather couch against the wall.

I almost say: Lost *has an amazing pilot!* But before I can spit it out, Pilot speaks again, "Yeah, my parents are really, really into TV," he adds.

"What?" Babe exclaims in disbelief, at the same time I blurt, "Oh my gosh, I'm really, really into TV!"

Atticus and Pilot laugh.

Oh no, that was a joke. My cheeks burn, and I bow my head. Whilst interacting with attractive boys, I have a tendency to experience incoherent babbling and sluggish brain activity.

I chuckle, keeping my eyes trained on the tiles under Pilot's feet as the embarrassment wave ebbs. A moment later, the kitchen door opens behind us and Agatha sticks her head into the room.

"Hey, Flat Three, I'm making my rounds. Orientation is about to start. If you could make your way upstairs, that would be great."

3. Breathe, Just Breathe

It's now been thirty hours since I last slept. Orientation ended twenty-three minutes ago. We were shuffled outside onto the sidewalk and divided up into groups by four different twenty-something resident advisors. I ended up being separated from everyone. I watched, crestfallen, as Pilot, Atticus, Babe, and Sahra walked off in the opposite direction with a different tour guide. I know it was just a stupid orientation tour, but it felt important in the moment.

The RA took us around the general area, pointed out the laundromat (I've already forgotten where this is), the movie theater (it's called the ODEON), and brought us to Orange UK (a cell phone place).

My new phone is a little gray plastic box straight out of 2003. It has real buttons and no flip-top to protect them. When I powered it up, the background was set to a stock photo of a rock garden. There weren't many options, but I've changed it to a close-up of a tiger's face. Tiger's face has more of a brave vibe than rock garden. On the way back to the Karlston, we stopped at a cafe where I ravenously ordered quesadillas. Note to self: Don't order any more Mexican food in England. It's not their thing. I'm already getting hungry again. The RA mentioned something about a grocery store somewhere close, but the details have already fallen out of my brain. I can't be expected to remember complicated things like which way the grocery store is while running on zero sleep.

I've now gleaned the code to the kitchen (which was, in fact, buried in the blue folder paperwork), grabbed Sawyer, and settled in at the table to write. I want to write about my experiences in England, so I've started working on a blog post about my first few hours here. I have my Horcruxes to house my personal musings, but I have a blog to post more polished writing pieces, like short stories that I've finished. While I'm here in the UK, I want to turn it into a study abroad blog of sorts and post short story versions of my adventures.

I let words drain out of me and into the digital space, until my doc is brimming with all the travel-related thoughts I've been wrestling with throughout the day. "Lucy in the Sky with Diamonds" is playing softly, and my fingers are still dancing across the keyboard when I hear the door open behind me. I straighten, anticipating the need to make conversation. *You got this.*

I turn in my seat. The *hi* I've loaded up dies on my tongue when I see Pilot. I glance around nervously as the door clicks shut behind him. *Do not be silent.*

"Hey," I force out.

"Hey. Shane, right?" He meets my eyes.

I nod as he walks around the table and sits across from me. "Pilot?"

"Like the first episode of a TV show," he drops casually.

I bring my hand up to cover my face.

He chuckles. "What are you working on?"

I look at my laptop and back up to his eyes. They're green. Like olives.

"Oh, um, nothing really, just writing. I like to write short stories and stuff."

He grins. "Looked like some super-intense typing was going down when I walked in."

I grunt-laugh. "I mean, just a rambling account of my first fourteen hours out of the country."

"Is writing, like, what you want to do? Be an author or something?" He eyes me curiously.

I falter a bit, fidgeting with my hair. "Um, yeah, I love reading and writing and stuff, so, that'd be amazing."

"That's awesome. Can I read something you've written sometime?"

I blink in surprise. What's going on? We've exchanged two words, and he wants to read something I've written? I look at my computer screen for a second because I can't handle the prolonged eye contact that's happening. Is this flirting? He looks and sounds so genuinely interested. This internal struggle needs to end, because of course he can read something I've written.

I look back at him, a smile crawling onto my face. "Um, yeah, sure. I have a blog where I post stuff sometimes." I pause, trying to maintain eye contact. "Do you write?"

He smiles. "Yeah, I do."

My lips drop into a surprised *O*. "Really?"

"I mean, I write music."

He. Writes. Music. "Oh my gosh, that's so cool! Do you play an instrument, then?"

"Yep, good ole guitar. I'm working on an album; gonna try to finish it while I'm here." He drums a quick little beat on the table with his hands.

I push Sawyer over to the side a little. "Whoa, what kind of music do you write?"

"You know . . . like, acoustic jazzy stuff."

I smile again, trying to imagine what acoustic jazzy stuff sounds like. "That's great! Is that what *you* want to do?"

He looks at the table. "Eh, I mean, I'd love to be able to do something music-related, but it's more of a hobby. I'm a finance major—I'm doing the business track here."

"Oh, well . . . I'd . . . I'd love to hear some of your stuff sometime," I squeak out. He shoots me a modest grin.

We're having a conversation!

"We should all do something in here tonight," he suggests, clapping a hand down on the table. One side of his mouth kicks up. "A flat bonding activity or something. Maybe get some beers and hang out."

My eyebrows shoot up. "Oh, yeah, we're legal here! I really want to go to a grocery store and get some food, too. I know we ate on our orientation tour thing, but I'm already starving again."

"You want to go now?" he asks.

Butterflies hustle through my veins. "I, um, I don't know where the grocery store is or anything," I stutter.

"The guy who did my tour talked about it, so I know roughly where it is. I think I'll be able to find it. I'm good with directions."

"I, um, okay?"

"I'll go grab my jacket. Meet by the stairs in a minute or so?"

I stare at him for a second in disbelief. What the heck. I've only been here for like four hours. This seems conveniently wonderful.

"Cool," I manage. I follow him out of the kitchen and . . . toward my room. At the last minute, he veers left to the door across from mine.

"Hey," I blurt loudly. "We're neighbors!"

He looks over his shoulder and laughs before heading into his room.

"Well, I'll be," he says in a fake Southern accent as I dive into my room for a coat.

4. I Think I'm Gonna Like It Here

We're walking down the sidewalk in London together. Pilot and me. Me and Pilot. A cute boy who's being nice to me. Who I held a conversation with. My heart is having a dance party. It's also wondering, is this, like, a date?

No, it's not a date, but it's like . . . a something.

The sun sits low in the sky and the streets are full of people hustling about. Big red double-decker buses swish by every few minutes. I can't help the stupid smile that plasters itself to my face as I gaze around in wonder like someone who's never been outside before. When I try to rearrange it into a more relaxed expression, the smile pops back up of its own volition.

"There are red double-decker buses like you see in the movies!" My voice is thick with delight. "It's so surreal. I've never been out of the country before, and now I'm just here."

I look over at Pilot quickly, and then back in front of me, and then back at him, and then back in front of me. How often should I look over? Is it weird to keep looking over or is it weirder not to look over? I look over at him again. He's smiling in a more subtle sort of way. His eyes shine like he's excited about London too, but he's got it smothered under a nice layer of chill.

We trot quietly down Kings Gate in the general direction of where the grocery store is supposed to be. Pilot has his hands jammed in his jacket pockets. We pass pretty white house with pillars after pretty white house with pillars, all the way down the road until we come to a stop at a busy intersection.

"Is this where we turn, you think?" I ask.

I gaze around for the tall metal posts with green signs labeled with the names of the streets that we all know and love in the United States—and come up empty. I already miss my phone GPS.

"I think . . ." He squints across the way. "It's another block down."

I turn away from the street to gaze at him warily. "You only sound, like, sixty-two percent sure about that."

He raises a hand to stroke his chin and glances dramatically from right to left. "I'd say I'm more like thirty-seven percent sure."

"Where are the street signs?" My head swishes from one corner to the next. There are no poles. This is so disorienting.

The *So You're Going to Study Abroad* pamphlet did extensively delve into a phenomenon called culture shock. At the time I scoffed, because come on, it sounds dumb. But dang, I guess it's starting.

"Okay, I'm, like, forty-three percent sure now that we go straight for another block," Pilot decides.

I smile and shrug. "Okay."

I look to my left and take a few steps forward into the street.

"Shane!" Pilot grabs my arm and heaves me back as a car races by a foot from my face.

My lungs suck up all the air in a ten-foot radius as adrenaline spikes through me. Pilot drops his hand from my arm as I spin to face him, mortified.

"Holy shit, I forgot about the cars coming from the other way. Oh my god!" I bury my face in my hands for a second.

Four hours in, and I've almost gotten myself hit by a car and killed via a flight of steps.

"Don't worry. I almost died a few times after I got here yesterday." Pilot starts crossing the street. I silently scurry after him.

"But I mean, I didn't, because I remembered and looked both ways before actually stepping out into oncoming traffic." He turns around as we reach the curb to smirk at me.

I shoot him a surprised grin. "Shut up!" I burst, reflexively whacking him in the arm. A half a second later, I stare at my own arm aghast. "Oh my god, I'm sorry. I didn't mean to hit you. I have this habit of smacking people sometimes—"

He laughs, interrupting me. "You have a habit of smacking people?"

"No." My voice rises a few pitches. "I mean, not smacking people. Jeez."

"Uh-huh."

"I mean, hitting people, lightly, sometimes."

His eyes narrow. "Is this a serious problem? Do you go to meetings for this?"

I bite back a laugh. "No!"

"Uh-huh." He's still smirking at me.

"Why are you smirking?" I protest.

He continues to smirk.

"Stop," I squeal. Before I realize it, I've whacked him in the arm again. Oh god. I stutter to apologize.

His smile widens as he jumps away in mock horror. "There she goes again with the violence. I just saved your life, and this is how I'm treated."

I bury my face in my hands, laughing.

We come to the end of another block and turn right down whatever nameless road we've reached. I'm having trouble focusing on anything other than Pilot. How close we're walking. How he's looking at me with his lips pursed like he's suppressing a grin.

I blow out a breath. "Maybe I do have a problem," I concede as somberly as I can. "I'll try and keep it under control."

"First step is acceptance," he says, putting on a haughty voice and bumping me lightly in the shoulder. Another laugh huffs out of me. Up ahead I can make out a sign with red glowing letters that reads TESCO. The name rings a bell.

"That's the grocery store, right? Tes-co," I test the word on my tongue. "Interesting name for a grocery store."

"Shane. Interesting name for a girl," he teases.

I narrow my eyes. "Pilot. Interesting name for a human." He snorts.

When Tesco's doors slide open, we're greeted with an onslaught of familiar sounds: carts squealing, elevator-esque music playing overhead, and the repetitive beeps as people check out.

"So, Shane, what kind of music do you listen to?" Pilot asks, as I scoop up a basket.

"Music? Who brought up music? We're getting food." I snicker shamelessly at my bluntness. I don't usually say stuff like that to people I've just met. I look at Pilot again. "I don't want to answer that; it feels like a trick question."

"I'm just curious!" he says innocently.

"You write music, so I think there's a ninety percent chance you're a music snob."

"I am not a music snob." He pauses and his lip quirks up. "I'm only a little bit of a music snob."

My smile is big and stupid again. "Do you want to go through all the aisles? Is that okay? Because I really, really want to go through all the aisles." I power walk into the first one, and Pilot trails behind.

"Pilot, look at these soda bottles. Are you seeing this? They're slightly skinnier than our soda bottles!" I gesture wildly to the soda lining the shelves.

He grins. "So you were about to tell me about the music you listen to," he prompts again. We turn into the next aisle.

"I listen to all types of music," I answer diplomatically, as I reach down and pick up a tub of Nutella to drop into my basket. "I have a general appreciation for music." We stroll past the peanut butters and the jellies. "I like the Beatles . . ."

"Wait." Pilot comes to an abrupt stop mid-aisle.

"What?" I say hesitantly.

"The Beatles?" he breathes. "No way. You like them? No. Way. No. Way—"

I roll my eyes. "Stop—" I interject.

"No. Way!"

"Stop!" My voice hits squeak levels yet unknown to mankind.

"I love them! I thought I was the only one who knew about them." He beams.

I run away into the next aisle. I hear him laughing behind me as I enter the bread section. I definitely like this boy. I skid to a stop in front of the UK pasta spread. All the pasta is bagged. What even! In America we box pasta!

"The pasta is all in bags!" I turn to Pilot, expecting him to share my sentiment.

He looks like he's about to make fun of me again.

I try not to smile. "No, 'cause in the United States, most of the pasta is in boxes!" He shakes his head, grinning. "This is an interesting tidbit, Pilot. You'll be happy I pointed this out in the future when you need to know it . . . for a game show trivia question about how England packages their pasta."

I drop a bag into my basket and skip—oh dear lord, did I really just skip?—down the aisle to find the tomato sauce and skid to another abrupt stop. I shuffle back a bit to make sure I haven't missed anything before emitting an involuntary gasp.

Pilot appears at my side. "You okay?"

"It's just this sauce section," I explain.

His mouth twitches. "Did the sauce offend you?"

"No, but look. There's only two types of tomato sauce here. What kind of world does England live in where there's only two types of sauce!" I gesture around wildly for emphasis.

He takes a step back, smiling broadly now, and points casually toward the sauce and then back to me. "Did you . . . did you gasp because of the sauce?"

Blood seeps into my cheeks. "Sauce is a big deal."

I flounder to grab a jar so we can move on and out of this aisle. As I snatch it off the shelf, a second jar slides to the edge along with it. My breath catches, and I lunge to snatch it out of the air, but I'm not fast enough. I leap backward as the second jar crashes to the ground. The glass shatters, and a mild splattering of sauce lands across my feet.

I freeze, staring at the floor. I can't believe I dropped a jar of sauce in front of Pilot. Shit. Shit, shit.

After a second, someone takes my arm and pulls me out of the aisle, away from the destruction zone. It's Pilot . . . He's touching my arm again. He's laughing. We turn a corner into an aisle full of alcohol.

He lets go and looks at me pointedly. "You murdered the sauce, Shane."

I shake my head. "Accident," I squeak.

Pilot scans the shelves before reaching down to scoop up a case of English cider called Strongbow. He clucks his tongue, shakes his head, and suppresses a smile as we head toward the checkout counter. "And the violence continues."

We make our way back to the Karlston at a slower pace. I've suddenly decided that I want to call Pilot *Pies*, and I don't know if that's okay. Pies is fun to say, and then we're friends, right? Or, we're something? Where there's a nickname, there's a bond. That's what I . . . always say.

"Can I call you Pies?" I blurt into the night. "Sorry. I wouldn't ask, but I really want to call you Pies," I finish hesitantly.

When I look over, he's smiling. My shoulders relax a smidge.

"Sure, you can, Sauce Killer."

I beam. "Oh, but I'd prefer if you didn't call me Sauce Killer," I respond politely.

He snorts.

"Do a lot of people already call you Pies?"

"Nope, that's a new one."

My heart sings a tiny bit at the idea of having created a new nickname that no one else uses for him.

"What do people call you?" I ask, curious now.

"Pilot . . . or Pi."

"Pi? Like in math? You're not Pi like in math, though. That feels kind of cold. You're more of a pie-pie. Pies are warm and wonderful and delicious—" I cut myself off. Okay, there's outgoing and then there's *this*.

He looks at me funny. My eyes fall to the ground as a new wave of embarrassment courses through my system. We walk in silence for a few moments.

"So, are you going to write about this grocery store adventure in your blog?" Pilot asks.

"Oh, yeah," I answer, grasping at the subject change. "I'm planning a whole exposé about this pasta in bags versus boxes phenomenon."

"I can't miss that," he says seriously. I laugh. "What's your blog called?" he continues.

My eyelids snap up. I didn't think about the part where I'd actually have to tell him what my blog is called. He's smiling at me again. My heart hops around idiotically. I can't handle all this.

I focus on the ground again. "Um . . . you know what? It's nothing. You don't really want to know." I pick up the pace a little. I think we're only a block away from the Karlston now. Maybe I can deflect this question.

"Hey, you said I could read your stuff," he protests quietly.

"It's a weird name," I confess.

"What is it?" he asks again.

I stay quiet, power walking.

"Shane!" He speeds up to match my pace, laughing as he catches my eyes. "You have to tell me."

He's full-on beaming now, and it makes me feel all floaty. Fluttery and floaty. He stops walking and I stop walking, and we smile at each other.

"It's FrenchWatermelonNineteen," I mumble, the words running together.

Pilot laughs. "I'm sorry, what was that? French. Watermelon. Nineteen?" he clarifies slowly.

"FrenchWatermelonNineteen." I smoosh my lips together so my smile isn't as toothy. His smile is toothy.

He shrugs, nonchalant. "Okay. French Watermelon Nineteen. What's so weird about that? It's so normal. Practically boring. I know, like, five other people who go by French Watermelon Nineteen on the internet. Are you French?"

"Nope." I feel sheepish. I try to make my face look sheepish.

He raises his eyebrows.

I drop my gaze to his shoes. "I'm . . . a big fan of French toast."

He answers immediately. "Oh, me too. Who isn't?"

I look up again, and he's closer. How did he get closer? I think I'm shaking. Anxiety springs up through my legs. I'm all unsteady, like I could be blown over by the next gust of wind. I'm not sure what happens now. Eye contact game is strong. My words come out quiet. "Also I love watermelons and the number nineteen, and so, I did what any rational human would have done—smashed them together into a weird blob of a word that would follow me around for the rest of my life."

He nods. "So, French Watermelon."

Is he closer?

"Nineteen," I finish.

What's happening? Is the sidewalk moving?

"I think it's a fantastic name."

We're standing so close. His eyes are inches away. I'm holding on to the grocery bag for dear life. Freight train has replaced heart.

And then my eyes swing down to look at a crack in the super-clean London sidewalk. When I raise them a moment later, Pilot's three feet away again. He's turned towards the Karlston.

"Look at that. We made it back." He looks back at me. "Ready to round up the flatmates and get the bonding rolling?"

I stare at him. "Um, yeah, of course. I've been awake for thirty-four hours now, what's a few more . . . I have some icebreaker games loaded on my iPod that'll be perfect."

He grins and jogs up the front steps to the door. I expel the giant breath I've been very aware of holding for the past thirty seconds.

It's so dark in our room. Sahra's asleep, but I've caught a second wind. Up in the bunk, I turn on my laptop for light, grab a pen, and throw open a fresh page in the new Horcrux.

1/11/11 1:03 a.m.

I just added all my new flatmates as friends on Facebook (Babe Lozenge, Sahra Merhi, Atticus Kwon, Pilot Penn), and finished off a short email to the parents letting them know everything went well today. I haven't figured out the best way to actually speak to them yet since I only have a certain amount of allotted minutes on my burner phone. The lights are off, so I'm scribbling via the light of Sawyer's screen. It works.

After grocery shopping with Pilot, all of us (minus Babe, who left earlier after orientation to visit a friend she has upstairs) met in the kitchen and sat tentatively around the table. Which, by the way, has terrible chairs. Atticus chatted easily for a few minutes about how excited he is to immerse himself into the London theater scene while the rest of us listened, politely inserting a word or two, but not really furthering the conversation. I was about to descend into a cone of social anxiety, but Pilot broke the silence by pulling out the ciders he bought. And then I broke out the Taboo. Well, the version of Taboo I have on my iPod Touch called Word Kinish. Nothing breaks the ice like a good game of Word Kinish. (In the interest of being outgoing, I obviously prepped my iPod full of group activities).

I got a little competitive, but I think we all had fun. We kept switching up the teams. My team always won because I'm a professional Taboo/Word Kinish player. The cousins and I used to play this all the time during summers back in our early teens.

Sahra was the worst of us at Word Kinish. She was easily flustered when she couldn't think of ways to describe the word she needed to make her team guess without using the illegal buzz words. Instead of talking it through, she would make angry noises until time ran out. I'm not sure what to think of Sahra. She's kind of nice, but she also seems kind of cold. She doesn't smile when she talks to me, and she always speaks in short, chopped sentences. I don't know if she doesn't like me or if that's her demeanor.

I regret not having brought a deck of cards with me. I've got to get myself one out here. There's something magical about a good game of cards when everyone's into it. It used to be that at every Primaveri gathering after dinner, we'd play cards. In general, the Primaveris are a loud and opinionated people. Normally, I observe rather than participate in their discussions because I'd rather be overlooked than potentially judged or scolded for saying the wrong thing. But when we're playing cards, that fear kind of falls away. Awkwardness with the cousins falls away. I'm automatically more confident and all of a sudden I have things to say.

I hope Pilot likes cards. He was totally into the game today. Not quite on my level of into it, but into it in a way that was fun. Atticus too.

Atticus is a drama major. He's really easy to talk to. There's this dorky charm about him that automatically makes me feel less alone. He just finished _The Lost Symbol_. I'm totally pumped to talk Dan Brown with him when we get a chance. He's super-passionate about theater and wants to intern in the West End while he's here. He recently broke up with his boyfriend because of study abroad, but he seems okay about it. He talked about being excited to mingle with the British. While Sahra and Pilot played Word Kinish tonight from a calm sitting position around the table, Atticus joined me, jumping up and yelling things.

I'm trying really hard to hold back the tsunami of Pilot excitement that's been building in me since I first saw him in the kitchen this afternoon, but now that I'm just sitting here in the dark, pre-sleep, I can't stop all these giddy thoughts from flooding my brain. Could we be a thing? There was a moment tonight where I'm pretty sure we almost kissed.

Pilot's so . . . like, cool. He's definitely kissed people. Having never been kissed feels like a giant Achilles's heel. I hate feeling so inexperienced. I hate that this isn't something I can study. I hate that I get sweaty at the mere mention of the game Never Have I Ever because I'm so scared of broaching sexual topics. How am I twenty years old and I've yet to even hold a boy's hand? It'd be fine if I didn't want to hold a boy's hand, but I do. And I've never even been close.

But now, the potential's, like . . . right in front of me.

The word "boyfriend" is already dancing around my brain. My family's been pestering me about the existence of a boyfriend every few months for the last seven years. How could I not be thinking about it? I've been fine by myself these past million years, but I want to know what's it like to have someone care about me that way. To put their arms around me from behind. I don't want this Achilles's heel.

5. Open Your Eyes and See

My eyes snap open. A high-pitched bleeping noise is blaring. It takes a second, but yesterday slowly gurgles to the forefront of my mind. I'm in London. That noise is my new plastic phone. It must be 9:00 a.m.

One of the four wardrobes in here is smashed up against my bunk and the top of it is level with my bed, so I've turned it into a makeshift bedside table down near my feet. That's where my phone sits now, bleeping away. I shut it off and make my way down the ladder to start getting ready. Everyone on the program is going on a boat tour down the Thames today to Greenwich.

We're supposed to be upstairs by 10:15. At 9:40, Babe and I are both dressed, so we head to the kitchen together for breakfast. Sahra's running behind, but she assures us she'll met us there.

Babe's sporting a new Canon DSLR around her neck.

"Nice camera!" I admire as we butter our bagels at the counter. I have my Casio digital camera in my purse, but a DSLR—those pictures are on another level.

When we finish eating, the kitchen door opens, and Pilot and Atticus stride in, all ready to go. My heart speeds up. I check my block phone for the time: 10:05.

Pilot grins at us, his gaze landing on me. "You guys ready to do Greenwich?"

Atticus yawns.

"Hell yeah!" I push up from my seat at warp speed to deposit my plate in the sink. "We've got—" There's an enormously loud crash behind me. I gasp, jumping three feet in the air, only to find that it was my chair falling over. Heat flashes up my neck.

Babe laughs next to me. Atticus is cackling. My eyes find Pilot's. He's laughing too.

"Dammit!" I grin in spite of myself, annoyed, but absolutely overjoyed to be around people who are laughing. My family's conditioned me to expect the frustrated sigh.

The four of us join a massive group of students on a pilgrimage to the nearest Tube station. Pilot and Atticus walk and chat about five feet ahead of me and Babe.

I'm wearing my long, black, puffy winter jacket because it's the only one I have. Under it, I'm wearing my favorite black jeans and a white, long-sleeve sweater. Over that is my new purse that slings across my chest. There are all these horror stories about how thieves in Europe carry knives and run around chopping off women's purses—the purses fall off their arms, the thief catches it, and runs. It's been recommended to me by American society (mostly my aunts, uncles, and parents) that I wear a cross-body purse to make chopping it off more difficult. I'm sure the degree to which America harps on this fear is slightly exaggerated, but, in the interest of better safe than sorry, I have also chosen to wear the purse under my jacket. It doesn't look too strange because the purse is really small, but it does look a little strange. There's an extra butt cheek-like thing protruding from the area behind my hip. *But, try to cut off my purse now, thieves. You'll have to find it first!*

"So, what did you do last night?" I ask Babe.

"I hung out with my friend Chad. He's here on the program with us. We're in the same school at YU and stuff. We got food, and then I went back to his flat upstairs and hung out with some of the people there." Babe is wearing her pretty green coat and sophisticated beret again. Her lips are painted a bright, cheery red. I feel under-fashioned.

I pause, looking ahead rather than at Babe. "Are you and Chad, like, a thing, kind of?" I ask hesitantly. I'm not sure if we're at the point in our friendship where boy talk is permissible. But Babe seems nice, and I want to be friends. Friends talk about that stuff.

When I glance back over at Babe, she's looking at the ground. She considers my question for a few seconds before meeting my eyes. "We're . . . I . . . I'm not sure. Kind of, it's a long story." She's goes quiet.

Guess we're not there yet. I quickly change the subject as we turn left onto Gloucester Road.

"So what do you study at YU?"

"Hospitality!"

"Oh, cool! What do you want to do when you graduate?"

"I want to work at Disney World. I, well, actually my goal is to make my way up to president of the park!" She smiles at me, excitement building in her voice. Her enthusiasm is contagious.

"So, like, President of Disney World, then?" I clarify, awed by this idea.

Babe walks me through the process of how one would make their way to eventual President of Disney World.

We get off the Tube—the surprisingly clean London subway system—near the London Eye, and our giant posse shuffles onto a ferry waiting along the edge of the Thames River. Once we're loaded on, I catch sight of Sahra and flag her over to our group.

The five of us stand together on the upper deck level of the boat. It's open, like one of those double-decker tour buses you see in New York City, and a scratchy microphone projects the voice of a tour guide. We *oooh* and *ahh* as we float under the London Bridge, and past the pickle-like building London calls the Gherkin. I snap pictures of everything.

I want to get a picture of the Flat Three crew. Would everyone be okay with being in a picture together? Do we not know each other well enough yet for me to suggest it? Is it too soon for friend pictures? Is this a stupid thing to worry about? I glance around at the people outside our little circle.

Fresh anxiety billows through me at the thought of asking someone to take it.

We pass under another bridge, and I bounce on the tips of my toes as it becomes a backdrop for a potential group shot. I brace myself, mashing my lips together determinedly, and make eye contact with a shorter guy wearing a beanie, standing near Atticus's shoulder. It's just a picture.

"Hey, do you think you could take a picture of us?" I ask quickly.

"Yeah, sure," Beanie Dude responds. I hand him my camera. Flat Three turns and gathers together for the shot. I didn't even have to ask them. Pilot stands to my left, and when he leans in and puts his arm around me, my insides twirl around. I know it's just a picture, but he didn't have to put his arm around me, right?

Beanie Dude counts down, snaps the shot, and hands me back the camera. I beam. I have a real-life picture of this moment. Real-life proof that this happened. Real-life friends I've made myself are with me on a real-life trip in a real-life other country where I'm living now. And an attractive, nice, funny boy had his arm around me. I take a quick second to inspect the shot. The framing's a little wonky, but I'm too triumphant to care.

Greenwich looks like a giant fancy green park. It's littered with enormous white marble buildings and structures with columns. Together, the five of us head to the National Maritime Museum (all museums in England are free). Babe, Atticus, and I laugh our heads off taking silly pictures with all their statues. Pilot laughs at us, agreeing to participate in the occasional shot. Sahra hangs back, watching with a small smile.

After the museum, we hike up a steep grassy hill to the Royal Observatory and wander through the exhibits. I take a picture of all our hands touching the oldest rock on Earth on display: 4.5 billion years old. We take turns standing on the prime meridian of the world. I snap pictures of everyone as they straddle both the eastern and western hemispheres. Babe takes the camera to snap one of me. I suck in a deep breath as I plop one foot over the line and then exhale, knowing I'm standing on both sides of the world at once. In my mind, I see the globe I used to play with in elementary school and the raised line that I would trace with my finger, down the world. A weird trill of wonder zings through me. I didn't think I was going to enjoy these museums . . . this much.

The five of us are starving as we tromp back down the hill from the Observatory, so we stop at the first pub we find and settle in at an empty table. A waitress comes over to greet us and hand out menus.

"So, are you guys all wanting to travel while you're here?" Pilot asks as we look over the selection. He's sitting across from me, smiling with his mouth closed.

"Yes!" Babe and Sahra exclaim immediately in response. My head cocks to the side in surprise.

"I want to travel eventually, but the theater track is super-demanding," Atticus adds. "I have to be here to see shows most weekends."

I'm not sure how to respond. I haven't really thought about traveling more. I already traveled all the way across the world to get here. We're in a foreign country right now. I can't cross the street yet without almost dying. I just learned that street signs are on the sides of the buildings instead of metal poles stuck into the corners of the intersections. I thought we were done traveling, and now we were going to explore the place we've traveled to.

But after today's adventure in Greenwich, I don't know. I would like to do more of this. I like adventuring with this crew. I've had more fun with these people in two days than I had with my roommates all last year. When else am I going to be living so close to other European countries? Italy! I've been taking Italian classes since I was fourteen. I could go to Italy.

Pilot's gaze has fallen on me. I feel it before I see it, because when you like someone, you develop a superpower that enables you to subconsciously hone in on all their movements.

They can rotate to face you all the way across the room, and the second it happens, you know: They're facing me from across the room, ON GUARD!

With a deep breath, I meet Pilot's eyes. "Yeah, I really want to go to Italy," I tell him as our waitress distributes waters around the table.

"Let's go this weekend, then!" he responds immediately.

My jaw drops.

"Oh my gosh, yes!" Babe chimes in.

This weekend? But that's, like, now. We literally got here yesterday.

"I'm on board with this," Sahra adds, picking up her water and taking a sip.

I fumble for words. "Like, go to Rome—for the weekend?" I ask in disbelief.

"Rome for the weekend," Pilot echoes confidently. I blink at him.

"Okay!" I blurt.

"Rome for the weekend!" Babe raises her glass of water to toast. We all join her, clinking our glasses.

"You guys are going to have an amazing time!" Atticus cheers.

I take a big gulp of my water and drop the glass back to the table. Across from me, Pilot jumps like someone pinched him.

"Whoa." He holds his hands up in front of him.

I raise my eyebrows. "Whoa, what?"

"Don't murder the glass!"

My head twitches to the left. "What do you mean, murder the glass? It's fine."

"Take a drink again."

I eye him suspiciously and slowly raise the glass off the table. I take a quick sip and drop it back down. An amused smile breaks across his face. Babe's starts laughing.

"What?" I demand.

"He's right!" She giggles.

"What are you talking about?" I laugh.

"You slam your glass down," Babe explains. "Like a sailor after he chugs a beer!"

"I don't . . ." I pick up my glass and take a sip again, concentrating now. I drop the glass back down, and it makes a loud thunk as it hits the wood. My breath *whooshes* out in surprise. I've never paid any attention to it. Realization must dawn on my face because across the table Pilot's silently chuckling.

"I . . ." I start, bewildered. "I didn't even realize. Are your cups, like, silent?"

Pilot picks up his glass. His eyes lock with mine as he brings it to his mouth, drinks, and puts the glass back on the table. It barely makes a sound. "It's all in the technique," he says. "Be chill. Be Zen."

Next to him, Babe takes a drink and puts down her glass experimentally. It makes a muffled clunk.

"See? There, she's got it," he says, pointing to Babe.

I pick up my glass and sip again. I watch Pilot with narrowed eyes as I lower it back to the table at snail speed. It makes a small sound as it comes back into contact with the wood. He grins.

"Was that to your satisfaction?" I inquire with a melodramatic flourish.

He squints at me. "With a few months' practice—"

I cut him off with a scoff, and he breaks into laughter.

6. Nothing's Standing in My Way

Last night we bought plane tickets to Rome! Two more nights until we go to Italy!

We all start class today. None of my flatmates are in class with me, so as I settle into my seat, I feel like a bit of a loner again, but then the professor struts in. The first thing he does is distribute postcards, one to each student.

"So, as you know, this isn't going to be our normal meeting day. Starting next week, class is Monday and Friday," he begins. "We're going to be delving into creative writing prompts every class, and to warm you up, get your juices flowing, each class you're going to get a postcard. Write to someone back in America about your experiences here. It's simple, easy, and effectively gets you putting words to paper. You have ten minutes. Take out a pen and go."

I gaze at the 4×6 shot of the London Bridge on my postcard, flip it over to the blank side, and start writing. I want it to look nice, so I break out the cursive writing I haven't used since elementary school.

January 12, 2011

Mom and Dad,
I'm still having trouble wrapping my head around the fact that I'm in London. Yesterday, I rode on

*a ferry under the bridge on the front of this postcard.
I'm in my first college-level writing class, and I'm
pretty sure I already love it. The professor's last name
is Blackstairs, which reminds me of a book series I
love, and he says we're going to be doing creative writing
prompts every class. I could play with creative writing
prompts all day, so I'm overjoyed right now.*

    Love you guys,

    Shane

Soon after I've finished, Professor Blackstairs stands. "Time. Great. You feeling good? Postcards away, laptops out. Let's jump into the fun stuff."

I slip the postcard into my book bag. It was nice to write those words on paper, even if I can't actually send them out. The professor hands us all strips of paper, each printed with the first sentence of a well-known book. When he drops mine onto the desk, I snatch it up.

`There is no lake at Camp Green Lake.`

I chuckle softly, excitement blooming in my belly as a new story starts to lace itself together in my head.

"Write me a short story with this as your opening sentence," he says. "You have an hour—starting now."

I yank out Sawyer, open a blank document, and let my ideas spill onto the page. My fingers jet across the keys as I spin a story from the point of a view of a sassy young girl about a camp on the moon where her parents met. I beam at my screen for the next fifty-nine minutes. When time's up, Professor Blackstairs starts an in-depth discussion about the importance of an opening sentence. We go through loads of examples. The three hours fly by. It's honestly the most fun I've ever had in a college class.

———

Babe is in our room Skyping with her parents when I return at three, so I head into the kitchen to put the finishing touches on my Camp Green Lake story and work on a blog post about yesterday's trip to Greenwich. The kitchen is more social than our room anyway, and I'm trying to put myself out there.

Sahra stops in at about 3:30 to grab a drink before heading back out to get groceries. Atticus storms in at 3:45, stuffs a microwavable meal down his throat, and runs out, sputtering about being late for his internship interview. It's about 4:00 p.m. now, and I'm staring at my Gmail.

My parents emailed asking for more details about my first few days here. I heave a shaky breath and type up a brief update, describing my new flatmates. I link them to my first two blog posts: "American Moves to London: The First Eight Hours" and the most recent, "What's Greenwich?" And press send. I yank Horcrux Nine from my bag.

1/12/11 4:04 p.m.

I think I'm going to organize a Flat Three card night. It feels like a good, outgoing step forward toward long-term friendship. That sounds pathetic, but this is where we're at right now. Last night, there was some tentative talk of us all going out to a pub tonight after our first day of class, since we're legally allowed to drink here. Maybe tomorrow we can stay in and have a card night. Friday morning, we have class again, and afterward Pilot, Babe, Sahra, and I head to the airport for Rome! INSANITY.

I startle as the door opens, quickly shutting my notebook and dropping the pen to the table. Pilot strides into the kitchen with a long, thin sandwich. My heart runs around like a puppy when there's a visitor at the door. *Please be cool, heart.*

"Hey!" He takes the seat across from me and unwraps his food. "You writing?"

"I was." I push Horcrux Nine to the side.

"Wow, with a real live pen and everything!" He hops up to grab a glass of water. "What are you working on?"

I fiddle with my fingers. "Um, well, nothing really. It's kinda like a journal, I guess."

"Ah, nice, that sounds like something an author would do." He comes back into view and sits across from me. "Have you started writing your book yet?" He smiles.

I blink in surprise, before huffing a laugh. "My book?"

"I hear authors write those," he adds, as he picks up his sandwich.

I laugh again. "One of my goals this semester is actually to start my"—I raise air quotes—"'great American novel,' but it's a pretty daunting task, so we'll see."

"Really? That's awesome," he says enthusiastically. "I read some of your stuff last night." I go still, shock zipping through me as he takes another bite of sandwich.

That was so fast. What does he think of my stuff? I can't believe he sat down and read stuff that I wrote. What does he mean, he read my stuff? He read my stuff! *He read my stuff!*

"Really?" I squeak. Is it chill to ask which story he read?

He swallows. "Yeah! Don't sound so surprised." There's laughter in his voice. "How could I possibly resist hitting up FrenchWatermelonNineteen .com? Your stuff was funny. I really enjoyed it."

I feel like running in circles.

"Really?" I say again. *Shane, you* just *said really.*

"The post about your first day here, pointing out all the random differences like the walk–don't walk signs, that was great! And then I read that one about the hermit people from that random island going to McDonald's for the first time. That was hilarious." He grins.

I'm biting my lip while he's talking, like a young adult book cliché, but it's the only way to keep my smile level under control. Chill. I'm chill. He read my "The First 8 Hours" post and a short story I wrote over the holiday break. I really liked both of those!

"Thanks!" I spurt.

"We still all going to a pub later for dinner and drinks?" he asks.

"Um, yeah, I think everyone's still down."

"Nice! Looks like Flat Three is hitting the town tonight, then."

I bob my head up and down, "Yup!"

I want to ask him about a card night. A few moments pass while Pilot eats his sandwich, and I open my computer, trying to gather the courage to ask him if he likes to play cards. Why am I afraid to ask him?

"Do you like to play cards?" I ask quickly.

Pilot's eyes light up. "Do I like to play cards?" he says, smiling. "Does a bear shit in the woods?"

I grin and pull my eyebrows together. "Why do people say that when they can just say yes, which is so much faster and less confusing?"

"You play cards?" He smirks.

"Yeah, they're only my favorite—I was thinking about going out and finding a deck so we could have a cards night, maybe tomorrow with everyone?"

"I'm in. You want help finding that deck?" he asks.

I blink. "Do you . . . want to go find one?"

I stride down the sidewalk with Pilot. This is our second walk in three days. Is this a second date? I think this boy likes me. I think he's feeling what I'm feeling, and I can barely contain the urge to skip down the road.

It's still light out as we make our way down fancy-white-sophisticated-buildings lane. I like how the sidewalk on this street is never too crowded like in New York. And when I say never, I of course mean, in the last three days, it hasn't been too crowded.

"Okay, so possible suspects in this card case. I'm thinking either Tesco, Waitrose, or Sainsbury, that other grocery store I haven't seen, but people have talked about. I don't know where they'll be if they're not in a grocery store, so hopefully they're in a grocery store. Maybe some sort of convenient store?" I'm babbling. I look at Pilot. He's smiling to himself. "Sorry, I'm really excited about cards . . ."

"We're going to find cards," he replies confidently. "Let's go to a different area, though, so we get to explore more of the city."

"Okay." I shrug and tuck my hair behind my ears.

"How about we go through Hyde Park? It's right down the street." He points down the road toward a large gated area.

I raise my eyebrows. "Whoa, off the beaten track. We might get lost." That was meant to sound daunting and sarcastic, but it sounded happy. This excessive smiling has my vocal inflections all over the place.

"Don't worry, I'll Magellan us back if we get lost."

I smile at him. "Don't worry, I'm not worried."

"Good." He smiles back.

We walk in content silence as we make our way down the block and cross the street to Hyde Park. I don't almost die this time, so things are already going smoother than they did on our last walk. There's a large opening in the tall black gates that surround the park where we enter. It's a nice day, so oodles of dog owners are out and about. Some people are reading on blankets and under trees. We start down a paved trail in the grass.

I glance over at Pilot. "So, now you've read some of my stuff," I start.

"Yeah?" He grins. His hands are stuffed in the pockets of his jacket. I've got one hand in the pocket of the white zip-up I threw on and another clings to the leather of my cross-body purse.

"When do I get to hear your music?" I ask.

He snorts, but his eyes get bright like eyes do when you talk about something you're passionate about.

"Oh, man." He looks at the sky. "Well, my first album is on iTunes."

"What?" I smack his arm in disbelief with my purse hand. He shoots me a dramatic look.

"Oh crap, sorry!" My voice gets pitchy as I try not to laugh. I heave a steadying breath. "Sorry, what I meant to say was: Is your album actually on iTunes? And why didn't you mention this before?"

He's got this chill-modest-cool-guy half smile on. "Yes, it's actually on iTunes, and it's not that hard to get your album on iTunes."

"Pies, that's so cool! Can I find it under your name or—how do I search you?"

"It's under my band name."

44

"What! You have a band? You've left out so many details of your music life!"

"It's just me and my friend Ted, so it's not like a full band."

"What's your band name?"

"We're the Swing Bearers," he shares with a giant grin.

A short laugh bursts out of me. "Wow, I love that. It's almost as cool as my blog. I mean, not quite as witty, but it's got a nice ring to it."

He snorts. "Okay, calm down, French Watermelon. We can't all be on your level." The phrase *French Watermelon* sounds extra ridiculous when he says it.

"I'm gonna download your album when we get back."

He presses his lips together. "I'll excitedly await your review."

"Am I allowed to share with the roomies?"

He shakes his head, smiling. "Go for it."

"This is so exciting!" I don't exactly skip, but my feet do a weird jumpy-dance thing.

I take stock of our surroundings. I haven't been looking around enough. We're approaching an opening back out into the city streets.

"You think we go this way, then?" I ask.

Pilot stops and puts his index finger to his forehead. "Card senses are tingling . . . that way."

I roll my eyes.

We walk a little way down the street before coming up on a Starbucks. The familiarity of it amidst the *culture shock* of the last twenty-four hours actually brings me up short. I stop walking to admire it from across the street. Pilot backtracks a few steps and comes up on my right.

"Starbucks!" I point across the way. "Doesn't Starbucks feel like an old friend now?"

He shrugs slightly with his hands still in his pockets. "Have you been since we got here?" he asks.

"No, not yet."

"Shall we go give her a visit?" He smirks.

I snort. "A visit?"

"I mean, is she your friend or not? I don't want walk in on a random stranger," he answers with mock sincerity.

I scoff, "That was a stretch."

"Uh, actually I think that was pretty witty," he responds, using the male version of a valley-girl voice, his words all drawn out and over the top. I make weird smothered-laughter noises.

I take the steps two at a time into the Starbucks, coming to a stop at the end of the line. We shuffle along in silence for a few minutes, waiting to place our orders. I bounce on my toes, excited for my usual drink. When I reach the register, my mouth flops open. The barista is a tall woman in her forties with a knot of red hair—it's the rude airplane lady!

"Hi, darling! I see you're making friends!" She glances from me to Pilot, back to me, and winks. I shake my head, flabbergasted. *Dear lord, woman, please don't say anything else.*

"What would you like?" she asks.

"I . . . um, a green tea latte, please," I tell her.

"Oh, we don't have those," she replies.

"Oh . . . weird. Okay, can I have a tall pumpkin spice latte, please?"

"A what?"

"A pumpkin spice latte."

"We don't have pumpkin spice lattes." She smiles.

"Okay, I guess I'll have a tall cinnamon dolce latte, please."

She shakes her head, bemused. "Never heard of that either."

"You're kidding, right?"

"No, we don't have cinnamon . . . dolce lattes."

I can sense Pilot silently laughing beside me.

"What kind of Starbucks is this?" I mumble.

We leave five minutes later, both of us with tall vanilla lattes. That was so strange. I turn to Pilot to tell him about plane lady.

"So that was your friend?" He clicks his tongue before I have a chance to speak. "I mean, you didn't know what was on the menu, so I'd say you're mildly acquainted at best."

I run a hand down my face, trying not to snort at his terrible attempt to continue the Starbucks-is-an-old-friend joke. "I thought it was my friend, but, turns out, it was a regular coffee shop who took Polyjuice Potion and was pretending to be my friend."

"Oh, no, too far." He shakes his head, grinning. "You ruined it with the Polyjuice Potion reference."

"What are you talking about? That was clever! *You* had already pushed it too far!"

"No, I pushed it the perfect amount. Shane, you pushed it to extreme-dork levels."

My cheeks burn from the force of my smile. We're about to turn left at the upcoming intersection when I spot something colorful on the corner.

I gasp. "Pies. Look." I point toward my discovery and watch his eyes widen.

"Is that what I think is?"

"That's a Beatles store! A whole Beatles-themed store!"

"Oh wait, that's that band you like, right?" he says.

"I'm resisting the urge to smack your arm so hard right now." I'd actually like to grab his hand and drag him across the street, but my arm won't obey that command; it's too scared of rejection.

We rush across, hands unlinked. When the light changes on the next corner, we jog across and up onto the sidewalk outside the Beatles store.

"Wow!" I stare at the beautiful, brightly colored window display. "It's Beatlesful," I pronounce. I turn to Pilot wearing a giant idiot smile.

He smothers a grin and shakes his head. "I have no words for that."

"Did you get it?"

"Oh, I got it," he says.

"That was clever."

He shakes his head, smile still smooshed.

"Come on. It was clever!"

"Let it be, Shane. Let it be." He heads into the shop.

I stand on the sidewalk for a second, processing. "Oh my." I follow him in.

"Love Me Do" plays inside the store. We've stepped into a Beatles wonderland: CDs, vinyls, sweatshirts, hats, socks, key chains. I know Pilot likes the Beatles. He keeps a chill front, but I can see it in his eyes. They're all alight and eager as he inspects the trinkets. I squat down to get a better look at what appears to be a set of Beatles-themed Russian nesting dolls in a glass display case. Pilot squats next to me. His side brushes up against mine.

"Oh, man, look at the sizes! John is the biggest, Ringo's the smallest. The shade."

I turn away from the dolls to look at him. "Look who knows who the Beatles are." For just a second, he smiles like a goof, then it's back to cool-guy grin. When we stand up, he starts pointing out different vinyls that he owns as we walk through the displays.

"Shane," Pilot calls from behind me as we wander down another aisle. "Beatles cards!"

I whip around, leaping over to where he is. "What?"

"Beatles playing cards, Shane. Target acquired. Mission accomplished."

We walk back through the park as the sun ducks below the horizon.

"What's your favorite Beatles song?" Pilot asks.

"What's *your* favorite Beatles song?" I throw back.

"Shot, you answer first," he says calmly.

"What do you mean, *shot, you answer first*? You can't shot that I answer first!" I laugh.

"Uh, first rule of shotting, you can shot whatever you want to shot," he responds with his voice all goofy.

I comply, trying to roll my eyes sarcastically and failing. "My favorite is 'Hey Jude,' I think, or 'Yellow Submarine,' or 'Hello, Goodbye.' Or, or . . . 'Ob-La-Di, Ob-La-Da,' I love that one!"

He closes his eyes and nods with a closed-mouth smile. "Nice picks, nice picks."

A pack of runners *whoosh* past us on the trail. "Now you share yours," I say expectantly.

"'Helter Skelter,' probably, or 'I Am the Walrus,' or 'Octopus's Garden,' or 'Eleanor Rigby'—they've got so many great ones."

"How dare you have mocked me for saying I like the Beatles!"

He shrugs. "You look more like a Taylor Swift kind of girl."

"Um, excuse me," I protest, "I am a Taylor Swift kind of girl, thank you very much. She's marvelous." I take a second to glare and dramatically toss my hair over my shoulder. "Music snob."

He throws his head back with a laugh. Warm fuzzies bubble up inside me. I don't know the science behind warm fuzzies and how they bubble, but they do.

7. Never Mind

I find Babe sitting on her bed, watching an animated movie on her computer. She looks up as the door closes behind me. Out the creeper window, I see Sahra on the couch in the kitchen, talking to her laptop.

"Hey!" Babe exclaims.

"Hey! Whatchya watching?"

"*Ratatouille*!" She's smiling ear to ear.

"Never saw that one."

"You never saw *Ratatouille*? It's so cute!"

I drag a chair up to Babe's bed, so we can properly chat. "Did you know that Pilot has an album on iTunes?"

"What? I didn't even know he made music!" She minimizes *Ratatouille* and pulls iTunes up on her computer. I scoot over so I can look on.

"Is it under his name?" She starts typing in Pilot Penn.

"No, it's under Swing Bearers."

"Swing Bearers!" She giggles. "Ah! I love it." She types it into the search box and taps the enter key. We watch in suspense as the internet loads. An album called *Porcelain Trampoline* pops up, purchasable for $6.99.

"Oh my gosh, it's real!" I laugh.

"Seven bucks? Heck yes!" Babe clicks the buy button.

We spend the next hour listening to the Swing Bearers while we sit on our computers. I like it. It has a relaxed, jazzy, vintage feel. When it comes time to get ready for the pub, I switch the music selection over to Britney Spears. Sahra comes back to the room, and we all get a little more dressed up. I change into my favorite skirt—a black high-waisted one with buttons—and a crop top with a blue-eyed tiger on it. Nothing too fancy, but more so than the jeans and blue New York T-shirt I was wearing on my walk with Pilot earlier.

The five of us sit around a circular table in the Queen's Head pub. I'm halfway through my first legal ordered-at-a-bar alcoholic drink: a glass of red wine. I dislike wine less than I dislike any other alcohol, so in the spirit of trying new things, I've decided to give it a chance. People say wine is an acquired taste, so I'm working on acquiring it.

Pilot, Atticus, and Babe are on their second Guinnesses, and Sahra's almost done with her glass of red wine. She's telling us about her boyfriend, Val, and how much her family loves him. They took him with them last summer to Lebanon.

When the conversation dies down, Pilot suggests we play a drinking game called 21 that I've never heard of, but turns out to be amazing. We cackle our way through the entire game. Everyone gets to make all sorts of random rules that correlate with the numbers between one and twenty-one. Babe creates a ridiculous one that has us all standing up and rotating to the chair on our right. Every round sends us moving around the table like we're performing some weird, poorly choreographed dance, and every time we get up to rotate, we start laughing uncontrollably. My abs are sore when we finish.

"Have you guys used Skype to call home yet?" Sahra asks, as we sober up from the game. "You can purchase minutes, and then use them to call the US, instead of spending a million dollars on your phone. It's great. I've been talking to Val on it because the internet for video-chatting kinda sucks here."

"I guess I should do that," I pipe in. "I still haven't actually spoken to my parents since I got here. I've never used Skype before, but I've heard legends," I add dramatically. "It can't be too difficult, right?"

"How have you never used Skype?" Pilot says in disbelief.

Babe laughs. "It's super-easy—my parents can do it. We have a Skype date tomorrow afternoon, to talk about the Rome trip."

"Yeah, you'll be fine. It's self-explanatory," Sahra adds with a smile.

I smile back happily (Sahra smiles are rare) and take another small sip of my wine. I try not to wince as the sourness coats my tongue.

"I Skyped with my parents earlier," Atticus says. "Which reminds me, did you get to Skype your girlfriend, Pilot? Sorry I was on the phone for so long." Time slows.

I blink.

Um. What.

What does he mean, *girlfriend*? What does *he mean*, girlfriend? *What does he mean, girlfriend*? My stomach does five hundred backflips as I turn my head to gauge Pilot's reaction. He's mid-gulp of Guinness. I try to meet his eyes, but he focuses on Atticus.

"I, uh, no. It's okay, no worries," he says before looking down into his drink.

I catch Babe's eye, and her expression of shock mirrors what I'd imagine my own face looks like right now. My eyes whip to Sahra—composed, as usual.

Babe speaks first. "You have a girlfriend?" she exclaims, voicing my thundering thoughts aloud.

My mouth feels dry. I think I'm slowly sinking down through the floor. I've hit an iceberg.

"Yeah, you didn't know?" Atticus says, sounding excited to reveal something we all didn't know first.

Pilot looks up at Babe. "Yeah, but we've only been dating for three months," he adds dismissively. His eyes bounce around the table and stop on mine. I hold his gaze for a split second before looking away.

Only three months.

"Oh," Babe says, like that explains something.

"Yeah, I asked her if she'd be up for putting things on hold . . . while I went abroad because I wanted to travel, and so we wouldn't have to worry about the long-distance thing, but she didn't like that idea." He chuckles nervously. "Do any of you have a boyfriend? I mean, I know you do, Sahra."

"Nope," Babe answers cheerily.

"Single," Atticus sings.

Pilot's gaze falls on me.

I'm underwater. I stare at him for a moment before he repeats himself directly to me. "Do you?"

Resurface. I clear my throat. "Um, no. I, I've never, um, dated someone that I, um, I liked enough to keep dating," I say softly.

I can practically hear my cousins snickering: *You've never dated anyone.* A flush burns its way up my neck.

Pilot's expression lights up. "Same!"

Babe nods her head at him in vigorous agreement. My armpits feel hot.

"I never really felt like I wanted a relationship, er, and then I met Amy, and we started dating and now, um, she's the first real relationship I've had," he continues.

Inhale. Exhale.

"So you're going to stay together long distance, then?" Babe asks.

He frowns for a moment. "I don't know, really. We'll see what happens."

We'll see what happens?

There's the lifeboat. I clamber onto it and try to breathe normally again while Pilot brings up my idea for a Flat Three card night tomorrow. I don't comment. Babe proclaims her excitement. Sahra might join us, but doesn't sound too enthused. Atticus might be able to join us after theater.

1/13/11 2:00 a.m.

He has a girlfriend. Of course he does. How could he not? My stomach's a churning pit of steaming embarrassment. And guilt! He has a girlfriend?!?!?

I keep replaying the conversation from the pub and feeling like an idiot.

What have we been doing, then? It's only been three days, but I feel like we've been taking walks and flirting forever. It felt like we were kind of, sort of, dating. I built up all these hopes. Now they're all withering around in pieces on the floor of the pub.

HE HAS A GIRLFRIEND!!!

It seems like he's not serious about this girlfriend. Why have a girlfriend long distance if you're not serious about her? You definitely don't ask a girl you're in love with if you can put your relationship on hold for four months while you're in another country. You don't introduce the idea of your girlfriend to people with the phrase "we've only been dating for three months" if you're in love. You don't say, "I don't know, we'll see what happens" in response to a question about staying together long distance if you're in love. You don't, you just don't. You don't. You don't. You don't. You just don't. You don't.

Why wasn't this on Facebook?

How do I act around him now? As if everything's fine? As if everything's the same? Are they going to break up?

He said, "We'll see what happens." Like, what the actual fudge? *Metaphorically rips hair out.*

In other, less depressing news, I'm prepping to use Skype for the first time.

8. I Want to Be the Rainstorm, Not the House of Cards

It's Thursday, and it's pouring. I can hear the rain pummeling the Karlston. I've set myself up in the kitchen with Sawyer and a bagel. In my email, I find a letter with the name and address of the place I'm going be interning: a travel magazine called *Packed! For Travel!* I have to interview with them before things are definite. My interview is scheduled for tomorrow afternoon, a few hours before we catch the plane for Rome.

I've been conditioned to think of creative jobs like mystical beings. Finding one would be like finding a unicorn. When I filled out the Common App for college three years ago, both of my parents were in the room, hovering over my shoulder. When I scrolled down to creative writing and added it as my major, Dad jolted behind me. I knew it wasn't what they were expecting.

"What are you doing?" Dad yelped.

"I'm choosing a major."

"Honey, we've known for years you want to be a doctor." Mom smiled encouragingly.

"Well, I've been thinking—"

"No." Dad tried to end the discussion.

"What about journalism?" I moved the cursor to select it.

"Where is this coming from? You've got straight A's in all your math and AP science classes; you're going to be a great doctor," Mom pushed.

"*Yeah, just, I took that creative writing elective last year and it was so fun. It got me thinking, maybe—*"

"*There is no maybe. We talked about how that class was just for fun. I'm not going to drop fifty thousand dollars a year for you to graduate with no job prospects. What are you tryin' to pull here?*" Dad said.

"*I'm not trying to pull anything—*"

"*Look at me,*" Dad commanded. I twisted to look him in the eye. "*Do you trust me? Do you trust your dad?*" I felt my lips start to quiver. I smashed them into a line, gave him a quick nod. "*We know what's best for you.*"

I get where they were coming from, but—*Packed! For Travel!* is a real-life, well-known magazine that can lead to a real-life job prospect.

I spend the morning in the kitchen, alternating between researching *Packed!* and reading book three in the Vampire Academy series: *Shadow Kiss*. When I break midday and head out into the hall, it's full of music. Guitar. I tread lightly down the corridor and stop outside my room.

Across the way, Pilot's door is wide open. He's sitting inside on a navy-blue twin bed, fiddling with a shiny tan guitar. There's a big map of the UK pinned up on the wall behind him. It takes a few moments for him to register that I'm watching. When he does, he stops playing.

"Hey," he starts.

"Hey." I hesitate a moment before crossing the hall to lean against his doorframe. *Be outgoing and act normal.* "You were able to bring your guitar here with you?" I say softly.

"Oh yeah, of course! I can't go four months without playing. I carried it on the plane."

I feel myself smile. "Does she have a name?"

"What, my guitar?"

"No, your bed," I quip.

He looks at me nervously and I feel my cheeks redden, oh my god. *Oh god.*

"Yes, your guitar!" I add quickly.

"Hmm." He considers for a moment. "She doesn't have a name, but now that you mention it, maybe she deserves a name."

"She deserves a name," I agree. "My computer is Sawyer."

He laughs. "As in Tom?"

"As in James Ford, the con man with a heart of gold, who changed his name to Sawyer, as in Tom Sawyer."

Pilot narrows his eyes in confusion.

"It's a *Lost* thing."

"Ohhh," he says, understanding dawning. "I never watched that show."

I put on my best snob voice. "It's only one of the greatest shows of all time."

He purses his lips. "I'll add it to the Netflix queue."

"So, your guitar?" I prompt.

"So, my guitar." He rests it on his lap so it's facing upward, and runs a hand reverently along the edges. "I'm thinking she feels like a Lucy."

"'In the Sky with Diamonds'?"

"'In the Sky with Diamonds,'" he confirms with a half smile.

There's a beat of silence. My heart rams nervously. "I listened to Porcelain Trampoline yesterday," I blurt.

His eyes light up. "And . . ."

And—why didn't I prepare a beautifully thought-out review? I'm not quite sure what to say. I liked it, but I'm still upset about last night, and it's making me wary of complimenting him.

"It was really good. I rated it four out of five stars."

His grin stretches. "Four out of five? Why not five out of five?"

I stammer for a response. "Uh, with five out of five, there's no room to grow! Maybe next time will be five stars."

He laughs. "It's okay, I'm just kidding."

I nod and focus on the guitar instead of his face. "Are you working on new stuff?"

"Yeah, like I said, hoping to put out that next album while I'm here."

"Oh, yeah! So, the five-star album is already in the making. Has London inspired you?" I say teasingly.

He blows out a breath. "Actually, a lot of family stuff," he says more quietly. The way his demeanor changes throws me. Guarded. I shouldn't have asked such a personal question. I falter for a second. *Change the subject.*

"You should start a YouTube channel so people can hear your music!"

He picks up the guitar, strums something, and stops. "I don't know, maybe," he muses unconvincingly. "Anyway, new album's almost done. I'm just adding in little things here and there, and then sending it to Ted so he can make final tweaks."

"You almost have two albums under your belt. That's awesome . . ." I trail off as he starts to play again, and back away toward my own room, not wanting to impede on his guitar time.

"Shane," he calls out, as I'm shoving my key into the lock. I pivot around. "Yeah?"

He's smiling now. "What time are we playing cards tonight?" The fuzzies bubble again.

The Skype call I scheduled with my parents rolls around before I'm ready for it. At 4:00 p.m. I dial them, swallowing hard at the nervous lump in my throat. Seconds later, their pixelated faces swim up in front of me—nicely framed, I may add. My how-to-frame-a-photo lectures have paid off. We exchange hellos and basic pleasantries. My palms are sweating.

"So, how's it going?" my mother probes excitedly. "How's class? Are your roommates on the premed track? I was looking at that brochure today and it sounds like it's gonna be tough—you should make some friends in your program."

My parents have a *YU London Study Abroad—Premed Track* brochure that I forged last semester. I trekked down to the YU study abroad office, took a brochure for each track offered in London, and put together a masterpiece.

"Guess what? I'm going to Rome this weekend!" I deflect.

Mom full-on gasps. "But you just got there."

Dad's brows knit together. "How much is that gonna cost?"

"Don't worry, I'm using the money I've saved from working over breaks."

Mom's lips fall into a worried frown.

"And what happens when that runs out?" Dad asks bluntly.

Mom's eyebrows shoot up. "Sal!"

"Hey! I'm just lookin' out for our daughter."

"I'll work over the summer. Dad, this is a once-in-a-lifetime opportunity."

He sighs. "Well, that's great, I guess. Headed to the homeland, eh?" He smiles like he's been to Italy.

"And you guys said learning Italian wouldn't come in handy," I add in a silly voice. Dad waves his hands dismissively.

Mom scoots her chair closer to the desktop and leans in toward the camera. "Make sure you're careful! You're wearing the cross-body purse like we talked about, right?"

"How's class? This travel won't affect your studies?" Dad asks.

"Have you made friends in your program?" Mom smiles. "Are you sleeping well? Eating healthy?"

"Yeah, I'm fine, Ma, and everything's going great! And yeah, um, one of my roommates is in my program . . . Sahra's premed."

Mom's smile stretches. "Good! That's great, Shane." And then, just as quickly, it droops. "Oh my god, Shane, your nails!"

I quickly move my hands out of the shot. "Ma!"

"What did I tell you about leaving old nail polish on? It's not professional. Let me see your nails again. They look terrible, Shane. Go out and get some nail polish remover."

"Okay. I'll pick some up."

Dad interrupts. "You seeing any guys out there?"

I drop my head into my hands. "Dad," I groan.

"Shane, really, your nails."

I shove my hands under my thighs. "No! I'm not seeing any guys, gah! I've only been here for, like, three days. What's going on there?"

Dad looks pointedly into the camera with his eyes all wide. "You know it's okay for you to date people. I never said you can't date!" This is, like, the third time we've been through this spiel. Dad's already worried I'm going to die alone. Either that or he's worried I'm gay. I have to check Dad and Uncle Dan on homophobic crap all the time.

I roll my eyes. "Oh my god, Dad, I never thought you did."

"You gotta stop sitting around with those books all the time!"

I close my eyes and suck in a cleansing breath.

Mom sighs. "Are the classes harder or easier than YU?"

I shrug and wave my hands. "Um, yeah, they're different. My teachers have accents and stuff."

"What does that mean? Do accents make things harder—"

"Oh my god. Wait! I haven't told you about the grocery store. You guys . . ." I jump into my Tesco story, and it's extremely satisfying to see them react just as drastically as I did when I tell them about the sauce selection. When the story concludes, I tell them I have to go.

Mom comes close to the camera again, "Okay, love you! *Be very careful! Be smart!*"

"Yeah, listen to your mother!"

I roll my eyes. "I always listen to my mother, and I'm always smart!"

"Do something about your nails!" Mom exclaims.

I hang up, sagging as a breath *whooshes* out of me.

1/12/11 11:45 p.m.

Bad news: Hardcore lying to my parents is already eating me up from the inside.

Good news: Card night was a giant hit!

I think I bonded with Sahra! Just when I thought she didn't want to be friends, she offered to pick up dinner for card night. She was on the way out for her internship interview, and she turned around and said: "Hey, should I grab everyone shawarma for card night later?"

I had no idea what the heck shawarma was, but I obviously said yes. Babe, Pilot, and I were all shawarma noobs before tonight.

SHANE MEETS SHAWARMA: A RETELLING

Sahra carefully unloaded wrapped food items from a white paper bag and distributed them among us. Before I had even touched mine, Pilot had unwrapped his and taken a bite.

"It's SO GOOD," he told us through a mouthful. Babe agreed around her own mouthful with a vigorous head bob.

"I know." Sahra plopped down at the table with us.

I dropped my gaze to the wrap before me. There were pickles in it. I'm not a pickle fan, but it smelled great, like really well-marinated chicken, so I kneaded away the paper at snail speed before hesitantly taking a bite. And then another. Because it was delicious and full of new taste combos I've never had together before. Pickles were made to be in shawarma.

"This is amazing!" I raised the wrap. "We should do this again next week."

"Totally vote we make Flat Three shawarma a weekly thing!" Babe seconded.

Sahra laughed, looking pleased. "Shawarma Wednesdays?"

"Shwednesdays," Pilot pronounced.

"I'm down." Sahra smiled.

And so, tonight, Shwenesday was born.

We used my Beatles cards. I showed off a little and shuffled the cards fancy. Leo and I once spent a whole day teaching ourselves card tricks. His little brother Alfie was our official shuffle-off judge.

Babe was all impressed with me. "How did you do that?"

I told them I was a professional, and then proceeded to mess up my bridge, spewing cards across the table. Embarrassment hit me hard for half a second, but then I snorted, Pilot made fun of me, and we all broke into laughter.

I taught everyone Rummy 500. Sahra put up a good fight. It came down to one hand in the end, but I won. Pilot's girlfriend came up once. Out of the blue, Babe asked if Amy (that's her) liked to play cards. Pilot said it wasn't her thing. The question was followed by an extended moment of awkward silence. I started sweating, stood to grab a glass of water, and my chair flipped backward, filling the void with the clash of metal on tile. I growled involuntarily, Babe and Pilot exploded into laughter again, and Atticus walked through the door just in time to join us for the next round. So, all in all, a good night.

9. Maybe We Can See the World Together

I'm twitchy with a fifty-fifty blend of anxiety and excitement as I head to the kitchen for breakfast. I have my book bag with me as usual, but today it's stuffed to the breaking point with my clothes and toiletries for Rome. I'm leaving Sawyer here because there won't be any internet at our inn. I'll have my dinky block phone, and Horcrux Nine. As I'm climbing the stairs to leave for class, Pilot comes into view, heading toward the kitchen.

"Rome for the weekend, French Watermelon!" he yells without pausing to look back. I jog up the steps, beaming.

As promised, Professor Blackstairs's class begins with another postcard.

January 14, 2011

Mom and Dad,

I haven't told you this yet, but after class today, I'm interviewing for a job at a magazine! It's only an internship, but an internship can lead to a paid job. I know you think my obsession with reading and stories is silly, but I don't agree. I know you want me to let

*this go, but I can't. I hope you give me the chance to
prove you wrong. I think I can do this.*
    XO,
     Shane

I slip the London Eye postcard into my bag next to the London Bridge from Wednesday. Class is wonderful again. We talk about writing suspense, and then we take the last hour to tackle a suspenseful short story of our own. I write about a nanny who's attacked unsuspectedly by her employer.

When we're dismissed, I run off to catch the Tube to Covent Garden for my interview. My legs nervously jiggle up and down as I watch the stops blur through the windows.

I'm a couple minutes early when I step up to the tall white building matching the address for *Packed!* The first level is a coffee shop, which makes things a little confusing. I wander around the side of the structure until I find another door. This one is outfitted with a buzzer and a little silver plaque above it that reads PACKED! FOR TRAVEL! It's on the second floor. I reach up and press the button.

"Hello?" a voice asks through the speaker.

"Hi. I'm Shane Primaveri. Here for an interview?"

A loud buzz makes me jump back a foot. The door in front of me unlatches. I pull it open and ascend the stairs. At the top of the steps is a white door with a frosted circular window decorated with the *Packed! For Travel!* logo.

I let loose a practically inaudible *whoa* as I step inside the office. A smile itches at my lips. The room is shiny, white, and modern. The walls are lined with gorgeous poster-sized photographs of cities all around the world. My eyes quickly locate New York among them. A pang of pride runs through me. I bring my attention to the half-moon silvery-white receptionist desk before me. A pale, tiny, twenty-something woman with freckles and a strawberry-blond bob looks up at me.

"Hello!" She has a heavy Irish accent.

"Hi! I'm Shane Primaveri. I'm here for an interview with Wendy." I shuffle my feet together.

The receptionist introduces herself as Tracey. I take a seat in a modern-looking silver chair adjacent to the door while Tracey goes to fetch Wendy. I watch as she scurries across the floor to the opposite wall and carefully opens a glass door to what must be Wendy's office. The center of the open space is littered with silver desks, big high-def computer monitors, and youngish employees. Tracey turns toward me, and I quickly drop my gaze back to my lap.

"Shane?"

I look up again to find a tall woman with long, straight, dark hair and golden-brown skin. She's wearing high-waisted black slacks and an orange blazer. She looks like a model.

"Hi!" I jump out of my seat as the woman extends her arm for a handshake.

"Hi, I'm Wendy! I run things around here. Great to meet you. Let's talk!"

I follow Wendy into her office. She has an enormous, sleek glass desk. I timidly seat myself in one of the two silver chairs in front of it. A whole corner of the desk is covered with tiny trinket versions of iconic landmarks: a pyramid, the Eiffel Tower, the Colosseum, the Statue of Liberty, the London Eye.

"Give me a little rundown about you, Shane. We're excited to hopefully have you interning here these next few months."

I press my hands against my knees, forcing them into stillness. "Um, well, I, I'm studying abroad, and I'm doing the writing program. I love reading, writing, telling stories. I'd love to work as a writer someday. And I have some interest in photography . . . Um, I have a blog! I post my pieces there sometimes, and I'm turning it into a study-abroad blog for these next few months."

"That's great!" She smiles at me. It makes me feel better. I grin back. "Well, here at *Packed!* we're currently working on expanding our online repertoire. I don't know if you've checked out our website—"

"I have! I love it!"

She laughs. "Then you've seen our city guides."

I have. They have travel guides for cities all over the world, the best places to stay, the best tourist spots to hit, where to eat, where to go out. It's great.

"So, we're working on expanding that series and adding some more exotic places. We're also always looking to add new series and points of view. Maybe as a final project here, you could even do a piece for us? We can work together on *A Guide to Studying Abroad in London*? I think study abroad guides could bring in a whole new demographic."

I choke on air for a second. Me? Do a piece? For their real-life magazine? It's a struggle not to gasp. "I . . . I'd love that. That sounds amazing!"

"Good!" She smiles at me again. "Have you done much traveling?"

"Um, not yet. Well, I traveled here, but I want to travel more. I'm actually going to Rome this weekend," I blurt excitedly.

"Fantastic! You're going to love it!" She shrugs enthusiastically, while still managing to look sophisticated. "We're a laid-back group here. We all love traveling, so if you ever want any recommendations or tips, don't hesitate to talk to us. While you're here, I hope you learn a lot! Tracey will be your go-to gal for questions, and she'll introduce you to the staff on your first day. We're looking forward to having you."

"Thank you so much!"

She stands and shakes my hand again. That was it? I'm going to work at a travel magazine!

10. Rome Ma-Ma

Our seats end up being scattered throughout the plane. Babe's in the window seat directly behind me. Sahra's a couple of rows up. Pilot's a few rows back, across the way in a middle seat. There's a drunk couple sitting next to me who keep trying to pull me into their conversation. I laugh feebly at their jokes and then go back to reading *Shadow Kiss* or staring out the window. Every so often, I sit on my foot and twist around to check on everyone. Babe isn't a constant reader, but she's currently working on *I Am Number Four* because the movie's coming out soon. I should give her a list of book recommendations for when she finishes. Maybe I can convert her to constant reader-hood. Pilot's ordering a bloody mary because drinks are complimentary on this flight (as has been made glaringly obvious by the couple in my row). I can't quite see anything other than the tip of Sahra's head. She's probably reading an intellectual book. I spotted something nonfiction sticking out of her bag earlier.

It takes us less than two hours to get to Rome. As we stride through the airport, I'm struck over and over again with jolts of excitement as I read the signs around us. They're in Italian, and I know what they all mean! It's probably annoying, but I can't help reading them out loud every few seconds and translating them.

"*Uscita!* That means exit!"

"*Cibo,* that's food, guys!"

"*Farmacia,* that's a pharmacy!"

It's obnoxious, but since everyone's equally excited, I'm tolerated without complaints. We pass through customs in a daze of enthusiasm. They add a Rome stamp to my barely used passport. I smile at it before stuffing it back into the purse inside my book bag.

On the way to the inn, our taxi drives right past the Colosseum. *The Colosseum!* We just casually pass it on the road. It's all lit up from the inside with gold light. Not two minutes later, the cab driver tells us we've arrived.

We file out onto a narrow cobblestone street. Old-fashioned buildings line both sides of the road. We shuffle up to number 42—the address of our inn. The numbers are carved into a gray stone mounted next to a giant arched wooden door—the kind of door you see on castles in movies.

We glance around at each other with hesitant expressions.

"This is it, right?" I ask Babe.

"This is it." She reaches out toward a small, dark doorbell to the left, dwarfed by the size of the door. It makes a buzzing noise, and after a few moments, the door opens to reveal a tiny Italian man.

The inside is quaint, cozy. The man introduces himself as Paolo, the innkeeper. He gives us a map of Rome (which Pilot immediately takes from him) and a set of two keys (which Babe takes): one for our room and one for the castle door outside. They're big, decorative iron ones straight out of a fairy tale.

The normal-sized door to our room clicks open as Babe twists the proper ancient key in the lock. We take quick stock. There are two twin beds with bright red comforters and one queen. It's spacious and full of color. We're all ravenous, so we drop our stuff. I fish my purse out of my bag and leave everything else behind.

Outside I can see the Colosseum in the distance, glowing in a haze of yellow. That's our heading. The four of us waltz through tiny brick alleyways, around endless colorful Fiats. All the architecture has an ancient feel to it, like these structures were built into the landscape of the city.

The area around the Colosseum is gloriously empty. We gaze at it from atop a hill inlaid with a set of long, curving steps that lead down to the ground. I can't believe this is real. I can't believe it's been standing for thousands of years. We can't go in till tomorrow when it's actually open, but Babe and I take out our cameras, and we all have a mini photoshoot outside the deserted piece of history.

We end up at a trattoria nearby that's still abuzz with customers. Babe requests a jug of red wine for the table.

"Italy is famous for its wine!" she explains. "Getting a jug for the table is a must."

We all order copious amounts of Italian food—I get ravioli, and it's exquisite. Sahra raises a glass to Rome, and we clink ours against it. We chat for hours, making our way through the entire jug. I can feel the alcohol as we mosey back to the room together, joking and laughing at everything. My chest is hot and fuzzy as I slip into my bed at the inn.

I wake with a jolt, taking a few deep breaths before remembering where I am. My mouth feels dry. My eyes zip to the tiny black digital clock on the night table. It's only 7:30 a.m. I shuffle to the bathroom and decide to start getting ready because we planned to get up at 8:00 a.m. My lips are chapped, so I head back to my area of the floor and look for my purse, aka the keeper of the Chapstick.

I don't see it on the floor, so I kneel on the ground and start rummaging through my book bag. My hand flails through clothes and toiletries without skimming over anything that even vaguely resembles my cross-body. Fear sizzles up my chest.

No, no, no, no. My passport's in that purse. My block phone's in that purse. All my money's in that purse . . . I had it at the restaurant. I had it on the back of my chair. Did I leave it?

My three travel mates are still asleep. I snatch my book bag off the floor and run to the bathroom to get changed. I have to get to the restaurant. I need to find my purse.

What an idiot. I'm such an idiot!

I emerge from the bathroom two minutes later, and position myself in front of the full-length mirror outside it to frantically throw on some makeup.

"Shane . . . why are you running around?"

I freeze and look down to my left, eye pencil held aloft. Pilot's propped up on his bed, squinting at me with sleepy eyes. His brown hair's all mussed up.

My answer comes out in a hushed rush of words. "I can't find my purse. It has my passport. I think I left it at the restaurant, so I have to go back and get it."

As I say it out loud, a string of frantic images run through my mind: me detained at the airport, me stuck in Rome by myself, my flatmates heading back to London without me, me on the phone with my parents, my parents having to make all the calls to get me out of this, finding out there is no premed program in London, my father disowning me—

Pilot's voice snaps me back. "Okay, I'll come with you," he returns simply.

I bob my chin up and down a zillion times. "Okay, okay, thank you."

He heads past me into the bathroom with his own bag. Ten minutes later, we're ready to go. It's almost 8:00 a.m. Babe and Sahra stir as we head for the door.

"Hey," Babe croaks, sitting up abruptly.

"Hey." I speed through an explanation. "I lost my purse—I think I left it at the restaurant, so we're gonna go see if we can get it back."

"Wait, we can get dressed . . ."

"No it's fine," I start, but Pilot jumps in.

"We'll go, and we can meet you at the Colosseum. I have my phone, so just let me know when you're heading over."

I nod in agreement and shoot Pilot a grateful look. I can't sit and wait for them to get ready while my purse, laden with passport and money, is indisposed.

"Okay," Babe mutters. She rises and heads toward the bathroom.

I turn for the door, feeling naked without my cross-body. How did I leave the restaurant like this? It feels so wrong!

This is your fault, wine.

Pilot and I walk in silence toward the restaurant. I'm so strung out about the purse that I barely appreciate the fact that Pilot volunteered to come with me—and not regular me: silent, sweaty, slightly angry, panicky me. She's no fun. *What was I thinking letting him come?*

As the trattoria comes into view, I speed up, power walking until I'm face-to-face with its closed door. My eyes lock on the tiny paper in the window displaying the hours. It's closed. I didn't even think about the fact that it's 8:00 a.m. It doesn't open till 3:00 p.m.

I whirl around, throwing my hands up in the air. "It's closed!" I yelp hopelessly.

Pilot comes up next to me to read what the sign says.

"Pies, it's closed," I repeat. I pace a few feet away from the door and pivot, turning back. "It's closed, and I have no money and no passport and no purse, and we're in a foreign country, and it might not even be in there, and it's closed!" My palms seize the sides of my head, and I focus my eyes on the ground.

What now? I have to stay here and wait for someone to open the restaurant so I can get my purse. It's too important.

I shouldn't have had that wine. Why did I leave London? I haven't even started my internship! If I've lost my passport, I've already blown everything to pieces. I didn't think this through. This whole experience hinges on my parents never having to look further into this program. What was I thinking taking a risk like leaving the country!

I feel a cool hand close around my forearm and look up.

"Hey." Pilot gently pulls my arm away from my face. "Shane, you're spinning in circles. Maybe sit down for a sec."

His hand slides away as he lowers himself onto the curb in front of the closed restaurant. I shake out my arms, trying to throw off the fidgety feeling crawling over my skin, and collapse next to him. My heels dance up and down. We're silent for a whole minute before Pilot speaks again.

"Hey," he starts, "it's stressful now, but think about it this way: However today goes, you're going to have a great story for the blog." He grins.

I shoot him an unamused look and shake my head. "I shouldn't have trusted myself to leave the country." I drop my head into my hands and ramble to the cobblestones, "I'm sorry. You should go meet up with everyone else. I'm gonna wait here. I have to wait for them to open 'cause this is too important; my passport's in there—I'm sorry I made you come with me. You can go back. I just have to stay. My parents are gonna kill me if I . . . if all my stuff gets lost." Stress curdles in my gut.

"Shane."

I stare at the ground. "What?"

"You didn't make me come with you. I volunteered."

I snort, thinking of *The Hunger Games*. He nudges me lightly with his shoulder, and I lift my head.

"Your parents will understand."

"You don't know them." After a few seconds, I continue, "My dad *grounded* me in high school for reading *The Da Vinci Code*."

"What?" He chuckles. "Why?"

"Because we're Catholic, and the church had a problem with it, blah blah blah."

"Are you guys super-religious?"

"I mean, I'm not." I pause for a second, curiosity rising. "Are you?"

"Nah, I mean, my family's Jewish. I do Hanukkah."

I nod, understanding. "So no awesome indie rock-themed bar mitzvah for you?"

He smirks. "Well . . ."

"Oh my god, you had an indie rock-themed bar mitzvah?" My mouth turns up in a tiny, closed-lipped smile.

"More punk rock." He grins.

I snort, turning away to watch the restaurant door. Off in the distance, I can make out the Colosseum. Pilot follows my gaze.

"So, if you could go back in time, would you want stop by there and watch a gladiator match?" he asks.

Trying to distract me. I click my tongue. "I guess so," I answer. "Would you?"

"Uh, obviously," he answers in a silly voice.

I smother a smile, storyteller mode switching on. "What if you only had three points you could choose to go back to? Would this be one of the three? And you can't do things like kill Hitler; you can only sit in on events and stuff. Maybe you can put in your two cents at said events."

Pilot frowns for a moment.

"That's a tough one." He stares into the distance. "I think first, I'd have to hit up one those epic concerts your favorite band used to put on back in the day."

I smile. "Taylor Swift or . . . ?"

He makes a *pfft* half-laugh sound. "I'd have to check out the Beatles . . . and—I feel like I gotta think out these second two."

"I think I'd want to be in the room when they wrote the Constitution." I ponder. "Maybe dressed as a guy, so I could insert my two cents and they'd listen to me."

Pilot shoots me a surprised grin. I return my attention back to the restaurant door. Silence stretches for a few moments. My panicked twitchiness returns.

"So, I guess we should go meet Sahra and Babe," Pilot says.

I turn to look him in the eyes. "Yeah, you go ahead. I'm going to stay here and wait."

He tilts his head forward. "Shane, it doesn't open till three."

"Yeah, you go, and I'll stay here."

"You think I'm just going to leave you here huddled on the curb by yourself?"

I look away from his face, feeling guilty. "Just go meet up with them. I'm fine!"

I wonder what the protocol actually is for losing your passport in a foreign country. Why wasn't this in *So You're Going to Study Abroad*?

"Let's go grab some food, and then we'll track down Sahra and Babe," he suggests.

My eyebrows furrow again. I do my best to keep my voice level. "Pilot, I don't have any money. I have nothing; I have to stay and wait for my purse."

His eyebrows descend as he responds with all seriousness, "Oh, is it meeting you out here?"

A breath huffs through my lips, and I fiddle with my numbers bracelet, spinning it around on my wrist. The idea of carrying the added guilt of ruining Rome for both me and Pilot is too much. Losing a passport is a trip ruiner.

"What does your bracelet mean?" he asks.

"It's a *Lost* thing. You'd have to watch it." I dismiss his next distraction attempt and instantly feel shitty about it.

"I lost my wallet once—" he tries again.

I interrupt him. "This isn't the same, Pies."

"Excuse me, can I tell my insightful story?" He raises his eyebrows. I deflate, caving in on myself and staring at the ground.

"So, I was in Florida with my roommates, freshman year spring break, and we took a cab to the beach."

I'm distracted momentarily, imagining Pilot all shirtless on the beach. I raise my gaze and watch him talk.

"When we got there, we set up camp near the water, and then I realized my wallet wasn't in my pocket."

I raise my eyebrows sarcastically.

He continues. "It was our only beach day there, and I spent about an hour retracing my steps all over the sand before heading back to where my buddies were. I had to borrow one of their phones to try and get ahold of the cab company. I gave them my hotel info and my friend's number so that if they found it, they could return it. Then I spent the day stressed out, pacing around and worrying."

"Uh-huh." I narrow my eyes.

He smiles. "And then I got a call around four that a driver had found a wallet and dropped it off at my hotel. When we went back, it was there."

I study him skeptically for a moment. "What's your point?" I say, trying to sound aloof.

"It's not worth the stress of stressing. We're here for two days. You can't spend one of them sitting on the curb of a restaurant for six hours."

"But what if—"

"Let's go get a gelato." He stands and offers me a hand.

"What? It's, like, nine in the morning," I say from the curb.

"And?"

"And I don't have any money," I add gloomily.

"I've got this one."

I twist back to frown at the trattoria behind me. *Why are you closed? I need you now!* When I turn back, Pilot's still holding out his hand. I am hungry. I won't be able to eat if I pass up this offer and insist on staying—because money.

"And then we'll come back and check on the restaurant?" I ask, grabbing his hand.

He pulls me up off the curb and releases my palm. My hand is fangirling as I return it to my side. I begrudgingly follow him down the cobblestone street.

"And then we'll meet Sahra and Babe at the Colosseum."

I let this sit for a moment. Maybe he's right. Am I being stays-in-her-dorm-and-misses-everything-out-of-fear Shane? But, if they happen to open early, I'd be here the second they open.

I sigh. "But what if I need Chapstick and start to deteriorate due to withdrawal?"

In front of me, Pilot turns back and shoots me a sarcastic look. I can see him trying not to smile behind it.

"If it gets bad, I'll take you to the hospital myself."

The corners of my mouth twitch up. Pilot hooks a left at the next corner, and we stop abruptly outside a gelato shop. It's open. What the heck? "How did you know this was here?"

"We passed it last night."

"It was dark!" I exclaim in disbelief.

He puts a finger to his temple. "Good with directions."

Pilot buys me a watermelon gelato, and we make our way down to a tourist-swarmed Colosseum. We find Sahra and Babe in the line to get in. While we're waiting, I express my extreme disappointment in not being able to document the day because my digital camera is in my purse—and immediately Babe offers to let me borrow hers whenever I feel like snapping a picture. I fight the urge to wrap her in one of those abrupt, emotional thank-you hugs because I don't want to come off as too dramatic. I go a little boneless for a second, looking from her to Pilot. I got real lucky being assigned to Flat Three.

1/16/11 11:50 p.m.

I thought I would be tired, having spent the last two days flouncing about in Rome and then traveling all the way back to the Karlston, but I'm invigorated right now. I'm riding this weird post-travel high. I already edited all the pictures, put them up on Facebook, and finished dramatizing a first draft of the harrowing tale of almost losing my passport for my blog ("That Time I Lost My Passport"). I'm happy with it, but I need to put down a more personal recounting of the weekend so I don't forget any of the details that made it super-wonderful.

THE ROME TRIP 1/14–1/16/2011: A HIGHLIGHTS REEL

<u>We Explored the Colosseum</u>

When the time was right, I switched into photographer mode, borrowing Babe's camera and snapping solo pictures of Babe, Pilot, and Sahra. Afterward, Babe took the camera away and shooed me and Pilot out in front of the lens. Immediately, I felt nervous and self-conscious. Is it okay to be in a picture alone with Pilot? Babe snapped the shot. Pilot then took the camera from Babe and instructed the girls to go stand at my side, and he snapped one of the three of us.

<u>We Saw Super-Ruiny Ruins</u>

We headed up the hills surrounding the Colosseum where temples and ruins of all sorts of ancient architectural grandeur were scattered. We took our time, stopping to gawk in awe at everything. I basically ended up hijacking Babe's camera for the entirety of the hike, directing everyone into different poses in front of all sorts of beautiful giant structures. You don't see things like this in the United States. We're too new. Everything in Rome feels old, weathered, and loaded with character.

I Ate More Ravioli

Around noon, we stopped for more Italian food. Sahra offered to cover my meal. I hugged her. She politely patted my back until I pulled away. I told her I'd pay her back as soon as I gained access to money. The three of them drank more Italian wine, and I worried more about my purse. Pilot promised he'd come with me to check out the trattoria again after we ate, so I quickly devoured the most delicious ravioli I've ever had.

We Found My Purse

Thank the heavens! When I raced us back to the trattoria, it was open, and they had my purse behind the counter. Babe whooped, Sahra smiled, and Pilot loosed an excited HEY of triumph. My relief was palpable. It was all I could do not to tear up as I described the items inside, and the owner handed the cross-body to me across the hostess table. I fell to the floor in a low squat and hugged it to my chest, feeling so blessed that I got to keep going—the adventure wasn't over yet.

We Saw the Pantheon

Pilot took the lead, paving our path to the Pantheon with the map he had stashed in his back pocket. We headed down a narrow street lined with little shops that emptied into an

open square dominated by one single, giant stone structure—
the Pantheon.

I did a whole project on the Pantheon in high school,
so walking up to it felt more surreal than any other
landmarks we visited. I reverently stepped through its
garden of pillars and into the circular cavern within. Niches
line the circumference of the chamber, each one filled with
some sort of historical statue or tomb, and when you look up
at the ceiling, there's an enormous uncovered hole in the
center called the oculus. You can look right up at the sky!
While I was ogling up at it, Pilot said, "Give me your camera,"
and when I dropped my gaze, he was right in front of me. I
handed it to him. He hurried back a few feet and snapped a
picture of me inside the Pantheon. Babe saw him take it,
came over, took the camera from him, and told him to get
into the picture with me. My skin buzzed as he sidled up
next to me and settled his arm around my waist. Another
picture of just the two of us. This one, on my camera. This
one would be (is) in my Facebook album.

The four of us made our way around the circumference of
the room, exploring all the niches and reading the signs inlaid
with small bursts of history. Robert Langdon–related trivia
kept zooming around my brain. I got to a point where I
couldn't help myself, and yelped about it excitedly.

Me: *flails* Guys, remember when Robert Langdon came
here in The Da Vinci Code?

Pilot, Babe, and Sahra: *crickets*

I proceeded to insist upon their reading of Angels and
Demons and The Da Vinci Code.

We Saw the Trevi Fountain

We all threw coins over our shoulders and made wishes. The fountain itself was fantastical! There was so much detail in every statue, I wouldn't have been surprised if it sprang to life (but that would be horrifying; there's one too many practically naked intense-looking men in that fountain).

We Climbed the Freakin' Vatican

Sunday (this morning), we spilled out of a bus into an area cordoned off with an impressive array of giant pillars. It legit felt like we were walking into Mount Olympus. The four of us wandered into the most breathtaking square thus far. I've never seen architecture this grandiose, this—epic.

Inside the Vatican, we climbed this endless winding staircase. The steps actually twisted sideways and up onto the wall as we reached the uppermost domed portion of the church. I loved it.

We were all out of breath when we finally reached the top. The path led us outside, onto a narrow balcony that encircled the tip of the dome. The four of us diffused, spreading out among the rest of the tourists. When I spotted an open area of railing, I flung myself against it to stare out at the city. I tried to memorize the view, the feeling of wonder and accomplishment, the joy pumping through my veins.

We Saw the Pope

Back in St. Peter's Square, there was a massive gathering of people looking up at a taupe-colored building. We wandered over to see what the fuss was about, squinting our eyes against the sun. There, five stories up, looking out over a balcony, arms extended, was the Pope. What even!

I can't believe we were only gone for two days. We saw so much. I never dreamed so much could be done in two days. But it can! I can't wait to do this in other countries. There's so many possibilities. I'm so much more excited about my _Packed! For Travel!_ internship!

11. What Comes Next?

January 17, 2011

Mom and Dad,

I got an email this morning confirming that I got the internship at the magazine, <u>Packed! For Travel!</u> I start next Tuesday! I'll have to lie to you about where I'm working when we Skype, and I'm not looking forward to it. I hope BBQ this past Sunday went well. Did anyone notice I was gone?

XO,

Shane

I slip today's postcard in with my growing collection as Professor Black-stairs hands back our first assignment. I almost leap out of my seat when mine falls onto my desk. I got an A.

An hour and a half into class, Professor Backstairs dismisses us for a fifteen-minute break. A lot of students head out into the street to grab a snack or some air. I guess I could do that. There's a Café Nero down the street, and I could go for a latte. I push up out of my seat and make my way outside.

"Shane?"

I pause on the front steps of the class building, my gaze snapping up to find Pilot ten feet in front of me on the sidewalk.

"Hey!" I walk over to where he's stopped.

"Are you done with class?" he asks, confused.

"No, I'm on fifteen-minute break. I was going to grab a latte," I tell him, delighted I decided to leave the classroom.

He shakes his head with a disbelieving grin. "Dang, me too. I guess our professors coordinated today."

He's all casual, hands in his pockets, hunched slightly against the breeze as we start down the block. I stuff my hands into my pockets too.

"So, Rome for the weekend is over," he says, a half smile on his lips.

Residual Rome hype spills out of me. "Yeah, it was so fast, but we saw so much stuff! I mean, yeah, the Sistine Chapel was closed but—"

"But," he interjects happily, "we got to chill with the Pope."

"That we did, that we did."

"How would you rate it out of ten?"

I consider this for a moment, pursing my lips. "Hmm, eight out of ten, I think, which is excellent, but leaves room for improvement. If there's ever a trip that's out-of-this-world superb, like if we got to hang with Taylor Swift and the Pope, that would be a ten."

Pilot nods approvingly.

"And what would you rate it?" I ask, raising my eyebrows.

He answers in a cheeky, over-the-top version of his voice. "I mean, I'm pissed Taylor Swift wasn't there, but I guess I'd give it an eight out of ten too."

I snort as we come to a stop, waiting for the walk signal to cross the street. "Where else do you want to travel while you're here?"

He jumps at the question. "Oh, man, everywhere! Scotland, France, Germany, the Netherlands, Belgium, Hungary, Denmark, Austria. I really just want to go as many places as I can."

I bite back a smile at the enthusiasm in his voice. "It's so cool that everything's so close. I didn't realize we're like two hours from so many places." The light changes, and we scurry toward Café Nero. "When do you fly back to the States?"

"I don't have a return ticket yet," he says.

My head whips over to meet his eyes as we reach the sidewalk again. "You don't have a return ticket?"

"Nope. Playin' it by ear. We'll see what happens."

There's that phrase again.

"Wow." I pause as he pulls open the door to Café Nero. We step in and join the line. *People go places without getting a return ticket?*

"I never even realized that's . . . like, an option when you travel," I say slowly.

"What countries do you want to hit?"

"Um, I don't know. I didn't think about it enough because I didn't realize everything was so close, and now I want to go everywhere I can." I meet his eyes again.

He smiles and straightens his arms, stuffing his hands farther into his pockets. I float a few inches off the ground. His smiles aren't like mine, which typically etch themselves onto my face for various stretches of time. Pilot's are fleeting; they come and then they're gone again, and he's back to his normal resting chill expression.

"Next!" the barista snaps. *Get back on the ground, Shane. He has a girlfriend.* I whirl around to place my order. After Pilot places his, we huddle in silence for a moment at end of the counter, waiting for our drinks.

"How goes the music making?" I ask. "Are you going to tour with this new album you're coming out with?" Amusement dances through my words.

He looks at the ceiling and lets go of a laugh. "Well, I'm hoping to do some gigs around New York City over the summer, like open mics and stuff, try to get our name out there."

My mouth falls open. "Really? That's awesome."

"Yeah, I really want to take this summer to do it because I don't think I'll get another chance with graduation coming and everything."

"Are you going to invite us to your gigs?" I grin.

His cheeks flush. "I don't know . . ." he answers shyly.

"What do you mean, you don't know? I want to come!"

The barista drops our drinks on the table. Pilot smiles at his latte. "We'll see."

"We'll see?" I repeat with mock frustration as I grab my own. "We're going to come and support your musical talents," I insist.

"What about you?" he says when we're back outside. "How's the book-writing plan going?"

I laugh in surprise. "I haven't started. I have ideas but, I don't know, none of them feel good enough. Or I guess, I'm not sure I could write them. We'll see," I finish slowly, staring into my drink.

"You should just go for it," he encourages.

We cross the street, approaching the class buildings again.

"We should all plan another trip for this weekend," Pilot suggests before we part.

"Yeah!" I call eagerly, as he strides toward the building next to mine.

This morning, Babe and I agreed to meet up for lunch. So after class, I wait for her on the corner. I wave happily as she approaches.

"Hey!" I greet her. "How was class?"

"Boring. You?" she says. We fall into step.

"Mine was excellent! We talked about structure, specifically the break between act one and two!"

She laughs. "Cool—you ready to try this burger place?" she says excitedly. Ninety percent of what Babe says is said excitedly.

We head into Byron's, a gourmet burger place we pass on the way to class. Once we're seated, a waiter comes to take our drink orders while we study the menu. They have milkshakes! Shakes and burgers—it feels so American! I've only been gone a week, but it already feels like I've been out of the country for ages. Weirdly, American things are starting to feel rare and special, in a way they've never felt before.

"So, you know that friend Chad that I was talking about the other day?" Babe starts as we peruse the menu.

I glance up at her with a knowing look. "Yeah, the one from upstairs who you hung out with that first day?"

"Okay, so, I do kind of really like him."

I nod and raise my eyebrows slightly to show I'm listening. I expect her to get giggly about it, but she's all business.

"Well." She puts down her menu. "This Sunday is his birthday, and I, um, I usually plan things we do for his birthday."

"You—plan his birthday?"

"We've been friends for, like, three years now, and I planned it last year and the year before, and he likes when I plan it," she explains carefully.

"Okay . . ." The waiter arrives, and we both order specialty burgers and shakes. We're quiet as he takes our menus and walks away.

She starts again, "Okay, so, I had class with Chad earlier, and he was talking about going to Paris this weekend maybe, to celebrate. And did you know we don't have class this Friday? It's Thursday instead. So, I think we're gonna go! Do you want to come? Maybe Pilot will come too? It'll be really fun . . ." She trails off.

I feel my forehead scrunch up. Is she suggesting a double . . . date . . . situation? I'm afraid to voice the question aloud. She knows as well as I do that Pilot has a girlfriend. But I want to go to Paris.

"Yeah, I'd love to come!" I spout.

"Really?" She relaxes back into her seat. "Oh my gosh, thank you! I didn't want it to be just me and Chad, but I kind of want it, you know, to be just me and Chad, sometimes—you know?"

I study her carefully. "So, what's the deal with you two, then? Have you guys had moments and stuff? Are you, like, almost a thing?"

"Well, I mean, like last year I tried to tell him once that I had feelings for him, but before I could get it out, he started talking about how he likes tiny short girls."

"What?" I drop my milkshake back to the table, instantly annoyed with Chad. Babe's tall and curvy. She must register the look on my face because she hurries to defend him.

"No, but he's really nice, and we both love Disney. He's great, you'll see! I don't know what was up that night. I think he was acting out and nervous about losing our friendship. I don't know, but he's great. I promise!"

"Okay," I say quietly. We'll see about this Chad.

———

Back at the flat, Babe and I retire to the kitchen to work on our laptops. When I pull up Safari, it opens to Facebook where I have twenty-three new notifications—probably people liking my Rome pictures.

I smile, opening them, but my insides shrivel when I see who the majority are from: Leo, Alfie, Anthony, Angelo. Not just likes, *comments*. I race down to the first one and open it in a new window. It's the picture of Pilot and me in the Pantheon. They all liked it.

> **Leo Primaveri** Who's this?
> **Alfie Primaveri** Breaking News: Shane's with a dude.
> **Anthony Primaveri** No. Fucking. Way.
> **Leo Primaveri** Do you actually speak to each other?
> **Alfie Primaveri** Can't wait for the wedding.

I'm gonna throw up.

Babe's voice. "Shane? Are you okay?"

Pilot's tagged in this photo. I'm gonna die. My mouse scrambles up: *Delete. Delete. Delete. Delete. Delete.* I speed back to the notifications and open another. There's a post on my wall from Leo and Alfie's mom, my aunt Marie.

Marie Primaveri

Miss you, sweetie! It looks like you're having a great time. Leo tells me you have a boyfriend out there. I hope it's the cutie in the pictures!

The computer's pulled away from my face. "Shane, seriously, you've been muttering *no* repeatedly for, like, a solid sixty seconds."

I pull it back. "Sorry, family thing," I mumble. I pick it up and run out of the kitchen. I hear my chair fall, but there's no time to stop. This is dire.

I slam into a seat at our bedroom table and delete the post. Another new notification pops up from Leo. He's online. He posted on my wall.

Leo Primaveri

You deleted our comments about your new boyfriend?
I'm hurt.

Delete.
Another new notification on my wall.

Leo Primaveri

You keep deleting my posts about your boyfriend.
What's his name—Pilot?

Delete. Angry tears sting my eyes. Why is Leo leading this parade? I sit back up, opening a private thread in Facebook Chat.

> **Shane**
> WHAT ARE YOU DOING?
>
> **Leo**
> Relax, cuz, just having fun.

"Ahhh!" I scream at the screen. It's one thing to do this when we're at a family party—I swallow at the lump in my throat and type.

> **Shane**
> GET THE HELL OFF MY PROFILE,
> ASSHOLE.
>
> **Leo**
> Whoa, calm down, you don't curse.
>
> **Shane**
> I THINK I JUST DID.
>
> **Shane**
> ONE MORE COMMENT AND I'LL
> BLOCK YOU.

A new notification pops up. Another post on my wall for the world to see.

Leo Primaveri
BITCH.

A tear sears down my cheek. *Delete.* I storm through Facebook. Leo: *Block.* Alfie: *Block.* Angelo: *Block.* Anthony: *Block.*

I return to the kitchen ten minutes later. Babe's still here. She looks up from her laptop as I settle back into the chair across from her. She must have picked it up for me.

"Is everything okay?" she asks, pushing a dark curl behind her ears. She's wearing adorable gold Mickey-shaped studs.

"Yeah, it's fine. I took care of it," I breathe. Babe rises from her seat, comes behind my chair, and wraps me in an awkward hug.

"I don't think he saw," she says quietly.

She saw. My face burns.

Babe sits back down and tells me that her older brother is constantly making fun of her obsession with Disney. She tries to make me feel better. "Pilot's been in class. We don't have smartphones here; he probably didn't see."

She's right. She's probably right.

I throw myself into proofreading the "That Time I Lost My Passport" blog post about Rome. Babe lingers with me. I'm pretty sure she's just waiting for Pilot to get back, so she can ask him about Paris. Now, there's the added bonus of finding out if he saw the stuff on Facebook. He finally strides in at 4:00 p.m., a few minutes after I publish the Rome piece.

12. Has He Heard?

"Hey!" Pilot greets us. Normal inflection. Good sign.

We *hey* back casually. At least I try to. I think my eyes are a little too wide to really pull it off. He's carrying a store-bought frozen dinner that he pops out of its cardboard box and throws into the microwave before dropping into the seat at the head of the table. Babe and I are seated on either side of him.

"So how's it going?" Babe asks tentatively.

"Good, good! I got my internship confirmed this morning so that was good," he answers normally.

"Me too!" I interject.

"Nice!" he adds with a grin/head-bob combo. He's wearing a red-and-black plaid shirt with a black T-shirt layered underneath. I nod, relaxing slightly.

Babe smiles at me like *see, we're fine* before turning back to him. "I'm trying to plan a trip to Paris for this weekend! You want to come?"

Pilot glances at me and then back at Babe. "Uh, yeah, I'm down. Who else is going?"

"Shane and me and my friend Chad—so far!" The room's slowly filling with the delicious smell of Italian food as the microwave defrosts Pilot's meal.

Pies makes a Soprano-esque frown-approval face and nods his head. "Sign me up. Sounds like a party. We can take the Eurostar train, right?"

I turn my attention back to my computer screen, a tiny relieved smile crawling up my face.

"Yes!" Babe beams. "Yes, we can. Great. I'm going to look up the things we can do and get everything planned, and it's going to be so much fun. I'm so excited! It's gonna be epic!" She gathers her things and *whooshes* out of the kitchen.

The microwave beeps. Pilot gets up to grab his lasagna and slides back into his chair. "So, we're going to Paris," he says casually, digging into his food.

I look up for a second to make eye contact. "Apparently."

He nods, his lips quirked up to one side. I turn back to my computer. When Pilot finishes eating and leaves the kitchen, I blast Ke$ha and give in to a brief celebratory he-didn't-see-the-posts-and-we're-going-to-Paris dance party.

13. Here Goes Nothing

1/19/11 11:05 p.m.

Tomorrow after class we go to Paris. What is my life now? I'm glad I've been hoarding my savings for years because I'm going to run out of summer work money faster than expected if I keep up this avid traveler thing.

Earlier today I Skyped with Mom. She mentioned that she and Dad are thinking about coming out to visit. I did my best to discourage her without arousing suspicion or sounding mean.

I downloaded this game everyone's talking about called Angry Birds on my iPod this morning. Super-frustrating, but addictive as hell. I wasted an hour where I could have been reading or writing, throwing birds at green pigs.

Tonight was Flat Three's first official Shwednesday! I went out for the shawarma. It was even better the second time around. Afterward, we all played a game of Rummy 500. Atticus gave me a run for my money.

———

Past Eurostar security, I find myself in an area that feels very much like an airport terminal: lots of tired people sitting around in chairs, a Café Nero, and a little restaurant. Babe and Chad already left on a 4:00 p.m. train because they get out of class earlier than me and Pilot. The two of us are set to catch a 6:30 p.m. train, and we're all going to meet at the hostel Babe booked for us.

I spot Pilot chilling in a seating area off to the right with a backpack at his feet. He's dressed in an unbuttoned red-and-blue plaid button-up with a gray T-shirt underneath and jeans. His green jacket is tucked under one of his arms, and white headphones trail from his ears down to an iPod in his hand.

Nerves prickle my skin. I wonder if he feels weird about this. Not only are we going to Paris in a foursome, but we've broken off into twosomes to actually get there. Why couldn't Babe wait these two hours and go with us? I roll my stuff toward the seating area.

"Hey," I say brightly when I'm about two feet away.

Pilot hadn't seen me, and he startles, yanking out his headphones.

I chuckle and take the seat next to him. "What were you listening to?"

"Secret snobby hipster music," he says without pause as he wraps his headphones and stuffs them away in a backpack. "You wouldn't know it."

"Are you embarrassed to tell me? Was it super-mainstream? Was it the Backstreet Boys?"

Pilot's mouth falls open. "How'd you know?"

I blink in surprise. "Wait, really?"

"No." He laughs.

I scrunch up my face and extend my arms in a pushing motion, without actually pushing him. "This is me mentally pushing you over."

The seats on the train are divided into sections of two. It's going to be a two-and-half-hour ride, and we're going to spend a lot of it under the English Channel.

Pilot takes the window seat, and I plop down next to him after storing my roller bag above us. I fish my iPod Touch out of my book bag before stuffing it down by my feet. Right on time, the train pulls forward, and we're on our way.

"Have you played that game everyone's talking about, Angry Birds?" I ask as my iPod powers up.

"No, I've heard of it, though," he says. Pilot shifts a bit so we can look at each other more easily when we talk.

"I just got it on my iPod and tried it the other day. It's pretty fun. Do you want to play?"

"Sure."

"Okay, we can switch off. I'll go first so you can watch my technique," I say.

He grins, leaning in to see the tiny screen in my hand. I'm only on level three. I don't have much technique, but I play my round leaning slightly to the right so Pilot can watch. Our heads get close as we hunch over the little iPod. My heart gets excited. My hands get sweaty. When I lose, I pass him the iPod so he can give it a go.

Soon, we're completely lost, having an excellent time strategizing together about how best to take out our targets with the allotted amount of birds. Some levels go quickly, but others stump us for rounds and rounds of going back and forth between the two of us, and all the while, we're sitting so close.

All the alarms go off in my brain when I realize his shoulder's leaning against mine. We're touching shoulders! *Shoulders are touching.* This is something! *THIS IS ROMANCE.* Must stay still. Can't. Lose. Shoulder contact.

"Awww," he croons sympathetically as my last bird dies. "You were so close. I got this." He gently takes the iPod from my hands. *Yeah, sorry I missed that last pig, I'm a little busy trying to be a statue over here.*

We're on level twenty-seven now. I don't know how long we've been doing this, but I can finally see out the window again. When Pilot loses the level, he takes notice of the change and suddenly sits up straight, breaking shoulder contact.

"Oh, man, we must be getting close!" He hands me back the iPod. My chest deflates a smidgen as his body heat leaves my arm.

"Yeah, that was fast," I say, trying to sound casual and not at all distracted by romantic shoulder-contact nostalgia as I turn off my iPod and repack it in my bag.

A Parisian taxi drops us off outside a building that looks kind of like a rundown diner. It's decorated with faded signs proclaiming it to be our hostel, so we head through the door. The inside looks like a diner too. To the left is a cafeteria-looking area, and ahead of us is a young girl in a red tank top standing behind a tall hostess-like desk, texting. To her left, Babe and a pale boy with dark hair are waiting for us on a bench.

"Hi!" Babe jumps up. "We've been down here for thirty minutes now. I figured you'd be arriving within the hour window, and since our phones are shoddy, I wanted to make sure we were here to meet you. We've just been hanging out, so you haven't missed anything. I got the keys for our room and your room."

I bring my roller bag to a stop behind me. "We have two rooms?" I ask, confused.

"Well, they didn't have four beds available in one room, so we're in one room, and you guys have two beds in the other room. I figured this way we both have guys in the room with us, so we'd feel safer about the random strangers," she says coolly.

I swallow hard. Pilot and I don't comment. This is weird. I wonder if there really isn't a room available with four beds, or if this is a ploy to give Babe and Chad time by themselves. She hands me and Pilot keys.

"Come on, let's go drop your things off and get some food—oh!" She turns, remembering Chad, who's still sitting quietly behind her on the bench. "This is Chad. Chad, this is Shane and Pilot."

Chad gets up. He's a little shorter than Pilot—about five-nine with spiked-up dark hair, brown eyes, and a long straight nose. He stretches out his hand, so I shake it. "Yo, yo, nice to meet you," he says.

I nod and smile.

"Nice to meet you, man," Pilot says, taking Chad's hand. I keep sneaking glances at Pilot to see how he's gauging all this. He doesn't look caught off guard or uncomfortable. He looks chill. I relax a little bit. If he's not uncomfortable, I shouldn't be uncomfortable. He's the one with a girl-friend.

"You guys are on the sixth floor," Babe explains as we follow her down a bland, gray corridor. We pass a shelf full of brochures and tourist maps. Pilot snatches a couple as we go by. The corridor leads to an elevator. We load in and press six. I stare at the other buttons; they're different from the usual elevator. The ground floor is labeled zero and then there's a nega-tive one floor . . . and a negative two floor.

"Guys, look, floor negative two!" I laugh stupidly.

Babe snorts. "Oh my gosh, I didn't even see that."

"Must be where they store the dead bodies," Chad adds. Babe laughs enthusiastically at his non-joke.

I exchange a look with Pilot, and his eyes go round with amusement. There's a ding, and we file out into another dimly lit corridor, stopping outside a door labeled *62*. It swings open to reveal a large room with six beds: all singles, with white sheets, spaced about a foot apart. It looks like an old-fashioned infirmary. Everything glows a greenish-yellow under the outdated overhead lights—the same kind we used to have in my elemen-tary school classrooms. To the right of the door are a half a dozen blue lock-ers. It looks like gym class.

"Wow, cozy." Pilot grins. He throws himself onto the bed nearest to the door, opens a map, and starts studying.

Babe and Chad linger near the door as I inspect the lockers.

"This is a little scary," I start hesitantly. It doesn't appear that anyone else is currently staying in the room, but I see that two of the lockers have locks on them.

"You guys have more beds in here than us," Chad says. "We only have four."

"Oh boy, more strangers for us." I chuckle nervously and test out a locker.

"Don't worry, we'll be fine," Pilot says, dropping the map down onto his lap.

Pilot and I don't have locks.

Babe reads my mind. "They have locks you can buy downstairs! I got one for me and Chad to share. You guys can get one."

"Cool, cool," Pilot says, rolling off the bed. He hangs his backpack in one of the lockers, and I shove my carry-on into another.

After we sort out our lock situation, the four of us find a Chinese restaurant that's still open and grab dinner. My chest feels tight as we head back to the hostel, and my pits are sweating up a storm.

We're sharing a room and bathroom with random strangers who could be ice-pick killers. And I'm going to be sleeping in a bed a foot away from Pilot. What do I do about makeup? Do I sleep with my makeup on? I'm not ready to be makeup-less around Pilot. I've never been without makeup, close up, around a boy I like. I'm going to have to take it off when I know it's dark and he can't see me, and run to the bathroom in the morning to put it on before he wakes up.

Babe and Chad get off at the third floor, leaving Pilot and me alone in the elevator as we head up to six. When we get to our room, the lights are dimmer than before, and there are bodies asleep in two of the beds in the far left corner.

Pilot sighs and collapses onto his bed with a grin. "I'm gonna crash. I'm knackered."

I snort. "*Knackered* sounds so wrong without an English accent."

Quietly, I maneuver my suitcase out of the locker and roll myself to the other end of the room. There's another door here, and it must lead to the bathroom. When I push it open, heavenly light blazes out into the sleeping area. I stumble in as quickly as possible and lock the door behind me.

It's a restroom. There's another door across from this door, which suggests that you can enter from another room as well. Joy. I lock that door too before catching sight of myself in the mirror. My mass of blond hair looks matted and disheveled.

I strip down and switch out my boots for flip-flops before stepping into the shower with my travel soaps. It's a tiny claustrophobic white rectangle. I imagine this is what it'd be like to stand vertically in a casket lined with white tile. I close the flimsy plastic curtain behind me and look for a shower dial. There's only a button. *One button.* A giant, rounded silver dome amongst the tiles. *What the fudge?*

I step as far out of the way of the showerhead as possible (not far at all; any oncoming water will be inescapable) and smash my hand against the button. Water sprays out of the showerhead right onto my face. It's warm, but nowhere near comfortable levels. I sigh, speeding through my cleaning ritual. About twenty seconds into wetting my hair, the water goes off.

And now I'm freezing.

"Are you kidding me?"

Oops, I didn't mean to say that out loud. I smash my hand against the button again. More lukewarm water falls over me. I soap up my hair. Forty-five seconds later, the water turns off again. Deadpan, I smack the button. What the heck is this shower that only turns on in forty-five-second spurts?

Five minutes later, I step out, seething, and pull on a tank top and sweatpants. Do I have to wear a bra? I bra up. I'm not ready to be walking around braless in a room alone with Pilot and two strangers. After brushing my teeth and taking several deep breaths, I exit the bathroom.

It looks like I had nothing to worry about. Pilot's already asleep. He lies on his side, facing the door. I tiptoe over and slide into the bed next to his, shifting myself into a comfortable position, facing his back, when suddenly Pilot turns to look me. I nervously yank the thin white blanket up to my neck.

"Night, Shane," he murmurs sleepily.

"Night," I whisper as he turns back toward the door.

14. Sail?

I'm up at 7:00 a.m., washing my face and doing my makeup in the bathroom. I pull on dark blue jeans and a black turtleneck, because it's freezing outside, and leave my hair down. Back in the room, one of the strangers is gone, but the other is still asleep. He looks oldish, in his forties or something, and he's wearing a sleep-apnea mask.

I'm sitting on my bed playing Angry Birds, dressed and ready to go, when Pilot stirs awake a little before 8:00 a.m.

"Morning," he says, sitting up.

I drop the iPod in my lap. "Morning."

"What's that?" He yawns, nodding at it. His eyes narrow. "Are you Angry Birding without me?"

"Um." I smile guiltily.

He laughs, bringing his legs over the side of the bed and pulling on jeans. "How dare you?"

Pilot grabs his bag from our gym locker. He eyes me with surprise. "Are you already ready?"

"So, guys, I signed us all up for Paris Pass," Babe explains as we walk toward the Metro. "It's this all-inclusive thing that gives us unlimited access to the Metro for the next two days and includes tickets to the Louvre and

Versailles. We have to go pick it up first, but maybe then we head to Versailles and do the Louvre and everything else tomorrow?"

"Saturday night, we hitting the club scene for my birthday, yo! It's gonna be sick," Chad adds.

"Sounds good," Pilot says. "I took a look at the map. Our hostel is kind of far from everything, but we'll make it work."

It takes us an hour to get to the convenience store and pick up the Paris Passes. Pilot wasn't exaggerating when he said we were far from everything. But once we get there, it only takes Babe a minute to run in and emerge with our tickets. She hands us each a pass.

"So, how do we get to the palace now?" I ask with a hop.

"Now, we catch the RER," she answers cheerily.

"The what?" Chad interjects as Babe leads us away.

"What is this, RER?" Pilot questions in a ridiculous French accent.

"It's a bigger train that goes to farther places," Babe explains as we trot behind her down the street.

"So we're taking the Rerr?" I say goofily.

Babe laughs. "The R-E-R," she repeats.

"The Rerr," I repeat back.

"We're hitting up the Rerr," Pilot backs me up.

"I'm so pumped for the Rerrr, you guys," Chad pipes in. I laugh, and Babe starts chuckling along.

"Okay, the Rerrr," she concedes loudly.

Babe leads us to another underground platform much like the Metro, except cleaner. We stand in a little circle, waiting for the train. There's a distant rumble as it approaches, and with a rush of wind, the RER pulls into the station. It's a double-decker, and we're all thoroughly impressed by it. The seats are arranged in groups of four, a set of two across from a second set of two. Pilot takes the seat next to me, and Babe and Chad sit across from us.

"How long is the ride?" I ask Babe.

"I think around thirty minutes," she answers. Chad leans his head against the window and closes his eyes. Babe pulls a brochure for Versailles from her bag and starts to read. I watch them for a moment before Pilot turns to me.

"Angry Birds?" he says with quiet excitement. I smile and dig my hand into my purse.

Versailles doesn't look real. A massive stretch of gravel spans before us. Is this a driveway? Maybe for a family of giants with twenty cars. It leads to an endless sprawl of gold building.

When we get inside, a tour guide escorts us up to the second floor. On the way up the stairs, I catch sight of the backyard (if you can call it that) through the windows.

"Holy crap, do we get to go out there?" I look to Babe anxiously.

"Yes, don't worry!" She giggles.

Pilot's mouth quirks up his right cheek. "I'm excited about this."

We come to a stop in an overwhelmingly lavish foyer area that leads into the legendary Hall of Mirrors that everyone talks about. After snapping a few pictures (Babe snaps one of Pilot and me, and Pilot takes the camera to get one of Babe and me while Chad hangs to the side), we stroll on in.

It looks like a ballroom. Gorgeous chandeliers drip from the ceilings. Tall golden candelabra line the edges of the room, and mirrors decorate the walls. Are they mirrors? They're more like old, decorative reflective glass.

"Wait, this is the Hall of Mirrors?" I ask hesitantly as we make our way across it. "Where are all the mirrors?"

"Right there!" Babe points to the decorative glass panels along the wall.

"But those aren't mirror mirrors, those are like glass . . . that reflects you," I fumble. That didn't come out right. Pilot starts laughing.

"Glass that reflects you? Like a mirror?" Chad asks sarcastically.

"But there are no real mirrors!" I protest.

"Is this the real Hall of Mirrors? Are we in the faux Hall of Mirrors?" Pilot exclaims, pretending to be outraged.

"This is it!" Babe cackles.

"I was expecting, like, a fun-house maze of mirrors . . ." I explain, full-on laughing now. I guess I heard about this when I was really young, and that's the image I conjured in my brain. Pilot appears on my right, grinning broadly.

"No, I was expecting a fun house too," he says quietly.

"Right?" I exclaim.

"I mean, when you think Hall of Mirrors you think *hall full of mirrors*—mirror maze."

I snort. "They should add a mirror maze for, like, Halloween."

Pilot's expression goes blank. "I'd be so down for that."

"Maybe they have a suggestion box," I add. His head kicks back with a laugh. I bite down a pleased smile.

Babe veers off toward the blurry, foggy-ish mirrors, and the three of us beeline after her. Once we're all in front of a mirror, Babe frames up a mirror pic. In the Hall of Mirrors. I stick my hand up and do a queen's wave.

"It's like the Mirror of Erised!" I grin.

Babe laughs. "I'm not seeing what I desire."

Room by room, we wind through the palace. We see Marie Antoinette's bedroom, and where King Louis the somethingth slept. We see a painting that literally takes up a ballroom-sized wall! I've always thought of palaces like castles, I guess. Stone and cold, ancient-looking—nothing like the ridiculous grandeur we tour through.

Then comes the backyard. I know backyard isn't the right word—it's more like an endless expanse of park, complete with a lake, fountains, hedges, and statues. It looks like photo-shoot heaven. Park heaven. It's like an ocean in park form; you can't see an end, there's *no edge*! It just keeps going.

I don't know how long we're out there making our way through the jumbo-sized courtyard and taking pictures with the different landscapes. We meander farther and farther in until we reach a café where we stop for lunch. I could frolic around this place forever.

"So are you, like, into photography?" Pilot asks as we make our way back to the RER.

I turn to look him in the eye. "Yeah, it's one of my things." I smile.

"Really? You've never said anything about liking photography."

"Well, it hasn't really come up, and it's more of a hobby."

"You do take great pictures; my mom loved all the ones from Rome."

I chuckle. "Glad to hear I have your mom's approval."

"You need one of those nice pretentious cameras."

"I'd love one of those pretentious cameras. One day!" I smile up at the sky longingly and then drop my eyes back to Pilot. "Are you not into photography?"

"I mean, I appreciate a good picture. I respect that." A grin tugs at his lips.

"You're a good co-photographer."

"Co-photographer?"

"Yeah." I turn my oversized grin away from his face. I need a second without eye contact to gather myself. "I mean, usually I end up having to give people lessons about how a picture should be framed." I turn back to gauge his reaction.

He gives me a funny look.

"Like, they don't ask for the lessons. I kind of obnoxiously teach them after they take a picture for me and it's framed poorly—like, I give them a mini-lecture and make them do it again."

Pilot laughs in disbelief. "What?"

"Yeaahhhh." I look at the ground. "You didn't get a lecture, though, and you've taken quite a few pictures for me."

When I meet his eyes again, he brings a hand to his heart. "Wow, I'm so honored to have passed this secret photography test."

I look away, trying to get my expression under control. "Mentally pushing you over again."

He shrugs. "Sorry, mentally dodged you. Didn't get me."

A wave of giddiness roils through me, and I'm so distracted that I trip walking up the train stairs.

"I'm so pumped for tomorrow, y'all. I'm turning twenty-one. Shit's gonna be amazing." Chad's voice snaps me back. I got lost in a Pilot-related thought spiral while eating my quiche. We've stopped in a French restaurant for dinner. Chad raises his drink off the table, and we all clink our glasses.

"It's gonna be great," Babe confirms. "I asked the girl at the front desk about the best area to go to."

"I'm pumped to go to the top of the Eiffel tomorrow," Pilot adds.

Chad nods his head past us at something. "Check her out, man," he says in his bro voice.

I turn around to see a petite dark-haired girl walking over to the bar to get a drink. I'm about to turn back and serve Chad a dirty look when I notice the bartender. A woman with a shock of red hair piled up on top of her head moves toward the girl to get her order. It looks like plane/Starbucks lady? Why the heck would she be—? The woman looks up, makes eye contact with me, and winks.

"What the fudge?" I bellow, abruptly standing from my seat.

"Shane . . ." Babe mutters, embarrassed. I turn to face her. She thinks I'm about to yell at Chad. I glance at Pilot.

"You okay?" he asks.

"Yeah." I look back at Babe, who's silently urging me to sit. I raise my eyebrows. "No, I, it's not that. I know the lady at—" I look back at the bar. She's gone. There's a guy there in her place, talking to the dark-haired girl. I blink, shaking my head. *What the hell?*

"I— Never mind." I settle back into my seat. *Why am I hallucinating a middle-aged British woman?*

Back at the hostel, we split off to our separate rooms. Pilot brushes his teeth and gets into bed. I take a ridiculously short shower and snuggle into the single bed next to Pilot's around midnight. He's asleep facing the door again.

"Night," he mumbles as I settle in.

I yank the covers up to my chin. "I always think you're asleep, and you scare the crap out of me," I mutter.

He turns toward me, wearing a mischievous smirk. "Muahahahaha!"

We're only a little more than a foot apart. I grab my pillow out from under my head and whack him in the face. He snorts.

I pull it back under my head with a smile. "Night."

15. Fail

I've always been under the impression that the Louvre was a museum under that iconic glass pyramid. We're now standing in front of said pyramid, but it's surrounded by what looks like another palace.

"Is all of that the Louvre?" I ask, stunned.

"Yeah, of course!" Babe answers.

"Holy crap."

I've been dreaming about visiting this museum since I first learned about it in sixth grade, when we were all forced to take Intro to French and Spanish. And then of course *The Da Vinci Code* only added fuel to that fire.

I'm particularly hyped when we come upon the *Winged Victory* statue—the famous, armless angel missing a head. It's from, like, 200 BC. I did a report on it in that sixth grade French class. I skip up to it. I'm only there alone for a moment before Pilot appears at my shoulder.

"You want a picture with it?" he asks knowingly.

"Yes, please!" I hand him my camera.

As I step out in front of the sculpture to pose, we make eye contact—he smiles and my brain malfunctions. I raise and lower my arms like they've just sprouted from my torso. *Oh god, not this again. Hand on hip? Both hands on hips? Arms out in glee? One hand up? Pop a foot? Jazz hands? Stand sideways? Shit.* I snap my arms down and smile with them straight at my sides like a soldier. And then it's over, and I'm offering to take one of him, desperate to get back behind the camera as soon as humanly possible. He stuffs his hands in his pockets doing his cool-guy stance. Chill as ever.

I check the camera to see what pose he got. Jazz hands and Soldier. Cool.

We spent forty-five minutes walking from the Louvre to the Eiffel Tower. Now it looms over us, dark and daunting. While the four of us are gazing up in awe, a man wearing a winter hat and puffy jacket walks up to us with a giant metal ring threaded with oodles of tiny Eiffel Tower replicas.

"Five, one Euro?" he asks anxiously. We just stare for a moment. "Five for one Euro?" he repeats.

"No, thanks," Babe answers. The man hurries away to a new group of tourists.

"Ready to scale this thing?" Pilot beams.

"Let's do it!" I cheer. After climbing the Vatican, I want to climb all the things.

"Yo, heights freak me out, but I guess I'm down to climb, 'cause how often am I in freaking Paris," Chad comments.

Babe looks from Chad (who's paler than usual) to Pilot to me. "I don't think I really want to—Chad, I thought you'd want to take the elevator. I'd really rather take the elevator," Babe says, turning to him.

"Come *on*, Babe, let's do the steps. When do you get to climb the Eiffel Tower?" he whines.

Babe frowns and stares upward for a moment before her gaze drops to me. I nod at her encouragingly. She heaves a giant sigh and mildly rolls her eyes.

"Fine."

"Yay! To the stairs!" I exclaim.

Minutes later, we're at the base of another never-ending staircase. I hurl myself upward, taking the steps two at a time, leading the way, Pilot climbing at my heels. Three hundred and twenty-eight steps later, we make it to the first tier of the tower. We spend a few minutes snapping pictures, leaning against the wire fencing, and admiring the view.

Babe heaves a sigh. "Okay, guys, I'm going to take the elevator the rest of the way." She looks at Chad expectantly.

"Okay," he answers, oblivious to her obvious hinting that she wants him to come with her.

"Chad, can you come with me, please?" Babe asks pointedly.

"Oh, um." He sighs. "Yeah, sure."

"Thanks." Babe looks at us. "We'll meet you guys at the bottom!" They walk off into an indoor area.

I look over at Pilot and raise my eyebrows.

"And then there were two." He smiles at me again.

"Ready to head for the top?" I squeak.

"Am I ready? Please, Shane." He smirks, striding toward the next set of stairs.

A sign lets us know we have 341 steps till the next tier. We climb in silence for a few minutes, our feet against the metal providing the soundtrack to our ascent.

"So, I've been pondering that back-in-time question," Pilot says out of nowhere.

I grin in surprise. "Oh yeah? And?"

"And I like your Constitution idea. I think I'll hit that one up with you and sit in on that meeting."

"Oh cool, I'll have a buddy to back up my I'm-a-man charade. You can jump in and be like, 'No, I grew up in his town, he's legit. Listen to all his genius, forward-thinking ideas,' when they accuse me of female-ery!"

Pilot smiles at the ground, and we continue up. "Have you cemented a second choice?" he asks.

"Uh." I look anywhere but his face because I'm blushing. "Yeah, I think I'll hit up that Beatles concert with you."

He looses a breathy laugh. "Damn, when we find this time machine, it's on." I laugh too, releasing some of my pent-up giddiness.

The wind whips at my cheeks, throwing my hair around as we step up onto the second tier. Pilot and I find a spot and lean against the protective grating that encases the area. In New York City, I've looked out from the windows of tall buildings at an endless sea of gray skyscrapers. Rome was a chaotic explosion of reds and burgundies. Paris . . . Paris looks like a painting. A work of art that was carefully laid out and organized to look beautiful from every angle.

"This . . . is so cool." The words fall softly from Pilot's mouth. The wind is loud; I only hear him because we're standing shoulder to shoulder. Chills run over my arms. Pilot pivots around, and I bounce nervously on my heels as he stops the first person who walks by. "Hey, could you take a picture of us?"

He wants a picture of us? A white-haired woman takes the camera from my outstretched hand, and we pose, smiling next to each other, his arm at my back, against the edge of the Eiffel Tower.

As the woman returns the camera, Pilot turns to me, excited again. "To the top?"

"To the top!" I cheer, new energy zipping through me. Who knows what will happen when we reach the top—it's just the two of us and I don't know. I feel good about getting to the top *together*. It feels like things are . . . possible.

We circle the tier, eager for the next set of steps, but end up back where we started.

My smile wilts. "Is there no other staircase?"

"What the heck?" Pilot's expression falls.

We venture inside to ask someone. It turns out you can only take the elevator to the very top, and today even that route is closed due to high winds. As if to prove a point, an aggressive spool of freezing air rams into us as we exit back out through the doors. My mental list of romantic reaching-the-top-of-the-Eiffel-Tower-together fantasies spins away on the breeze.

Disappointment looms over us as we wind around and around, back to earth. *Is he feeling what I'm feeling? Or is this just normal I-didn't-get-to-scale-the-Eiffel-Tower level disappointment?*

When our feet hit solid ground, Babe and Chad are there waiting. The four of us cross a bridge and head along the bank of the Seine, moving toward an area populated with shops and restaurants. We're still strolling alongside the river when Babe stops short to pivot around and look back at the Tower in the distance. The sun's going down and the Eiffel's golden lights have switched on.

"Wait!" she shouts. We stop and look at her. "What time is it?" she asks, her hazel eyes alight.

Chad looks at his watch. "5:45."

"We have a good view here!" she says.

"A view for what?" I ask. My stomach growls restlessly as I glance at the Eiffel Tower. Now that we've stopped, the cold air cuts right through my boots. I scrunch my toes up against it.

"Something cool is going to happen to the Eiffel Tower at six o'clock," Babe answers, leaning against the barrier that lines the river's edge. "You want to see this," she says confidently.

"What's going to happen to the Eiffel?" I shoot, rubbing my hands together for warmth. I pull my puffy winter hood up over my head against the wind.

"How cool?" Pilot asks skeptically, narrowing his eyes. He's got his sweatshirt hood up and his jacket hood up over that.

"Pretty cool. I think we should wait—if you guys are okay with that," Babe answers.

"It's frickin' freezing," Chad says, leaning against the wall now, hugging himself, dark peacoat buttoned all the way up. "I hope this is good, Babe."

"Okay, I guess we've got fifteen minutes," I say wearily.

Five minutes pass. We're all antsy, but we've begrudgingly stayed put.

Babe paces back and forth. "I hope it works now that I'm making everyone wait." She laughs nervously.

"I can't feel my hands," Chad announces.

"The Eiffel Tower's preppin' for takeoff," Pilot announces.

"If the Eiffel doesn't go off, it's going to be really upsetting." I laugh.

Six minutes left. I can't feel my fingers, and I'm wearing gloves.

We've all staked out spots against the barrier now, staring eagerly. The sun just disappeared behind the horizon. The Eiffel glows with the remnants of its orangey-gold light.

"Are you sure it doesn't just light up like this?" Pilot asks. I snort.

"No, that's not it." Babe chuckles.

"Come on, Eiffel Tower. Let's go," Pilot demands. We all cackle. He turns to smile at me, and I feel a little less cold. "Gosh, the Eiffel Tower is just letting us down," he continues.

"Two minutes!" I announce. "I can't feel my feet, Eiffel Tower. I hope you're happy."

"Come on, Eiffel Tower," Pilot repeats.

"One minute! I've got T minus one minute," Chad adds.

"You sure about this?" Pilot asks Babe again. She smiles and shakes her head.

"Babe's definitely wrong, and we're definitely throwing her in the river," Chad answers jokingly.

And then, it happens. Glitter explodes all over the famous structure. Lights sparkle up and down its iron legs. It looks like Tinker Bell threw up all over it, and it's having a sparkly seizure. We erupt into whoops and cheers.

"Ohh snap," Chad calls out.

"OHMYGOD, OHMYGOD, OHMYGOD," Pilot yells with mock fangirl-esque excitement, and I can't stop laughing for a good twenty seconds as we dance around in the freezing air, admiring it.

We indulge in a dinner full of red wine, ham, and cheese at a French restaurant before taking a taxi to the area recommended to us by the girl at the hostel check-in desk—Bastille.

The taxi releases us at the mouth of a street full of lights, buzzing with activity. Because it's his birthday, we let Chad lead the way. He stops outside a building where music floods the street each time the door opens, and looks back at us with an overexcited smile before heading in. We follow, a few steps behind. Through the door is a coat check booth at the foot of a twisting staircase. The music is coming from the second floor, so we check our jackets and head on up.

A live band is playing. The band's at the far end of a large, open room full of people bopping around to the music. Here, on the opposite end of the room, is the bar. We grab drinks before zigzagging through the crowd to find an opening where we can watch and nod along. When the indie rock song they're playing ends, they start a song I definitely recognize. I find myself bobbing around more purposefully.

I took her out. It was a Friday night. I wore cologne. To get the feeling right.

Babe and Chad are dancing too. Pilot's smiling and singing at me on my left. I join him, throwing my arms about as the chorus comes in.

"And that's about the time she walked away from me," we scream at the top of our lungs, laughing and throwing ourselves around. *"Nobody likes you when you're twenty-three."*

We bounce and laugh our way through the weird mix of oldies the band continues to play—mostly classic rock and punk rock from the early 2000s. When "Eye of the Tiger" comes to a close, Pilot asks if I want to get another drink. Another familiar tune starts up as we head to the bar.

Pilot orders a beer. He turns to look at me as the bartender fills his order. I hold eye contact, the lyrics to the latest song automatically flowing out of me, my head whipping side to side with the beat. *"This is the AN-THEM, throw all your hands up!"*

He laughs.

When the bartender returns with his drink, I lean up against the bar. "Um, water, please," I request before turning back to Pilot's eyes. Music pulses around us so I lean in as close as I dare (not very close; there's still at least a foot of space between us). "Do you not like to dance?" I talk-yell with a smile.

"I'm not really a dancer," he says as my water is placed in front of me.

"But anyone can dance. We're all dancers!"

He grins and rolls his eyes.

We stroll back to approximately where we were standing earlier, but we've lost sight of Babe and Chad. The band has started playing the Beach Boys "Wouldn't It Be Nice." We sway back and forth, casually singing along. We're not close enough that we're touching, but now that Babe and Chad have moved, it feels like it's just us here, out alone together.

Fifteen minutes later, we head back to the bar. I order another water. *"When we live such fragile lives, it's the best way we survive. I go around a time or two, just to waste my time with you,"* belts the lead.

"This band is like my iPod on shuffle," I comment, lazily leaning up against the bar and gazing out at the singer. "Except without the Beatles. Where are the Beatles? And also Lady Gaga."

Pilot snorts. "Don't forget Taylor."

"Oh my god, it would be amazing if they played some T-swizzle rock style." I sigh. "You should play at bars like this, with your music," I suggest cheerily.

He grins at the floor. "That would be cool."

We head back out. Twenty minutes later, we're at the bar again. Pilot orders another beer. He watches me as we wait for his drink.

"It's been a really great day," he says, "a really great day, I've had a lot of fun—" He's smiling with teeth, like an adorable goof. Heat spreads across my chest. We have an eye contact moment before he continues. ". . . with Chad, of course. What would Paris be without Chad to see it with?" he finishes. I convulse in laughter.

Back on the dance floor, a song I don't recognize finally blasts though the room. It's a punk-rock song I'm not as familiar with, but it demands movement all the same. I sing blindly, making up words. Pilot is still smiling. I've never seen him hold a smile for such an extended period of time. He's standing right next to me now, and we're bumping into each other as we jump and sway. My skin sings in response: *Houston, we have contact.*

He keeps turning to smile at me. I smile back and follow up each burst of eye contact with a giant swig of water. It's a good excuse to break away and center myself. I'm slowly morphing into an anxious ball of nerves. *What's happening right now? Are we flirting? Like, flirting more intensely than before? What do I do? Nothing, just be cool, keep doing what you're doing.* I'm hyperaware of my movements as this unknown magical song that made Pilot more smiley comes to a close.

I think this is flirting. It has to be flirting. The band starts up a new, more mellow song. I know it—I gasp and break into a little happy dance as everyone starts singing along. "Yellow Submarine." Pilot's smiling so big at the band. He starts to sing along and I start to sing along, and then his arm comes to sit around my back.

I go full statue. He's not looking at me this very second, but his arm is on me. His arm is wrapped around me like we're together. My heart is drumming too fast for the music.

Okay, it's fine. Just keep singing. I can't remember the words.

I can't think of anything but his arm. His hand has settled around my waist. I look up at him. He's still singing. We sway together. He sways normally. I sway like a statue that someone's knocked into by accident. At least I'm moving.

He pulls me closer to his side, and my heart kicks up to light speed. *Oh my god.* We're smooshed together now. Body contact all along my left side. His warmth mingles with all of mine.

Stay cool, Shane, stay cool. What is staying cool? More swaying. Is the band still playing "Yellow Submarine"? *Concentrate on the song.* Yes, they are. The overhead lights keep whirling over us, the band keeps playing, and I keep my movements to a minimum in an effort to ensure our skin-to-skin contact stays intact.

I don't know if he's looking at me now. I haven't looked over at him in ages. The idea of looking at him now stresses me out.

You have to look at him, Shane. This is it, this is a moment.

Slowly, I'm talking at molasses speed, I turn my head to the left. He's already looking at me. Chills race up my limbs. It feels like when the band stops, this moment is going to stop, and I don't want this to stop. Anxiety shoots up through me, bouncing off the walls of my insides.

His green eyes study mine. We're looking at each other, but I don't even know what I would do to initiate something. I've never kissed someone, and I don't want him to know that. If we kiss, will he know that? *Oh my god, he'll know.* How could he not know? I have no idea what I'm doing. I don't even know what I would do with my arms! Where do arms go when you kiss? Do I just, like, grab him? I can't just grab him! What if I do it wrong? Is grabbing him an invasion of personal space? *Oh my god, I'm going to stand still like I'm doing a pencil dive with my arms flat against my side, aren't I?*

He leans forward a bit. *His lips are right there.* Panic takes the wheel, and before I even realize what I'm doing, I've raised the glass I'm clutching back up to my mouth, and turned forward to face the band.

I chug a cowardly swig of water. Disappoint torrents through my system.

My eyes glaze over as I stare unblinkingly at the guitarist. He wasn't going to kiss me, right? That wasn't a big enough lean, was it? Oh god. I don't know how to reinitiate whatever almost happened. I have to pee. I have to go. His arm is still there. I don't know how long we've been like this.

Abruptly, I spin toward him. "Hey, Pies, I'm gonna run to the BR. I'll be right back."

I've startled him with my sudden transformation from unmoving statue back to living, breathing human being.

"Oh, okay!" he projects over the music. "Do you want me to—" he starts, but I'm already leaving, weaving back through the people to the hall off the end of the room where I saw restroom signs earlier.

I plow into the bathroom. The stalls are painted black, and the lighting is all neon blue. I walk over to the sink area, which is just a big trench across the front of the room, and stare at myself in the mirror. My hair is wild and extra big from the humidity. Tears burn in the corners of my eyelinered eyes.

What is wrong with me? A choked sound escapes my mouth. I take a few more deep breaths in front of the mirror. *Do not cry.* I curl my hands into fists, a physical threat to the salt water gathered in my eyes. *You're okay.* I pee, wash my hands, and head back out into the abyss of the dance floor.

Rather than navigate directly through the sea of humans, I edge my way back along the perimeter of the room.

"Hey, girl!" I hear a familiar voice and stop, spinning around to find Chad walking over with a fresh vodka cranberry.

"Hey!" I say, a little relieved to catch a glimpse of him after losing him and Babe pretty early on in the night. He walks up to me until he's a little too close. I find myself up against the wall as I step back, trying to maintain a bubble of personal space. "Where's Babe?" I ask over the music.

"At the bar, I think," he says offhandedly. "How are you liking this place? It's dope, right?" He smiles, eyes drooping drunkenly.

"Yeah, it's good. I like the music. I was just heading back to find Pilot." I crane my neck, looking over Chad's shoulder.

"You have really pretty hair," he says, staring at me. I narrow my eyes.

"Okay, thanks." I turn my head, still searching for Pilot. When I turn back . . .

"What the—" I'm cut off as Chad's squishy lips hit my face, landing half on my own lips, half lopsided on my check. I bend my legs, sliding down the wall toward the floor before falling sideways slightly and jumping back up, a foot to the right of where I had just been. Chad's gawking at me with his jaw hanging open.

"What are you doing?" I demand.

"It's my birthday!"

"Babe likes you," I scold. I bolt away from him, weaving in and out through the crowd now. That didn't happen. My first kiss isn't from some drunken doofus who's supposed to be here with my friend. It isn't. It doesn't count. It didn't happen!

Relief floods through me when I spot the back of Pilot's plaid shirt among the damp crowd of dancers. I bump into him lightly as I step up on his right.

"Hey," I greet him gratefully.

"Hey! Welcome back." He grins. To my surprise, he pulls me in next to him again. His arm resettles around my waist. And, as expected, I turn back to stone. My whole body hums. He looks so calm and content, but my mind won't stop whirring. Maybe I didn't mess everything up when I turned the other way? Where is Babe? Chad is an asshat. I do not like that guy. I didn't like him before, but I definitely do not like him now.

The music stops at some point. Pilot leads me toward to back of the room with his hand still at my back. My eyes find Chad and Babe. They're near the bar, clutching half-empty drinks, and Babe is yelling. I can tell from here.

"Are they fighting?" I ask Pilot nervously.

"Looks like it." We power walk over. Before I can make out anything they're saying, Pilot speaks over them, "Hey, you guys ready to head out? I think the band's done."

Babe jerks her attention to us, eyes red and puffy. Oh no.

"Oh yeah, we should get going so we can catch the Metro," Babe agrees, her voice cracking on the words *get* and *Metro*. She places her drink on the bar, grabs Chad's drink out of his hand, and slams it down next to hers. The remnants of his vodka cranberry fly around the clear plastic cup as she pivots and storms past us toward the stairs.

"Happy birthday, man," Pilot says, giving Chad a manly clap on the back with the hand that's not on me. I watch Chad's eyes drift to Pilot's hand.

"Yeah, happy birthday," I sputter nervously like nothing happened.

Chad throws a slick grin at me before looking at Pilot. "Thanks, man."

"Let's go," Babe yells up ahead. I should try to talk to Babe.

"Wait, Babe!" I yell, "I think we should pee before we go!"

She turns to glare at me, but after a moment she nods, and we head toward the restroom. There's a line snaking out the door now. She adds herself to it, and I step up behind her.

"Babe, are you okay?" My voice comes out small and hesitant.

She turns to face me, glaring again for a good five seconds before exploding, her voice pained and low. "I don't know, Shane! I finally try to make a move on the guy I like, he jumps away yelling, and I quote 'Dammit, Babe, I don't like you like that,' and then he makes a beeline right for you." Her eyes shine.

"Babe, I'm so sorry. He's an assbucket!"

"What, is Pilot not enough? You need every guy's attention on you?"

"What?" Tears strangle my voice as I squeeze out the next two sentences. "What are you talking about? He came over to me, and I ran away from him!"

"I don't want to talk to you right now." She turns away pointedly as we make it into the actual bathroom. Babe strides into the next open stall. I turn and leave.

I wait outside next to Pilot, who's chatting with Chad about bears. When Babe emerges, we follow her to the stairs and join the slow trickle of bodies headed to pick up their jackets. We shuffle along the coat check line. Babe's a few people ahead of Pilot and me. Chad stands behind us, looking off into space.

Pilot ducks his mouth close to my ear as we take a step closer to the coat check window. "What do you think their best song was?" His voice tickles my face.

"Um, I think my favorite was that cover from that band I like." My stomach rotates like a washing machine.

He smiles. "That weird hipster band? Same." He holds my eyes.

"Next!" the woman behind the counter calls us forward. We break eye contact and step up hastily, handing over our tickets and paying the Euro for our jackets.

"Come on, Chad," Babe demands with attitude as we all file back out onto the street. She spins on her foot and heads down the road toward the Metro. Chad starts after her.

Pilot and I hang back, walking slowly. "That looks dramatic," he starts.

I take a deep breath, trying to quell my anxious stomach. "She went to kiss him, he said some nasty things, and then he tried to make a move on me in front of her when I was on my way back from the bathroom, and I ran away from him."

"What?" His eyebrows pinch together.

"Yeah." I exhale a gust of air. "It was weird. I don't really want to dwell on it."

Pilot studies me for a moment, his eyebrows low, before nodding and pressing his lips together. He looks down, watching the ground go by under our feet. I drop my gaze.

"So where should we go next?" he asks.

My head snaps back up. I stutter, "Um—like tonight or in life?"

He huffs a breathy laugh. "Where should we go for our next epic weekend trip? What else do we need to climb?"

"I'm down to go anywhere really, maybe Scotland?"

"Scotland! Let's hit that up. *Braveheart*!" he yells enthusiastically.

"Scotland it is, then! That's where Hogwarts is."

"Oh, did you go there?" he asks in a serious voice.

"Class of '08." I force down a smile.

"Me too."

I put on my best Scottish accent, "So, you're a wizard, Pilot?" It's terrible. Pilot snorts.

Up ahead, Chad and Babe descend into the Metro station. We start down the steps a moment later and make our way to the platform. The station is packed. Everyone's trying to catch the last train. We linger on the grungy platform for twenty minutes before an announcement is made to tell us the last train has already left the station.

Wearily, the four of us join a mass exodus back up to the street. On the left side of the staircase, there's still a steady flow of people going down into the station despite its lack of trains. On the right side, we're all packed together streamlining our way up. The four of us are slightly separated, a human or two between us. I'm in the middle of the pack.

We're nearing ground level again. I can see the sky up ahead, but as I take my next step, there's a tug on my cross-body purse and the strap yanks down on my right shoulder. The pull intensifies, and the strap slides up against my neck. I stumble back and turn my head in alarm. There's a man, heading down the stairs, his hand is in my now-unzipped bag. My chest seizes. *What do I do?* He's being pulled away with the downstream current of humans, and I'm being yanked backward.

"Ahhh!" a yell bursts from my lungs as I lunge upward and to my right, hopping over three steps, ripping my bag away from him.

"Shane?" I hear Pilot shout back.

"What's going on?" Babe asks.

"I think she just tripped," Chad's voice hits my ears.

I flail over my feet, fumbling upward, pushing off the ground with my hands to regain my balance like a child running up the stairs. I grasp at my purse, pulling it up to my chest, and run up the remaining steps, pushing my way past everyone, not stopping till I've broken away from the mob and I'm back on the sidewalk outside.

I'm shaking as my hands pry the sides of my purse open, taking stock. I unzip the second pocket where my wallet is and exhale a relieved breath. It's here.

It's okay. A hand falls on my shoulder, and I look up to see Pilot's olive eyes. I breathe breathe breathe breathe, pumping the fear out of my system.

"Are you okay?" he asks.

Babe appears in front of me with Chad next to her.

"What happened?" Babe cries.

"A guy." *Breathe.* "Had his hand in my purse." I look frantically from Pilot to Babe.

"What the fuck?" Pilot's concern morphs to outrage. He takes a step back, runs a hand through his hair. Chad looks at me blankly, and Babe's hand whips up to cover her mouth.

"He had his hand in it and he was pulling me back down, and I lunged away and his hand fell away 'cause he was going down the stairs. And I—it's okay, he didn't get anything," I babble softly.

"Oh Mylanta," Babe whispers. "We have to get a cab. Let's get back. Come on." She shoots me a sympathetic look, turning toward a cab stand in the distance. Chad follows, and I fall into step robotically. I focus on trying to quell the panic circuiting through my veins. Pilot's hand is on my back again.

16. A Million Little Shining Stars

I sit in the middle of the taxi bench. Pilot's on my left, Babe is on my right, and Chad's in the front seat. I want to lean into Pilot's shoulder. I don't have much shoulder-leaning experience, but I think I could handle it. I don't do it.

In the silence, my brain replays the night on a loop, my stomach going up and down, like on one of those milder roller coasters with lots of little unexpected drops. I focus on the good parts. Something is happening with Pilot. It makes my heart balloon up in my chest.

After an eternity, we spill out onto the gray concrete outside the hostel.

Babe and Chad get out at their floor, and as the elevator doors close behind them, I blow out a breath. Babe and Chad's anger made for a quiet, tense cab ride. I want to lighten the mood again. Pilot's leaning against the railing along the back wall of the lift, staring at the doors.

"Finally," I say, breaking the extended silence. He turns to me expectantly, and I freeze up.

Finally? *Finally what?* Jesus Christ. I curve my lips up into a small smile. Smiling is always good. He smiles back, but doesn't say anything, and then abruptly stuffs his hands in his pockets and looks at the floor.

The elevator dings. Nerves snap around inside me as we walk toward the room. I feel like one of those crackling orbs of electricity you see at science museums. When we reach the door, I dig around in my purse for the key. Another eternity passes before I yank it out and plug it into the lock.

"Shane," he says.

I turn around. He was right behind me, right in front of me now. He's leaning toward me again, and the world slows. I still don't know what to do. Where will my arms go! I'm having a hot flash. My hand grapples at the key behind me. I rip it out of the lock and drop it to the floor, jumping slightly as it clashes against the white tile. Pilot jerks his head back. I whip around, swoop to collect the key, plug it back into the lock, twist the door open, drop my purse, collect my suitcase, and speed to the bathroom to get ready for bed.

When I emerge fifteen minutes later, Pilot's seemingly passed out on his single. I slip quietly into my bed. My heart's in overdrive. I can't get it to calm down. I snuggle up in the covers and pull my legs into the fetal position. Almost immediately, tears spring into my eyes.

No. Why am I crying? No crying! I twist onto my back, letting the saltwater slide down my cheeks. I gasp in a shallow breath, staring at the ceiling. Seriously, what's wrong with me? I flash to Pilot at the club, Chad's face on mine, Babe's glare, the man's face on the steps of the Metro, Pilot again outside the door. My study abroad goal list would be ashamed. I wasn't brave tonight; I was pathetic. And I almost lost my purse. *Again.* I suck more oxygen. Close my eyes. *Stop. Crying.*

There's light tap on my shoulder. My eyes snap open. Pilot's standing next to my bed. I frantically wipe at any still dripping tears and jolt up to my elbows.

"Hey," he says, quietly hovering above me. I just look at him. What is he doing? He nods his head in a move-over gesture.

Hesitantly, I scoot to the left side of the twin bed. He sits and *lowers himself down next to me,* on his back, facing the ceiling. Holy shit. I flatten onto my back again. I suck in one last steadying breath, damming up the waterworks through sheer force of will.

He's still wearing his jeans and a white T-shirt.

"Are you okay?" he says softly.

I talk to the ceiling. "Yeah . . . I'm sorry, this is stupid." Another breath. "I'm just feeling overwhelmed or something."

"Someone almost mugged you; it's not stupid to feel overwhelmed."

I blink up at the ceiling.

"Can I ask you something?" Pilot continues.

"Yeah."

He turns onto his left side, propping his head up with his arm. I rotate to my right to match—insides in full freak-out mode.

Pilot purses his lips. "Do you think Chad is Santa?"

A laugh bursts out of me. "Dear god, I hope not," I say shakily.

Pilot grins. "Do you have any siblings?" he asks.

Master of distraction. My eyes drift down to his mouth and quickly back up to his eyes. "No, I've got a load of cousins, though. You?"

"Two younger sisters," he says.

Two younger sisters. Is that why he's so nice? I smile to myself.

"What?" he asks, lips turning up.

"Nothing," I say quickly. I rotate onto my back again, falling under the pressure of prolonged eye contact and opting to stare at the ceiling. I feel Pilot shift next to me until we're side by side again. Sharing a pillow.

I swallow. "What's the scariest thing you've ever done?"

He purses his lips for a moment. "I— What do you mean by scary?"

"I mean, not scary commercially, but scary to you, you know?"

There's a beat of silence before he answers. "I'm not sure . . . I kind of left my . . . I mean"—he blows out a breath—"I guess change has always been scary for me."

I'm quiet for a moment, nodding in agreement and working up the courage to speak.

"This is the scariest thing I've ever done," I whisper.

"What—"

"I mean, not this-this—I mean, coming out here for study abroad. I'm not very good at trying new things, and I've never been this far from my family. Um, but more than that, I'm, I'm always the good child, you know. I get great grades, and I don't talk back. I do what they tell me to do. It's only me, and I want to make them happy, and I've never lied to them. So, when I lied to them about this, they believed me."

"They don't know you're out here?" he asks quietly.

I huff a sad chuckle. "I'm premed, so I told them I'm out here doing a premed program. I, like, made a fake brochure and everything. I took care of all the paperwork and stuff. But there is no premed track out here . . . and they're gonna be pissed when they find out."

"I thought you were an English major."

"They wouldn't pay for college if I didn't major in something that lined me up for a *lucrative* future." I blink at the ceiling. "My grandpa did the struggling-artist thing, wrote poetry and stuff, worked a bunch of temporary jobs. It made him a pretty shitty dad. He was never around, and when he was, he was distant and tired, had a short fuse with my dad and his siblings.

"Now my dad's obsessed with financial stability, in this macho Italian, I'm-a-real-man sort of way. I'm his only kid so . . . he . . . it's a lot. Like, I know in his own way, he's just trying to be a good dad—and writing, being creative, it's not exactly known for being a pragmatic career path.

"I'm good at math and science, and I like numbers. My mom was gonna be a doctor. But she had to drop out of med school when she got pregnant with me, so it just makes sense. She's really excited." I turn my head to get a read on Pilot. His face is right there, a breath away. There's a sadness etched in his eyes.

"I don't hate being premed, I'm just not particularly, you know, it doesn't have the same—and it's so all-consuming. I don't know, I want to make things. These past two weeks here, studying something I really care about, and writing, it's been the best.

"I hadn't really found a place at YU, so I'd been going home like every other weekend. And everyone in our year was prepping to studying abroad, and I felt like maybe this would be a way to start over. Make new friends and have new experiences and not spend all my time in the dorm.

"I started looking into programs, saw this writing internship track in London, and I knew it was my chance to try to do . . . what I would really love to do because there's the internship—a writing internship . . . like a real job, and if I did well there, maybe they could help me get a real paid summer internship job somewhere in the US, and maybe then I could show my parents that, you know, I can do this.

"I can do it. I'm good at it, and I can do it. I'm gonna do it." I swallow hard. Pilot's watching me attentively. I meet his eyes for a moment before shifting back to the ceiling tiles. "So, um, when I get jumpy, that's me doing my best to deal with all the residual paranoia and fear swirling around. Like when I lost my purse, I thought, you know, it could ruin everything. They would find out and, I don't . . . I don't know . . . I haven't told anybody any of this."

Pilot's fingers weave through mine. He squeezes my hand. Warmth shoots up through my fingertips.

It's quiet for a minute before Pilot says, "Shane. That's insanely badass."

Unexpected laughter rises in my chest. My shoulders shake as I try to contain it. I don't know what to say. I gently squeeze back. We lie like that for another twenty minutes. I don't know what to do with myself. I couldn't possibly sleep. My heart is ping-ponging around like a Super Ball. After a while, he finally gets up. Carefully, he scoots back into his own bed. I pretend to be asleep.

"Good night, Shane," he mumbles from his bed.

My words wobble nervously from my mouth. "Night, Pies."

17. Such a Breakable Thread

1/23/11 8:30 a.m.

THINGS I'M PRETTY SURE ABOUT:
1) It's time to leave for the train back to London. (100%)
2) Pilot and I have almost kissed multiple times now. (91%)
3) Pilot has a girlfriend. (73%)

Does this thing that's been happening mean he might break
up with his girlfriend? Would he break up with his girlfriend?
Has he already broken up with his girlfriend? Would he have
told us? I can't bring myself to ask. I never ever bring her up,
and he hasn't brought her up since, well. . . he's never
brought her up.

If something were to happen between us, he would have to
make the first move. Not that I would even know how to
initiate any sort of move . . . he might have been making
moves last night. Moves that I blocked? I wish I could ask
Babe. It feels taboo to share any of this with anyone, because
as far as I know, Pilot has a girlfriend. It's against the rules
to like him. I like to follow the rules.

But, maybe they did break up? It's not like he would have shouted it from the rooftops. He could have. He said he wanted to go to Edinburgh together next weekend. I mean, the signs are saying yes!

"Shane?"

My head snaps up. Pilot's at the foot of my bed, waving his hands around. *Whoa.* Last time I looked up, Pilot was heading to shower. I slam the cover closed on my notebook, hastily click off my pen, and smile at him. "Hey! Yes! Ready?" I shove Horcurx Nine into my book bag.

Pilot and I find Babe and Chad in the lobby, sitting on opposite sides of a bench with their arms crossed.

"Hey," Pilot says as we step up to their bench.

"Morning!" I greet them.

"Ready to get a cab?" Babe jumps up.

"Yeah, sho—" I start.

"Great!" Babe interrupts. She power walks out the door with her suitcase.

It takes us ten minutes to flag down a taxi in this outskirt area of Paris. When we do, I step up and open the door to the back seat. Babe jumps forward and scoots in immediately. The driver pops the trunk and gets out to help load our bags.

"I'm not getting in that taxi," Chad announces from the sidewalk. There's a thump as Babe's bag flops into the trunk.

I whip around. "Why? What's wrong with this taxi?"

"I'm not going in the same taxi as *her.*"

I hear the thump of my bag dropping into the back. The boys both hold onto their packs, so the driver closes the trunk with a bang and gets back into the car.

"What do you mean, you're not going in the same taxi as her? We're all going to the train station. There are four seats here." I try to speak calmly, but bits of anger edge their way into my voice.

"I want to get a separate taxi!" he yells. Pilot and I exchange a look.

"Man, it took us, like, ten minutes just to find this one taxi," Pilot reasons.

I duck my head down into the cab to gauge Babe's reaction. She's looking determinedly at the back of the seat in front of her.

"I will not ride in this cab," Chad repeats loudly.

"Shut up, Chad," I say, whirling back to him.

"You guys go. I'll stay with him, get another cab. We'll meet you there," Pilot offers.

I blow out an angry breath, but concede with a nod and slide in next to Babe.

"Okay, good luck," I say before closing the door. I shoot a glare at Chad and slam the door. "Gare du Nord, please!" I tell the driver.

My eyes are on Pilot as we pull away from the curb. He nods at me before turning to say something to Chad. I settle into the back seat, my puffy jacket swishing against the leather. Babe pouts next to the window.

I heave a great sigh. "Babe, did more stuff happen with you two? I'm sorry about last night, but please don't be mad at me. Chad came at me with his face to make you angry or something, but nothing happened. I ran away from him."

Babe sighs as well. "I'm not mad. I'm sorry I yelled at you. I drank too much." She's still looking at the floor. "Chad's just being an asshole and making a scene. He gets really dramatic sometimes."

"No kidding."

Babe snorts and meets my eyes. Hers are glassy. "Last night at the bar I thought things were going really well. He freaked out—and then later when we got back to the room, I wanted to explain, but he wasn't having it. He just talked over me: 'Babe, we've talked about this! I like short girls, you're not my type, god, why are you trying to ruin this? We're having fun and you have to ruin things. It's so frustrating.'" Her Chad impression is pitchy but I like it.

She continues, "And I was like, 'I don't understand why would you ask me to plan your birthday, then!' And he had the nerve to say, 'I didn't ask you to plan anything.' And I was like, 'You sure as hell didn't ask me not to; here we are in Paris together for your birthday!' And he goes, 'Don't try to turn this into some romantic thing.' And then I told him he was being an asshole, and then he stormed out of the room."

"What kind of douche kabab says those things to their friend? Who treats anyone like that? He doesn't deserve you in his life."

"He eventually came back in and went to sleep."

"And apologized?"

"No, we didn't speak this morning."

"What the heck? And that's why he had a hissy fit outside and wouldn't share a cab?"

"I tried to talk to him again while we waited for you guys to come down . . ."

"Babe, there are other guys out there who like Disney. This whole situation is so weird and melodramatic. It was like you were married for ten years, and he caught you with another man in bed this morning."

"He's just passionate."

I slap a palm to my forehead. "You're not going to pursue him anymore, right?"

She's silent for a moment, before shrugging coolly. "You're one to lecture. What's going on with you and Pilot?"

My lips clamp shut. I swallow slowly, debating whether or not to share my breakup theory. I stay quiet.

She raises her eyebrows. I turn to look out the window.

We pick up burgers on our way back to the Karlston. I eat mine in the kitchen with Babe, both of us surfing the internet and catching up with the world. I import all the Paris pictures, edit them, and get an album up on Facebook. I spend some time on the *Packed! For Travel!* site, getting ready for my upcoming first day of work. At some point, Atticus comes in and asks us about our trip.

As we fill him in, he stabs animatedly at a frozen meal and stuffs it in the microwave. When we finish our highlights reel, he launches into a story about a strange show he had to go see for class that revolved around the life of a toad. We get a play-by-play of the entire thing, and it's ridiculously entertaining through Atticus's sarcastic retelling.

Thirty minutes into the toad show recap, the kitchen door swings open.

Pilot strides in and flops on the black leather couch, looking exhausted. I feel a nervous smile pop up onto my cheeks. Last night—I mean, something changed between us.

"And then the whole cast is just squatted on the ground ribbiting for, I swear, five minutes straight with no dialogue—" Atticus, who had been pacing around the table, stops short, looking at Pilot.

"Hey! I'm telling them about the toad play!" he says cheerily. Pilot huffs a sarcastic laugh and lets his head fall back against the couch. "How'd your call go?" Atticus asks.

A call? I push Sawyer aside so I can see Pilot better. Could it be a break-up-with-Amy call?

Pilot runs a hand down his face and looks at the ceiling. *Oh my god, something's wrong. Was it a breakup call?*

"Um," he starts, "Amy's going to come visit me next month during her break. She wanted to see me, so she bought a ticket to come. Visit."

I suck in an audible breath as the cloud I've been dancing on dissolves under my feet. Pilot's eyes flit to mine and then down to the floor. Babe shoots me a sympathetic look.

"That'll be nice!" Atticus exclaims from his position leaning against the counter near the sink. "You guys should go back to Paris together, city of *love* and all that."

I pull my computer screen in front of my face and stare at it blindly.

"Yeah that's . . . that's where she wants to go," Pilot mumbles. He doesn't sound excited. I don't know if that makes this better or worse. I need to get out of here. I need to leave the room.

"Even though you were just there?" Babe asks hesitantly.

My limbs refuse to move. They need to hear all the details.

"Yeah, she really wants to go."

"It'll be fine. There's always more to see in Paris," Atticus says, taking a seat at the table.

Pilot stands abruptly and strides for the door. "Yeah, I have to—I have a paper," he says.

I give it a minute before I pack up my computer to leave too. I want to be sad in the privacy of my top bunk. As I stand, the chair I was on topples backward, clanging obnoxiously against the floor.

I whip around to glare at it. "Fuck off!"

Babe and Atticus watch me silently with wide eyes. I swallow before placing Sawyer back on the table, picking up the chair, and breezing out of the room.

18. I Can Learn to Do It

January 24, 2011

Mom and Dad,

My internship starts tomorrow. My boss's name is Wendy, and she's already the coolest. She said if things go well, I might get to write a piece about studying abroad in London for the magazine! I spent the morning researching the company to get a better feel for their posting style. This afternoon, I'm going to put together a list of touristy things in London to try out these next few months. This way, if I get the chance to write that article, I'm prepared. Wish me luck!

XO,
Shane

P.S. I miss your cooking.
P.P.S. I like a boy. He has a girlfriend who isn't me, and it's the worst.

I'm outside the door of *Packed!*, jittery with freshly consumed caffeine pumping through my veins.

I glance at my phone again: 9:52 a.m. Eight minutes early. That should be fine. I push in the doorbell and step back as the buzzing sound blasts from the speaker.

Tracey the receptionist welcomes me in. She brings me to a little table outside the office kitchen and sets an old white MacBook on it. This is where I'm to sit. Then she speeds me around the wide-open space, introducing me to the employees. I try to take note of everyone's name, but we only exchange quick hellos, so it's difficult (Donna, Janet, Declan, George—and Jamie?). They're all trendy-looking, and they all have English accents.

Then I get a rundown of their kitchen–tea station. They have cool cubed sugar, a stainless steel electric kettle, ten different types of tea, and a chart pasted to the wall with everyone's specific tea preferences. I'm to make tea for whomever requests it. It's a quick tour, and she finishes by leading me back to the little table with the white MacBook.

"So you can reach me on IM if you need me," she adds before heading back to the front desk.

I carefully pull out the chair and sit. I open the MacBook and bring up iChat. Tracey's name is there as my sole contact online.

For the rest of the morning, I obediently man my station. Any time someone walks by my table, I sit up straighter, ready to be asked to make tea. *I can make you tea,* I think toward them, *ask me to make you tea!* But no one asks me for a cup of tea. They just walk on by and start making it for themselves. Don't they know I'm here to make their tea?

I catch pieces of conversation about different cities around the globe as people go by, but not enough to feel like I know what anyone's working on. I watch the office breathe for hours, utterly clueless about how I should be spending my time. I instant message Tracey, asking her what she'd like me to work on, and she messages back: *I'll let you know.* But what do I do in the meantime?

During high school and over breaks, I've always worked at my dad's office (he's a financial advisor). Every morning, he has his assistant email me a list of things to do. It was mostly numbing, mindless work, but from that extreme mindlessness came some of my best ideas. I'd zone out and plot stories in my head while inputting financial stats for hours. The thing is, I don't want to zone out here. I want to zone in.

I love the cool, modern office environment. Indie, alternative music plays lightly from Spotify on an unmanned computer at the editing station in the center of the room. The editing station is a group of five big Mac desktops grouped together. The cute, young male employee I noticed during the tour works over there. He's pale and skinny, with square black-rimmed glasses and curly brown hair. I remember his name: Declan. Then there's the pretty brown-skinned lady with long, flowing locks who works at a desk adjacent to the editing bay: Donna. And across from her desk is I think the oldest man in here, George. He's got pasty skin, round black-rimmed glasses, and a receding hairline. Across the room are two other desks positioned back to back. One is Janet's, a petite black woman with cool red glasses and voluminous shoulder-length bronze curls, and the other is Jamie's: a posh, fake-tanned, might be in her forties, intimidating, tall woman with bleached, straight hair and bangs.

The boss, Wendy, stops by at the music computer every once in a while to switch up the tunes before returning to her office. This morning, she announced that she loved Neon Trees, and we've been listening to their music all day. Now I like them too.

At 3:30 p.m., Tracey finally comes over to my table with a task. I straighten excitedly as she hands me a Post-it. It's a grocery list. She wants me to pick up some groceries down at the supermarket near Covent Garden.

It's not magazine-related in the slightest, but I happily get the groceries, eager to be helpful. When I return, Tracy tells me to search the internet for a creative-looking coatrack for the office. I spend the rest of the afternoon gathering links to weird coatracks and emailing them over to Tracey. At 5:00 p.m., she gives me a bag full of packages and tells me I can go home after dropping them off at the post office.

My shoulders slump as I thump down the stairs and out the door. That was not what I expected. I felt more like a burden that no one knew what to do with today than any sort of assistant. On the trek home, I try not to be disappointed. This was just the first day.

"I love my office!" Babe exclaims, as she drops a bag of food onto the kitchen table. "It's covered in Disney-themed things. Everyone has little Disney stuffed animals on their desk. Oh Mylanta, it's amazing!" The entire flat has congregated in the kitchen to discuss their first days at work. I just finished up the shawarma I picked up on the way home; it's not Shwednesday, but I was craving it.

"I have to go back in to work in an hour," Atticus calls from the couch. He's typing away on his laptop. Atticus is always moving, juggling, multitasking.

"I ran errands all day: food, dry cleaning, groceries." Sahra sighs as she puts a pot of water on the stove.

"Yeah, I did data input on a computer," Pilot adds as he unwraps a Byron burger.

"I researched artistic coatracks for a good two hours," I tell everyone. I glance over at Pilot sitting two seats away at the end of the table. He doesn't meet my eyes.

"Coatracks?" Babe asks in disbelief.

I twist to look at her. "Yep, I really got an inside look at how a magazine is made." Babe laughs.

"Sahra and I have decided we're hitting a club in Soho this Friday. You guys want to join?" Atticus asks.

"I'm staying in this weekend," Babe answers.

"What about you?" Sahra points her wooden spoon at me.

I can't help glancing at Pilot again. Why isn't he saying anything? He always wants to do things. Right now, he's concentrating intently on eating his burger. *Is he not going to come with us?* I look from Atticus to Sahra.

"Okay," I answer.

1/28/11 8:30 p.m.

Days two and three at <u>*Packed! For Travel!*</u> *went slightly better than day one. I genuinely want to learn, so on Wednesday* after 1.5 hours of panicked internal anguish, I got up—out of my seat and everything—with a plan. I traipsed around the office like an anxious kitten and quietly asked each employee if they would like a cup of tea. This led to mini conversations.

They would open with something like: "Hi, how are you, darling?"

And I would come in with something brilliant like: "Hi, would you like a cup of tea?"

And they would return with an excited "Yes, please!" or "No, thank you!"

I made two cups of tea. One for Donna and one for Janet. I was super-nervous concocting the first cup. I mean, I'm American and they're British. By default, they have higher tea standards. But that chart in the tea station was a lifesaver. I've never used these sugar cube things before, and I'm very amused by them. They should make sugar stars! And other shapes! Sugar octagons!

On Thursday, all the employees acknowledged me with a "Hi, Shane!" or "Morning, Shane!" when they came in for the day. They know my name. I'm one step closer to learning how every detail of their job works. I did a tea sweep at 11:00 a.m. and then another at 3:00 p.m. because that's about the time I start finding it difficult to keep my eyes open at my lonely little island table.

After the morning tea circuit, Tracey gave me a task that was vaguely related to the company. They ordered five hundred canvas tote bags with the _Packed! For Travel!_ logo on them. I had to go through them all to sort out which ones were printed correctly and which ones were printed slightly crooked, or "wonky" as the British call it. I'm learning so many new words.

At the end of day three, Donna (Irish Breakfast, one sugar, extra milk), got ready to leave, and the whole office came alive. They stood, gave her hugs, and wished her luck on her trip to Moscow. She's going to research travel ideas for _Packed!_ Part of her job is going to different cities, staying at different places, and exploring different attractions.

Today's Friday, so this morning I had class and wrote another sad postcard to my parents to add to my collection. And oh, it's been five days since Pilot and I have had a conversation. It's almost like he's avoiding me.

I've been hanging around the kitchen every night after _Packed!_ to work on various writing projects (the Paris blog post and trying to really flesh out an outline for a novel idea about adopted twins in college who learn one of their professors is their birth dad). When I walk into the kitchen, if Pilot's already there, he suddenly has to leave. If I'm already in there, and he's coming in, he just grabs something and heads out again.

Babe's been spending a lot of time on her bed watching various editions of _Cinderella_. I caught her watching _Ever After_ yesterday, and this morning she was watching the Brandy one. I tried to get her to reconsider coming out tonight, but she says she still isn't up for it. I AM up for it. Tonight, I stop dwelling on Pilot.

I check my appearance in our full-length mirror one last time and straighten out my high-waisted black skirt. I paired it with a plain red crop top today, and, inspired by Babe, I painted my lips a matching shade of ruby. Avril Lavigne's new song "What the Hell" plays on repeat from Sawyer over on the table by the giant window. Sahra's putting the finishing touches on her makeup. She's wearing a loose, cream-colored dress that falls right above her knees with blue dangly earrings and cream heeled boots.

"Ready?" she asks in her usual assertive tone. I'm getting used to it now, and I'm starting to respect her for it. She's confident in a way that I'm only pretending to be, and I don't think I'm even pretending up to her standards.

"Yep!" I say, pulling a stained finger out of my mouth and popping the top back onto my lipstick. I zip up my boots and grab my purse. Sahra's first out the door. I glance back at Babe. She's wearing headphones and watching the animated original Disney *Cinderella*. I wave goodbye, trying to catch her eye, but she's engrossed in the film.

We take the Tube to central London. Sahra leads Atticus and me through the streets and to a bright red bar in Soho. The place pulses with music and laughter. We grab drinks (I order a glass of red wine), and the three of us sit on one of the red trendy-looking couches lining the walls. At first we try to chat, but it's too loud. Atticus perseveres, trying hard to talk over the music, but despite his efforts, our conversations die quickly. There's a mildly crowded dance floor in the center of the room. The DJ's playing Top 40 pop music, and after a few conversationless minutes, I'm itching to get up and move to the beat. I tap my foot against the floor to Rihanna's "Who's that Chick."

"Want to dance?" I ask.

"Why not?" Atticus agrees.

Sahra shrugs. "Sure."

I give myself to Rihanna, twirling and throwing my arms around. Wine sloshes over onto my wrist, but I embrace it, cackling. Sahra dances more conservatively, sticking to one or two basic back-and-forth motions. Atticus busts out hilarious old-fashioned nerdy-looking moves. After a few songs, someone taps me on the shoulder. I whirl around to find an attractive black man in a blue button-up shirt.

I smile at him. "Hi!"

"Hey! My friend would like to dance with you," he shouts over the music, pointing over his shoulder to another guy. Behind him, a broad-shouldered, freckly, red-faced man built like a rugby player is looking at me. *Are we in middle school?*

"Um, okay," I say. Rugby Guy walks over and the two men join our little dance circle. Eventually Atticus goes off to get a drink by the bar. Sahra stays with me and the two guys.

When we've danced for ages, Rugby Guy asks if he can talk to me for a few minutes away from the floor. After checking with Sahra via eye contact—and receiving an aggressive *go!* head nod—Rugby Guy and I find an open spot at the bar. I spot Atticus at the other end, talking to an attractive man-bun guy.

"So, this is really fun! What do you do?" Rugby Guy talk-yells over the music.

I turn away from Atticus to respond. "I, um, I write! What about you?"

"Like books or articles? I'm a lawyer!"

"Cool, um, both, I guess." I take a sip of whatever wine managed to survive the dance session.

He stares at me for few beats. It starts to feel awkward, so I fumble to make conversation. "Um so, what are your thoughts on *Legally Blonde*? Was that an accurate portrayal of law school?" I try to smile.

His face lights up. "You are so cute."

He doesn't say anything else, so I laugh nervously and pull on a British accent. "Um, so, what kind of lawyer are you?"

"What's that accent?" he exclaims happily.

I continue, "I don't know to what you're referring?" Before I can register what's happening, he pulls me to his face and we're kissing. *Whaa?*

I clutch my wineglass in one hand and the other hangs limply at my side. He's kissing me, but I'm not sure what the hell I'm doing. It's wet and warm and—my mind flashes to a time Leo unexpectedly grabbed my head and forced me underwater in the deep end of the pool.

We break apart. That was weird. I look at the ground, eyes wide. I've never been so close to another human's face before, but *I did it . . . I kissed someone.* Someone whose name I don't even know. How anticlimactic.

He takes my limp hand and holds it between us as we lean up against the bar. We make forced small talk for another ten minutes. It's not much fun because I have to propel the whole conversation, and he responds with quick, boring answers whenever I ask him things.

Finally he asks, "So, could we go out sometime? Can I get your number?"

How do I say, *Lol, no thanks,* without sounding mean? I slowly retrieve my block phone.

"Um, yeah, hold on a sec," I say, navigating through to my address book with the stupid tiny buttons. I don't have my number memorized. I had to put myself in my own contact list. I click on the contact and turn the phone so he can see it. He plugs the number into his phone.

"Thanks!" He puts his iPhone away. "This was fun."

He pulls me in, and we start kissing again. I let it happen because this is still such a mystery. I want to feel it out, so I'm not floundering when there comes a time I care about the human I'm kissing. This kiss is better. I kiss back for sure this time, and it goes on for a little longer before we break apart. Okay, that was better. That was kind of nice.

1/29/11 10:30 a.m.

It happened. I sit here eating breakfast and writing to you as a kissed human being. It doesn't technically count as accomplishing a goal on the list because I didn't really like that guy. But I put myself out there a smidgen, and I experienced the thing! And I feel slightly less left out of general society because of it. Now, I shall relax and begin my reread of Cassandra Clare's City of Glass—which, yes, I brought to London in my suitcase—as a reward.

"Morning, Shane! You hear from Rugby Guy yet?"

I slap my notebook closed and look up at Atticus. He comes over waggling his eyebrows and sits across from me with his laptop.

I snort. "No, have you heard from Man Bun?"

"I have indeed. *Nathan* and I are getting dinner on Sunday." He grins.

"Wow, that was fast." I smile at him, before pulling over *City of Glass* from where I left it on the table.

"Whatcha reading?" he asks, curiously glancing at it.

"*City of Glass*, one of my favorites!" I tell him happily. "The fourth book in this series is coming out soon and I'm rereading in prep."

"Never heard of it!" he says cheerfully.

"You're missing out!" I tease. "What are you reading right now?"

"Currently *The Poet* by Michael Connelly. It's creepy as hell, but it's good."

"I'll add it to my TBR!" I proceed to pitch the Mortal Instruments series until he agrees to check them out.

Before heading back to my room to read in the bunk, I decide to ask Atticus if he'd be up for exploring some more of London with me this afternoon or tomorrow. I have to start building my repertoire of knowledge for the potential *Packed!* article. He politely declines because he already has theater-related plans and then of course, his date.

I head out of the kitchen and freeze halfway down the hall when I hear Pilot's guitar. We haven't talked in six days now. Should I see if Pilot would want to come with me? Maybe the only way to fix the weirdness happening between us is to push back against it with forced normalcy?

The door to his room is wide open.

I don't give myself the chance to chicken out. I walk right up and lean against the doorframe. He's strumming Lucy, wearing big old-fashioned headphones, and watching his computer screen.

"Hey," I say a little louder than normal. He startles, dropping the headphones back.

"Hey, I didn't see you." He laughs weirdly. Nervously?

He glances down at the computer screen again and back at me. Oh god, is he Skyping with someone? But the door was open!

"Um, sorry!" My heart sledgehammers in my throat. "I wanted to see if you wanted to, um, explore places in London, later today or Sunday with me and maybe the girls? It should be fun. I'm doing research for an article I might get to write for *Packed!* and I'm working on this list of places I want to go check out and, uh . . . yeah."

He blinks. "Um, I actually made some plans with the guys down the hall. We're going to Bath today and staying till tomorrow, but—good luck, that sounds great."

An uncomfortable sinking feeling fills my gut. "Oh, okay, wow, um, have fun." I spin around, bolt into my room, scurry up the bunk, and lie on my bed clutching Horcrux Nine and *City of Glass*.

That was weird; he was weird.

1/30/11 2:17 a.m.

Pilot left for a trip to Bath today . . . why didn't he tell any of us about it? I mean, yes, I guess he's not obligated to tell me about his life. But he didn't invite me. Or any of us.

I hate that this is hurting my feelings.

Babe, Sahra, and I are going to explore the city together tomorrow which should be fun.

I got a text from first-kiss Rugby Guy asking if I'd go out with him this coming Wednesday. I didn't know how to say no nicely, so I panicked and told him I'll be in Germany.

I can't get to sleep. The day I landed here in London—it felt like my life lit up with a thousand strands of fairy lights. I've been walking around all aglow for the last few weeks, but with Pilot edging away, a bunch of the strands are going out. Blergh.

19. Drifting

"What's this I hear about you havin' a boyfriend?" Dad opens.

I got back from Monday class a couple hours ago and have been nervously anticipating this Skype call ever since—it's our first since I started the internship.

I shift against the wall in my bunk. "I don't have a boyfriend."

"That's not what I heard from Leo."

"Well, Leo's an ass."

"What's wrong with you? I'm just askin' a question!"

"Come on, Shane, don't talk about your cousin that way," Mom chides.

I harrumph.

Mom changes the subject. "Tell us about work!" She grins at the webcam. "What did you wear? Who are you working with?"

"I'm working at an urgent care office, and I'm shadowing the receptionist right now, her name's Wendy, and my roommate Sahra works in the same building at the pediatrics office there." I pull up a forced smile.

Mom beams. "Wow, Shane, that's great! You know I'm proud of you, right? I'm so proud of you! I just . . ." She trails off, putting a hand to her heart. "And that's so nice you that have Sahra there. Do you two get to take lunch together?"

My heart hurts. "Yeah."

"You learnin' a lot?" Dad asks.

I nod vigorously. "Yeah! I've already been exposed to all sorts of medical issues and emergency situations."

Mom's eyebrows shoot up with curiosity. "Any particularly interesting ones you want to share?"

"Um, no, I mean, well—"

Dad conveniently interrupts me with a new question. He'll never admit it aloud, but he's squeamish. We sign off a few minutes later. I feel like I just swallowed a cup of mud. I want to tell them about *Packed!* I want to tell them how great the writing course is going, that I got another A on an assignment in class today. I love the way they look at me when they hear I'm doing well—the way my dad smiles and my mom's voice wobbles because any heightened emotion brings her to the brink of tears. I like being their perfect daughter.

It's inevitable that they find out I lied about all this, but I need it to be after the semester's over. Once I've sorted things out. Dad's good at being proud. He's good at providing, protecting, playing games. But he's not good at being angry. It swallows him up. He goes into sleep mode and someone else takes the helm. I've experienced as much when the cousins and I have broken things by accident, or when I haven't attended to a chore fast enough. Mom and I make Bruce Banner jokes after the fact, but there's nothing funny about it in the moment.

But it's going to be okay when I come back to them with a job. He can't be too mad if I get a job. I close my laptop. Through the window wall, I can see my flatmates in the kitchen, engaging in various stages of dinner. I climb down to join them.

I flop onto the leather couch, not wanting to crowd the cooking area where Babe and Atticus move about chopping things. Sahra and Pilot are eating at the table.

"How'd Skype with the parents go?" Babe calls from the counter as Atticus wraps up the story he was telling when I walked in.

"Fine." I smile.

"Any change in status with Friday night Rugby Guy?" Atticus asks in a silly this-is-scandalous tone.

"Who?" Babe exclaims, spinning around.

I swallow. It takes all my willpower not to glance at Pilot. I stare at Atticus. "Um, he texted me last night. How was your date with Man Bun?"

"You missed it. I was just telling everyone how great it was!"

"Oh my gosh, that's amazing!" I smile.

"Shane, who's this Friday night Rugby Guy?" Babe puts down the knife she's been chopping vegetables with and crosses her arms.

I glance at Pilot. He's pushing microwaved lasagna around with his fork. I open my mouth and close it wordlessly.

"Shane made out with some Lawyer Guy at the club on Friday," Sahra says casually.

"Sahra!" I yelp. I stare at my keyboard now, cheeks blazing.

"Way to fill me in!" Babe accuses.

"It wasn't a big deal," I tell her.

"So did he ask you out?" Atticus asks.

"He wants to go out on Wednesday," I mumble.

"That's exciting!" Atticus grins.

"Well, I told him: No, sorry, I'll be in Germany," I add sheepishly. Out of the corner my eye, I see Pilot's fork stop moving.

"You're going to Germany?" Sahra asks.

"No," I answer guiltily.

"Shane!" Babe giggles and turns to resume her cooking prep.

Atticus breaks into a full-on cackle.

Pilot turns his head and meets my eyes for the first time in over a week. "Why don't you want to go out with him?" he asks.

My heart rams against my chest. *You should ask him if we can talk outside.*

I swallow. "I just . . . didn't like him." I can't make my mouth form any more words. We hold each other's gaze for an extra second in which I desperately try to communicate *But I do like you, can we talk, do you have any interest in me, what happened in Paris?* with my eyes. Sizzles and pops permeate the room, disturbing the moment. I look away to find Babe breaking up a blob of ground beef on the stove.

Atticus pipes in from the sink where he's about to drain his pasta, "Well, don't worry. I'll help you draft something to let him down easy."

20. Spinning

2/15/11

It's been a while.

Other than interning at _Packed!_, which is fine (I'm still running basic errands), and doing writing assignments for class, which is going great, basically three things happened in these past two weeks:

<u>1) Babe and I decided to plan a flat family dinner.</u>

Because all of a sudden the whole flat got super-busy. We haven't hung out all together in ages (weeks but it feels like ages). I barely see Sahra, Atticus has always been busy, and Pilot's MIA. Babe and I go out of our way to chat most days, but even that's been difficult. I guess the combo of internships and class can do that. Babe and I discussed our lack of hangs and decided the way to fix it was a scheduled flat activity: an American family dinner with the works—baked ziti, wine, cards, and beer pong. She started a group Facebook chat to work out what day would be best for everyone.

2) *I didn't speak to Pilot.*

After that night in the kitchen when we talked about Rugby Guy, I didn't even see Pilot for six whole days, let alone exchange words. I was writing in my bunk when I finally caught sight of him walking into the kitchen through the bedroom window. He set his open computer down on the table and chucked a frozen meal into the microwave. For a minute, I debated going in there to "write," but then I realized he was talking—Skyping again. My heart slunk further down into its metaphorical chair as he shared a laugh with the screen.

3) *We scheduled the family dinner.*

It might as well be a hundred years from now. When four of us can make of it, one of us can't, and when three of us can make it, two of us can't. The date we picked was so far in the future that Atticus suggested we just save the dinner as a big last-day-in-London flat celebration.

So now, it's scheduled for our last day in London (April 22).

I feel a little like I've lost control of my raft. Like, I came to this river with the boat, and I was rowing toward my destination, but somehow I got caught in a tide. How do I reestablish control? Was I ever steering? I must have been. I got myself to London, didn't I?

"Do you know what you're doing for spring break yet?" Babe asks as she twirls some spaghetti Bolognese onto her fork. We coordinated our dinner eating times today, but I finished way before her and am currently working on character bios.

My eyebrows furrow, and I push my computer screen down a bit so I can see her face at the end of table. "We have spring break? When?"

"Next week, Shane." She laughs.

"*What?* That's so soon. Don't we all have work?"

"It's written into everyone's internship schedule; it's part of our program," she says matter-of-factly. "I'm going on a tour of Ireland! And I'm going by myself. It's going to be great, like an epic adventure!"

"Wow, good for you," I say halfheartedly.

"Yeah, I've never gone somewhere by myself before, but traveling alone is supposed to be an amazing experience. And I'll be on a bus tour, so I'll meet people, and it should be kind of like a journey of self-discovery, you know. And Guinness was invented there. I think I'll get to go to the factory."

I smile at her enthusiasm. "Well, that's awesome. Do you know what Sahra's doing?" I ask.

"Yeah, she's meeting her boyfriend in Barcelona to celebrate her birthday!"

"Wow," I respond softly.

I wonder what Pilot's plans are.

Why are you wondering? You haven't spoken in two weeks.

The door bangs open as Atticus races in with a bag of groceries. "Hey, guys!" he greets us before reaching into the bag and whipping out yet another frozen meal. "I'm running late for a play, but I've gotta take ten minutes and eat!" He rips the food from the box and stabs at it with a butter knife.

"Atticus!" Babe laughs from the table. "That's so loud!"

"Yeah, I enjoy drama. What else is new?" he cracks.

The two of them cackle. I pull my computer back in front of me, so I can stare into space angstily without looking like I've just had a lobotomy. What if everyone's already doing things for break? I'm going to be stuck here alone in London all by myself for a week?

"We were talking about spring break plans!" Babe announces. "What are you going to be doing?"

I jump into the conversation. "Yeah, At, do you want to do something together?"

He turns to me. "Actually, my family is flying out here! We're road-tripping across the UK, up to Scotland!"

Babe rinses her dishes in the sink. "Oh my gosh, that sounds great. I'm going to Ireland on a tour, and I'm going by myself. I'm so excited! Traveling alone is supposed to be an amazing experience of self-discovery! And I'll be on a bus tour so I'll meet people . . ."

Hearing this a second time is depressing. I duck down under the table to grab headphones from my book bag. As I'm digging around, the door opens again. Four of us in the kitchen at once? *It's probably Pilot!* I yank my head up to check.

There's a loud thud as my cranium slams into the corner of the table.

I'm catapulted forward with the rebound momentum and topple sideways, crumbling into a heap on the floor. My chair clashes onto the tile next to me.

The microwave bell goes off as I yell, "Freakin' A!" and Babe yelps, "Jiminy Cricket!"

When I look up, everyone's hovering.

"What happened?" Atticus asks.

"Are you okay?" Babe demands. "That was an epic bang!"

When Pilot steps into view, I cringe. Of course he's here. The first eye contact we've made in weeks, and I'm in the fetal position on the floor.

"Did you really just use the phrase *Jiminy Cricket?*" I grumble to Babe, moving to get my legs back under me. "I'm fine. Evil chairs are out to get me, falling every five seconds."

As I get to my feet, Pilot shakes his head. "Devil chairs," he accuses in an exaggerated Southern accent.

I want to be mad at him, because I am. I want to say something like: Where the hell have you been the last fourteen days? But instead, I loose a flustered huff, pick up the chair, and flop back onto it.

"These chairs are a hazard to myself and others." I wince, touching a finger to the bump forming on my head.

"Sure you're okay?" Pilot asks.

"Yeah, fine," I say dismissively. Atticus is at the table now, stuffing pasta puttanesca down his throat.

Babe swoops into a seat. "So, Pilot, what are you doing for spring break?"

I glance at him. Cross my arms. Uncross. Raise a hand to hold up my chin.

"I'm going with Steve and Quail from Flat Four to Vienna and Amsterdam," he tells her. Again, looks like we're not invited.

Well, ask. Take charge of your raft.

I open my mouth. "Oh man, that sounds cool. Um, I don't have any plans yet. Do you think maybe I could join?" I'm already having a hot flash. I can't believe I just said that. Pilot drops his gaze to the table.

Oh god, he's going to say no. I think I'm going to cry. My face is burning. It's gonna melt off.

"Uh . . . I'm sorry, Shane. It's actually already planned, and it's just gonna be a guys' trip. I'm sorry." He looks up at me. He is sorry. I see it in his conflicted mossy eyes. "If things weren't—"

I cut him off, waving my arms around. "Oh my god, of course, I'm sorry. Why would I assume? I didn't mean to . . . that was . . . forget I said anything."

You're fine. No crying. Atticus is looking at me with his head cocked to the side. I shoot Babe a wide-eyed look: *Help!*

She jerks into gear. "Wow, well, that's going be awesome, Pilot! Guess what? I'm going to Ireland! And I'm going by myself on a bus tour . . ."

21. Ticking Away

2/17/11

TODAY WAS MOMENTOUS. Declan asked me to shadow him while he edited a photo spread of Moscow! We didn't speak much, but I learned things. I got to watch how he used their software to craft things together for the next printed installment of <u>Packed! For Travel!</u> They release new articles weekly on the site, but only publish a hard-copy issue once a month.

And then . . . wait for it: A fancy guest photographer called Lacey Willows came into <u>Packed!</u> for a meeting with Wendy and Donna about a new piece on Istanbul, and Wendy invited me to listen in on the meeting. I sat there smiling like an eager beaver throughout the entire thing.

In other news, the flat is preparing to go their separate ways for break, which starts tomorrow. I couldn't bring myself to book a trip alone, so I'll be here. Everyone at work today wished me an amazing spring break. I kind of wish we didn't have a spring break.

In other, other news, this all-consuming crush for Pilot Penn has come to a crux. I think I need to tell him because this unrequited thing isn't working for me. I hate missing him all the time. I miss him, and I feel like an idiot. He's so obviously been avoiding me. He materializes in passing from time to time, and it's like catching sight of a ghost or finding yourself in reach of a butterfly. I step toward him, and he floats out of reach again—he's on the way to class; going to meet with the guys down the hall; just "headed out."

2/26/11

THINGS I DID ON SPRING BREAK 2/18–2/25:
A HIGHLIGHTS REEL

Went out and bought <u>The Poet</u> by Michael Connelly.

Read <u>The Poet</u> by Michael Connelly.

Watched <u>Ratatouille</u>.

Got shawarma on Shwednesday.

Stared into space for long periods of time, imagining what everyone else was doing.

Tried to start my book but kept getting distracted by thoughts of what everyone else might be doing and second guessing every word I put on the page.

Started a <u>Lost</u> rewatch (got to mid-season two).

Skyped with the parents more about working in an
imaginary doctor's office.

2/27/11 11:20 p.m.

Everyone got back today, thank god. I gave Babe a giant
welcome-back hug and gushed with her about all her
adventures, trying to live vicariously through them. When
Atticus got back, we spent a beautiful thirty minutes digging
into _The Poet_. He said he's going to check out the Mortal
Instruments series. I'm so excited! I have a reader friend
now! Sahra showed me all the stunning pictures she took in
Spain and told me she's in the middle of reading _The Da Vinci
Code_ on my recommendation, and she's tearing through it.
Can you believe it? Sahra trusted my judgment. Smart,
independent, wise Sahra!

I stayed in the kitchen all day on Sawyer, going back and
forth between character bios, the blank document that is my
book, and Twitter—while waiting for everyone's return.

After Sahra, I waited for Pilot because it's time to have the
scary talk, so I can stop being sad with every passing day
that we don't interact. He never came.

Now I'm in bed with Sawyer—it's 11:30 p.m. We have class
in the morning, and there he is through the window. In the
kitchen with his computer. Skyping with Amy again! Is that
all he does now? Must he do it in the kitchen?

February 28, 2011

Mom and Dad,

Last week was spring break. I spent it alone. I think it's the loneliest I've ever felt. I miss our house. I miss Mom's perfume. I miss Dad's milkshakes. I miss Aunt Marie. I miss my obnoxious cousins. Who do they make fun of when I'm not around? I miss having a variety of sauces to choose from when I make pasta. I miss telling you guys everything.

It's time to start our writing prompt for the day. Is it weird that I spend the weekends looking forward to this class?

XO,

Shane

22. I Must Dream of the Things I Am Seeking

The Tube is packed with people today. I'm smooshed up against the rear wall, but I can't bring myself to care because I had the most wonderful day at work. Honestly, it's been amazing these past two weeks. I finally feel like things are clicking! Everyone said they missed me when I came back last Tuesday after break, and I've been shadowing people every day since. Today, Donna asked if I'd like to sit with her as she organized a piece about Rio. She walked me through her process, and she talked to me like I'm part of the team, not just *the intern*. She asked me for opinions!

I step off the train at the South Kensington stop today. It's Thursday, not Wednesday, but today calls for a celebratory shawarma. *Donna cared what I thought about her piece!* As I close in on Beirut Express, I throw myself into a little happy twirl, landing with my hand on the door and yanking it open.

Inside the restaurant, I take a seat at the bar. There's no one manning the area right now, so I dig Horcurx Nine from my bag, eager to document the day.

I'm clicking on my pen when I hear someone swish back in behind the counter. "What are we having today, doll?"

"Oh, I'll have—" Before me is the copper-haired woman from the plane and Starbucks and Paris. I almost slide off the stool. I drop the pen, grasping at the table so I don't fall over. "Jesus Christ! Are you stalking me? What's happening?"

"How's it going?" she asks casually.

I'm so confused. I look behind me and then back at her to make sure I'm not hallucinating. Now she's holding my notebook.

"Oh my god, give that back!" She's riffling through it. "What are you doing?" I throw my hands up in frustration, trying to make eye contact with anyone else in the vicinity, but no one looks at me. She wraps the cover around to a certain page and drops it back on the bar in front of me.

1/1/11

COLLEGE, TAKE TWO: STUDY ABROAD GOALS
1) Kick ass at internship—turn it into a paid summer job.
2) Make friends you like to hang out with and who like to hang out with you.
3) Kiss a boy you like. Stop kiss-blocking self.
4) Have adventures in the city you're in. You've done nothing in New York City during the 2.5 years you've been there, you idiot.
5) Maybe try getting a little bit drunk. Don't black out or anything, but find out what it's like in a controlled, self-aware environment. You're legally allowed to in the UK!
6) Start your great American novel. You've spent an absurd amount of time trying to think of the perfect first sentence. Stop it. Just write.

I blink at the list.

"How's the internship?"

I struggle for words, flabbergasted. "Fine. Great!"

"Friends?"

I roll my eyes. "I have them!"

"Have you kissed that boy you like?" She winks.

"Stop winking at me!"

"Well, have you?"

"Well, no!"

"Your novel?"

"I'm trying."

I drop my head into my hands. *What's going on? Am I hallucinating, for real?*

I look back up. "Why are you following me?" I growl slowly, enunciating each word as if she doesn't speak English.

"Get on it, darling. Steer the raft."

I shake my head. "Who are you? How did you—? Did you just read that in my—?" I hop off the stool, swipe the notebook off the counter, and sprint out into the street.

I'm out of breath, freaked out, starving, and shawarma-less when I throw open the door to the blue kitchen back at the Karlston. *Who do I tell about this? Do I tell people about this . . . or will that make people think I'm insane?*

"Hey, Shane!"

I jump, whirling to my right to find Atticus and Babe seated on the couch in front of a laptop, laughing.

"Holy crap. I didn't see you guys there."

"We're about to watch *Glee*. Want to join us?"

"I . . ." I breathe in and out a few times, calming my heart.

"What, did you run home?" Atticus chuckles.

I shake my head and make a dismissive motion with the hand that's not white-knuckling Horcrux Nine. "No, I, nothing, okay." I walk over and flop down next to Babe.

On *Glee*, Mr. Schue's class is prancing around and singing "Blame It on the Alcohol." Babe and Atticus are singing along. I can't stop thinking about the lady. *How does she know where I'm going to be? Did someone hire her? Could my parents have arranged for a babysitter? Has she been mere steps away this entire time?*

The door to the kitchen swings open, and Babe and Atticus seize up midnote. I look up from the screen as Pilot walks through the door with a girl.

You've got to be shitting me.

A slim girl with long, brunette locks tags behind him. It's her. She's smiling up at him. I still haven't talked to him. Atticus pauses *Glee*.

Guilt seeps into my cheeks. *But I didn't do anything! I haven't done anything!*

"Hey," Pilot says, as the door thunks closed. They stand facing us. Amy only glances over before fixing her stare at the floor and positioning herself mostly behind Pilot.

"Hey," we answer in chorus.

"This is Amy," he says quickly. Dread builds in my chest at the thought of conversing with Amy. *I can't talk to Amy. I can't.*

"Hi!" I throw up my hand up in a nervous wave.

"Hi, Amy!" Babe says enthusiastically.

"Hey, nice to meet you!" Atticus exclaims.

Amy makes a face almost like a smile, but it doesn't quite get there. She doesn't say anything. Is she anxious? She's wearing tight, skillfully ripped skinny jeans and a white sweater, and she's naturally pretty in that way that makes me feel insecure about the fact that I feel the need to wear makeup.

Pilot moves, walking over to the sink, and Amy shuffles up right behind him, grabbing his hand as he fills up a clean glass with water. She leans into his ear and talks softly so none of us can hear. I stare blatantly. I don't want to stare. But I can't *not* stare. Pilot chugs his water and places the glass down in the sink.

This silence is deafening.

"Okay." He turns to look at us again. "I'm off to go show her the—" He's cut off by an obnoxiously loud rapping at the door. As one, all five of our heads whip toward the sound.

I leap off the couch like a spooked gazelle at the sight of my dad's face in the window.

23. Thunderbolt and Lightning

Is this a nightmare? Am I asleep? I walk slack-jawed toward the door and open it. My parents spill into the kitchen. My parents are in our kitchen. My feet glue themselves to this spot on the floor. Mom's in a stylish black jacket, her hair a blaze of bronze waves around her face. Dad's in slacks and a button-up shirt, dark hair slicked back.

"Hi, sweetheart!" He sweeps me into a hug.

When he releases me, Mom swoops in. "Shane, surprise!"

I say nothing. Have I lost the ability to speak? Mom pulls away. I glance about the room. My flatmates and Amy watch us, unsure of what to do with themselves. Pilot and I make eye contact for a second, and I watch as understanding dawns in his expression.

A nauseating panic courses through my veins. *This is too much right now. This is too much.*

"Shane, who is everyone? Aren't you gonna introduce us?" Dad throws up a hand and gestures around the room.

I swallow hard, vocal cords jolting to life at his command. "I, um, um, yeah, um, that's um . . ." I glance over at the couch. "These are my parents." I gesture to my mom and dad.

"Hey!" my father's voice booms.

"Nice to meet you all," adds my mother pleasantly.

"This is Atticus, and Babe . . . and . . ." I swivel to face Pilot and his girlfriend. *Dear lord.* "This is Pilot and Amy . . ."

My flatmates chorus a round of greetings.

"Great!" my dad announces. "We're taking you all out to dinner right now. No exceptions. Let's head out. Is anyone missing?"

Oh no, we can't go to dinner. No no no no. It's late, 7:00 p.m. It's . . . no.

"Ahhhut," is all I manage to get out. I just stand. Rooted to the floor. Gagging on protests. The flatmates remain silent.

"Shane? I asked you a question," prods my father.

My brain switches to autopilot. "Sahra's not here . . ."

"Text her and tell her to meet us— Where are we going, honey?" He looks over at Mom.

"The Covent Garden Tube stop."

He turns to me. "Tell her to meet us at the Covent Garden Tube stop." He looks pointedly around the room with raised eyebrows. "Everyone ready?"

Pilot glances from Amy to me to my father. "Uh, well, sir, we actually had plans to go to dinner."

"Great, come on. My treat!" he responds.

"But we're kind of—" Pilot starts again.

"You don't want a free dinner? Come on!" he insists. Loudly.

I meet Pilot's eyes with an expression of extreme desperation and/or embarrassment. There's no mirror in the kitchen, so I can't be completely sure, and I'm currently drowning in both. I drop my gaze to the ground.

"I won't take no for an answer. It's gonna be fun, let's go," Dad bellows again. He pivots and holds open the door. Mom looks at me expectantly. My flatmates hold still, like somebody hit the pause button on time.

Babe breaks the spell and hops off the couch. "Thanks, Mr. Primaveri!"

We're corralled out of the kitchen. I do as I'm told and text Sahra.

"So all of you been traveling every weekend, huh?" my father asks as he drops his glass back to the table. I wince at the small *boom* that reverberates when it makes contact. We're seated at a large circular table at Delia's, the

Italian restaurant my mother led us to. Me, my parents, four flatmates, and Pilot's girlfriend.

"Oh my gosh, we've been following all your Facebook posts. The pictures have been beautiful. It looks like you're all having so much fun." Mom smiles.

Babe answers with over-the-top enthusiasm. "Yeah! Paris and Rome were amazing, and I was in Ireland last week. I went by myself on a kind of an epic journey of self-discovery!"

She's taken up the role of me for the time being, since I've become almost mute, uttering one- or two-word answers, if any, before descending back into my cone of anxiety.

"Yeah, um, I was all over Europe last week for spring break," Pilot pipes in.

"How exciting! I know Shane was in Paris with you a couple weeks back, right?" Mom looks over at me with wide eyes, trying to drag me into conversation.

"Yeah, she told me about Paris!" Atticus answers. He starts retelling a story I shared with him about a little crepe shop we ate at. He doesn't know what's wrong, but he's trying to help. And Babe's trying to help. Pilot's trying to help. Sahra injects words every so often when she feels they're necessary. She wasn't there when they walked in, and she seems a little confused. I'm surprised she even made it. They've all been struggling to engage my parents in conversation for the last half an hour, while I sit in silence, quietly trying to master the art of teleportation.

Why'd they have to come? They never leave the country. They barely leave New York.

"We've never even been to Europe! But we're so proud of our genius girl here." Mom gestures to me sitting next to her. Heat floods up my neck. "We had to come see her here in her element!" She laughs lightheartedly. "How about we play a game and go around the table and everyone shares where they've traveled since they got here and how they liked it?" Mom suggests. "Atticus, kick us off!" She grins and tucks a wavy chunk of hair behind her ear.

I feel like an anvil's floating over my head, and I can't get out from under it. Like Wile E. Coyote. I wipe my sweaty palms over the napkin in my lap. *Keep it together, or they'll know something's wrong. You've made it this far. You can lie if they ask. You're just trying to follow your dreams. There's nothing wrong with that.*

I don't know how to lie to their faces like this. I've never kept anything from them. I've never had to.

Conversation comes to a screeching halt when Mom's where-have-you-traveled game hits Amy. There's a long pause while my parents wait expectantly for her to speak.

"I, um . . ." she sputters. *Come on, Amy, say something. Keep the focus on travel.* She shakes her head slightly. My feet bounce against the floor. Too long. She's taking too long. Dad's uncomfortable with long silences. He's going to change the subject!

"London?" she offers just as Dad jumps in with, "Everyone's working! Is it going well?"

I'll stay silent. I can't raise suspicions if I never speak.

I pull out my brick phone and fiddle with it absently. I'm busy. I'm not suspicious. I'm phone.

"Yeah! I'm working in the West End, and I've seen so many plays. It's been such a once-in-a-lifetime opportunity," Atticus shares.

"I work at Disney headquarters here! And it's so much fun. I can't wait to actually work for the company someday," Babe adds.

"Wow, great." Dad's head swings from me to Sahra. "Sahra, you work with Shane at the health clinic, right?" I put down the phone.

If I were a mute cartoon character, I'd hold up my sign for the audience—*Help!* I find myself looking at Pilot.

Before Sahra can answer, Pilot abruptly offers his own response, "I'm actually working for an accounting office. Are you interested in accounting, Mr. Primaveri? You do something in finance, right?"

Did I tell him that? I must have. Dad's expression scrunches into one of distaste. I'm immediately nervous for Pilot.

Dad shakes it off. "What? I was talking to Sahra," he says dismissively. He brings his attention back to Sahra. "Sahra, I was sayin', how's it workin' at the health clinic with Shane?"

"I don't—" Sahra starts.

Pilot speaks over her. "Sorry, sir, I was, accounting's really interesting, and I thought—" he interjects again.

"Excuse me, would you stop—I'm talking to Sahra." Dad shakes his head in disbelief. "Sahra—"

I would smile if I wasn't already busy being terrified.

"Yeah, I actually work at a la—" Sahra insists.

Her words are muffled as Pilot continues to loudly babble: "Sir, I'm sorry. I didn't mean to interrupt. I know Sahra's tired, and I was just excited to talk about accounting . . ."

"Pilot, what the hell?" Sahra exclaims.

Dad swivels his gaze back to Pilot. "What's your name again? Pilosh?" he bellows.

"Pilot, sir."

"Wouldja shut up for just second and let me talk to Sahra, please? You can talk next." He uses his angry-joking voice.

Pilot swallows visibly. He catches my eye as he surrenders, shoulders sagging. "Yes, sir. Of course."

Dad huffs. "Now I'm gonna say this one more time, *Sahra*." He widens his eyes at Pilot and turns to Sahra. "How's it been at the health clinic with Shane? You enjoying it?"

Sahra's eyebrows pull together. "Yeah, I work at a law office . . ."

I squeeze my eyes shut. Open them.

Dad's looking at me. "What?"

"Yeah, I work at the law office of Millard J. Robinson and Associates," I hear Sahra continue. Dad's eyebrows draw together as he holds my gaze. My lips flop up and down, but nothing comes out.

The conversation descends into chaos.

"Uh, Sahra must have gotten conf—" Pilot starts.

"Our mistake, sweetie. For some reason Shane told us you worked with her at the clinic."

"I don't understand. Why are you working at a law office if you're premed?" my dad booms at Sahra. "They're allowed to give you an irrelevant internship? That's not right!"

"Shane, how'd you confuse that, sweetie?" my mom coos.

"I'm not premed. I'm prelaw," Sahra explains.

"Prelaw?" echoes Mom.

"What?" My father's face flushes a bright shiny red, and he turns his attention back to me.

This is bad. This is bad.

"She means premed!" Pilot exclaims from across the table, but Dad's done listening to him.

Sahra turns to Pilot. "What are you talking about? I don't even think there is a premed track in London."

Dad's glare hardens. "What?"

I stare at the tablecloth and start hyperventilating.

"Oh, that can't be. Shane is in that program, Sahra, there's a whole brochure," my mother starts to explain.

"Well, maybe there . . . is a premed program?" Atticus adds.

"Shane's in the creative writing program," Sahra states with oblivious nonchalance.

"Sahra," Pilot scolds through his teeth.

"I'm not sure what's going on—" Babe interjects.

"What do you mean creative writing? She's premed." Dad's voice is low and furious.

Babe blurts, "She's premed?"

"Shane," Dad demands.

Scalding hot tears materialize without warning as I raise my gaze.

"Shane, what's going on?" Mom's concerned blue eyes lock onto mine. My heart constricts.

"Is there no premed program here?" Dad's voice explodes to fill the room. I shrink down an inch in my seat.

"I, uh, no, not technically, but."

"YOU LITTLE SHIT."

Those three words knock the wind from my lungs.

Mom gasps, "Sal!"

Shit. I've heard Uncle Dan call Leo a little shit. I've never been a little shit. Dad called me a little shit.

I heave oxygen into my chest. "I'm sorry! I didn't mean to. It was an accident—"

"An accident?" His hand slams on the table. "Where did that brochure come from?"

I am shit. "I, I made it," I whisper.

"You. You made it?" Dad's eyes bulge as he sucks in a new breath. "You conned us?" He turns to Mom, *"Do you hear this, our daughter fuckin' conned us!"*

People can probably hear him in space. Mom's eyes have glazed over.

Dad's gaze returns to me. "You've lost an entire semester of required courses, Shane! How are you going to catch up?"

"What about the MCATs?" Mom sounds heartbroken.

"I'm sorry. I was just trying . . . I just wanted to try—"

"I can't believe this. I can't believe what I'm hearing! Number one: *What about the MCATs?"* Dad snarls. "Number two: I'm home working my ass off, shelling out thousands of dollars for your education, and you're out here completely disrespecting me and your mother! Lying to our faces! Repeatedly! *Who the hell do you think you are?"*

"Dad, I'm sorry! Mom, I didn't mean to. I'm sorry! I just wanted to—"

I watch his eyes drop to my phone on the table. He snatches it up and jerks out of his chair. Stands. Drops the phone to the floor and violently brings down his foot. The gasps of my flatmates echo around the table as the plastic smashes to pieces.

My lungs spasm. Oxygen. I need oxygen. The shame is suffocating. The air is too thick. I can't. Breathe.

"Sal," Mom scolds softly.

He looks me up and down with—with disgust. "You're done, and you're on the next flight back to New York."

"No! Please! Dad, please!" My voice rises. "I just want to finish the semester. I . . . I'll take classes, please! I'll make up the classes over summer! I'll do summer classes! And I'll work at your office! I'll make it up. I'll be ready for the MCATs. I'll do it. I can do it! I'm sorry! Please, please let me finish this up, please."

I am snot and tears and desperation. He stares me down, fury billowing off him, before he digs out his wallet and drops a few hundred pounds in the center of the table. "End of semester, the second you're home, you start work at my office. Don't call us for money. Don't call us for anything. You're on your own."

He stalks out of the restaurant.

Don't call them? What?

My mother's studying her still-pristine dinner plate. We didn't even make it to appetizers. She looks up. "I'm so sorry, everyone. Please, enjoy dinner on us." She meets my eyes. Shakes her head in disappointment. "Shane, what were you thinking?"

She strides out after my father, leaving us in absolute silence. I'm standing up. When did I stand up? My ears are ringing. I glance around. The entire place is watching me, plus my four flatmates and Pilot's fucking girlfriend.

I stare at the door.

Activity starts up again at other tables. Not mine. We hold onto the silence. I can't look at anyone. Numbly, I sit back into my seat and drop my forehead to the table. *What now?* We've gone a whole two minutes before I feel a hand fall onto my arm.

"Shane . . ." Babe starts sympathetically. I wait for more, but she doesn't continue because what does she say? What do you say when you witness something like that?

"I'm sorry," I mumble to the table.

"Shane, don't apologize," Pilot answers quietly.

"Shane, we're sorry," Atticus exclaims.

"I'm sorry!" Sahra says suddenly.

I raise my head an inch and rest my chin on my arm. "I think I have to go."

"Shane, don't go. Let's at least eat dinner," Babe says in an extra-gentle voice.

I stand from the table and grab my purse. "I'm so sorry," I blubber. My eyes find the broken remnants of the phone on the floor, and I beeline for the door.

"Shane, don't leave," Atticus calls as I throw myself outside.

24. Broken Dreams

I pace outside the Karlston for ten minutes, trying to compose myself for the security guard at the front desk. Inside, I close the blinds in our room and climb into my bunk. Then I lie down and stare at the wall. I'm still staring at the wall when the girls come back. I'm staring when they ask me if I want to talk. I'm staring when they go to bed. I stare until 1:00 a.m. when my mouth feels so dry and my nose is so stuffed up that I have to get up and go to the kitchen for water.

I pad my way over, watching the ground with half-lidded, swollen eyes and hoping to god that I don't run into anyone on the way. I push the kitchen door open slowly and rush to the sink when I catch sight of the empty table. I pull a glass from the cabinet, fill it at the sink, take an enormous swig, refill, and turn to lean against the counter.

An involuntary gasp slices down my throat. I am not alone in this room.

Amy is on the couch with a bag of pretzels, watching me. She's all the way at the end, in the spot closest to the far wall, where I couldn't see her through the windows. My eyes travel from hers down to the book open in her lap. She's in here reading. It actually looks like a notebook.

She's reading— *Oh my god.*

The glass slips from my hand and smashes across the tile.

"What are you doing?" I shriek. My voice comes out hoarse and gravelly.

Even from across the room, I recognize my scribble, my pages. That's my notebook. That's . . . that's mine. "What the fuck do you think you're doing?" I screech.

She inclines her head slightly. "It was on the couch, so I opened it. Once I realized what it was, I needed to know."

My lips curl into a mortified jumble.

"I see him in all your pictures—" She shuts the notebook and holds it out. I lunge around the broken glass and yank it from her hand. I press it against my stomach. Stare at her. I don't know what happens now. She read my . . . she knows my—Fresh tears cloud my vision. I feel—violated. *What do I do? How long has she been in here with it?* Finally Amy's eyes slide away from mine. She stands, sidesteps me, and walks to the door.

She turns back with her hand on the knob. "I knew it," she whispers. "I knew this was happening. Keep your distance."

I watch her slip out of the room.

I must have left Horcrux Nine on the couch in all the chaos earlier.

Is she going to tell him? What have I gotten myself into? Why did I come here? This was such a stupid idea. My parents don't even want me to call them any-more. I don't want to like someone else's boyfriend! I don't want to make anyone upset!

I fall to my knees on the kitchen floor with my head in my hands.

I skip class and stay in bed Friday, doing nothing. I don't feel like writing or reading or watching. I feel like nothing. I send an email to my parents apologizing and wait for them to respond. Snapshots of their disappoint-ment plaster the inner walls of my skull, the backs of my eyelids. They've never looked at me like that before—like they put all their eggs in my bas-ket, and I crushed them. How do I uncrush the eggs?

I avoid Babe and Sahra's attempts to talk all weekend. I don't have to worry about running into Amy because she and Pilot are in Paris.

It's been over twenty-four hours, and no response has come from my apology email. I think I made a mistake begging to finish out the semester. Why did I make such a scene? I should have just shut up. I'm never going to get up to speed with the science classes I've missed if I'm spending all my time at the internship.

If this train's going to run out of track, why should I wait till the last minute to jump off?

Sunday night, I'm in the kitchen, eating and doing nothing, when Atticus comes in and sits at the table across from me.

"Hey," he greets me. I nod in acknowledgment.

"How long are you going to keep to yourself about this?" he says gently. "We should talk about it."

"I don't want to talk about it."

He smiles. "Well, I think we have to. I think you need to so we can move past it." I push the ravioli around in my bowl.

"We all have family drama, Shane. You don't have to be embarrassed about it. We're your friends. We've all got our crap . . . My dad didn't magically accept me when I came out, things were weird for a good long while. He still doesn't ever ask about my dating life. Families aren't perfect. You didn't have to lie to us about your major. You can talk to us about that stuff."

"How old were you when you came out to your parents?"

"Thirteen."

"Wow, brave thirteen-year-old."

He nods proudly. "Gryffindor."

The corner of my lip turns up. "So, I'm premed."

"Yeah, so I've heard." He cracks a smile. "It's okay to want to also study other things."

I shoot Atticus a small smile. "My parents have been bragging to literally everyone and anyone about how I was going to be a doctor since I was eleven. I think the local grocery store clerks are aware of my impending doctor-hood." I smash a ravioli with my fork.

Atticus rests his head in his hand. "What do you want to do?"

I shake my head. "I don't—know anymore. I don't want to be a disappointment. I wanted to be premed for my mom . . . I mean, I want to. I'm the reason she didn't get to finish med school. She got pregnant and spent her life taking care of me. . . . She's been there helping with all my math and science homework for as long as I remember.

"Like, for all of forever, whenever I didn't understand something, she explained it in a super-fun way and sat with me until it clicked. And it means so much to my dad that I have opportunities like this because he didn't.

"I know he came off pretty horrible the other day. . . . He's not always like that." I gnaw at my lip.

Atticus stays quiet.

"Growing up, whenever I hurt myself, he'd stop everything and make me a chocolate milkshake with a slice of watermelon on the glass because it's my favorite. And then as I got older, he started making them whenever I was feeling sad. It sounds silly, but it always makes me feel a little better. He makes them now when I come home on the weekends from YU." *Because I always come home sad.* I swipe at a fresh tear dribbling down my cheek. "Sorry."

Atticus presses his lips together and catches my eyes. "Don't be sorry. It's complicated. I get it." He pauses, studying me. "Try not to be too hard on yourself. College is to, like, get a job and everything, but it's also about finding yourself—and all that jazz. Out here, doing your own thing, you learn stuff. It's good to shake things up. Haven't you had the time of your life the last couple months? I know I have."

"Yeah, I guess," I whisper. "But my parents aren't even responding to my emails."

"I'm sure they'll come around, Shane. Maybe they haven't checked them yet," Atticus reasons.

I pull out my laptop because I'm crying, and I can't continue any sort of conversation. I really want to write in Horcrux Nine, but I can't open it without feeling like my stomach is going to fall out my ass.

"I'm here if you want to pick this back up," Atticus says quietly.

"Thanks, At."

He takes out his laptop, and we sit in companionable silence.

I get an email response from Mom.

Re: I'm sorry! <3

___

Cara Primaveri <MathMama68@aol.com>   3/6/11
to Shane

We'll discuss it when you get home.

A lump forms in my throat. There's another email under it. From Leo.

hey

___

Leo Primaveri <LeoBaseballPrimaveri@gmail.com>   3/6/11
to Shane

Heard you fucked up. Are you coming home? My mom won't go into detail.

What does he care?
Not yet.
I press send.
A response pings in sixty seconds later.
What happened? You okay?
I blink, eyebrows furrowing.
Why are you asking? Looking for more shit to hold over me?
Send.
Another almost instant response:
I know how they are when they're mad.
My vision blurs. I close the computer and retreat to my bunk.

———

I miss class again on Monday.

I spend Tuesday morning at *Packed!* staring in the general direction of the Paris poster across the room. I haven't been given a task today, and I haven't asked for one. When Declan and Donna walk by and say good morning, I nod in response. I haven't made any tea. I haven't gotten up. My limbs feel heavy.

At noon, I wander robotically toward Wendy's office. She's in there wearing a trendy yellow dress, working on her computer. I knock softly on the molding of the doorframe because the door's propped open.

"Shane?" she asks in her posh accent. She closes out of what she's working on and her brown eyes dart over to mine. "What's up?"

"Hi, Wendy, I'm sorry to bother you. I just, I had to tell you—I'm quitting."

She shakes her head quickly as if she's hearing things. "I'm sorry?"

"I can't work here anymore. I'm sorry," I speak slowly, trying to keep my voice steady. "Thank you for giving me this opportunity." I turn to leave.

"Shane! Sweetie, wait!"

I stop. Turn back.

"What's wrong? Why would you quit? You're not going to get the school credit," she says softly.

"I'm sorry. I just can't work here anymore." I turn and power walk back to my desk. I pack my things. Donna stands from her desk as I start toward the door.

"Shane?" she asks. I turn around. Her forehead's wrinkled with worry. Wendy's standing watching me from her doorway. I don't want Wendy to think poorly of me, but I can't stay. I need this time to play catch up. I need to study. I need to earn my parents' forgiveness. I need to pass the MCAT. I spin on my heel and leave, without saying goodbye.

What's the point anymore? I can't get a writing job when I go home. I have to take summer classes so I can fulfill the course requirements to graduate on time.

I'm too embarrassed to tell anyone I bailed at *Packed!* I can't think about it for more than a second without feeling sick. My flatmates are so busy with their own jobs that I get away with it pretty easily. I spend my free time during the week in the kitchen and at Café Nero, trying to teach myself the class material I've missed these past three months.

Time goes by so much faster now that I'm not enjoying it. The days smear into one another. It's Monday and then it's Friday and then it's Monday again.

I continue to barely see Pilot. It's killing me not knowing what he knows. Does he know? How much does he know? What did Amy tell him?

I guess it doesn't really matter. What matters is that he has a girlfriend. A serious, flew-across-the-Atlantic-Ocean-to-see-him girlfriend. I'm not even supposed to be here. I keep telling myself that. But—the Pilot-related sinking sensation in my gut isn't fading with time apart like I want it to. It's intensifying as we near the semester's end. I need to know. I need to know what he knows. I need to talk to him. I need this feeling to go away.

April 1, I get an email from my father detailing my work and class schedule starting the Monday I get back to New York. It's a schedule. No words. It's been weeks since they spoke to me. I've sent four more I'm-sorry emails.

My apologies aren't working. They're still upset. How long will they be upset? *What else can I do?*

April 2, I dig the small bundle of postcards I've accumulated from the beginning of every writing class out of my bag, and head to the nearest post office. I send them all to my house in New York.

A week a half later I get another email from Leo.

Your postcards are the talk of the town. What'd you say in those things? The 'rents won't stop whispering.

I don't hear anything from my parents.

25. One Last Time

Our last full day abroad comes without warning. Yesterday, I made a new Facebook chat thread for us to exchange American numbers. I need these friendships to stick. Everyone leaves their numbers, including Pilot. I stare at the digits next to his name, anger sparking in my chest.

This morning there was a new message in our family dinner group chat.

> **Babe**
> FRIENDLY REMINDER: Our flat
> family dinner blowout is tonight!!
> 6:00 p.m. Be there!

I pull out two jars of sauce (my dinner contribution) and leave them on the table before heading out to do the Tower of London with Sahra and Atticus. Babe said she was too busy packing to come. Pilot just didn't come. Maybe he went to hang out with the guys down the hall.

Tonight, I'm confronting him.

We head to the kitchen at 6:00 p.m., per Babe's instructions. Inside, the table's all set, and the room is already brimming with the sweet smell of melting cheese and tomato sauce. Babe's leaning against the counter with a glass of wine. Atticus enters behind me, and we all chorus a round of *heys*.

"Did you start early?" I exclaim.

"Yeah!" Babe lifts her glass. "I just set the table, and I bought some wine yesterday. The ziti's been in the oven for around thirty minutes, so it'll be ready in like, fifteen. I finished packing early, and thought, why not get started!"

"Babe, we were going to help," Atticus protests.

"Don't worry about it. I love cooking!" She grins, picking the wine bottle up from the table. "Who wants wine?"

Atticus and I each pour ourselves a glass. I pull Sawyer out of my bag and put on a classic rock playlist. I place it on the couch at a low volume for background ambiance. Bruce Springsteen's "Born in the USA" kicks things off.

"'Merica!" Babe yells in the self-aware ironic way we do to make fun of ourselves.

"'Merica!" echoes a male voice. I turn around to find Pilot standing in the doorway, wearing one of his classic plaid button-ups. He holds up a plastic bag. "Got the ping-pong balls! I had to go to three places, but I finally found them at Primark so all is good!"

"I knew you'd come through." Atticus grins.

I tense up and head over toward Babe and Atticus, taking a spot against the counter. Pilot places the bag on the couch near Sawyer and slings his backpack off.

"It looks like they don't actually have solo cups here, but they had these." He pulls a sleeve of medium-sized white cups from his bag. Babe and Atticus laugh.

Pilot hauls a pack of beer from his bag and puts it in the fridge before cracking one open for himself. He leans up against the counter near me. We're all leaning against the nice wrap-around counter near the window. "What have you all been up to today?"

"Packing," Babe drawls.

"We went to see the Tower of London. Remember, I invited you this morning," Atticus teases.

"Oh yeah." Pilot blinks. "How was it?"

"Educational and great!" Atticus exclaims.

"Nice." Pilot takes another sip of his beer.

Sahra bursts through the door. "Woo! Family dinner night," she yells with fifty times the enthusiasm of her usual voice. "I'm so ready to drink and be American together." She throws her purse on the couch, strolls to the table, and falls into a chair. "How long do we have till it's ready to eat?" she adds eagerly.

When the timer goes off, Babe grabs an oven mitt and pulls a casserole dish of steaming ziti from the oven. We pick up plates, and Babe takes charge, deeming herself the official pasta distributer. Billy Joel's "We Didn't Start the Fire" starts playing from my playlist. It makes me smile.

"Do any of you know all the words to this song?" I ask. "It's one of my life goals to know them all one day." Babe drops a scoop of ziti onto my plate.

"I want to too!" She laughs.

"Doot doot doot doot doot doot doot," I sing along quietly.

"Wow, you already know so many of the lyrics," Pilot says from the table. I snort as I make my way to my seat.

We finish our baked ziti in merry chitchat, catching up on all the things we've missed in each other's lives. After dinner, we clear the table for beer pong. We play three on two and rock-paper-scissor for teams. I end up on Pilot's. We play, and Pilot and I are winning and laughing and high-fiving, and I almost forget that he's been avoiding me for ages and might know all my most intimate thoughts.

It's 9:00 p.m. when we finish up a game of Kings, gather our jackets, and head out to a pub in Camden that Babe found on Yelp.

The inside of the pub is littered with round, dark green, fancy-looking booths. Music plays low in the background, so speaking is still an option. We pick a booth, and Pilot slides in first, followed by Sahra and Atticus.

As I lean to slide in, Babe loops her arm around mine and pulls me in the opposite direction toward the bar. "We're going to go grab some drinks. Hold down the table and then we can switch," she tells them.

She leans into to my ear. "Is there something going on with you and Pilot again? You haven't talked about him in forever."

"Nothing is going on with me and Pilot," I mumble.

Babe shakes her head and meets my eyes, putting on a serious face. "Do you like him still?" She tries to study my expression. I never told her about Amy and Horcrux Nine. I haven't told anyone.

I blow out an exasperated breath. "I don't want to talk about it."

She sighs as we reach the bar. Babe orders her drink. I have to get Pilot alone. Maybe I should buy him a drink and lure him to a different table?

"Can I get a glass of red wine?" I ask the bartender. I hesitate for a second then add, "And a Guinness, please."

"You're getting a Guinness?" Babe asks beside me. I turn to respond to her and startle. There's a tall, curly-haired man standing right behind her. The guy introduces himself, shakes our hands, and quickly orders us all shots of whiskey. I exchange a look with Babe, but she's into it. They start up a line of small talk.

I glance back over at our booth and see Pilot watching us. He raises his eyebrows at me in amusement. I look away, trying not to smile. He's so stupidly charming.

Four shots come on a platter and the guy distributes them: one to me, Babe, and his dark-haired, lanky friend who appeared out of nowhere while I looked away, turning our little triangle into a circle. I bring the tiny glass to my nose, take a quick whiff, and pull away. It smells like a mixture of wood and rubbing alcohol.

"To tonight!" says the curly-haired guy. The three of them shoot the liquid down their throats. I take a sip.

"Oh my god." My face squishes up, and I spasm like a dog shaking the water from its fur. It burns.

"Shane!" Babe says, laughing. "You can't sip it!" The curly-haired guy laughs with her.

I hand the shot to Babe. "Here, you have mine," I tell her. I grab my wine and the Guinness from the bar and stroll back to our booth.

I slide in next to Pilot, holding both drinks—and freeze up. I can't lure him to another table if I'm already inside the booth. *Good job thinking this one through.*

A moment later, Sahra and Atticus slide out.

"Where are you guys going?" I ask quickly.

"To get a drink," Sahra answers, like it's the most obvious thing in the world.

"Pilot will stay here with you until Babe gets back." Atticus laughs before zeroing in on my Guinness. "You got a Guinness?"

"I, yeah, just," I flounder as they get up and out of the booth. Atticus grins but doesn't wait for my explanation. I watch them walk away. Babe is still chatting up the guys over there. I slowly look over at Pilot, widening my eyes and pulling a hmm-I guess-it's-just-us face. *How do I open?*

I look at my drinks. "Uh, I actually don't think I want this," I say, pushing the glass of Guinness forward. "You can have it if you want."

He smiles hesitantly. "Are you sure?"

"Yes, please take it." I push it toward him.

"Thanks." He picks it up and takes a swig. "How was that whiskey shot?" he asks with amusement.

"Oh god, it was nasty. I felt rude not at least trying it, though."

He smirks and shakes his head, bringing the beer to his lips. I feel myself smile and then force my lips back down.

I take a sip of the wine. It's so sour. *Okay, say your words, Shane.*

"How's the book going?" Pilot lowers his beer.

I never actually started my book.

I swallow. "Um, not going too much. I've been trying to catch up on some other studying."

He closes his eyes for a moment. "I'm sorry about what happened with your parents . . ."

"Um, yeah, I never got to say thank you for, you know, going to that, and um, attempting to prevent that dumpster fire of a conversation." I gulp down another sip.

His eyes find mine, and hold them for a beat, like a sort of metaphysical hand squeeze. "Anytime, Shane."

I glance over at the bar. Atticus and the girls are cheers-ing with the whiskey guys and downing another round of shots.

I turn back to Pilot, twitchy with nerves. "I have to ask you something."

"Shoot," he says.

I grip my glass tighter. "Um, okay, well, um, do you know about that night in the kitchen?"

He grins. "I think you're going have to be more specific."

"Um, the night my parents visited, I lost my notebook in the kitchen . . ." I trail off.

"Oh shit, did you find it?" he asks. "You must have a crapload of hilarious story ideas in there."

I loose a pent-up breath. *He doesn't know. Now tell him how you feel.*

"How's that album you're working on?" I find myself saying.

"Oh, it's um, kind of on hold for now," he says with a sad smile.

"What? Why?" I lean forward, forearms on the table.

"I don't know. I don't feel like I'm totally happy with it anymore, so I'm taking a break until I figure out what's not sounding right."

"Oh . . ." *Tell him.*

I watch as he looks down at his drink thoughtfully. He looks sad. I don't want him to be.

"Pies." I take another sip of wine and scoot the tiniest bit closer.

"Yeah?" His lips quirk up.

I moved closer and he smiled.

Do it, Shane. I clear my throat. "Are you excited to get home?"

Pilot exhales, tilts his head, and rests it in his hand. "Well, in a way, yeah, there are some people there that I want to get back for."

I blink, letting this sink in. He wants to get back for Amy. Amy is some people.

You should still just tell him.

"What about you?" Pilot asks, trying to catch my eyes because I've dropped my gaze to his earlobe. I let him catch them.

"Kind of, I guess, but, um, well, I'm really gonna miss, um, miss, I . . ." I swallow.

Pilot breaks eye contact. He never breaks eye contact first. My lips wobble.

"HEYOOO! We got free shots!" Babe interrupts. She's grinning broadly as she scoots back into the booth. Pilot and I snap back to a regular non-angled-toward-each-other posture as the rest of the flat returns.

"Let's play 21!" Atticus exclaims.

We play one last game of 21 in London. I'm all smiles and laughter and underscored sadness. Afterward, we chat about how we're going to spend the summer. Babe's coworkers have connected her with the Disney Internship program, and she's heading down to Florida in June. We discuss our flight times for tomorrow. Pilot's not leaving; he's staying for the royal wedding and then traveling some more with the guys in the flat down the hall. Babe's parents are coming, and they're going to do London and the royal wedding this coming week as well, then she's traveling for a week by herself. The rest of us will leave together for the airport at 12:00 p.m.

26. Bye Bye Bye

Babe and Sahra are last-minute packing when I emerge from the shower at 2:15 a.m. I venture to the kitchen for water.

I go home to my disappointed parents tomorrow. Disappointment that will have no doubt rippled through the entire family by now.

I manipulated my parents into paying for a study abroad trip completely irrelevant to my degree.

Standing at the sink, I close my eyes and heave a giant breath, pressing my palms up into my eyes. The door opens behind me. I turn to see Atticus. His happy-go-lucky expression drops.

"Jeez, Shane, are you okay?" He takes a seat at the table.

"I'm fine, just, um, sad that this is all over."

He presses his lips together and nods. "Yeah, me too. I wish I went to school with you guys." Atticus goes to a different university that sent him to our program.

"Me too," I agree. "But we'll still keep in touch, right?"

"Yeah, of course!" he says adamantly. "Are you going to be okay? Do you want to talk about it?"

I smile at him gratefully. "I'm fine. I think I just need a second, you know?"

"Yeah, I do," he agrees, understanding on his face. He gets up and fills himself a glass of water before heading toward the door. "Good night, Shane."

I slump down into a seat, resting my head and arms on the table. I'm going to miss Atticus. And Sahra and Babe. And Pilot.

There's a giant pit in my stomach. The kind you get when you know you failed the test the teacher's handing back, and there's nothing you can do about it.

In the morning, we're all up early cleaning out the kitchen. Everything needs to be thrown out or wiped down. It's our last flat activity. I don't know what I was expecting, but this last group hang isn't fun. Everyone's on edge. We don't make much eye contact, and we're all quiet.

We clean for an hour before Atticus, Babe, Sahra, and I make our way up the stairs with our luggage. Pilot helps us. We roll up to the door with our bags. Pilot gives Atticus, Sahra, and Babe each a hug, and then it's my turn. It's not the goodbye I've romanticized. It's barely a goodbye at all. He avoids my eyes and leans in for the same generic hug he gave everyone else.

"Bye," he says quietly with his arms around me.

"Bye," I whisper under my breath. It's quick. He turns his head, pulls away, and then he's heading back down the stairs.

Babe walks off to catch the Tube to her new hotel (we're all kicked out of the Karlston today). Atticus, Sahra, and I share a cab to the airport. We're all on different flights, so at Heathrow we part ways.

I wait in a long check-in line for Virgin Atlantic, and think about how I've let everyone down. Including myself. Wendy and Donna and Declan, and Mom and Dad.

I let all my writing goals go to shit, and I never confronted Pilot.

I'm going to be waist-deep in premed work when I get home, which will leave little to no time for book drafting. And things with Pilot are really going to change when we get back to the US—I'm never going to be able to tell him how I feel. He's going to go back to Amy, and it'll be like nothing ever happened. Maybe this wasn't a big deal for him, but feeling like this was . . . is a big deal for me.

"Next in line!"

I roll up to check in with my two bags and heave my giant suitcase onto the scale.

"I'm sorry, ma'am, this is fifteen pounds overweight," the woman says.

I blink at her and take it off. I pull on my carry-on. *I came here to do things. Not regret things.*

"This one's four pounds overweight." She points to an area behind me. "You can go over there and try to rearrange things. There's a max of fifty pounds per bag." I follow her gaze to where two other young girls have their bags wide open on the floor, repacking shit in the middle of the check-in area.

I came to take risks. I came to be outgoing. I don't want it to end like this.

"What?" I hear the check-in lady ask.

Did I say that out loud?

I pivot and drag my bags away. I don't stop near the repacking girls; I keep walking and head outside again, gaining speed as a surge of adrenaline courses through me. I wait for another cab. I give the driver the address of the Karlston, and we plow back into London.

My heart beats outside my body, running in circles around the taxi. I'm doing it. I'm gonna do what I said I was going to do: I'm going to tell him. I'm at the end of the rom com, not the drama. It's not going to end with me getting on the plane.

I practice what I'm going to say: *Pies, I really, really like you. I don't know how you feel, but I really, really like you and I had to tell you. I had to let you know.* Simple, straightforward, easy to remember. I can go off cuff from there.

I repeat it over and over in my brain the entire way.

When we pull up to the Karlston, I leap out onto the sidewalk. *Pies, I really, really like you. I don't know how you feel, but I really, really like you and I had to tell you. I had to let you know.*

"I'll be right back!" I tell the driver. "Can you please keep the meter running?"

I slam the door shut, beaming now as I hurtle up the steps. *I'm doing it!* I've committed, and god it feels great!

I have my ID out and ready to flash at security. I sprint past them and down the stairs, holding onto the railing so I don't trip and break my neck. I shuffle over to the kitchen and peek in through the windows to see if he's in there.

It's empty, so I run down the hall to his door, heave in a great breath, and knock. *Pies, I really, really like you. I don't know how you feel, but I really, really like you and I had to tell you. I had to let you know.*

"Pies?"

I laugh. I can't believe I'm doing this.

"Pies?" I knock again. "Pies!" I yell louder now. No answer.

Maybe he's listening to music. I put pressure on the doorknob and find that it's unlocked. I push the door open. The room is empty save for the black comforters we were told to leave behind.

"No," I breathe quietly. "No," I say again, wandering into the room, looking for any remnant of Pilot that might suggest he's still here, just not *here.*

"No." I run out into the hall.

"Pilot?" I call. I go into the kitchen to make sure he's not hidden from view on the far end of the couch. I run down the hall to the other flat where his guy friends live. "Pies?"

No one's here.

I can call him! He's still in London! I fumble for the phone in my crossbody for half a second before the idea crashes down around me. I don't have a phone. Dad broke my phone, and I never got a new one because I hardly used it anyway. I don't know Pilot's British number by heart. His US phone doesn't work here. I never thought to ask where he was staying after this.

Maybe he's on his computer wherever he is, and he can give me a location? I sprint back up to the taxi, dive into my book bag, and whip out Sawyer. I run back in and down to the basement to connect to the Wi-Fi. I open Facebook chat.

Shane
Hey, Pies?

I wait thirty seconds.

Shane
Pies, you out there?

Thirty more seconds.

A minute. Three minutes. The messages remain unviewed.

My face crumples. I close my laptop because my meter's running. My plane's waiting. I drag myself back up the stairs and into the taxi. Ask the driver to go back to the airport.

I miss my flight.

When I finally land back in the United States, Leo and Alfie are waiting for me at JFK. My expression falls as I step up to where they're standing, fiddling on their smartphones. I was expecting Mom.

"What are you guys doing here? Where's my mom?"

"Your parents sent us," Alfie answers, still texting.

I look to Leo. "Why?" My voice cracks.

He shakes his head like he's at a loss. "You tell us."

I start walking toward the baggage carousel, tears welling up in my eyes.

Leo trots after me. "Shane, come on. You never tell us anything anymore. You've never been in trouble your entire life. What the hell did you do to piss them off so much?" He steps in front of me, blocking my way.

I close my eyes and heave a breath. I'm so tired. "Leo—" I huff.

"Leo lost his baseball scholarship and dropped out of school," Alfie snickers from out of view.

Leo winces. Whatever I was about to say dies on my tongue.

I glance at Alfie over Leo's shoulder, but he's back to texting on his phone. I study Leo's eyes. They're blank, guarded.

"What is he talking about?" I ask quietly. "What's going on with you?"

"What did you *do*?" he asks again.

I slump forward and step around him toward the carousel.

Pilot responds to my message the next day, asking what was up. I tell him I needed Babe's British number because I accidentally packed one of her shirts.

Part 2

27. What Page Are You On?

"If you were a shape, what shape would you be?" The chair creaks as the man leans back and folds his hands over his knee.

If I were a shape? *If I were a shape.* A diamond? Would they want to hear diamond? Am I a diamond? I'm under enough pressure. What about parallelogram? I like how the word *parallelogram* rolls off the tongue.

What. Shape. Am I? What shape am I?

His fingers drum on the table. Shit.

"Uh, I would be a circle, or actually a sphere because I'm three-dimensional, you know, and, because I can always roll with the punches."

He blinks. "Hmmm."

I swallow.

"If you were a flower, what flower would you be?" he drawls.

Flowers? I don't really know flowers. Rose because *Red* is my favorite Taylor Swift album? Sunflower because I'm upbeat? What are those things at Christmas? Poinsettias! Also red. And poisonous. Is there something orange? Orange feels unique.

The fingers drum again. *Make a decision.*

"Okay, I'd say, I'd be a rose—"

His eyebrows shoot up to his hairline. Okay, *rose is bad.*

I choke. "I mean, no, that's too romantic. I'd actually be a sunflower because they're really bright and positive, and well, tall . . . and I'm just, like, average height. I retract that?"

He sighs loudly.

"I'm an orange tree!" I blurt. "I like to make . . . things that people can enjoy, and oranges are unique, but not too unique because . . . they're universally good for your health." I nod absently to myself.

"So, not a flower," he states gravely.

My shoulders droop. How does any of this trace back to my medical experience?

His frown deepens. "What was my last published work?"

His? Oh god, I found out I'd be interviewing with him half an hour ago. I'm bombing this. I can't believe I'm bombing this. I did so much research on their program.

"I, I . . . I'm sorry, um . . . I don't know."

Silence stretches.

"Okay, thank you for coming in." I'm dismissed.

"I, um . . . would you like to hear about any of my medical experience? I—"

"I've read about it in your file, Ms. Primaveri."

There's a moment of uncomfortable gaping on my end.

"Um, uh, okay, well, I just want you to know, I'm graduating top of my med class, and I think the world of the university and I really appreciate, um, your consideration for the residency position here at NYU."

He says nothing. I pick up my purse and stumble from the office.

Outside, students bustle around me, entering and exiting the building. I drop down, taking a seat on the stone steps. Well, that went poorly.

I check my cell. Still no return call from Babe. I have a few hours before my other interview—*that one will be better*. Now I know to expect random, obscure personality questions.

My gaze drifts over to my left hand. I'm still having a hard time processing what happened yesterday. Straight up out of the blue, Boyfriend asked me to marry him. The second the proposal left his mouth a different guy barged back into my thoughts. Both the proposal and the reemergence of Other Guy have been very inconvenient surprises to deal with while doing last-minute residency interview prep.

I couldn't sleep on the plane ride over because my brain was like: Um, you know what would be more fun than sleeping? Staying up forever and rehashing every waking memory that Other Guy's ever been a part of. Now I'm tangled up in a mile-long string of what-ifs.

It just so happens that Other Guy works here in the city at a company that makes golf equipment or something. I've seen the name of the place on Facebook. I've also looked up where it's located on Google Maps because apparently I'm slowly making the transition from Facebook stalker to actual real-life physical one.

I can't go see him.

What I'm going to do now . . . is get some work done in a coffee shop for a few hours, and then head over to Columbia for my other interview, and then I'm going back to San Diego, and over to see Boyfriend. There will be no pit stops. I will not complete the transition. *Rage, rage against becoming the stalker!*

I huff a breath, a wave of hair fluttering away from my face as I watch taxis weave through traffic.

It would be ridiculous. We haven't exchanged communication, other than a happy birthday on each other's Facebook walls, in six years. If I'm being honest, he missed my birthday last year.

I check my phone again. Still nothing. *Call me back, Babe.*

Stalker Shane thinks perhaps this inner turmoil means she needs closure; then she can go back to her pre-boyfriend-proposing mindset. Everyone talks about closure on TV. Closure is magic. Closure is the knife that'll sever the what-if strings and leave her free to dwell on other less irrelevant things. Like Boyfriend. And . . . marriage. Taxes. Gastroenterology. Important shit.

I speed-dial Babe one last time. It goes to voicemail again.

"Babe, where are you? I think I'm about to do something stupid, and I need you to talk me out of it. Or maybe tell me it's not stupid and I should go for it." I hang up and make my way down to the sidewalk, mind racing.

I come to a standstill at the curb. I have a missed text from Melvin:
Counting the minutes till your return

I blink at it. I think he's trying to be cute, but without emojis and punctuation, there's an underlying creepiness. I tap out of Messages and push away this new claustrophobic feeling that I now apparently associate with my boyfriend.

A yellow cab's approaching.

Don't do it.

I throw up my arm.

Full-blown stalker status, unlocked.

I can do this. I can talk to him again. I can say things. I'm a grown-up. I'm almost a doctor. This is casual. This is nothing.

When the taxi comes to a stop, my stomach's turning itself inside out, but I have a plan. It's simple and classy. Simple and classy. It's classy. And it's simple. I'll ask him to grab a cup of coffee. That's a normal thing that people ask people when they want to catch up.

I step out of the car. My tight, blue business dress rode up and got all twisted in the cab. I hastily pull it down while I crane my neck to get a better look at the generic, sleek silver building towering before me. A wide set of steps leads up to a row of glass doors.

I spend a good two minutes staring at the doors. *This is a terrible idea.*

Then I steel myself. *Do it for the closure.*

My tiny neutral-colored heels clack up the stairs. I fumble a little as I take the last two steps at once, before striding into a large, high-ceilinged, empty lobby. Gold elevators line the wall a little way in to the left, and a man with gray hair sits behind a desk to my right.

"Good morning!" I greet him.

"How can I help you?" he responds blandly.

I clear my throat. "I'm looking for Pilot Penn. I believe he works at FJ Golf. Could you tell me what floor I could find him on, please?"

"Do you have an appointment?"

"No, but it's all right. I'm a friend of his," I lie. I mean, we're kind of friends.

The security man stares at me for a second, contemplating whether or not I should be allowed up without an appointment. He seems to decide I'm not a threat to the building.

His face falls, and he mumbles, "You're going to need a visitor's badge. Name."

"Shane Primaveri. P-R-I-M-A-V-E-R-I," I respond automatically. He scribbles my name on a small white sticker, slaps it on a badge that says VISITOR, and hands it over the counter.

"Put it on and head up to the sixteenth floor."

I carefully clip it to my silver cross-body purse before ambling over to the elevators on the balls of my feet in attempt to be less conspicuous. Why is the urge to be stealth overwhelming? I don't need to be stealth! *This isn't weird. This is fine!*

Inhale. Hold. Exhale. I punch the up button with my index finger.

The arrow over the elevator all the way to the left glows yellow. I nervously float up to the crack in the gold doors until I'm right up on them. There's a muted ding as they slide out. There's already a guy inside, holding a bunch of paper. When he looks up my eyelids snap back.

"Shit," I breathe, stiffening as insecurities I banished years ago materialize instantaneously. *It's him.* I was counting on having a few more seconds to prepare and he's just here.

He's sporting khakis and a white button-up shirt today, carrying two big stacks of paper. He stares at me blankly for a half a second before actually registering that I'm me. I know when he does because his eyes widen like he's seen a ghost, and the paper slips from his hand. It flops to the floor of the elevator with a hard thud.

"SHANE?" he spurts.

I inhale sharply. *You are a grown lady who's been successfully networking her ass off at medical conferences the last four years. You can and will confront Pilot Penn.*

I take the step forward into the elevator. "Hey, Pies."

The doors start to close. He gathers the paper off the floor before snapping back to a normal, standing-with-two-packs-of-paper stance.

"What are you doing here?" His voice is still laced with shock, but he's trying to regain his composure.

"I'm actually here to talk to you . . ."

His forehead crinkles up. "*To talk to me?*" He's loud and confused again.

My instinct is to laugh, but his eyes catch mine and instinct drowns real fast in my ever-growing pool of anxiety.

I suck up some air. "Yeah, I'm sorry to disturb you at work, but I kind of really needed to talk. To you . . . Can we go grab a coffee or something?" I resist the urge to fiddle with the zipper of my purse.

The doors slide open to reveal floor sixteen: a large, bright open room lined with windows and divided into gray cubicles. Pilot steps out, and I follow as he strides along the edge of the room.

"I haven't seen you in"—he pauses, turning to look at me—"six years?" He takes on a higher pitch with those last two words.

He rounds into one of the cubicles, drops the two packages of paper on his desk, and collapses into a desk chair. He closes his eyes and takes a breath before looking back up at me.

I hesitantly smile and wave. "Hi, cup of coffee?" I repeat.

He glances around and scratches his neck. He looks almost the same— different haircut, maybe broader shoulders?

"Why are you here?" he repeats, calmer this time.

"I had an interview at NYU earlier, and I have one at Columbia later." I pause. "I mean, that's not why I'm here, here. I'm here, here because I need to talk to you and I'd like to get a cup of coffee," I repeat, leaning a little against the thin gray divider entrance to his cubicle.

"For?"

"Their internal medicine program," I say. His eyebrows pull together. He looks down, propping his elbows up against his knees.

"So, you just randomly decided to come to the building where I work and ask me to go get a coffee?" He meets my eyes.

"I mean, kind of, yeah," I say with a strained expression.

He tilts his head. "Who does that?" Amusement creeps into the question.

"Crazies," I answer sardonically.

"I'm not really supposed to leave right now," he says quietly.

"Oh, um." I glance around uncomfortably.

Pilot stands. He swings his head around, taking stock of the room until he finds who he's looking for: a heavyset man in his late thirties walking along the opposite wall.

He locks eyes with him. "Hey, Tom, I'm going to have to step out for an hour. Family emergency." I straighten abruptly and try to look solemn as Tom's eyes dart from Pilot to me and back to Pilot again.

"Okay," he responds slowly.

"Okay!" Pilot replies, hopping out of the cubicle. He puts a hand on my back and silently leads me from the room.

He drops it as we load back onto an elevator. We're quiet until the doors slide closed.

"Okay, let's do it. Coffee," his says with small smile, stuffing his hands in his pockets. He studies me for a moment. "It's weird to see you."

"Weird to see to you too."

"Sorry about"—he shakes his head—"that minor freak-out; don't know what happened there." He leans against the wall of the elevator.

"I know. That's out of character for you." I cross one foot in front of the other and bobble slightly in my heels.

Pilot huffs a laugh and purses his lips. We're both quiet for a moment before he says, "So are you a doctor now?"

I nod. "Almost. Interviewing for residency programs, working toward becoming a gastroenterologist. What have you been up to? What do you do here?"

"Oh, you know, computer programming, writing code, solving IT issues, exciting stuff." He crosses his arms, inspecting me like a riddle he's trying to crack. I turn away to glance at the doors.

That's when I realize—we're not moving. The buttons are on Pilot's side. I grin and mirror him, leaning against the opposite wall.

"Hey, Pies."

He tilts his head. "Yeah?"

"You never pressed any buttons, so we're just chilling in a metal box."

Surprise dawns on his face. He releases a quick laugh before jabbing the lobby button.

"You know, I usually travel the building with an assistant. He does all the button pressing when I elevator," he relays in a haughty voice.

A laugh busts out of me. The doors ding open, and we emerge into the lobby.

"You have a coffee place in mind?" he asks.

My heels clack onto the tile. "Um, I'm haven't really—"

"You're looking for a coffee place?" The guy at the front desk casually interrupts me. He grins at Pilot.

"Hey, Jack," Pilot greets him. "You know a place?"

"Somebody dropped off flyers for some new place just ten minutes ago." Lobby Jack waves us over and pulls a stack of lavender paper from behind the desk. "I was like: lady, this isn't the grocery store, we don't hand out flyers, but she left 'em anyway. After reading the thing, I mean, it actually sounds like a pretty cool coffee joint. Take a look." He pushes the stack toward us.

"Interesting." Pilot picks one up and holds it upright so we can both read it. *Quirky hidden coffee place, complete with secret elevator?*

I raise my eyebrows, catching Pilot's eye as we head for the exit. This place on the flyer is at least a ten-minute walk.

"You up for this? We could just hit a Starbucks if you want," I tell him.

He pushes the door open and gestures for me to go first. "Hey, I'm always game for an adventure."

A smile pulls at my lips as I lead us out. "Okay. Let's go for it."

Pilot folds the flyer and sticks it in his back pocket as we fall into step on the sidewalk.

"So," he starts, "how did you hunt me down?" A sideways grin kicks up his cheek.

I shrug. "You know, had to call in favors, get a background check."

His eyes grow.

Another laugh bursts out of me. "Pilot. I looked at your Facebook. It says where you work. I Google-mapped it."

"Ohhh! Dang." He grins. "I'm impressed! You had me there for a second."

We cross to the next block.

"So you wanted to talk about . . . ?"

I blow out a breath. "Let's save it for this quirky-ass café."

He chuckles. "So, you're gonna to be a—what is it, a gastroenterologist?"

"Yup, working on it."

"Why gastroenterologist, may I ask?" he asks curiously.

I purse my lips for a moment. "Well, I wasn't really sure what I wanted to do, so I just kinda picked gastroenterology."

"Just picked it?" He chuckles. "Isn't it, like, a really giant life commitment?"

"Yeah, I've got six years of residency coming my way . . ." I trail off like a wind-up toy running out of steam. I decided I was working toward gastro somewhere between my first year of med school and now. Melvin was so passionate about it.

"Wow, that's a lot of years."

I shrug and pull a small smile. "Yeah, I don't know. I'm graduating top of my class, though. It's going well."

He nods and drops his gaze. "How are things um, with your family? Better? I still think from time to time about that night they showed up."

I pause. "Things are still kinda shitty, but in a more boring way. We don't really talk. I'm out in San Diego—I kind of needed to get away—but I'm doing well in school, and they're happy with my progress."

He's quiet for a beat. The blare of New York swells in the silence.

"Wow," he finally breathes.

"Wow what?" I ask as we make our way across another block. I grip my purse, one hand on the chain and one on the actual bag.

"I can't believe you're an almost doctor." He raises his shoulders in a shrug-smile. God, it's really cute. "You still writing all the time?"

I shake my head. "Nah, not really. Things are so busy, and I haven't really had the time to write for fun . . . Do you keep in touch with anyone from London?" I ask, changing the subject.

"No, I'm completely out of the loop." He speaks slowly. "Do you?"

"Well, yeah. Sahra graduated from Harvard a year back and she's, like, a real lawyer. I track her success via Facebook. Atticus and I grab lunch in

LA every few months—he's producing a play there right now—and Babe and I still talk all the time! She just got engaged, actually."

Pilot's quiet as we cross to another block.

After a minute, I meet his eyes again. "Have you been back since we left?"

He shakes his head. "Um, no, haven't been back, but I want to someday. Have you?"

"No—there have been times where I've really, really wanted to." I even spoke to Melvin about maybe going during one of our breaks the first year we were together. He didn't want to spend the money, which is understandable. "But like I said, things have been so busy with school and working, and I haven't been able to take the time off."

I heave a breath. "In my head the whole place has taken on this almost magical quality."

A fresh wave of nostalgia washes over me. I catch a wistful glimmer in Pilot's eye before he looks away.

Two more blocks and the café should be up on the right. Traffic roars down the street as we weave through a light crowd of midday walkers: middle-aged women, couples, and businessmen speed by.

Pilot's studying me again. It lights me up with nerves.

"Are you still making music?" I ask suddenly. We've come to the edge of another sidewalk. I stare at the walk–don't walk sign across the way. It feels so important that he's still making music. *Please say you're still making music.*

"Um, nah, not too much."

I turn to catch his eye. "What? Not even, like, on the side?"

He shakes his head, passes me a small smile.

I blow out a breath and refocus. "I think it's up here, on the right." I point to a shiny silver business building up ahead of us. The number *5184* glimmers along its edge.

Pilot smiles, pulling out the flyer to check the address and looking back at me. "You think when they said quirky coffee place they meant corporate block of cement?"

I smother a laugh. "Maybe it's camouflage. It says *hidden café*, Pies. There's gonna be"—I hold up air quotes—"a '*secret elevator.*'"

He snorts as we climb the steps. I throw the fancy glass doors open, a little excited now. There's a lobby desk much like the one in Pilot's building. This one's unmanned. A string of silver elevators line the wall to our left. Straight ahead at the far, far end of the room, a hallway stretches off the left and right corners.

The flyer says the elevator's down that hallway on the right. I power walk toward it, and Pilot strolls behind me.

I clack around the corner into the hall and skid to a stop. *Holy wow.*

The entire corridor is painted black. Fifty feet away at the end of the hall is an elevator. This one's covered in words. It looks like someone ripped a page from a giant book and plastered it onto the wall.

"Whaaat!" Pilot exclaims behind me. "That's pretty sick."

"It really is."

I suck in a breath as we start toward it. I wasn't expecting to go somewhere this cool—I can't let myself get too distracted. We're now moments away from sitting down and getting deep in uncharted conversational waters. I reach out and jab the up button, or the button; there's only one button next to this elevator. It's a tad sketchy, but the bookish decor on the doors has sort of put me at ease. They slide open a moment later to reveal a shiny black interior.

We step in silently. There's one button inside as well. It's labeled RE-WRITE, the name of the cafe.

"Check this out." I point, before pushing it. We lurch upward.

"This is kind of creepy," he notes.

"Me or the elevator?" I half joke.

"Oh, definitely you, but the elevator too." He grins.

I hesitate. "I'm sorry if I am actually creeping you out with this surprise visit. I didn't mean to—"

He interrupts, "Shane, that was a joke. You're way too . . . you to be creepy."

"What's that supposed to mean? I can be creepy," I protest.

"No, not really, no, you can't."

"I can creep if I want to—" The ding of arrival interrupts my argument. We spin around as a second set of doors behind us slides open.

"Whoa." Pilot's jaw drops. I echo the sentiment.

We must be at least twenty stories up. Before us is a quaint rectangular space. One full wall is just window, providing a fabulous view of the city. The other three walls are plastered in the aged, browning pages of books. The ceiling is covered in words. Lanterns hang off long chains hovering over delicate-looking French tables and chairs scattered throughout the room. Even the floor is in theme. It looks as if it's been littered with thousands of discarded book pages.

There's one other customer: a middle-aged man in a business suit reading a paper and having a cup of coffee in the corner. A barista stands behind a large counter on our left. I stumble forward, gawking at everything.

"Welcome to Rewrite!" the barista greets us.

"Thanks, good morning!" I reply automatically as I make my way to a table near the far wall (aka the giant window). Pilot follows closely behind me.

The metal chair scrapes lightly against the floor as I pull it out and sit. Pilot sits across from me, still glancing around at the decor.

"This place is really cool." He nods, impressed.

I'm smitten with the ambiance, but nerves chase away further comment from me. The barista comes over and places two small Rewrite menus in front of us. I glance up at her. She looks familiar.

"Thanks." Pilot shoots her a smile before she leaves us be.

The menu's typed in Courier New so it looks like a movie script. I put it aside and bring my attention back to Pilot. He's watching me, waiting.

He raises a brow. "So this mysterious meeting we're having?" he prompts.

My eyes travel up from the raised brow to his unfamiliar haircut. The sides of his head are shaved, and the top is long, flopping over his forehead.

I blow out a breath. "So—"

I'm cut off as the barista steps up to our table. "Can I take your orders?"

I look up at the woman again. She's maybe in her late forties, pale and freckled, with a nest of bright red hair tied up on her head.

"I'll have a cup of English Breakfast tea with milk and sugar please." I hand over my menu, studying her features.

"I'll have a cappuccino," Pilot says, handing her his menu as well. The woman retreats.

Our gazes fall back to each other. I press my lips together, trying to gather how best to start this conversation. "So . . ."

Pilot scoots a little closer. "So, I was trying to crack this visit open . . ."

I gaze out at the view of New York, take in a deep breath, and—the woman's face snaps into place.

"Oh my god." I jump up out of my seat and whip around. My hair smacks me in the face before resetting over my shoulders. The woman's moving around behind the bar.

"What?" Pilot asks.

I look back at him with wide eyes. "Do you see that redheaded lady over there right now?"

He glances between the bar and myself with a confused expression. "The woman making our coffee? Yeah . . ."

My eyes zips back and forth between the two of them a few times before I swallow and sit back in my chair.

You're acting insane.

"Are you okay?" Pilot asks. I blink.

Forget the lady. Get your head in the game, Primaveri. You came for closure.

"Yeah, I'm fine. Never mind." I blink some more.

"You were about to fill me in on why we're here."

"Yes!" I concentrate on Pilot again. I can do this. *Just go.* "My boyfriend proposed to me yesterday—" I start.

"Oh, wow—" Pilot's expression shifts in surprise.

Not the opening I had in mind.

"We were sitting on our bed, and I was reading, and he was doing something on his laptop and out of the blue he said"—I deepen my voice—"'You know, we probably should get married; it makes sense for tax reasons,' and I put down my book to look at him, but he wasn't looking at me, he was still looking at the computer. And I said, 'Did you just propose?' And he said"—I put on my deep voice again—"'Yeah, I guess, what do you say?'"

Pilot's head tilts to the side.

"And I told him . . . I had to think about it—"

"Shane, why are you telling me this?" he interjects quietly.

I continue like I didn't hear him, "It's like I've been living through a macro lens and all of the sudden everything just zoomed out—"

"What's a macro lens?"

"—And I don't think I want to be with him. I'm not sure why we're even together anymore. I barely remember how I got to this point. I thought I was tethered. I knew where I was going, but then he said that thing about taxes and whatever imaginary rope was holding me just snapped and I'm floating away into oblivion. Even you just asking me that question, *Why gastroenterology?* Like why? What? I don't even know! What am I doing—"

"Whoa, Shane. Take a breath."

I vacuum up an audible breath and begin again, more slowly. "I started thinking about London again, and I haven't thought about London in ages." I fix my gaze on a small nick in the table. "And I started thinking about you and— Do you ever think about our semester abroad?"

There's a pause before he answers, "Yeah, of course."

I meet his eyes. *Here we go*: "Do you ever think about us?"

He blinks. I sit back in my chair. He doesn't move or speak. My heels bob around under the table.

I give him a minute. A minute thirty.

Crap. I broke him.

"I. I, eh," he stutters over himself, finally breaking his silence. Blood seeps into his cheeks. "What do you mean, us?"

"I mean like you, Pilot, and me, Shane," I answer plainly.

The words hang there. I imagine them expanding to fill the space between us.

"There was no—" He stops and wipes a hand quickly down his face.

I swallow. "I've been thinking about it a lot. I thought I was past it, um, but I'm apparently—not past it?" I cock my head to the side, glancing away for a moment. *Eloquent, Shane.*

He's staring at the table now. This is embarrassing; why am I doing this again?

"I'm just here because I want to move forward from the whole *us* idea. It's still this open door in my brain," I blabber on. "It's been six years, and I'm still going back over these moments we had. So, I wanted to clarify, to know officially, that I'm just making this all up in my head, so I can stop wondering about it. Was there something there, with us, for you?

"I know this sounds ridiculous, but I was up all night thinking about the differences between how I felt then and how I've felt throughout my entire relationship with Melvin and—"

"What?" Pilot's voice cracks.

"—For me, there was always something there." I pause. "More than something, apparently, because I'm here, talking to you, out of the blue, during what future Shane might describe to friends and family as a psychotic break."

Pilot's shoulders move with what I hope is a suppressed chuckle. It takes another minute, but eventually he meets my eyes.

"Shane. I—I'm with Amy, and I was with . . ." He looks away and shakes his head. "I don't know what to say."

I heave in a breath. I can feel twenty-year-old Shane resurfacing, making a play to shut up and let this go. I close my eyes and push past her. *You have nothing to lose.*

"That's not what I asked," I reply softly.

The barista returns with our hot drinks and sets them down in front of us. I keep my eyes on Pilot. He pulls his elbows up onto the table in a frame around his drink and rests his head in his hands.

I watch the steam rising from my tea.

"I'm still with Amy, Shane," he mumbles from behind his hands. He lifts his head, fear in his eyes now. "I don't know what you're expecting from me."

"I just want to talk."

"Shane, I've been with Amy for six years," he says the words slowly, like he's proving a point. His forehead scrunches in discomfort.

"Okay, are you two engaged?" I ask quietly.

He looks into his cappuccino. "No."

"Is she the one? Are you happy?"

"I don't know!" He runs a hand through his hair in panic. "Why are you asking me this? You can't just waltz into my office and drop all this on me, Shane! What are you doing? Why aren't you talking to your boyfriend about this? It sounds like he's the guy you should be talking to!" He's almost yelling.

"*I don't know, Pies! I don't know. I didn't want to talk to him. I wanted to talk to you!*" I stop abruptly, my hand whipping up to my mouth. I can't believe I just shouted in this little coffee shop. A flush flashes up my neck, and I join Pilot in staring at the table.

I speak these next words in my best, calm, collected voice. "I'm just here for closure, and research, to put this to rest. Did I make this all up? Am I making this more than it was? Please. Just answer the question."

Pilot's silent for the longest minute known to man. Finally, he runs his hands down his face and mumbles: "You'renotmakingitup."

My head tilts, processing that jumble.

I'm sorry. I was prepared for: *Yes, you're ridiculous. Yes, you're making this all so much more dramatic than it actually was. Yes, please leave and let's never discuss this again.*

The emotion that comes out of the woodwork in response to that mumble is debilitating. It scares me. I can't speak for a full thirty seconds because I didn't know I cared this much. Christ, I'm harboring a full-blown Gatsby complex. I need to find a therapist.

I blink at him, struggling to maintain a calm front. "What?" I demand.

"You didn't make it up," he repeats, frustrated now.

"What?" Tears are pricking behind my eyes. "So—why didn't something happen?"

Because of me. Because I let fear make decisions for me. Because I've chosen to let the world push me around instead of pushing my way through the world. Why am I even with Melvin if I don't feel this weird magic with him? Because he asked me out? Because he was cute? Because he was convenient? Because he was there? The thoughts fissure through me. My shoulders roll forward with shame. *I have to break up with Melvin.*

"I was with Amy!" Pilot exclaims, breaking me from my reverie.

The force behind his voice unleashes a wave of anger in my gut. "Jesus, Pilot, you said in front of all of us that you asked her if she would put a pin in your relationship during the time you were abroad! You bought a one-way ticket to England!"

"It was hard! I was already with her, and you were there, and then she was coming, and it was complicated. Things were complicated!"

"Yeah, I get it." A tear slips out. Shit. I swipe it away, nauseated by my own complacency. Shakily, I bring the tea to my lips and attempt to take a sip. Pilot hasn't touched his cappuccino.

He opens his mouth again, eyes unfocused now. "There was something there. I was afraid of it because I was in a relationship. It was bad timing." He tries to take a sip of his cappuccino, but instead ends up setting the mug back down onto the table. "I think about it sometimes."

"About what?" Another demand.

"About what would have happened if, you know, things were different."

I can't stop blinking. This is *not* how I was expecting this to go. I knew he was still with his girlfriend. I knew I was walking into a dead end. I was expecting hard confirmation. I was expecting to be thoroughly humiliated— to kill the *what-ifs* once and for all, and move on. Melvin numbed them for a while, but before him, they were there, just as present as they are now.

He's not sure about the dead end? What do I even say now?

"Shane, anyone would think about it." His face is all squished up like I'm torturing him. "But I have a whole life with Amy."

I suck in a hard breath. "No, they wouldn't, Pilot," I say with finality.

We stare at each other for an eternity.

"Maybe we should go," I finally say.

"Okay," he says solemnly.

I push out my chair and stand. I hardly made a dent in my tea.

"I'll get the coffee." Pilot puts some cash on the table.

"Thanks." It comes out as a whisper. I'm devastated. Outraged. Annoyed. Ashamed. Frustrated. A small part of me is jumping up and down. You could make an *Inside Out* sequel out of these past forty-five minutes.

We head to the elevator, and I stab at the button. I don't know why I thought this was a good idea. Now that I know, how do I stop thinking about it? I'm supposed to just let this go? I forcefully cross my arms as we wait for the elevator.

"Bye!" the woman behind the barista counter coos. "Thanks for coming! Have fun!"

I snap my gaze to her.

"*Stop following me!*" I belt, pointing at her angrily. Pilot shoots me a horrified look.

There's a ding, and the doors in front of us slide open.

"I'm so sorry. Great place you've got here," Pilot tells the woman as we step into the elevator.

We take our spots against the two opposite walls. The doors close.

"What the heck was that?" he demands.

I study the floor. "I've seen her around before and it's getting . . ." I don't know how to talk about this without sounding bat-shit. "I don't know. I shouldn't have yelled. I'm having a day. I'm sorry."

I look up. Pilot appears to be in physical pain. I turn my attention to the button on the wall. It's in front of Pilot again.

"You didn't hit the button," I grumble.

"Shit." He jabs the lone button, and we descend in silence—until the elevator jolts violently and we shudder to a stop.

We're stopped. Oh dear god.

My eyes drop to the lone button on the wall. "Are we stuck?" I spin around.

"I don't know." Pilot gazes about, contemplating as he turns in a slow circle. "There's got to be a fire button or a phone or something."

I've already spun around in maybe seven circles in search of a fire button or a phone. I see nothing. We're stuck. *We're stuck!* Pilot catches sight of my expression and digs his phone out of his pocket.

"It's fine. We'll call the fire department or whoever it is you call when you have these problems," he reasons calmly.

"Okay, yeah, um." I lean against the wall and reach to into my purse, fumbling for my phone. "Are you dialing nine-one-one or should I?" I bite my lip.

Pilot is frowning down at his iPhone.

"What?" I ask.

"Um, I don't have service," he shares with a look of bewilderment.

"How can you not have service? We're in New York City, that's ridiculous!" I vigorously dial 9-1-1. Push the call button, whip it up to my ear.

Nothing happens.

"What the hell?" I stare at the phone in disbelief.

A new thought hits me like clean, sliding glass door to the face. "Oh my god, my interview's in, like, an hour." A sickening sense of helplessness joins the emotional tidal wave I'm riding.

"They should able to reschedule, right?" Pilot asks.

I exhale. "I don't even know. It's a really tough program." My voice comes out slow and defeated.

"Someone's going to get us out soon. That had to have caused some noise. Don't worry, we're gonna be fine," he says.

I heave a giant sigh, straighten my dress, and slide down to the floor.

28. More Than You Bargained For

It's been an hour. We're still here. We've been sitting in silence for fifty-four minutes when Pilot decides it's time to break it.

"Good thing we didn't finish our drinks, huh?" he opens.

My lips twitch. I look up from the floor and narrow my eyes.

He studies me for a moment before continuing, "You think you still feel whatever you felt before, even now?"

I blow out a breath. "Remember how we talked about what three places we would go back in time to if we could?"

"Vaguely." He's thoughtful for a moment. "We were going to hit a Beatles concert?"

"Yeah, and the Constitutional Convention, but I never came up with a third one." I fixate my gaze a few inches to the right of Pilot's head. "I think my third would be January 2011."

He stares, expression too neutral to read.

I stare back. "If you could go back and do London all over again, knowing everything you know now, would you do it?"

He looks up at the ceiling for a few beats before dropping his eyes to meet my gaze. "Maybe."

Another jolt rocks the elevator and it shifts violently to the right.

"*Holy!*" I slide across the floor toward Pilot.

"Shit," he breathes. Loud creaking noises cut at our ears. My arms clutch at the black railing running along the walls. The elevator's creaking. *What is creaking? Why is it creaking?* There's a bang. I close my eyes and scream.

1. Helpless

I wait for impact. When fifteen seconds pass and it doesn't come, I hesitantly unscrunch my eyes.

I'm sitting at a table in a light blue kitchen with a laptop in front of me. *What the—?* I jerk out of the seat, disoriented. The chair flips backward and clangs against the ground. I jump, whirling around.

No. I was in an elevator. Where's the elevator? The elevator was creaking.

My breaths come fast and shallow. I glance back at the computer on the table. On the screen, Pages is open to . . . a blog post about London? *Not possible.*

I slam the laptop shut. There's a white *Lost* Dharma Initiative MacBook decal on the back.

"Gah!" I jump away from it.

My legs tangle with the fallen chair, and in seconds I'm slamming up against the floor. Pain lances from my ass up my back. That's going to bruise.

That's my old computer up on the table. That computer's dead. Sawyer died at the end of 2011. I had to get a new one—Sayid.

"What the fuck?" I yell to no one. I smack my cheeks and shake my head, trying to clear the room from my vision.

Nothing happens. I scramble off the ground and spread my arms out in front of me, Chris Pratt raptor-style, and slowly back away from the laptop. My eyes fall to the white chair lying on the floor. My heart pounds.

"No," I insist. A scream crawls up my throat, so I let it out. It bounces around the room. Echoes around my head. I drop to the floor in a squat.

"This can't be real this can't be real this can't be real this can't be real. Inhale, exhale." I inhale and exhale. I focus on my feet. Black boots.

I was . . . I was wearing those little heels. I yelp again, leaping up off the floor. Horror washes through me. I'm also wearing jeans. Jeans! "Did someone change me?"

What happened? We were in the elevator. I was in the elevator with Pilot. In New York. *Did I pass out?* Did someone kidnap me and change my clothes and fly me to London? Where'd they get my old computer? *This can't be.* My head spins. I sink back into my squat.

There's a bang behind me as the door smashes against the wall. I spin in my squat and end up on my ass facing the door. Pilot's there looking wide-eyed and furious.

"*Shane?*"

I look up at him from my sad spot on the floor.

"What the fuck is going on? Did you set this up?" he yells.

I'm lost. I blink. "Set what up?"

His arms flail about. "What is this? Are you insane? Is this like some weird set-up you thought would be cute? Did you knock me out?"

I shake my head. "I— What?"

"Did you pay someone to recreate the flat? What the fuck?" His eyes bulge. He's scared. He looks up at the ceiling and takes two steps to collapse on the leather couch against the wall with his head in his hands.

"I don't understand," is all I manage.

He looks up at me, still wide-eyed. "I can't believe you called Atticus in on this!"

I shake my head again. "What are you talking about? What is *this*? I don't know what this is, Pilot. What the hell are you saying?"

"This!" He gestures around the room. "This creepy replica of the London flat, Shane!"

Why is he yelling at me? My eyes sting. *No crying.*

"I don't know what this is! Why the fudge and how on earth would I even go about getting a replica of a flat made? Christ, listen to yourself, you sound insane!"

I'm still on the floor, legs stretched in front of me like a rag doll. Pilot's expression clouds.

"What do you mean, Atticus?" I ask hesitantly.

"Atticus is here, he's in 'my'"—he holds up air quotes—"room."

How can Atticus be here?

"Did we get drugged?" I ask, my voice is ten pitches higher than normal. "Do you feel drugged?"

Pilot runs a hand down his face. "I . . . I don't really feel drugged . . . You mean at the café?"

"*Yes*. We were in a café." I grasp at the words. That happened.

"You only had a few sips of your tea, and I didn't even drink mine." His voice raises a few octaves. "Are you serious? You don't know what's going on right now?" His wild, panicked eyes search mine.

"*I don't know what's going on right now!*" I didn't mean to yell, but I'm having trouble staying calm.

My hands tangle up into my hair, smooshing it up and away from my face. I feel dizzy. I fold forward, letting my head hang between my legs.

"Shane?"

I stare hard at the ground. *You're fine, you're okay.* "I'll be okay in a second. Hold on," I mumble. A moment later, I feel Pilot's hand on my back.

"Here, get off the floor and sit on the couch," he says.

I lift my head to find his hand hovering in front of my face. I grab it. He pulls me off the floor. I drop his hand and fall to the couch. He sits three feet away from me on the other end of it. I'm trying to get a grip on the panic soaring around inside me, but it feels like a losing battle.

I pull my legs up and clutch them to my chest. "Someone changed my clothes."

His eyes expand as he looks down at his own clothes. "Mine too," he says, surprised. I watch his throat bob as he swallows his fear. "Maybe we should go talk to Atticus."

I bob my head okay. He bobs his head back, and we rise from the couch.

"Wait!" I say abruptly before we open the door. "We're unarmed, maybe we should be armed."

"Armed?" he says skeptically.

I run over to the utensil drawer near the sink and yank it open.

"Pilot," I say as I rifle through it and grab two steak knives, "what if someone knocked us out and brought us here?"

I pivot around, gingerly holding the utensils, and shove the drawer closed with my butt. Pain shoots through me. *Ow*, butt bruise.

"Okay," he concedes. He carefully takes a knife, holds it down by his side. I grip mine tightly and point it out in front of me.

I creep behind Pilot as he strides down the hall. The hall. It's just like the hall from London. This is the hall.

"Oh god." I stare dumbstruck at the two doors at the end of the corridor. *This can't be happening.* Pilot moves toward the left door, puts his hand on the knob, and twists.

He frowns. "Shit, I don't have a key." He instinctively drops his free hand to his pocket. A second later he pulls out a set of keys. He gapes at them, eyebrows pulled low.

"I don't know how I got these."

And then the door in front of him just swings open. Atticus stands there wearing his familiar goofy smile. "Hey, you lose your key?" He catches sight of the keys in Pilot's hand and laughs. "Apparently not." His gaze falls to me and he laughs again. "Are you cooking?"

I stare at him, confused. Why would I be cooking?

"What?" I ask.

"You're holding a knife . . ."

I gaze down at my hand, remembering. Oh yeah. I drop my knife hand so that it dangles by my side.

"Where are we, Atticus?" Pilot demands.

Atticus's expression screws up, and he turns to me, as if to share a look of bewilderment, but I just glare angrily. He brings his eyes back to Pilot.

"Uh . . . London," he says, not without sass. "What's with the theatrics?" He smiles expectantly, like he's waiting for the punch line of a joke.

Pilot and I share a look. Atticus takes this moment to walk back over to his bed where he's unpacking a suitcase full of clothes. *No . . .*

"What do you mean, we're in London?" I demand.

Atticus turns around holding a folded shirt in his hand. "Uh. London, like the city? London, England."

"How did you get us here?" Pilot asks in shock.

"What?" He whirls around with a laugh and sets down the item of clothing he's holding. "We met this morning. I'm pretty sure you both took separate planes of your own volition."

My head starts to spin again. I feel the knife fall out of my hand and thump mutedly against the carpet.

"Cut the crap, Atticus. Tell us what's going on; this isn't funny," Pilot says. He drops an arm to the doorframe, leaning against it for support. Atticus stands in the center of their room, now with his hands on his hips.

"Look, man, I don't know what you're talking about," he states simply.

"How can you not know what I'm—" Pilot's words muffle. I turn and look at the door across the hall. Head for it. A roar's building in my ears. It only takes a few steps and I'm knocking. The door creaks as someone opens it from the other side. Sahra's face appears in front of me. My jaw's gone slack.

"You misplace your key already?" she asks.

"Hey, Pilot," Sahra shoots over my shoulder. Darkness creeps at the edges of my vision. *Shit.*

2. Somebody Catch My Breath

"Shane? Shane!"

What happened? I pull my eyes open. Pilot's face floats into focus above me. He's saying my name again, anxiety spiking through his voice.

I gasp for oxygen. "Oh my god, I passed out." I squeeze my eyes shut. Everything comes slamming back. The elevator. *London?*

"I had this *Twilight Zone* dream we were back in London, and Atticus and Sahra—"

"Shane," Pilot cuts me off. I vaguely register that I'm awkwardly lying with my head in his lap, his arms stretched out under my armpits. He caught me trust-fall style. I stare past him at the white ceiling in confusion. The elevator was black.

Sahra's face pops into view.

"Oh my god," I croak.

"Shane, I got you some water. Don't worry, Atticus ran to get help," she says.

"Sahra, Atticus—" My eyes find Pilot's and he nods.

"Yeah," he says.

I sit up quickly. Pilot takes back his arms, and I scoot away. "I don't need help. I'm fine. I just need some water and some food. I'll be fine."

"Take it easy, Shane," Sahra says. I grab the glass of water from her outstretched hand and chug it down.

Frantic footsteps fly down the hall, and Atticus comes into view. He speaks through heaving breaths. "I found. Someone. They're coming."

"No, no, tell them not to come, please. I'm fine. I just need to eat some food."

"Are you sure? You were pale as heck," Atticus asks, heaving.

"Please, go call them off!"

"Um." Atticus looks from to me to Pilot. Pilot gives him a nod, and Atticus takes off running back upstairs.

I look back at Sahra, now leaning against the wall, watching me with a worried expression. "I'm fine, guys, really."

"Maybe it's the jet lag or something?" Sahra reasons. Her eyes catch on something behind me. "The hell? Why are there knives on the floor?"

I look over at Pilot, who's now sitting on the ground, staring blankly at the carpet. I turn back to Sahra.

"I'll take care of the knives. Can you, um, give us a second?" I ask quietly.

"Okay," Sahra drawls in a mildly suspicious tone. "Take it slow getting up," she adds assertively before heading back into . . . our room. She leaves the door open.

I turn to Pilot. "Pilot?"

He doesn't move or respond.

"Pies? Pilot!" I reach out and shake his shoulder. He looks up and meets my eyes, but doesn't say anything. I exhale in relief before slowly rising from the ground. I need food.

"Let's go get something to eat."

Pilot nods and gets up. I start to walk toward the staircase. It's the same staircase. When we reach the landing, we come face-to-face with the foyer of the Karlston. I mash my lips together and plow past the front desk, through the doors. I glance over my shoulder to make sure Pilot is behind me. He is, looking just as dumbstruck as I feel. We emerge onto the street with all the fancy white-pillared buildings.

I come to a standstill on the sidewalk, my head frantically swinging from left to right. Pilot stands next to me in silence. We stay that way for a minute.

Then Pilot puts a hand on my back and steers me to the right. "Food—this way."

I comply. We head toward Gloucester Road. His arm drops back to his side. We walk like aliens on a foreign planet: creeping cautiously rather than at a normal human pace, and silently ogling at our surroundings. London breathes around us. Cars swish by. Children pass on scooters. Men and women power walk home from work. Red buses race down the street.

At the end of the block we come up on a newspaper machine for the Telegraph. I stop walking and reach for Pilot's arm so he stops as well. We share a look before simultaneously stooping down to inspect the front page behind the glass. It takes me a moment to pinpoint the date. Under *The Telegraph*, on the top left in tiny print, it reads: *January 9, 2011.*

I collapse the rest of the way to the ground and land pretzel-style on the cold concrete sidewalk. Pilot grips under my upper arm and helps me back to a standing position.

"Food." He points down the street.

I nod, and we walk. Eventually we're in front of Byron's. I nod up at it and look at Pilot. He nods, and we go in. A tall, skinny, dark-haired waiter strides up to us.

"Table for two?" he asks.

I nod. Maybe I'll just speak in nods from now on.

The waiter directs us to a table near the wall. We sit. The place mats are menus. Neither of us speaks. I stare at my menu. Questions swarm my brain.

I take a deep breath. Inhale. Hold. Exhale.

I open my mouth and look up at Pilot. "I'm freaking out over here."

He meets my eyes. "Understatement of the decade."

The waiter returns. "Can I take your orders?"

I swallow and give him my Byron usual: burger and a milkshake.

"Byron burger and a chocolate milkshake," Pilot adds solemnly. The waiter leaves with our orders.

I look up at Pilot again. "So, do you think—"

"I don't know what I think."

"Do you think—? I don't really want to say it out loud."

The smallest of smiles flickers across Pilot's lips before they fall back into a blank expression.

He looks at the table. "That's insane."

"I agree."

"It can't be happening."

"It can't."

"Do you think that's what's happening?"

"It feels like it might be."

"But how could that happen?"

"I . . ." My brain struggles to put together a logical response, but the only explanations springing to mind are Harry Potter–related. "Mag . . . ic?"

"You think someone wizarded us back here?" he says in his high-pitched voice.

"You have a better theory?"

"Could we have gone through a wormhole?"

"Magic is more plausible than a wormhole," I argue.

"Wormholes are scientific."

"Magic is just science we don't understand yet."

"Shane, it's magic; that's why we can't understand it."

"Hogwarts could be real!"

"I can't believe this is a serious conversation I'm having." There's a shade of humor in his voice, but he drops his head back into his hands.

The waiter returns with our milkshakes. I pull mine forward and take a sip: delicious. I savor it for a moment before engaging again. Pilot's ignoring his own milkshake and now has his head pressed directly against the table.

"Could the elevator have been, like, a time machine?" I sound absurd.

"We didn't tell it to go anywhere. It was stuck," he mumbles into the faux wood.

"An involuntary time machine?"

Pilot stays silent.

"You should try the milkshake. It's really good," I encourage him.

He lifts his head from the table and takes a sip of the milkshake without making eye contact.

In a quiet voice, I add, "Do you think maybe we need to find our spirit guide?"

"Are you really thinking about *17 Again* right now?"

"Were you thinking that too?"

"God, this is so bizarre." His gaze falls back to the table. He's not making eye contact with me for more than a few seconds at time. I direct my gaze at the table too. *Table, do you know what's going on? Tell us your secrets!*

"Do you want to eat and then maybe look for someone who would maybe be our spirit guide?" I say as seriously as I can manage.

"That sounds like a ridiculous plan," he deadpans, and takes another sip of his milkshake, "but okay."

Our waiter returns right on cue with our burgers. My mind spins while we eat. I've thought about going back and doing study abroad again so many times. *So many.* But I never imagined what it'd be like if it actually happened. Does everything just start over from here? Will I be redoing my entire life from this point onward? A jittery feeling settles over me. This is horrifying, but also a little thrilling.

"Oh shit," I blurt out suddenly.

"What?" Pilot responds with concern.

"I don't have any money on me!" I whisper.

"Shit," Pilot pats his pockets. His face relaxes as he pulls out a wallet. "My old wallet is just chilling in my pocket."

I lean back against the seat. "Thank god." The last thing I want to do right now is dine and dash.

"Maybe my old purse is back in the kitchen near my old computer? Jeez." I press my head into my hands for a second. "This is so weird."

When we're finished with our burgers, we sit in silence until someone finally comes over with the check. It's a redheaded lady this time. Wearing a waitress outfit.

I do a double take as she puts the check on our table and quickly retreats.

"Are you kidding me?" I yelp in disbelief. I spring from the table and fumble after her.

"What is it?" I hear Pilot call after me.

The woman has stopped at a table with two older people at the back of the room. The room is divided into two different tiers, and I almost go flying as I fall up the four steps into the second tier. But I save myself, twisting in an unstable circle, and jump to a standstill beside her.

"What is going on?" I blurt in disbelief. She doesn't look at me, just continues talking to the table she's waiting on.

Pilot stops short next to me. "Shane!"

I nudge him in the side and angle my head toward the waitress. He surveys her quizzically.

"I recommend the Byron Burger," Potential Spirit Guide concludes before turning to look at me. I take in a breath to speak, but she beats me to the punch. "Now, dear, there was no need to run after me. I'll be back at your table in a moment to speak with you two."

It's definitely her. I can't believe this. *Has she been a spirit guide this entire time?*

"Go sit back at your table. I'll be there in a moment," she says.

"How can we trust that's true?" I exclaim.

"Shane," Pilot urges.

"Dear, there's no need to be rude. I'll be there in a moment," she repeats.

Pilot takes my wrist and starts slowly pulling me toward our table. I walk backward, afraid to lose visual. I've watched too many movies to make that kind of idiotic mistake. She's talking to the old couple again, taking down their burger orders.

"Shane, what are you doing?" Pilot whispers from over my shoulder when we get farther away.

"Pilot, that's her. That's our spirit guide!"

"What?" His eyes snap back to her. "Why would you think that?"

"That's the woman from the café! She served us our tea; she told us to have fun when we were leaving. And now she's here. That's her! And I've seen her before, just in random places. She was in Paris back when we were there. I thought I was going crazy!"

"Wha—?" Pilot breathes. We're now standing in front of our table, staring at the woman in the back of the room. She suddenly pivots to look at us.

I rip my gaze away. "Oh my god, she's looking. Sit down."

"Why does it matter that she's looking?"

I scramble back into my seat. "Sit down!"

"She's coming over."

"Sit down, Pilot. She said to sit down." Pilot gracefully slides back into his seat as she approaches.

My heart thrashes around. What's she going to say? What's she going to do? She comes to a stop in front of our table and smiles.

"Having fun?" she asks sweetly.

Pilot and I share a look.

"What did you do to us?" he asks in a shaky voice.

She answers swiftly, "This is what you wanted."

I blurt out the first thing that comes to mind: "Are you a wizard?"

Pilot's gaze whips over to me. He looks angry again. Why is he angry at me?

"Rewrite your past," says the woman.

"What do you mean? Are you saying this is real? We're in two thousand fucking eleven?" Pilot demands.

"*Deathly Hallows Part Two* hasn't been released yet," I add.

"You had no right to do that!" Pilot yells.

"There's a reset option if you so desire." She smiles at him.

"What?" He juts his head forward toward her for emphasis.

Airplane Lady/Starbucks barista/waitress/spirit guide continues calmly, "If in three days you don't want to continue down this path, a reset button can be found during your Rome venture."

"And Miley Cyrus hasn't released 'Wrecking Ball,'" I say.

"What do you mean, a reset button?" Pilot inquires skeptically.

She folds her hands together. "A portable button. If you choose to push it, you'll go back to the elevator. This opportunity will be lost and forgotten."

I swallow hard. "That sounds awfully magical. Is this magic or is this science?"

"It is what you make it." She smiles again.

"Where will the button be?" Pilot demands.

"It will be placed in Rome this weekend."

"But where?"

"You'll have to find it."

"Like a treasure hunt?" I sound like a curious seven-year-old asking her parents a question.

"We'll have to find it? Are you kidding? What is this, a game to you?"

"Have fun on your journey." She leans over to pick up our check and some cash that Pilot must have thrown on the table when I went running after her.

I catch her hand, placing my own over it. "Wait, will you be here to talk when we need you? Are you going to disappear in a minute? Are you technically our spirit guide?"

She heaves a great breath and looks me straight in the eyes. "Child, this isn't a film; this is reality."

Chills run down my spine. She pulls her hand out from under mine and walks away.

"That's not an answer at all!" I yell after her. I make to jump from my seat, but I can't get up. It's like I'm glued down. My ass is stuck. The chair won't move. I'm stuck. I yank and squirm.

Pilot tries to leap from his own seat, but it would appear he's found himself in a similar situation.

"What the hell?" he blurts.

We watch helplessly as she disappears into what I can only assume is the kitchen at the back of the restaurant. And then I fall sideways from my chair onto the cold tile floor, and Pilot flies up to his feet.

He breezes by me toward the kitchen. I scramble off the floor, my knees burning from the impact of the tile, and hurry after him. The whole restaurant gapes at us.

Pilot charges through the kitchen door, and I'm in there with him a second later.

Burgers sizzle on a giant grill a few feet away and a dark-haired man in his thirties stands behind it. A few other people bustle about chopping vegetables and preparing salads. Our spirit guide is nowhere to be seen.

"This is exactly what would happen in a film. What a load of bullshit," I growl.

Grill Man looks up with a confused expression. "What are you two doing back here?"

"S-sorry, we thought we . . ." I stutter, "um, and so we came to look, but—"

"You have to get out of here," Grill Man scolds.

Pilot shakes his head that way you do when you're having an argument with someone who's being ridiculous, and you can't deal with them anymore so you just shake your head and turn away. Pilot's mad, but I can't help but feel a trickle of excitement. He pivots out of the kitchen, and I follow at his heels.

"Pilot," I start as we descend the steps at the center of the room.

"Shane, I can't talk right now."

"But—"

A waiter up ahead is saying things to us. I'm too distracted to listen or respond. We barrel past him, toward the door, and back out onto the sidewalk. It's a nice night. Pilot heads in the direction of the Karlston with his hands stuffed in his pockets. He keeps his gaze focused straight ahead. I have to power walk to keep pace with him.

My mind spins back to our first night here: the grocery store, there's no food in the kitchen. That almost kiss. The Flat Three Taboo game we initiated.

I speak up as we round the block toward fancy-white-house lane, "Pies, we're going back to a kitchen with no food. Maybe we should grab something little, at least to have as a snack during the flat bonding game? If everything's the same as before, I should have a bunch of British cash in my purse that my mom gave me right before she dropped me at the airport. I can pay you back ASAP."

"I can't."

He doesn't turn to look at me. He keeps on toward the Karlston, walking even faster now. I stop moving and stare at his back as he gets farther and farther away. *What the hell?*

My hands curl up into fists against my jeans. I sprint to catch up to him. I'm out of breath when I grab his arm.

"Pilot!" I gasp-yell.

He turns to me with a flat expression. "Why are you out of breath?"

"I—" I suck in more air. "I fell behind, so are we going to get the flat together and play Taboo tonight? That's what we did last time we . . . did this," I say in my normal tone of voice.

"I'm not feeling up to it," he responds. There's attitude lurking behind those words.

"What is wrong right now?" I demand.

"Really?" he says to the sidewalk.

"I mean, yeah, apparently we've been thrown back in time, and yes, that's completely mind-boggling, and in a way, terrifying, and I understand being in shock. I understand being scared and uncomfortable, but what the hell is this drastic change in tone? Why are you acting like you're angry at me?"

He turns away, walking toward the Karlston again.

"Pilot!" I yell.

He pivots. "I am mad at you, Shane!" The words blow out of him, and I stumble back a few steps in surprise.

He rolls his head in an irritated little circle. "We barely know each other anymore. I didn't ask for this." He takes a breath. "*You did.* You drop in unannounced after six years without so much as a conversation. You just showed up at my office! *You* wanted to go for coffee. *You* wanted to dredge up the past. *You* needed closure. I didn't have a say in any of this." He throws his hands up.

I strain not to blink. We are at the foot of the Karlston steps now. He turns away. I find the control to spit out one more sentence before tears compromise my voice. "How can you blame this on me?"

He doesn't look back. He takes the steps two at a time and disappears inside the building. I look up at the sky for a moment before spinning away from the Karlston. I'm not going back there without groceries.

Halfway down the block toward Tesco, I realize I don't have any money. I pivot again and hurry back to the Karlston.

"Student ID, please," requests the security guard without looking up from his computer. Crap.

"I'm so sorry, I left it downstairs in my purse. I forgot my whole purse. Can I go grab it?" He makes eye contact. Immediately his expression softens; he can tell I'm crying.

"Go ahead, that's fine." He hastily waves me forward like I'd proposed a conversation about my period.

I run into the kitchen. It's empty. Thank the time-travel lord who brought me here. Sure enough, my old cross-body is lying on the floor, under the table. I pick it up, sling it across my chest, and tromp back out into the night for groceries.

When I return an hour later, I find Sahra on her computer in our room. I float the idea of heading to the kitchen to chill, and she's up for it. As she gathers herself, I dash across the hall and knock on the boys' door. Atticus pulls it open, grinning.

I smile back. "Hey! Um, so we're gonna go hang out in the kitchen and play some games, do some flat bonding. Want to join us?"

"Of course!" Atticus exclaims. He turns to Pilot. I catch a glimpse of him on the bed with his guitar. "Pilot, did you hear?" Atticus adds.

"Yeah, man, go ahead," he says without looking up.

"Okay." Atticus looks at me expectantly. I linger awkwardly, wanting to talk to Pilot alone. Across the way, Sahra emerges from our room.

"Go ahead to the kitchen. I'm going to get my iPod. I'll be there in a minute!" I tell them both. They head off. I catch Pilot's door before it closes and pull myself into the frame.

"Are you going to come?" I prompt.

He still doesn't lift his head. "I don't think so."

"But this was our flat bonding night."

"No, thanks, Shane. I think you should go."

"I just don't feel right about—"

"Please leave." There's force behind the words, and it hits me right in the gut. I halt midsentence and take a step back into the hall.

"Fine." I grab the knob and slam the door in place. I take a deep breath, run into my room, grab my iPod, and head for the kitchen.

3. I Thought Time Was an Hourglass Glued to the Table

Going to sleep after finding yourself six years in the past and waking up in the same predicament is a fucking trip. When I open my eyes, I'm still here, sharing a room with twenty-year-old Babe and Sahra.

Getting ready as past Shane is unsettling. My hair's at least eight inches longer than it was when I woke up yesterday in New York. My makeup bag is severely lacking—past Shane doesn't even own foundation—and all these old clothes in my London closet feel bland and out-of-date.

Babe and I chitchat endlessly about Disney World and movies on the way to Greenwich. I already know half the things she's going to say before she says them. It's disconcerting. She's one of my closest friends in 2017, but this Babe doesn't know me yet. I'm dying to discuss all the time-travel weirdness, but unfortunately the one person who'd understand is actively keeping his distance.

Pilot remains quiet and withdrawn all morning. He positions himself next to Atticus and Sahra in our group huddle as we float down the Thames. He stands on the opposite end of our group pictures. He physically walks to get to the opposite side of our lineup when I ask a stranger to take a group picture of us in front of the Maritime museum. Whenever I get close, he starts talking about nothing to Atticus.

I re-experience the day in a constant state of déjà vu. Things are slightly different because of Pilot's mood, but for all intents and purposes, Flat Three has the same Greenwich adventure. After exploring the Royal Observatory, it's time to head down to the pub where we had burgers and decided to go to Rome.

The five of us settle in at the same wooden table. Because Pilot's been lagging behind, he's forced to take the last remaining seat: the one across from me. My lips flip up into a snarky grin as he plops into the chair.

The waitress comes around, distributing waters and taking our orders. I so vividly remember living this moment: how tempted I was to take out my camera and ogle at all the pictures we took today, how Atticus laughed when he became the fifth person in a row to order the same burger for dinner, the way my heart stuttered when Pilot asked us if we wanted to travel while we're here. That question sparked my first taste of wanderlust and opened me up to possibilities I never even considered to be *possibilities*.

Pilot's currently staring past me at nothing. I try to catch his eyes so I can roll mine at him. Babe's watching and shoots a confused glance between the two of us before taking a sip of her water.

"So!" she starts cheerily, tossing her dark hair over her shoulder.

I straighten in my seat. "So," I echo, smiling at her and shifting to look at everyone. "Do you guys want to travel while you're here?"

"Oh my gosh, yes!" Babe exclaims.

"Definitely," Sahra asserts.

"Yeah, I hope I can find time to squeeze in some travel, but the theater track is really intense," Atticus explains.

The four of us turn to Pilot for his response. He's leaning against the table, head propped up on his arm. He treats me to a mildly irritated look before facing the rest of the group.

"Yeah," he answers tiredly.

"Great. Well, we should go to Rome for the weekend!" I say cheerily.

"Yes!" Babe agrees.

"I'm in," Sahra adds.

Atticus explains that he can't join us because of his internship.

"Pilot, are you coming?" Babe asks him carefully.

He scratches his head before responding blandly, "Yeah."

"Yay!" she cheers before raising her glass of water. "To Rome for the weekend!"

Sahra, Atticus, and I raise our glasses.

"To Rome for the weekend!" I repeat. I never carried around water bottles during this era, but nowadays I have one on me at all times. How did I live? Apparently in a constant state of dehydration. I end up chugging half my glass before I set it down. Across the table, Pilot's watching me carefully. His mouth twitches.

I blink at him. "*What?*" I ask.

"Nothing. I was just noticing how soft the landing was there," he says.

My eyes dart from the water to him. A smile tugs at my lips. "Yeah, I guess some dude yelled at me about the way I put down my drinks six years ago, and I've since gained a new respect for glassware."

"I don't think he yelled at you."

"Some guy yelled at you about the way you put down your drink?" Babe jumps in, appalled.

I drop my gaze to stifle a laugh. When I look back up, Pilot's smiling. He's looking at the table, but he's smiling.

I shoot Babe a grin. "It was nothing, I was exaggerating."

Back in the kitchen, we buy our plane tickets for Rome. Babe's Googling for the inn we're going to stay at, and Sahra's relaxed on the couch with her laptop. Pilot's in the seat across from me. He's trying to catch my attention over our computer screens. He gives a little jerk to the right with his head. I look to the right at the blue wall and furrow my brow. He does it again, stands up, and strides toward the door. I stand to follow. My chair starts to fall, but I scramble forward and forcefully set it upright. "You stay there."

"I *can't win* with these stupid-ass chairs," I find myself hissing as I step out of the kitchen. "Even when I get up carefully, it's like it doesn't matter, they still flip over just to piss me off."

Pilot's in the hall, leaning against the wall, arms crossed over his chest.

I fall against the opposite wall. "What's up?"

He visibly inhales. "How are we supposed to go off looking for some mystical reset button when we're in Rome with Babe and Sahra?"

I shove some hair behind my ears. "I don't know. I figured we'd figure it out as we go. Maybe we can break away from them at some point?"

"Don't you think it would have been easier not to tell them about Rome at all and go without them so we can fix this?"

I let out a frustrated sigh. "Well, she said *the Rome trip,* which alludes to the trip we previously took, and they were there, so maybe I didn't want to take any chances on changing the circumstances and the button not being there because of it."

I watch as he nervously runs a hand through his hair and looks past me at the wall for a moment. I turn to go back into the kitchen.

"I'm sorry I yelled at you yesterday," he says quietly.

I turn back around, crossing my arms. He uncrosses his and stuffs them in his pockets. I stay silent until he looks me in the eye.

"You know this is all a big shock for me too," I tell him.

He presses his hands farther into his pockets. "It just felt like, in the moment, you were trying to . . ."

My expression hardens, and he speeds up, "I was an ass. I'm sorry." He pauses, glancing at the floor for a moment. "I'm just as bad as the chairs."

I grunt a laugh and look away.

He sidesteps, his eyes finding mine again with a new sincerity. "Can we start over?" he asks.

I exhale, relief coursing through me. I turn and walk around the corner, stay there for a count to three, and stride back to where Pilot is still standing, now clearly confused.

"Hi, Shane Primaveri, almost doctor, hater of kitchen chairs, lover of watermelon, French toast, and writing." I hold out my hand.

He reaches out to take it. "Pilot Penn, no association with the Fountain Pens."

We shake. "So the Ballpoint Pens, then?" I add diplomatically.

He nods vigorously, eyes alight. "Exactly."

4. I'm the First in Line

January 12, 2011 (take two)

Mom and Dad,

We haven't really talk—talked in a while, so it's extra—weird to be writing these to you again. This is when everything really went to shit—for a couple of months, I stopped worrying about making you happy. I've been trying to make you happy for six years now, hoping somehow that would make me happy too, but I don't think it's working. You're not really happy with me because I'm not happy with you because I'm not happy with me.

XO,
2017 Shane

My mom's parents used to have this old-fashioned record player. We don't see them as much as I see my dad's family. But, when we did visit, I used to look forward to playing with that record player. Hunting through their album collection until I found *Mary Poppins*. Carefully pushing the record onto the device. Positioning the needle like my life depended on it. Grinning ear to ear as music magically began to play. Spending hours dancing around their living room to "Supercalifragilisticexpialidocious." This morning I got up and re-attended the first class of my abroad semester. The professor gave us our first blank postcards and the famous first-sentence writing prompts. I honestly don't remember the last time I sat down to write something that wasn't gastro-related. It felt like being back in that living room. Setting the needle down on a record full of music that lights you up from the inside.

We have two nights before we fly out to Rome. I'm sitting at the kitchen table, staring at the start of my first study abroad blog post. I'm not sure what to do with it. Rewrite what I wrote the first time around? I close out of the blog and open the file with the outline I have all prepped for my *great American novel*. Scrolling through it sparks excitement in my chest. I open a blank page and start typing, because honestly, *why not?*

I have three thousand words down on the page when Pilot strides into the room with a sandwich.

"Hey." He pulls out the chair across from me and sets down his food. "You writing?" He raises an eyebrow.

I bite back a smile and yank out my headphones. "As a matter of fact, I am."

He grins to himself, settling into the seat.

"This is so weird . . . going to class again." He shakes his head and peels the cling wrap from his food.

"Agreed, but I kind of had fun." I shrug.

"I probably should have cut mine, but Sahra's in the class so it felt"—he looks up, searching for the right word—"suspicious? Skipping."

I chuckle. "Yeah, I have this uncontrollable need to be good in school, so I didn't even think about cutting." Maybe I would have considered it if someone had brought up the idea before I got there, but not anymore. I forgot how much I actually enjoyed going to this class.

He takes a bite of sandwich, focusing somewhere on the wall behind me. "You remember what we did today the first time around?"

I close my laptop and give him my full attention. "Of course. Do you?"

He meets my gaze. "The Beatles store."

"Got those gorgeous playing cards."

"They were a great find."

"That they were." I bob my head nostalgically. "Remember the Russian Beatles nesting dolls?"

He snorts. "Those were fantastic."

"I love that they're a thing." I bite my lip a moment, hesitant to push this any further. "You want to go?"

Pilot sucks in a breath and leans his head forward. He runs his now interlocked hands up from the base of his neck over his hair and back down to the table in front of him before looking at me again.

"Uh . . . I don't think so, you know . . . We should probably keep our distance for now, ride out these last few days, find the button, get out of here."

I nod, absently. "Oh, yeah, okay, um, I'm gonna go find something for dinner."

I carefully stand up out of my chair with one hand locked on the back so it can't possibly fall over. I pull my book bag off the floor, snatch my laptop from the table, and head onto the streets of London to clear my head. Instead of taking my usual right toward Gloucester Road, I hang a left toward Hyde Park, hiking my way toward the main street near the Odeon and Orange cell phone place.

Twenty minutes later, I've picked up some new makeup that past Shane didn't know she was missing, and I'm crossing the street to TK Maxx. I find myself a black backpack with three different compartments and padded straps. Book bags are for travel rookies. I'll be backpacking it from now on.

Later, as a flat, we all go to the pub down the block. We play 21. Atticus brings up Pilot's girlfriend. Babe is shocked. Pilot looks at the table and quickly changes the subject.

5. Reaching in the Dark

The hustle and bustle of Victoria Station streams around me as I make haste for the Gatwick Express. My backpack bounces lightly against me as I weave in and out of swarms of travelers. I giddily make eye contact with strangers as they stride by. Some smile back, a lot of them abruptly look down. I don't care, I'm feeling wonderfully empowered right now—free.

I haven't been able to stop grinning since I left the *Packed!* office. I just re-interviewed for my internship. I forgot how cool the office was. I forgot how much I liked Wendy. When she teased the idea of writing a piece about studying abroad in London, my heart flew around in my chest all over again. Now, I can't stop picturing my name under an article in their magazine. I've written some stuff for scientific journals these past four years . . . but I don't know. I don't know why it feels so different for me with this travel magazine. But it does. The scientific journals felt like an obligation. An obstacle I had to hurdle for my impending medical career. This feels like a goal. A finish line I'd like to cross.

It's not till our plane has taken off and we're up there in the atmosphere that I remember *the button*. I'm not just going to Rome for the weekend. I'm headed on a wild goose chase for a mystical button.

We've been flying for about forty minutes. I'm currently treating myself to a free mini bottle of white wine. Beside me is the same drunk couple as last time. The two of them are chattering away, but all I can hear is the roar

232

of the plane in my ears. The uncaged feeling from earlier saps with every passing mile. Pilot's a few rows back in a middle seat across the way. I thoughtfully swig another mouthful of wine before turning to steal a glance at him. When I hitch myself up and twist around, I find him looking right at me.

Instinct is to drop back into the chair, but I fight it. *I don't have to hide.* Instead, I raise my eyebrows. Pilot dips his chin hello before dropping eye contact. I slide back into my chair, finish off this mini wine, and unbuckle my seat belt.

I stand the best I can to catch the attention of the drunk couple. "I'm sorry. Could I get out, please?"

Once free, I take the few wobbly steps to Pilot's row. He watches me curiously. The middle-aged woman sitting in the aisle seat next to him looks up at me. I put a hand to my heart.

"Hi!" I knit my brow. "Sorry to bother you. I just, that's my brother, and he's holding it together right now, but he has a crippling fear of flying. I can see he's having a really hard time, and I was wondering if you wouldn't mind switching seats with me so I can be next to him? I can calm him down when he's hyperventilating and stuff." I jut out my bottom lip.

She looks to her right, at Pilot. My eyes flit to him as well. He's gaping like I just grew two new heads.

The woman turns back to me. "Oh my goodness, of course we can switch. What seat were you in?"

I feel crappy about the lying, but I need to take advantage of this Babe-and Sahra-less time to discuss our current predicament. Thirty seconds later, I flop into the aisle seat next to Pilot with my backpack. Up ahead, the nice middle-aged lady scoots in past Tweedledee and Tweedledrunk to my window seat.

"What the hell was that?" Pilot asks.

Hmm, how to begin? I angle myself sideways so I can see him more easily. *Hi, Pies, so I'm not so sure about this reset button thing.*

I cluck my tongue and loose a sigh. "Pies, we haven't done shawarma yet." This is valid.

"What?" His eyebrows furrow.

"We didn't. Get. Shawarma this week," I try to enunciate, but my words bleed a bit more than I'd like. *Am I tipsy from that baby wine?*

He swishes his head from left to right. "So . . ."

Where am I going with this?

"So . . . we should have gotten shawarma."

"Did you switch seats to get this very important message to me before we landed? Do you need shawarma when we land?" he asks blandly.

My head tilts slightly to the left as I consider this. I burst out laughing.

"Shane?" he asks calmly.

I compose myself. "I came over here because I wanted to talk to you."

"About shawarma," Pilot says, eyebrows raised.

I choke on another laugh. "You remember in *Avengers*—you saw *Avengers*, right?"

He nods.

"Remember when Iron Man was like, *Let's get shawarma*, and then they did get shawarma?"

"Yeah." His lips turn up.

"Yeah, all I could think about when that happened was the amazing shawarma we had here."

"Shwenesdays," Pilot confirms nostalgically.

"And now it's all mainstream, you know. Everyone's all, *Yeah, shawarma like in* The Avengers, and I'm all like, *No, I knew about shawarma before it was cool.*"

He closes his eyes and shakes his head. "You know, you're completely right. How dare the Avengers want shawarma; we invented that."

I keel forward, cackling at the angst in his voice. "Yes! Totally ripped us off. But, there ain't no shawarma like Beirut Express shawarma! Because Beirut Express shawarma is da best!" I sing-talk.

Pilot's expression flatlines as he executes a dramatic blink: "Did you just make a random S Club 7 reference?"

My eyes ignite. "Did you just pick up on an S Club 7 reference?"

He squints, grinning now. "Touché."

I smile. "Have you had good shawarma since London?"

"Are we back to this?" he asks the seat in front of him.

234

"I've had okay shawarma, but not excellent shawarma, and I've tried like five different shawarma places."

He twists to face me. "You've said the word *shawarma* at least fifty times since you've sat down, and you've been here for like three minutes."

I smother another bout of laughter. "Well, I just wanted to say that we should have gotten shawarma."

"Sorry, so to clarify, you made a woman switch seats so we could discuss shawarma."

"Well, I came over so we could chat because we're about to go on some ridiculous mission through a foreign country to find a button to reset ourselves forward in time, and we haven't really thought out a plan."

"I tried to suggest a plan, and you said we could just"—he raises his hands to do air quotes—"'figure it out.'"

I lean forward. "Well, I was still kind of reeling from the whole we're-back-in-time reveal. I needed time to process."

"What is this conversation?" He scoffs in disbelief.

"What do you think we should do about the button?"

"We're going to find the button, and use it, so we can go back to our normal lives."

I click my tongue playfully. "But how will we find it? I'm assuming it's going to be somewhere we went the first time around."

"Yeah, that makes sense."

"Do you think she left clues maybe?" I widen my eyes dramatically.

His forehead scrunches up. "No?"

"If there were clues, this would like be just like *The Da Vinci Code!*" I beam. Pilot laughs toward the ceiling and I deflate. "Oh yeah, I forgot you haven't read that one."

His lips twitch. "Actually, I did read it a few years ago."

"What?" My heart does a little jig.

"Yeah, I've read all his books now." Color floods his cheeks. "You raved about them enough while we were here."

"Oh, man." I look at the seat in front of me while I process this. "Okay, come on, don't lie, the prospect of a baby *Da Vinci Code* is kinda exciting." I grin. He smirks back.

We fall into silence after theorizing a bit more about the mysterious button. I'm hoping it looks like one of those Staples *Easy* buttons. That would be nice and clear. But what if it looks like something else—like a random sewing button on the ground or if it's camouflaged to look like its surroundings? She wouldn't do that, right? That's too complicated.

I lose myself in button-centric thoughts, and then we're landing. I'm treated to a new swell of dread in my gut as we descend.

"You okay?" Pilot asks quietly.

Great, Pilot can sense my dread.

"Yeah, this is all still freaking me out a little bit," I whisper.

"Hey." He puts his hand on my knee. My eyebrows jerk up. "Just a little longer, and we're going back home."

I swallow hard. *Sentence so unhelpful in quest to ease dread. But hand on knee making heart perform "Swan Lake" across chest cavity.* A jolt shakes the plane, vibrating up through our seats as we touch down. Here we go.

6. What a Lovely Night

Babe tugs at my arm, pulling me back as we make our way through the Rome airport. I slow my pace to match hers. We trail a healthy distance behind Pilot and Sahra.

"Shane!" she stage-whispers. "What happened on the plane? I saw you move to the seat next to Pilot. You made someone switch?"

Shit, I forgot I'm not invisible. "Oh, um, yeah, I needed to talk to him."

"Is something going on between you two?"

"Ah . . ." I run through potential excuses as to why I would have had to sit next to Pilot: *I found out he stole my wallet. I accidentally stole his wallet. I lost my wallet, and I thought he might know where my wallet was.*

"Umm . . ." *Maybe he needed a piece of gum. Something with gum?* "Gum!"

"Gum?" she repeats skeptically.

"He lost his gum. And I had gum, and he wanted a piece."

"You made a woman switch seats so you could give Pilot a piece of gum?"

"I, yeah."

"How did you know he needed gum?"

"I . . . looked over and saw that he wasn't chewing any."

"You didn't ask me if I'd like gum."

"Uh—"

"Shane, is something going on between you two?" Babe demands.

I make a split-second decision. "Um, kind of."

"Oh my god," she gasps. "Are you serious? Are you like—"

"No! I mean, I don't know. It's so new so nothing's happened yet, but something's kind of happening, a little," I ramble. This way, when we need a few moments alone to be mysterious time travelers and look for the dubious button, maybe Babe will more easily give us some space.

She juts her chin forward, eyes doubling in size.

"I, um, I'll keep you updated. I don't know what it is yet," I fumble.

"Please do! Oh Mylanta! This is insane. He has a girlfriend!" she exclaims quietly.

My stomach drops. *Crap.* I'm too worried about the damn button to remember the girlfriend. Backtrack. "Yeah, no, I'm exaggerating. Nothing's happened, so don't worry about it."

"But something might happen?" she inquires dramatically.

"No, I mean, it's just a stupid crush I have on him, that's it. He's not available. Nothing's happening."

"But I think he might also have a thing for you!" she continues. Up ahead, Pilot throws a glance back in our direction.

"Whaaat!" I say dismissively.

"Yeah, I've caught him looking at you a bunch of times these past few days."

Pilot throws another look this way, clearly trying to get my attention.

"Look, he's doing it right now, Shane!"

"Shhhhh!" I exclaim. Babe chuckles as we power walk to catch up with the other half of our group.

When I'm on his right, Pilot turns to me. "Do you think we have to search the airport?"

"No." I glance around. "This isn't Rome; this is the airport," I answer conclusively. We cannot search an entire airport for *a button.*

"Okay."

"Okay," I echo.

I grin as our bags thump to the floor of the inn. This room's just as happy and colorful as I remember.

"Shall we food?" I suggest eagerly.

"Yeah, definitely, but first, I kind of want to explore the Colosseum. We just drove by it. It's got to be super-close," Sahra proposes.

"Oh my gosh, let's! We can get some great pictures," Babe adds, digging the camera out of her bag.

"You guys go ahead. I'll meet you out there. I need to make a call," Pilot says quickly. He plops down onto a bed.

"Okay," Sahra agrees easily. She looks to Babe and me. "I'm gonna head out and look around. I'll be right outside." She picks up her purse and marches out the door.

"You need to make a call?" I shoot Pilot a confused look as I sling my pack off the floor and back onto my shoulder.

"Do we even have service here?" Babe asks.

Pilot raises his eyebrows pointedly. I drop my bag back to the floor.

"Okay," I say. "I'll stay behind too. You shouldn't be walking around alone in a foreign city." Pilot scoffs.

"Maybe we should just all wait, then," Babe adds. She glances anxiously from me to Pilot and back to the door. I give her an it's-fine-go-on nod. She doesn't move.

"It's fine, go ahead," I encourage her forcefully. "We'll be right there."

"Shane," she says with concern.

"Babe." I shoot her another look.

"Okay. I guess we'll meet you at the Colosseum." Babe backs out of the room, wearing an extremely mom-like expression. The door closes very slowly behind her.

I turn back to Pilot. He's already on the floor, rummaging under his bed.

"Pies, don't we want to eat before we go tearing the room apart?" I put my hands on my hips. He's prying around near Babe and Sahra's bed now.

"Shane, this is important. Come on, let's find this thing." His voice is muffled by the blankets he's tearing through. I'm too hungry to argue, so I search the room halfheartedly.

Ten silent minutes later—no button. Added bonus: Now it looks like the room was ransacked by thieves. Pilot straightens near the door, study-ing the mess with crossed arms and a flustered expression. I pull the sheets back up onto my bed and walk over to stand next to him.

I break the silence. "Well, that was fun."

"It's not here."

"It would seem that way."

Pilot sighs. "This is going to be difficult."

"Agreed." We stare at the room a beat longer. "Food?"

"Food."

We meet Sahra and Babe down the street, outside the Colosseum, and head to the little trattoria I remember from Rome: Take One. I keep my purse on all through dinner, just to be safe. We all share a pitcher of Italian wine. I get my usual: ravioli. The four of us cackle and chat about YU—how we're so lucky to be here in Rome for the weekend, while all the other poor schmucks are still in New York. College-era nostalgia settles over me. I feel it like a tangible thing on my skin. The memories are sticky. I try to shake them off with laughter and wine, but they cling to my face, arms, legs, until I'm just one big collage of random moments, decisions, and regrets.

The four of us grow quiet as we mosey our way back to the room. It's late, but I'm not the slightest bit tired. Instead, I'm jittery and anxious like I've had too much caffeine. When Babe hauls open the giant castle door with the appropriately ancient key, I stay rooted at the foot of the shallow stairs. Babe slips inside, followed closely by Sahra. Pilot puts his foot in the door and turns back to hold it open for me.

"Coming?"

"I don't really want to."

Pilot disappears into the inn. He reappears a few seconds later, letting the door shut behind him. He skips down the steps, hands jammed in his pockets.

"What's up?" he says with a tilt of the head.

I scuff my boot along the ground. "I don't know. I mean, we're in Rome. We're in Rome again . . . and we may be leaving." My voice wavers. I clear my throat. "We could be leaving at any moment, and I just want to make the most of being here. I don't want to go to sleep if there's a chance we might be gone tomorrow morning."

Pilot takes a few steps down the street and looks back at me. "Then let's stay out and explore."

7. There's a Glow Off the Pavement

We wander quietly through narrow, cobblestoned alleys, full of old buildings and crammed with tiny parked cars.

"So, how much have you thought about time travel since we got here?" Pilot quips.

"Let me think. I thought about it a few days ago, and again today, so . . . just about every other minute since we got here." I smile sweetly.

He snorts.

I shake my head. "*Breaking Bad* hasn't ended here, and *Game of Thrones* hasn't even started! I saw a sign for it on a bus when I was walking to class the other day. It's mind-boggling!" I vent. "Have you seen *Hot Tub Time Machine?*"

He narrows one eye. "Yes?"

"You know how they release all these hit songs before they were actually released?" I grin. "How funny would it be to do a cover of 'Wrecking Ball' and put it on YouTube and just see what happens? We could do that!"

Pilot huffs. "While we're at it, why don't we film our own pirated version of *Deathly Hallows Part 2* and release it in May?"

"Pies, they've already released a trailer. Everyone would know it wasn't real."

A real smile spreads across his face.

We walk on: down more tiny streets, past closed shops, occasionally bumping shoulders.

I scuff the cobblestones with my foot. "So, why did you stop doing music?"

Pilot takes a moment to ponder this. "I mean, I worked on it a lot the summer after London. Did some little gigs in New York."

"I thought you were going to invite us to those so we could come watch you play? We never heard from you. Even when we sent messages . . ."

He sighs. "It was complicated."

"The album you released in September that year was great. Babe and I had a little listening party in our living room when you uploaded it. I know we tweeted you, but we never got to talk about it in person."

"Damn, a musical endorsement from a doctor. This is big," he says through a small smile.

I push him sideways. "Shut up."

He laughs, but then in a more serious voice, he says, "Really though, thanks. That was my last one."

"Why, though? What happened? What happened to the Swing Bearers?" I smile.

He shrugs. "I don't know. I got busy. Senior year was tough, and I had a lot to juggle. It's not like people were really listening."

"*We* were listening. You could have made them listen! I could have helped. I can help. You can start a YouTube channel! I was a blogger, I'm internet savvy. YouTube can open up so many other opportunities. I've seen it happen! We could kick it off with a 'Wrecking Ball' video, and then you can just perform your originals after it goes viral."

He grins at the ground.

"Do you miss it?"

"Of course. I mean, I still play sometimes on the side."

"Do you miss writing?" I ask.

He slows to a stop and looks at me hard, with his lips mashed together. Heat flashes down my neck.

"Do you?" he asks.

I hold his eyes. "Yeah I really, really do. I didn't realize how much till I went to class on Wednesday. I've been dragging myself through the motions of what I thought I needed to do for so long, I forgot how great it feels to do what I *want to do*." I shake my head slightly. "I miss that feeling you get when you create something, you know?"

He drops his gaze, and we start moving again. He nods slowly. "I do know."

We emerge into an open square—to my surprise, rising before us in the night is the Pantheon. I suck in a breath, taking it in. It's colossal and extra-impressive without the usual sea of tourists. I stride ahead, skirting around the fountain at the center of the square to stand right before the hulking structure.

Pilot's jacket brushes up against my arm a minute or so later. I smile at him. "I wish I had my camera. I could get some damn good night photos right now."

He walks off behind me and takes a seat on the wide steps that encircle the fountain. I shuffle over to join him, crossing my ankles straight out in front of me and leaning back on my palms.

"We haven't really talked about what happened in the café the other day," he says quietly.

My cheeks warm. I try and keep my eyes on the Pantheon.

"How many guys have there been since study abroad?"

I resist the urge to scoff. "Why are you asking?"

"Because you've been with other guys. You've had other crushes. You don't still feel . . . that way," he says hesitantly.

I turn to him. "What?"

"Don't pretend you're not attractive and smart and funny and . . ." He trails off. "You don't still feel that way," he repeats insistently.

I meet his eyes, which is difficult, because a windstorm of anxiety just materialized in my chest. How do I explain how rare it is for me to feel so ferociously about *a crush*?

"Pilot, I've dated people, but I've had one actual boyfriend . . . Melvin. And I don't feel the way I'm supposed to." I pause, picturing Melvin at the kitchen table, that last morning we spent together, going on about his latest medical research project while I fiddled around with the poached eggs he made me. He was trying to do something nice, making breakfast. But we've been together for four years. Why doesn't he know I don't like eggs?

"I'm gonna have to break up with him when I get back." I curl forward and hug my legs to my chest. How do you break up with someone you've been with for so long?

Pilot's quiet.

"Of course, I've had other crushes, but I've never randomly shown up at their place of work." I stare at a stone on the ground and loose a bemused huff. "I'm a mess. I can't believe I randomly showed up at your place of work."

"You're just going through some stuff. Come on, you're about to graduate at the top of your medical school class. That's unbelievable. You're going to be a real, live doctor."

"Yeah, but do I even like being a doctor?" It comes out like a plea. Panic sweeps through me.

I don't allow myself to think things like that, let alone say them aloud. It's a second before I feel like I can breathe again. "I don't know. I thought I was okay with it. It makes my mom really happy, but I'm, I don't know. I thought it'd make me happier. But I feel like I'm losing myself a little bit."

I stare blankly at the Pantheon. Pilot doesn't respond.

"So, in conclusion, yes, tons of other guys," I add.

He grins, shaking his head. "I don't believe you."

I exhale a breath and let go of my legs, relaxing back into a normal sitting position. As he meets my eyes, a memory resurfaces. An embarrassing, repressed, secret chapter of my Pilot chronicles.

"There was this one guy I met the summer after study abroad."

He raises his eyebrows, the hint of a smile on his lips. "Oh yeah?"

I heave in a load of oxygen. This has been locked up for a while. "Me and a high school friend went to visit our friend, well, more her friend, Matt, at college. The three of us went out to this bar. We got a table, and one of his friends from college ended up meeting us there.

"And my jaw dropped when he walked in, because he looked *just like you.* I clammed up for a second because I was so confused when he came over to our table and started talking to Matt."

I snort. "I sat there like some flabbergasted idiot. Like, *what the hell is Pilot doing here and how does he know Matt?* But then Matt introduced us, and his name was Rob. I swear to god, Pies, he looked just like you."

I shake my head and focus on the Pantheon again. "The four of us tried to talk while we had a drink, but it was a loud bar and the conversation wasn't going anywhere. And he kept looking at me, and it was driving my brain insane. I could not compute that it wasn't you.

"My friend and I decided to go dance, and the guys came with us . . . and eventually this guy and I ended up dancing together."

I take a beat, dropping my head to stare at the cobblestones. "And then he kissed me, and we were making out on the dance floor, and my brain was in emotional overload. Like: *This guy I've liked for ages, is making out with me, and we're dancing, and it's freaking great.*

"It was this whole weird, fake rush, and then we got off the dance floor and . . . he wasn't you."

New breath. "If it were you, afterward we would have laughed and talked about random shit. But when we walked back to Matt's place, this guy kept talking over me and my friend, and making a point to only talk to Matt. And then he barely said goodbye before disappearing back into his apartment, and we never spoke again.

"And that high I was riding, that trick my brain was trying to pull, just crashed. 'Cause study abroad was over. You hadn't been responding to any of our silly group messages over the summer, and . . . I . . . I went abroad to make bold decisions and be brave and do things I was always scared to do, but in the end, I didn't even tell you how I felt. And it hit me as the high crashed, that this fake version of you was probably the closest I was ever going to get.

"I don't typically tell people I like them. I actually have a track record of complete and total secrecy." I huff a sad chuckle. "So that whole café ordeal was kind of a big thing for me."

My eyes are now trained on a spot near Pilot's feet. I think I've ceased being Shane and become pure embarrassment. I shouldn't have shared that. Instant regret.

I slowly raise my head to face his reaction. His mouth is slightly agape. His eyes are round and conflicted, a dark forest green in the night. I swallow, unsure of what to say or do.

Babble into another subject, Shane. I open my mouth. I can't think clearly with him looking at me like that. "Um, well, anywa—" I'm cut off as his lips catch mine. Startled chills run up my calves.

The kiss is slow and careful. After a second, I kiss him back. My lips part. Head tilts. His hand glides over my waist. My skin . . . burns? In a good-fire way. I didn't know there was a good way to be on fire.

I thought people were making shit up when they described kisses like this. This is some Eiffel-Tower-at-6:00-p.m. shit. I'm glittery fire. And I like it. I break away and scoot back. Swallow. Pilot looks like he's been hit over the head with a rock.

My heart's playing hopscotch. "What was that?" I breathe.

"I . . . I didn't like that story with doppelgänger jerk version of me."

It takes a few seconds to spit it out, but I do. "Pilot, you're with Amy, in our time and in this one."

His breathing picks up. "I am with Amy." He drops his head in his hands. "Shit. Shit." He gets up and starts pacing back and forth. I watch him for a minute before I remember Melvin.

Did that count as cheating on Melvin? In 2011, we haven't even met yet. Maybe I should send a preemptive breakup message? I could mail it to his parents' house.

Pilot's been pacing for four minutes when I decide to stand. It's gotta be almost 4:00 a.m.

"We should go back," I suggest.

He looks up with a pained expression and nods. We walk back in silence. My entire being feels alight and aware, awake. I keep looking over at Pilot, but he's lost in thought.

The sun's rising when we slip silently into our respective beds (Pilot grabbed the key from Babe earlier). My brain has that kiss on a loop. It takes a long time to fall asleep.

8. Where Do We Go From Here?

Someone's shaking my shoulder. I shoot upright.

Babe leaps away from my bed with a gasp and a hand to her heart. I watch as her dark hair resettles around her face. "Jiminy Cricket, you scared me!"

I squint, taking stock of the room. Sahra's laughing as she runs a brush through her hair in front of the mirror. *Rome. Pilot and I kissed last night.* He's not in his bed.

A yawn muffles my response. "You scared me."

"Did you forget to set your alarm?" Babe asks.

"I must have. Where's Pilot?"

"Shower," Sahra answers. "We planned to leave in fifteen minutes."

I scramble out of bed.

Babe hangs back with me as we walk to the Colosseum. Today, she's dressed in a bright red peacoat (Babe owns four different-colored peacoats) with a sash at the waist and matching red lipstick. I feel like the living dead, and next to her, I must look like it. She sidles closer and loops her arm through mine. "What happened last night?"

"Nothing, don't worry . . . I couldn't sleep, and we walked around."

"You were out so late!"

"Babe, I don't really feel like talking right now," I mumble.

"Okay," she sighs. She unloops her arm and quickens her pace to catch up to the others.

My shoulders roll forward. Great, I'm eroding the fragile base of friendship we've formed thus far. I yank my hair up off my neck and pull it up into a puffy high ponytail.

The morning blurs. We go to the Colosseum. Pilot wanders around looking behind artifacts and under balustrades for the button like some sort of amateur Sherlock Holmes. I follow lazily. I find myself drafting and redrafting a breakup letter to 2011 Melvin in my head: *Dear Melvin: We haven't met yet, but when we do, maybe don't ask me out. XO Shane. Dear Melvin: We're not together yet, but in January 2017 I'm breaking up with you. Sorry sorry sorry! This is so hard. XO Shane.*

We move on to the Roman forum. Pilot quietly inspects everything we pass. I glance about and move on. Babe provides a constant stream of oohs and ahs. Sahra ventures off, taking pictures of things, always slightly separated from the group. I haven't taken any pictures.

This is not like the first time. *Are we ruining the Rome trip?*

Well, it won't be ruined once we reset. My chest feels hollow. As we near the end of the trail, Babe pulls me aside onto one of the surrounding grassy areas.

"Shane, seriously, tell me what happened last night. You're clearly not okay, and Pilot's acting like a mute. You need to stop moping. We're in Rome!"

I look at the ground, ashamed. "Sorry."

"Don't be sorry. Just let me help. What happened?" She takes my shoulders, her eyes roving over me like they're going to locate some unseen wound that's causing my pain.

I try to twist my expression into something less dreary. "We walked around and talked all night," I tell her again.

She folds her arms over her peacoat and eyes me wearily. "Then why do you look like your dog just died?"

I blow out a resigned breath. "We kissed last night."

Her arms drop. "*You kissed?*" she exclaims, way too loud. My eyes bulge. "Babe!" I hiss.

I whip my head around. Pilot's inspecting the base of an ancient Roman temple, and Sahra's taking a picture of the same Roman temple from a different point of view.

"Sorry! But holy crap on a cracker! You said nothing happened!" she hisses back.

"Well, I was afraid of how you'd react," I say pointedly.

"Who kissed who?"

"He kissed me, and then we were just kissing."

"Is he breaking up with Amy?"

"Not that I know of."

Babe looks at me with a sad expression and wraps me in a hug. "I'm sorry, Shane." I hug her back. She pulls away to look me in the eye. "That sucks. But pick yourself up, you're strong. Stop moping. How many times do you get to go to Rome? Try to enjoy yourself!"

I soften, nodding. "It's just the combo of this with the sleep deprivation. I need a latte or something."

"Then we'll get you a latte. Don't worry, it's going to be fine! Pilot has to figure out what the hell he's doing."

So do I.

We end up at the same empty Italian restaurant for lunch. Babe orders a pitcher of wine for the table. I order a cappuccino. When Babe shoots me an encouraging smile across the table, I can't help but grin back at her. Nowadays, we only really talk via phone call—I forgot how nice it is to be around her positive energy. It's contagious.

After a minute Pilot "drops his fork." I roll my eyes as he swoops under the red tablecloth to search the floor. He comes up empty-handed.

The waitress returns to take our lunch order bearing gifts—my cappuccino and the wine. I order ravioli again before tentatively taking a sip of the hot drink. I have to dump in a good three packets of sugar, but once I get some caffeine in me, I start to feel more alive.

Babe tells us a story I've never heard before about her friend who had an internship at Disney World. Said friend worked the Haunted Mansion ride. Apparently a lot of people get on the ride and dump their loved one's

ashes halfway through it over that balcony that overlooks the ghosts dancing in the ballroom. When that happens, everything has to be shut down,
cleaned, and re-dusted, with clean, non-dead-human dust.

"That's so weird! I would never think that would be a thing." I snort.

Babe laughs, and takes another sip of her wine. "Happens all the time."

"They want to haunt the ride forever." Sahra smiles.

"Guys, that's actually in my will, so . . ." Pilot comments. I scoff and
Babe cracks up.

When the time comes, a swarm of waiters surround the table. Like
a group of dancers, as one, they carefully place hot plates of food in front
of us.

The ravioli is delightful. I stab a second one, leaning over my plate and
positioning my head sideways to bite into it. When I do, my teeth crash
over something hard. Pain shoots through my jaw, and my free hand flies
up to cover my mouth.

What the fudge?

"Shane?" Pilot eyes me with concern.

"Shane?" Babe echoes. Sahra watches me carefully.

I gag. A mouthful of ravioli and a metal, half-dollar-sized object spill
out into my hand. *Ew* and *holy shit*. It's some sort of locket with an inscription on it. A bolt of fear rams through me. I clasp my fingers over the
thing.

"Are you okay?" I hear Sahra ask.

My head snaps up. Babe's fork hovers over her lasagna. Sahra's waiting
for an answer. Pilot's staring at my closed hand.

"Shane?" Pilot repeats more forcefully.

I bound out of my seat and break into a run. A second later, I'm outside,
boots slamming against the cobblestones, sprinting back up through the
ruins.

What in the hell am I doing?

I run until I'm far enough away that I feel confident in my solitude, then
I veer off toward one of the massive ancient structures along the trail. A
plethora of steps lead up into an expanse of crumbly archways. I clamber all
the way to the top step and drop to the ground in a heap, breathing hard.

Slowly, I peel back my trembling fingers.

In my palm sits a thick, round silver locket. I've been gripping it so tightly, there's an imprint on my skin. The bottom of it is flat, but the top's rounded. The inscription's on the flat side; it circles around in a spiral formation. I wipe away remnants of sauce and cheese with my hands and shine the silver clean against my black shirt. I hold it up for examination, slowly rotating the piece to read the inscription.

Open and press upon the heart
You'll return to the start
The adventure gained will be lost
Every shortcut has its cost.

I turn it over. The front's plain silver. It looks like it belongs on a necklace.

"Shane!" Pilot jogs toward me up the stairs. I tense as he comes to a stop a few steps away. He's shed his jacket, now sporting today's green-and-black plaid button-up.

"What happened?" he asks, catching his breath. "Is that it?"

I nod. He sags in relief, stumbling up the final few steps to sit beside me. Stones crunch under his sneakers as he leans forward and settles his elbows on his knees.

"Okay," he resolves after a moment. "Let's do it, then. Press it."

I look down, my hand closing back over the medallion.

"I . . ." I trail off, feeling childish.

"You what?" he prompts.

Dread. Anxiety. Fear. They balloon in my chest, making it hard to breathe. I don't want to. I don't think I want to go back.

"I don't know," I whisper.

"What do you mean, you don't know?"

"I just—don't," I finish lamely.

"You don't want to push it?" Bits of frustration leak into his voice. "Shane, why would you want to stay here? You want to redo a whole year and a half of college and then four years of med school?"

No, no, I don't. But I don't want to go back. Not yet.

"Why do you want to go back so badly?" The words reluctantly twist their way out of me.

"Are you kidding?" he asks in disbelief. "Haven't we already been through this?"

I shift to face him, expression hardening. "Have we? I remember you going off on me out on the street for quote 'disrupting your life,' but we never really *talked* about why we're here. Do you really think we both would have been chucked back in time to the very same moment if we both didn't *want*, and/or need, to be here?"

He glares at me. I glare right back. Frustration pulses in the space between us. I stand up. He joins me a moment later.

"There's a part of you that wanted to come back. Your whole '*I* brought us here' theory, that's bullshit. *We* brought us here. I'm not ready to go yet." I spin in an angry circle, throwing my hands up and letting them fall to my sides. "Are you living your best life? What are you dying to go back to? Your job? Amy?"

He squeezes his eyes shut for a second. "Why are you dying to stay? Are you that afraid to break up with your boyfriend?" he blurts.

"Are you?" I growl.

"What?" he shoots back in confusion.

"Clear this up for me: Our first day here, we went on that walk together, you remember?"

Pilot's lips grind together in annoyance. "Please, just hand over the button, Shane."

"Do you remember?" I repeat.

More glaring.

"We almost kissed that first night, and you said nothing about a girlfriend. We talked for over an hour by ourselves, and then we stayed up with the rest of the flat playing games and you said nothing.

"We were together the entire next day, you said nothing. We went out together again the day after that and you said nothing. It wasn't till that night that Atticus, *not you*, brought up the fact that you had a girlfriend at all! *And* when we were surprised, you said you'd only been dating for three months, that *you were going to see what happened*! Who says they're going to see what happens when they're in love with the person they're see-ing?" I yell the last few words.

His expression goes blank. "You're making a scene, Shane."

"What happened to seeing what happened? Did something change? Six years later, are you guys in love yet?"

His lips twitch.

"We have a reset button that will erase this and bring us back to the point where we started. A literal fail-safe switch. Why would we use it already? We get a second chance to do life, and we're going to waste it five days in? What are you so afraid of? Take a risk, Pilot! Make a change! Break awa—"

"You're yelling a Kelly Clarkson song," he interrupts.

I stop short and swallow. "I didn't mean for that to turn into a Kelly Clarkson song. Why do you even know that song?"

"Everyone knows that song."

"Well, she's says some good, poignant stuff in it—" I cut off as Pilot takes a step closer. I stumble backward. "Hey!"

He raises his hands in surrender. "Can I just see the button, please?"

"No," I respond automatically.

"Please, just let me see it with my eyes." His arms flop to his sides. "Shane," he says gently, "I promise I'm not going to press it right now."

I suck in a slow breath, trying to relocate a semblance of calm. "I'll let you see it if you let me hold it," I tell him, raising my button hand and holding it out.

"Shane, I can't see it with you holding it. It's too far away—" I shove it toward him at the same time he takes a step forward, and he rams face-first into my hand.

"Sorry!" I blurt as he exclaims, "Jesus!" He briefly touches a hand to his forehead and retreats a step.

"Sorry," I repeat sheepishly.

A small smile plays at his lips now. "Can I just . . ." He steps forward and carefully takes my wrist, holding it steady. My skin heats at the con-tact. I imagine glitter seeping up my arm.

I'm not quite sure why this feeling amounts to glitter. It's like my skin's sparkling.

His head tilts from left to right as he reads the poem. Finally, he looks back up at me with wide eyes. "The adventure gained will be lost? So, we won't remember any of this?"

I nod. "That's what it sounds like." He holds my gaze for a moment.

"Okay." He lets go and stuffs his hands into his pockets. I bring the medallion back to my side.

"Okay what?" I ask quietly.

"Okay, let's hold off on the reset," he says simply.

"You want to hold off on the reset?"

"That's what I just said."

"No, you just said, 'Let's hold off on the reset.' Do *you* want to hold off on it?"

"Let's hold off," he says quietly.

"Okay . . . I want to hold on to this thing, okay?" I add softly.

He nods. "Okay. Should we make a rule?"

I quirk an eyebrow. "What kind of rule?"

"We can't press it without the other's knowledge; we have to discuss it beforehand."

I nod. "Sounds good."

"Shall we rejoin Babe and Sahra, and do Rome?" he suggests.

I scuff at the ground, processing. "I guess that would be appropriate . . . We left without paying for our food."

"Oh shit." He laughs.

I carefully stash the medallion in my cross-body, inside the tiny zipper area inside the main section of the purse, for safekeeping.

9. Might as Well Embrace It

"What the heck was that in your food?" Babe asks as she uncaps her lipstick in front of the mirror.

"Um, it was like a coin or something. I dropped it outside."

"Oh my goodness, that's insane! You're okay, right?"

"I'm fine," I insist with a smile.

"And things are okay with you and Pilot?"

"Yeah, we talked. It's going to be fine."

"What does that mean? Is he ending things with Amy?" She pulls a towel from the dispenser and uses it to blot her lipstick.

I swallow. "I don't know, but I promise, I'll fill you in when I can."

She pops her lips, makes eye contact through the mirror, and nods. "Okay."

On our way back to the table, she recaps how Sahra yelled at our waiter and got all our meals for free because I almost choked on something in my food and got sick outside.

The overall mood of the group picks up exponentially now that Pilot's not completely distracted, and I'm not moping around like I got coal for Christmas. Pilot resumes his role of Map Man and leads us through Rome. I let my hair fall around my shoulders. I pull out my little, super-old digital camera and start taking pictures. I giggle and converse with Babe and Sahra. I feel a thousand times lighter.

When we stroll into the Pantheon, Pilot stops short at the threshold and throws his arms out in a *T*. "Wait! Guys." We all stop short. "Remember how Robert Langdon came here in *The Da Vinci Code*?" he announces with exaggerated enthusiasm.

Sahra takes him seriously. "I never read it."

"Nope," Babe says as she strolls off after Sahra to inspect one of the niches against the wall.

I mash my lips into a line, trying not to appear amused. "Ha-ha," I mutter. He shoots me a mischievous look that makes my heart do somersaults, before strolling away toward one of the niches.

Sunday, we go back to the Vatican. I'm the first to burst out onto the balcony at the top of the endless staircase. When I find an open spot, I grab hold of the railing and step up as close as I can.

Pilot comes up on my right. "This was the coolest thing we climbed."

"Agreed, it was definitely my favorite." I grin at out at the sea of red rooftops.

After a moment, a mass of my hair shifts. I turn, to find Pilot tucking it behind my ear. His face is so close. My chest aches as I pull back, searching his eyes.

"Pilot, what are you doing?" I ask.

"I don't know." He swallows. "I couldn't see your face. Sorry, it wasn't on purpose," he mumbles.

I catch his eyes. "Hey, Pies."

There's an unfamiliar diffidence in his expression.

"I don't want this to happen again until you break up with past Amy. If we're going to try this, I want to try it for realsies." *Why did I just say for realsies?*

Pilot nods, looking serious now. "I'm sorry," he breathes. He runs a hand down his face and walks away.

Pilot keeps to himself the rest of the trip.

10. The Green Light, I Want It

We've been home for twenty minutes. I'm sitting behind Sawyer in the empty Flat Three kitchen, editing the few photos I took and gearing up to maybe write a blog post about Rome.

I pull up Gmail and find four missed messages from Mom and Dad, each more panicked than the one before. I haven't checked in with them since the day I "got here." *This is so strange.* I quickly shoot back a response, log into Skype, pay the ten dollars for real phone call minutes, and dial my house in New York. My mom picks up. Mom, six years ago.

The whole experience is surreal. She talks about my younger cousins who're still in middle school. She tells me how worried she's been because I haven't posted anything on Facebook or responded to an email in days. I tell her about Rome. She's shocked and excited to hear more details. Talking to her is so casual and easy. When we get off the phone an hour later, my eyes are glassy. We've fallen into such an uneven cadence these past few years. I lost the desire to share anything but the surface details of my life with her. I love my mom, but I felt this need to step away sometime during med school, and I never stepped back.

I work on a Rome-centric blog post until Pilot walks into the kitchen. I glance at the time: 11:30 p.m. He looks at me expectantly. I give a tug on my old white iPod headphones, letting them fall to the table. "Hey."

"Hey, can we talk? You hungry? Shawarma?" he asks in quick succession. His face lights up with that last one. He's fidgeting. I close my laptop with an amused look.

"You writing?" he asks.

Using extreme caution, I slide horizontally out of my chair and stand. "Yeah, I figured I'd try to post something on my blog. I've been slacking."

He clicks his tongue disapprovingly. "Can't leave those French Watermelon readers hanging, Shane."

I grab my bag and jacket, grinning at the mention of my blog. "So, shawarma?"

"Relax, Shane, we're gonna get your precious shawarma."

I bark a laugh as I follow him out the door.

Almost everything in Kensington is closed by this time, so it feels like we have the entire sidewalk to ourselves as we stroll down fancy-white-buildings lane. I wait impatiently for Pilot to initiate whatever conversation he wanted to have. After four minutes of silence, I nudge him gently with my elbow.

"What did you want to talk about?" I ask.

He runs a hand through his hair, stuffs his hands in his pockets, takes a breath like he's going to speak, doesn't speak, runs a hand through his hair again.

"The suspense," I tease.

He laughs nervously, but we continue to walk in silence. London and I wait with bated breath for 108 more seconds.

Out of nowhere, he blurts, "I'm gonna do it."

I eye him sideways. "Do what?" I ask tentatively.

"I'mgonnabreakupwithAmy."

"You're going to . . . ?" He smooshed all his words together, but I got the gist.

He might not actually do it. Keep your hopes down.

Let's be real; there's no stopping my hopes. They pulse through me like an adrenaline rush. They run and jump and twirl down the street. I manage to hold onto a neutral expression.

"I'm gonna break things off with Amy," he says more clearly.

I inhale a slow breath. "You are."

"Yes."

We've come to an intersection. We get the walk signal, cross left, and continue on.

"Are you sure?" I ask quietly.

He nods. "There was some truth to your Kelly Clarkson speech."

I worry at my lip.

He exhales a long breath. "Things were kinda different with Amy and me after I came back from London. She was worried about my relationship with you while I was out here. And like, I felt so guilty about it because she was right to worry.

"And when I got back to New York, I tried so hard to fix it. I promised myself I'd never let something like that happen again . . . but in a way the damage was done. She, like, investigated every woman I interacted with.

"After a while, she stopped voicing her concerns aloud, but I catch her doing it to this day. I mean, not this day, but in 2017. And I can't fault her for it. I just go through this guilt cycle because she'll forever have a right to feel paranoid . . . because of how I felt about you.

"I always picture that image from the *Princess and the Pea* story. Like that one seed of distrust I planted years ago is buried under all these years we've spent together, all these memories, but we still feel it." He pauses as we cross to the next block.

Pilot shrugs, emotion bleeding into his voice. "I think, maybe, the best thing Amy and I can do is let each other go."

I blink at the ground, sadness welling in my chest.

"I'm sorry, Pilot. I don't know what to say."

"Don't be." He sighs. "I was trying really hard to do what I thought was the right thing for so long, and turns out maybe the right thing was the wrong thing. . . . It's hard to come to terms with that. And it's crossed my mind so many times before. . . . Confrontation is just so fucking hard."

I stay quiet. Beirut Express comes into view a little way down the side-walk.

"I'm gonna do it tomorrow," Pilot adds carefully.

I swallow, letting the words sink in as we approach the restaurant.

A couple minutes later, when we're right in front of the door, I open my mouth to speak again: "I'm sending Melvin a preemptive breakup letter, just to cover my ground, even though we haven't technically met."

A laugh blows out of Pilot.

I nudge him gently. "Shall we shawarma our troubles away?"

I'm high on hope and shawarma as we mosey back to the Karlson.

"So, Pies, while we're here, what's the plan to jumpstart your music career? Can we get you on YouTube? I'm gonna really push for this 'Wreck-ing Ball' cover."

He grins and shakes his head—default humble, cool guy response.

"I just want to sing 'Wrecking Ball' and claim we wrote it first. Just one time!"

He laughs now. "You're ridiculous."

"This is a great idea! I have a camera. Why not?"

"You have a video camera?" He perks up curiously.

"Uh, duh, my Casio has a video setting. I myself thought about starting a YouTube channel about writing and such many a time circa 2010, 2011."

"French Watermelon Nineteen: the YouTube channel?"

"But of course."

"How 'bout French Writer-melon?"

"That doesn't make any sense," I reply melodramatically.

"What do you mean, it doesn't make any sense?" he protests.

"The internet knows me as French Watermelon. I don't want to tarnish the good French Watermelon Nineteen name."

He smirks at me, eyes gleaming. "Ridiculous."

"You say ridiculous, I say tech savvy. Tomato-tomahto."

We cross another intersection.

"What country do we want to hit next?"

"I'm pretty sure Babe's gonna pull me aside tomorrow and convince me to go on a trip to Paris with you and that pain-in-the-ass Chad."

"Oh jeez, how could I forget Chad? You up for Paris again?"

"Am I up for Paris again?" I say in a mocking tone. "Does a bear shit in the woods?"

He snorts.

11. Come Together

I can't eat breakfast. I'm too worked up thinking about Pilot and Amy; my stomach is in knots. *Will he do it?* I get down on the floor and flow through some yoga before leaving for class. Babe asks if she can join me. I welcome the distraction and quietly walk her through it. She giggles as we struggle through poses in our jeans. Sahra snorts when she wakes up to find us both in downward dog. As I heave my backpack onto my shoulder to take off, Babe asks if I want to get lunch together. I stop at the post office on the way to class and send off my letter to a clueless past Melvin.

At noon, I meet Babe outside of Byron's. We grab a booth, and Babe proceeds to pitch Paris for Chad's birthday. I do my best to drag Chad, but past Babe won't be swayed by Shane-she-just-recently-met-who-has-never-even-met-Chad. I find myself studying her face, marking the differences between her and the Babe I talk to weekly in 2017. Future Babe's hair is different; she has voluminous curls instead of the polished upturned ends she has now. And future Babe has switched to a slightly darker red shade of lipstick.

She comes to a close with her double-date question as the waiter arrives to take our orders. It's not my spirit guide. I've had my eyes peeled since I walked in, but there's no sign of her.

"So, what's going on with you and Pilot? Are you up for this? Will you come?" She shoots the questions one after the other, without giving me a second to respond.

I vacuum in a breath. "Okay, so let's just keep this between us, right?"

"Of course."

"Pilot's supposedly breaking up with Amy today," I tell her quietly.

"*What?*" Her hands fly up.

"I know."

"What— Are you two going to be a thing?"

"I don't want to jinx anything," I say hesitantly.

"So, you'll come this weekend!" she says abruptly, her eyes lighting up.

I nod, a smile breaking across my face. "I'm so excited to go again!"

"You've been to Paris before?"

"Uh, no, I mean, like, go again . . . to a place . . . with you and the gang. Pilot. Again."

Later, Babe and I sit in the kitchen together. I'm working on another new blog post. I'm surprised to find a comment from Leo on the Rome post. On my blog. Using his lame old screen name.

LeoBaseballPrimaveri
Why aren't you posting anything on Facebook?

I don't even know what Future Leo is up to. He got a job at the local gas station for a while after he dropped out of school, and then moved out to New York City. 2017 Mom never talks about him in our bristled conversations, and Future Leo doesn't use Facebook.

I haven't posted all the Rome photos, but I included a bunch in this post. They're not on Facebook because I'm not in the market for a running life commentary from the fam. If they want to see what I'm up to, they can read it on the blog.

Next to me, Babe's plucking away at a paper, waiting patiently for Pilot to return so she can pop the Paris question. She jumps to attention when he finally walks through the door with a frozen meal.

"Hey, Pilot!"

"Hey, Babe." He turns to me with a smile. "Shane."

"Happy Monday." I grin.

"So, Babe, I was thinking we should go on a trip again this weekend," Pilot says casually.

Babe eyes me with a suspicious smile, and I raise my eyebrows: *I didn't say anything.*

"Yeah, I was thinking the same thing," she says slowly.

"Where do you want to go?" he asks.

"Where do you want to go?" she asks suspiciously.

"How about we both say where on three?" Pilot suggests cheekily.

"Why?" Babe asks as I start counting.

"One, two, three!"

"Paris!" they exclaim simultaneously. Pilot laughs, and I cackle behind my computer.

Babe is amused. She thinks I told him. "Okay, you two talked already. Does this mean you're down?"

"Why not," Pilot agrees as he pops his frozen meal into the microwave. I glance at Babe, and she waggles her eyebrows at me. I roll my eyes, suppressing a grin.

Babe and I make ourselves pasta while Pilot eats his frozen meal. When he's finished, he takes out his laptop, pulls on his headphones, and retreats to the chair in the corner to work. I settle in at the table to eat and watch something on Sawyer.

"Hey," Babe starts. I look up to where she's dressing her pasta in a bolognese sauce. "Do you play cards at all? I picked some up earlier."

A smile tears across my face.

We buy our train tickets to Paris. We're leaving on the same schedule as last time and staying at the same crappy hostel. I let Babe plan it the same exact way because I've been itching to redo this trip for years. It wouldn't feel right changing the setting.

The three of us spend the evening playing Rummy 500. Sahra *whooshes* in and out during our first few rounds before finally settling in to join us. Atticus shows up at eight and suggests a game of BS. We chat and cackle until my cheeks hurt from smiling.

Atticus leaves the kitchen first because he has an early morning. Babe, Sahra, Pilot, and I play one last round of BS. It's not till then that I remember: Pilot was supposed to break up with Amy.

My stomach lurches. *How the hell did I forget?* From that point on, I have a hard time focusing on the game. When Babe wins, she and Sahra pack up and walk back to the room. Pilot shows no sign of leaving, so I linger, pretending to do something on my computer.

"You going to sleep too?" he asks. I swallow, suddenly feeling nervous.

"Um, yeah I guess so." I close Sawyer, pick him up, and hop out of my chair. A millisecond later, I sense it falling. I whirl around with a gasp and snatch it awkwardly by the seat with my one free hand. Carefully, I lower myself and the off-kilter chair to the floor.

Pilot stands, watching me across the table with an amused expression. "I've noticed that you're trying super-hard to make peace with the devil chairs."

I shake my head. "I'm being so nice to them, and they just *continue* with the rudeness." I gather my feet under me and pop up off the ground. Pilot's here now; he picks up the chair and pushes it back into place at the table.

"Some chairs never change," he says.

I snort and head slowly around the table toward the door. He follows me out. We walk together down the hall, veering off to our respective doors. I dig in my bag for my key.

"Hey," Pilot says behind me. I turn around. He's leaning against his door, so I stop fumbling and lean against my own door.

There's a long pause where I look at him expectantly. *Oh god, he's having second thoughts. He wants to leave. He didn't break it off. Is he waiting for me to speak?*

"Hey," I respond belatedly.

"I broke up with Amy," he says.

My heart jumps two feet outside my chest. *Shit. Get back inside me.*

"You—" I start.

He cuts me off. "Yeah."

I swallow, pausing to look at the ceiling. *He did it! What do I say?* My head bobs around, not in a nod or a shake, just in a weird bob.

I decide on, "Okay."

He pulls a thoughtful Soprano frown, jutting out his bottom lip, and nods. "Okay."

I nod in return, still at a loss. "So, good night . . . uh, I'll see you tomorrow."

A smirk flickers over his lips. "Good night."

He doesn't move to unlock his door, so I don't either. I wait a few seconds.

"Are you going in?" I ask, amused.

"Are you?" he challenges.

"Yeah, I'm going in." I smile.

"Okay, so am I."

"Okay, same." And then the door supporting my weight flies out from behind me, and I'm falling to my death. "*The fuck?*" flies out of my mouth as I twist in the air to catch myself before hitting the ground.

"Jiminy Cricket!" Babe's voice comes from somewhere near my crashing body. I manage to fall on my right forearm, but that's going to leave a bruise. Pilot's in front of me, grabbing my hand, helping me up. Babe's apologizing profusely.

"Oh my goodness, I kept hearing someone outside the door. And I thought maybe you didn't have a key, and oh Mylanta, I'm sorry."

"Don't worry about it, Babe," I breathe.

"You okay?" Pilot asks when I'm upright again.

"I'm fine," I insist with an embarrassed chuckle. And then I keel over laughing. Babe and Pilot join me.

"Good night, Pies," I repeat one last time. He nods and I nod back. He retreats to his door again.

"Night," Babe adds. He finally turns around to put his key in the lock, so Babe and I close our doors. Sahra's on her laptop with headphones in.

"What was that about?" Babe asks excitedly.

I snort as I head for the bathroom to take a shower. "Nothing, we were just saying good night."

"Did he break up with her?"

I pivot, make my eyes super-wide, squeeze my lips together in a line, and nod.

"Oh my goodness!" She falls into her bed, giggling.

"What? What happened?" Sahra says, lowering her headphones.

"Pilot broke up with his girlfriend!" Babe squeals excitedly.

"What? Why?" Sahra asks.

"Because of Shane!" Babe laughs.

"No!" I say immediately.

"What?" Sahra says in surprise.

I lock myself in the bathroom and hop in the shower to avoid an inquisition.

12. The Rush at the Beginning

I'm at the kitchen table Wednesday morning, working on a bagel, when Pilot strides in. My heart kick-starts. We head to Paris tomorrow.

"Morning," he greets me casually before flipping on the electric kettle.

"Morning." I smile at him before returning to my studious Twitter scrolling on Sawyer. He fixes himself a cup of tea and sits across from me, grinning.

I pull away from the computer and raise my eyebrows in question.

"So," he starts, "ah . . . I don't want to come off super-forward, but would you maybe want to come to Paris with me this weekend?"

"Like on a date?" I say with mock surprise.

"Yes?"

"Sure."

"Okay, good." His grin widens. "What time does your class get out tomorrow?"

"Four thirty."

"Four thirty," he repeats. With that, he stands, puts his tea in the sink, and leaves.

Thursday has come. I'm in class. We're discussing world-building by dissecting Harry Potter and it's everything. I've got my backpack and rolling suitcase with me at my desk because I have to leave straight from here to make the six-thirty Eurostar. When the lecture ends, I'm the last one out, bringing up the rear with my luggage. As I drag my bag over the building's threshold, I catch sight of Pilot standing out on the sidewalk, wearing his backpack and carrying a plastic bag.

"What are you doing here?" I ask cheerily, as I step up to where he's waiting.

"Got us some travel food." He holds out the plastic bag.

I gasp dramatically at the contents. "Shawarma! How did you know I liked this?"

"I don't know. I've never heard you talk about it."

We sit side by side on the Tube. We're nice and smooshed with the incoming rush-hour crowd. *We're on a date.* A first date. Which is weird because we already know each other. First dates are usually so . . . new.

But how much do I really know about Pilot's life outside of London? I turn to where he is on my right, and he meets my eyes.

"Pies, we've never really talked about our lives outside of . . . study abroad. Is that weird? I felt like I knew you, I feel like you knew me, but did we?" My eyebrows pull together.

"That's a loaded question." He tilts his head. I watch, freely admiring how attractive he looks right now, because I'm allowed, because we're on a date! The Tube lady's voice rings overhead: "Mind the gap."

His eyes refocus on me. "We knew each other. I guess I kept stuff about life back home private because it just didn't come up. There were so many other things to discuss because everything was new."

"Yeah, I never really offered much information about life at home either. I guess it was kind of like an escape, being here and not having to dwell on anything but the novelty of *being here.*"

He frowns slightly, nodding. "I mean, just because we didn't talk about our lives back in the US doesn't mean we didn't know each other." He smiles a bit now. "I knew that when you got up in the kitchen, the chair would fall."

I snort.

He continues matter-of-factly, "I knew that if a song you knew came on, or if someone started singing randomly, you'd sing along. I knew that if you tripped on the street, you'd do a crazy dance and manage to stay upright. I knew I could probably always find you writing in the kitchen. I knew your eyes were ice blue. I knew I could always poke fun at the weird stuff you do because you'd laugh right along with me. I knew enough to know you."

I stare, speechless for a moment. He drops his gaze, smiling at his hands and fiddling with a strap on his backpack. "You know, you never really gave me any shit back then, when I'd give it to you," he finishes.

My lip quirks up. "You're not as weird as I am; it's harder to make fun of you. Back then, I barely knew how to make fun of myself—not jaded enough yet, I guess."

"And you're jaded now?" He smirks.

"In terms of me, I'm jaded," I answer with a scoff. "I came here so sheltered. It's hard to be cynical when you're constantly spinning around in awe of the stuff around you. So many times, you'd crack a joke or say something ridiculous, and so many times, I wouldn't realize it for a good three minutes because I was too distracted by the world to pick up on the sarcasm and I'd feel like an idiot for having missed it and not reacted in the moment."

He grins, shaking his head.

I continue in earnest, "We were gallivanting around in foreign countries I've never seen before! It was a lot to take in." I laugh, looking at my knees. "Now that I've been here before, it's a little more familiar than foreign." I meet his eyes again. "I feel a little less like a newborn puppy than before."

Pilot nods with a small smile. "I've noticed."

"Noticed what?" I ask with a smidge of attitude.

"You're bolder than before."

We eat our shawarma in the Eurostar waiting area. Once we're settled in on the train to Paris, I turn and ask him something that's been on my mind for a while. "Why did you want to do study abroad?"

"To get away from everything and travel, see the world."

Everything? "Really?"

"And get a break from school. It's a lighter semester, and when else are you going to be able to live in a different country?"

I nod and look down at my lap.

"What about you?"

I purse my lips. "I mean, I needed to get away, I guess, but at the time I was fixated on starting college over."

Pilot tilts his head. "What do you mean?"

"My roommates from freshman and sophomore year had gone ahead and booked a double without me for junior year. They were my closest friends at YU. I was left super-alone in a single apartment, all sad and friendless. I was going home every weekend. I found the writing program on the study abroad site—and the rest is history."

He studies me thoughtfully. "And you're glad you did it?" He raises his brows, eyes twinkling because he already knows the answer.

I fiddle with the edge of my jacket. "Best unintentional decision I ever made. You?"

He grins. "Are you kidding? I wouldn't have missed this for anything." He reaches for his backpack on the ground and plunges his hand inside. It comes back out holding . . . a pack of Beatles cards!

I gasp and he chuckles. "Picked these up yesterday. Didn't feel right not having them."

"You went to the Beatles store without me!" I nudge him playfully.

"I wanted them to be sort of a surprise."

"Well, thanks." A fire stirs to life in my chest.

"Shall we play?"

13. Close

My hand smacks over Pilot's as a second queen shows up. I topple sideways, cackling in defeat. I might lose this round of Egyptian Rat Screw.

I'm all smiles and smothered competitiveness. There's a palpable air of hesitancy when it comes to closeness, much like real first dates. We did kiss last weekend, but it's different now. He's single. Closeness is expected now, anticipated.

Pilot snorts as I rattle off the address of the hostel to the cab driver.

"You know what I didn't realize till now," he starts dubiously. "We're going back to *that* hostel."

I laugh. "*Yeah*. I didn't forget."

He scoffs, "If you didn't forget, why didn't you push Babe toward something different?"

"Because then we wouldn't be redoing this trip. We'd be on a different trip. Where's the struggle there?" I beam. He shakes his head, grinning, and I continue. "Think of all the things we'd be missing out on. We wouldn't get to room with that forty-year-old and the sleep apnea machine."

"You're right, and we wouldn't have that banging wall of lockers to put our stuff in."

"They were the perfect shade of gym-locker blue," I coo. "And don't forget the shower. You remember the shower?" I ask excitedly.

His head kicks forward. "I forgot about the shower."

I throw a hand over my heart. "You know how I love a good forty-five-second shower."

The hostel's just as unimpressive as it was the first time. Babe's waiting with our keys when we arrive. She introduces us to the same brosef Chad I remembered. I purchase a lock, anticipating the need for one before we head up. Pilot snags a map from the brochure stand next to the check-in desk. Upstairs, we drop our things in the lackluster lockers and go out to find food.

When Pies and I get back to the room post-dinner, I head to the shower because I'm not sure what protocol is now. It's strange to share a room on a first date. When I reemerge, he's lying on his bed, head propped up on his palm, waiting for me.

"I feel like this first date is ending rather anticlimactically," he says thoughtfully as I climb into my own bed. I throw my damp hair over my shoulder and mirror his posture.

"Well, it's not really the end, though. We have all of Paris," I reason.

"Yeah, but a date is a day, it's right there in the word, if a date was a weekend, it'd be called a wate."

"I mean, if you're gonna do that, I feel like week-ate makes more sense."

"I guess this is the end of our first date, but we can come back around to rating the wate as a whole, Sunday night."

I snicker. "I'll write up a full review for Yelp."

Pilot makes an irritated *tuh* sound. "Shane, you know I'm only on Trip Advisor."

I drop my head, cackling. "Well, our date isn't completely over yet."

He perks up. "Oh, are we continuing it with our new friends: forty-year-old-sleep-apnea man and random teenager in the corner?"

"We could play a game," I suggest.

"Are you going to wake them, or should I?" Pilot teases with a nod toward the far-right corner.

I snort. "It's a game just for us; we don't need them."

Pilot squints at me. "I'm intrigued. Tell me more."

"The opposite game." I smile goofily.

"The opposite game?" he repeats in an amused, ridiculous voice.

"Yeah, the opposite game."

"I hate the opposite game," he says in a fervently serious voice.

"I hate the opposite game too," I whisper.

He smirks. "I love this pillow."

"I love this pillow too."

"You're just taking all my opposite ideas. I win the game," he says.

"Yes, I win the game."

Pilot snorts and I giggle deliriously.

"This isn't the opposite game," he retorts.

"This isn't the opposite game!" I say cheekily.

"I like brussels sprouts."

"I like lemons."

"I'm from the future."

"Ha!" I beam. "But you *are* from the future. I think that means I win."

He falls onto his back, looking up at the ceiling now. I can see the white of his smile in the dark. I fall on to my back and look up at the ceiling as well. We lie there like that for a few minutes.

"Hey," he breaks the silence. "I really hate this situation we've gotten ourselves into."

I rotate so that most of my body is belly-down on the bed. My arms fold under my pillow, propping up my head. "I don't like you," I whisper, smiling like a five-year-old.

He rotates onto his stomach to mirror my position. "I don't like you either."

I bury my face in the pillow, laughing, and pull the blanket up over my shoulders. I'm still smiling when I close my eyes. "Morning, Pies."

"Good morning."

I get up early to beat Pilot to the bathroom and get myself sorted. I'm back waiting on my bed before he's even opened his eyes. I realize too late that I never did download Angry Birds. I should have brought a book.

"Hey." Pilot's sleep-ridden voice stirs me from my thoughts.

"Hey."

Spikes of his hair stick up in weird directions. "Why are you already ready?" he grumbles.

"I needed to beat you to the bathroom. This way you don't have to wait around and deal with zombie Shane."

He smiles lazily. "Zombie Shane? I want to meet zombie Shane."

I scoff, "Maybe another time."

We meet up with Babe and Chad, grab croissants from the hostel's built-in diner, and stroll down to the nearest Metro station. Babe and Chad walk a few feet ahead of us. My hands are jammed in my pockets, like Pilot's beside me. The streets are fairly empty—to be expected given that we're in the East Jabip sector of the city. Around the next corner, a Metropolitan sign comes into view. The sight sends an unexpected bout of happiness bubbling through me.

I'm on a date *in Paris*. I smile to myself, feeling fearless as we approach the underground. On a whim, I extricate my hand and take hold of Pilot's arm. Delicately, I pull it from his pocket and slide my hand into his. Pilot looks taken off guard for a second and then, doing his best to strangle a smile, glances down at our now intertwined hands. Glitter pulses through my fingers. Nerves shoot around in my stomach.

"What's this?" he asks, amused.

I hold our hands up for inspection, squinting dramatically. "I think this is a move."

Pilot's head shoots back with laughter.

"Is there some separation anxiety happening between your hand and the inside of your pocket?" I ask.

He narrows his eyes. We're only ten feet from the Metro steps now. Babe and Chad are already descending. Pilot takes an unexpected left, crossing in front of me. He leads us away toward a brown business building. When we're right up on it, he swings me around so my back is to the wall, and raises our held hands up above my head. They press against the wall as he brings his face close to mine. My pulse shoots up.

"What's this?" I manage to breathe. He closes the gap, and we kiss for the first time as single humans, and it's ridiculous and spontaneous and— all the swoon.

I feel like I just threw back a few espresso shots when he pulls back to meet my eyes.

"That was a move," Pilot whispers smugly.

I push him away and step off the wall. "Show off."

Over Pilot's shoulder, I catch sight of Babe and Chad standing with their arms crossed, watching.

"Oh my god." I choke. My cheeks flush. Pilot follows my gaze and laughs.

"We'll be there in a minute!" I yell to Babe. They turn around and go back down the Metro steps.

"Give me your hand!" I demand. "Trying to out-move me with your movie-worthy, stupid, really great moves," I mutter as I snatch at his palm and drag him toward the steps.

"I'm not the one who threw down the gauntlet with the super-intense hand-holding."

I shake my head, giddy as we descend into the yellow-tinted tunnels of the Metro. We find Chad and Babe waiting for us by the turnstiles. When we get close enough, Chad looks at Pilot and nods his head approvingly before saying, "Duuude."

I roll my eyes and turn to Babe. She widens her own like, *Oh my god, so now are you guys a thing?*

14. Don't Stop Me Now

"You know what I just realized? We haven't played Angry Birds." Pilot's grin kicks up his cheek. The countryside shoots by the window. We've settled in on the RER, a few rows back from Chad and Babe.

"Because I completely blanked and forgot to download the app on my iPod Touch before we left."

"That was really fun, back in the day. You ever get past that level we were stuck on?"

"No, it got to the point where I was irrationally angry at the game, so I thought it best for my mental health to put it down."

I study him again because I'm allowed. His smile doesn't fade like it usually does. My eyes wander up to his hair. Can I touch it? I suck in a breath to speak.

"What?" he says with a laugh.

"I'm going to make another move."

"Another move? Was it the eye contact we made before you started staring at my forehead?"

I purse my lips together. "No. And I'll have you know, eye contact is a great move."

I clear my throat and look away for a moment. "Okay. It's coming. Brace yourself."

He watches me carefully as I reach out my hand. Starting at the left corner of his forehead, I comb my hand back slowly, letting the hair slide through the *V*s between my fingers. He closes his eyes for a second, leaning into my hand like a puppy. I bring my arm back, feeling triumphant.

He opens his eyes. They hold mine for a few charged moments before he smiles. "Is this a move-off now?" One of his eyebrows quirks up.

I shrug, shooting him a competitive look. "If we make this a real game, I think ground rules have to be established."

He laughs, bringing his face close to mine. "Lay them down, Primaveri."

I pull back to a safe distance, taking a moment to think this through. A move-off, *a move-off* . . . well, kissing shouldn't really be a move in a move-off; it's not creative enough. And we shouldn't be making out when we're with Babe and Chad anyway.

"Okay," I reason, shifting my body to face Pilot, "so the rules of the move-off are: We'll take turns making moves, but a kiss is no longer a move. It was taken and is no longer creative. First contestant to break and kiss the other before midnight loses the move-off. We both make it to midnight, it's a tie."

His lips fold back into a smirk. "You're on."

"It's on like Donkey Kong. There's more hair-brushing and hand-holding where that came from," I say, pointing a finger at him.

He laughs again. I feel so warm and fuzzy. I let my smile pop on full-force because it's too hard to keep it under wraps.

"Your hair felt really nice," I add.

"Thanks. I grew it myself."

"I grew mine too!"

Versailles still steals my breath away. I whip out the camera immediately. We make our way into the palace and up the stairs. When I'm satisfied we've taken enough pictures in the room before the Hall of Mirrors, we move on in. Pilot and I amble lazily, letting Chad and Babe take the lead again. This second time around, they're really getting the double-date experience. I hope things are going well. Babe hasn't left his side to come to mine, so it must be going at least okay.

Pilot pauses about five feet into the room, so I pause beside him. He glances around, making a show of scanning the area.

"Disappointing," he concludes, shaking his head.

"Excuse me?" I retort, my abs seizing.

He frowns. "Still haven't installed that mirror maze."

Laughter rocks through me. Pilot shoots me a delighted grin before striding onward. I catch up to him a second later at the center of the room because he's stopped again. Tourists trickle around us. Babe and Chad are posing for a selfie in a mirror up ahead. I let my gaze soften on the cloudy glass lining the wall.

"I like it better this second time around," I muse. "My expectations were less eccentric going in."

I startle slightly as Pilot twists his arms around me from behind. His left hand carefully takes hold of my right, and his right hand takes my left. I look up over my left shoulder, a smile burning my cheeks. "What is this?"

"Brace yourself." He grins.

I don't have time to respond before he sways us gently to the right, then left. When we go right again, he releases my right hand and instinctively I twirl outward, laughing. He gives a pull, and I go twirling back into his arms, ending with my back to his heart. A few tourists have stopped to watch us.

I look up at him over my shoulder again. He releases my left hand and twirls me toward him. We end up face-to-face, my hand on his chest.

My heart jumps around. "Damn it, that was a great move." His green eyes capture mine, drawing me closer. I make a conscious effort to pull back before it's too late.

"I thought you didn't dance," I chide him.

"But you do," he says simply.

"I . . ." I search his eyes, bright with adrenaline and certainty.

My lips mush together. I spin away, metaphorically floating now. I keep hold of his one hand, squeezing it as I lead us out of the hall. I can feel the eyes of random spectators on us as we go. I'm enjoying myself too much to care.

I spot Babe and Chad talking and pointing animatedly at a painting in the next room. My brain whirrs, trying to figure out my next move. How do I retaliate? What other moves are there? I'm not good enough at moves.

Once we reach the outdoor area, I snap into photographer mode, power walking ahead with Babe, who also has her camera out. She poses, and I crouch into weird gotta-get-that-shot positions to frame the best possible picture of her with the endless expanse of park.

"Chad," I throw over my shoulder. "Do you want one?" Chad scurries up for a picture. I snap it. "Pies?" Pilot switches in. I snap a picture.

"Your turn." He takes the camera. I switch into the photo spot. He squats down, finding the position I was in and then twisting into a more awkward version of it, angling his head ridiculously.

"This look right?" he asks confidently. I snort.

Babe and Chad start down the steps into the landscaped abyss. Pilot places the camera back in my hand.

"Thank you." I sling the camera safety strap back around my free wrist. "Shall we?" I ask in an English accent, jutting out the crook of my arm like ladies do in old-timey movies.

Pilot pauses and sidesteps to look at me from the front. "Is this your next move?"

"I . . . no," I declare defensively. I drop my arm and head down the stairs without him. Dang it—I should have learned to play guitar and brought one with me in the event that a move-off should occur and played one of his songs. That would be the move of moves.

Pilot catches up with me easily. We veer off left on a trail and come up on a path lined with skinny, dead, leafless trees. It's stunning. I whip up my camera to snap a shot. I'm concentrating on the shutter when I feel Pilot come right up next to my face.

"Brace yourself," he warns again.

"Wait, but I didn't—"

I freeze as his nose lightly brushes the side of my face. His lips dance against my ear as he whispers, "I watched all six seasons of *Lost* that summer after study abroad, and they were fantastic."

The idiot smile takes over. I drop my camera hand and rotate to face him. He doesn't move, so his face brushes against my cheek until we're nose to nose.

I hold his eyes in challenge. "No, you didn't."

"Yeah, I did." His smile stretches.

My heart flutters around. "No."

"Don't tell me what I can't do," he says.

My jaw drops a smidge. "No . . ."

"Four—" he starts.

My head tilts slightly as I beam in disbelief.

"—Eight. Fifteen. Sixteen. Twenty-three. Forty-two."

"Are you talking *Lost* to me?" I ask, incredulous.

My skin hums. Our faces are so close.

"We have to go back," he whispers.

"Stop it," I protest half-heartedly. I'm very much into this, and it's definitely working.

"If something goes wrong, be my constant?"

Too. Attractive. Can't. My arms twirl up around his neck, and we kiss in the backyard of Versailles. I lost.

The four of us have lunch together in the café buried amidst the landscape. There's more hand-holding, but it's always when Babe and Chad aren't paying attention. We ride the RER back into the heart of Paris, explore Notre Dame, have dinner, and make fluffy conversation.

At the hostel, we drop Chad and Babe off on floor four, and ride up to six. Hands intertwined, we come to a stop outside our room.

"So this is me," I say, casually turning to face him.

"You're kidding. I'm here too."

I roll my eyes, trying to clear out the overwhelming googly-eyed feeling that's taken hold of my brain, and put the key in the lock. This sensation is so new. I always get anxious, shaky, but swoony? Is *swoony* a word?

I push open the door. Sleep-apnea man wheezes away in the corner. I drop my purse onto the floor and sit on my bed, feet resting on the ground in the space between our singles. Pies sits across from me on his own mattress. My skin zings as our knees graze.

"So, is this the end of our second date?" I note quietly.

"Looks like it. How'd we do?"

I purse my lips. "Four and a half out of five stars." He smiles.

"Congrats on winning the move-off." I hold out my hand to shake his.

He squeezes it gently. "You put up a valiant effort."

I grin and reposition so I'm lying on my side like last night. "If you can't tell, I'm not a big move maker."

The bed next to me creaks as Pilot mirrors my posture. "You hold some damn good eye contact," he says with his trademark cool-guy smirk.

"Yeah?"

"Yeah," he says softly.

"Good. I've been practicing for years now."

His eyes light with a smothered laugh.

"The whole move-making thing is tough." I purse my lips together for a moment. "Putting yourself out there like that makes you feel like a vulnerable idiot."

"Sometimes we have to be vulnerable idiots," he says simply.

"Yeah, I've been a vulnerable idiot since we got here, but I mean, like, even more of a vulnerable idiot."

He chuckles. I push myself up and off the bed. His eyes follow me as I step toward him.

"Move over, please," I instruct.

He raises his eyebrows in amusement and scoots to the opposite edge of the twin bed. I settle myself on my side and prop my head up. We're inches apart, but nothing is touching.

I bite down a grin. "Look, literal and figurative move."

"Respect." He smiles freely. He studies me for a moment. "Just for reference, I know I acted like I was angry about what you told me at the coffee shop when we first got here, but in retrospect, I'm glad you made that move."

My heart swells. I imagine my lungs crushed against my rib cage.

I swallow. "Pilot, I know this is kinda weird to talk about, but I feel like I need to know more about your current 2017 life."

He exhales and flops onto the pillow, staring up at the ceiling. A minute passes. I drop my head onto the pillow too, but stay on my side, watching him.

"I don't know . . . My job is good. Stable. Amy and I, we live, lived . . . together. You asked if we were engaged that day at the café . . . I've thought about proposing. I guess I'd kind of fallen into this Sisyphean cycle, though, where I felt like I was constantly trying and failing to reach a point where Amy and I were back at a hundred percent. It wouldn't be fair to her or me to get engaged if we weren't at a hundred percent." He lets loose a long breath before rotating to face me. "Shane, my parents were going through a tough divorce the first time we were here."

I study his eyes for a second. "What?"

He stares back up at the ceiling. "Yeah, and I guess it's happening again now. They separated right before I left for London. I didn't really understand why, they tried to explain it, but I didn't really—I guess they just didn't want to try anymore. I don't know. They never really argued much, but all of a sudden, everything was a fucking crap show. They were debating whether or not to sell the house, where my sisters would live. My sisters were a mess. Holly was only twelve and Chelsea was fifteen. I was Skyping with them a lot while I was here, trying to help them figure everything out. My parents were asking them to choose where they wanted to live, and they didn't know what to do. My home life was changing so much, and I had no control over any of it."

He pauses. I stay silent, heart clenched up. All those times he was on a call or Skyping in the kitchen, it could have been with one of his little sisters? I always assumed it was with Amy. I take his hand and give it a gentle squeeze. He returns the gesture.

"It was hard to imagine anything else changing, you know?"

I exhale a breath. "Pies, I had no idea. I'm so sorry."

"Yeah, it's okay. Things are okay now. At the time, you know, it was hard being so far away from it. And at the same time, I didn't want to talk about it here because it's kind of like what you said the other day—it was a nice escape not to have to think about it all the time. It's surreal now. I mean, I just talked to Holly this past week, she's eighteen in 2017, and she was so little here. It was such a trip."

He turns onto his side and props his head up again. I prop mine up too, so we're on the same plane.

He shoots me a small smile. "Sorry, that was kind of a downer. I just wanted to tell you."

"I'm glad. Thanks for being a vulnerable idiot. I appreciate it," I say quietly.

"Maybe let's change the subject," he adds hesitantly.

My lips turn up. "Okay." I think for a moment. "How about you tell me the stuff you like? Stuff you find out on dates."

"What kind of stuff?"

"Everything. Like things! Stuff! I know some things, but give me more."

He purses his lips.

I snort. "Do you need an example? Go ahead and ask me what I like," I prompt.

"What kind of stuff do you like, Shane?" he asks, amused.

"Obviously *Lost*—Juliet inspires me. Harry Potter always makes me happy. I love walls full of pictures. If I ever build my own house, I'm making a room just for pictures, where I'll plaster them on every surface. Extreme photo-albuming!" I pause for a second. "Black raspberry ice cream because it's delicious, but mostly because it's a wonderful purple color, and it doesn't taste like grape. And I like when thunderstorms make the lights go out at night, and you're stuck inside with your family using flashlights for hours. Everyone acts like it's the worst and such an inconvenience. And it is, but the bigger part of me gets excited by the darkness, and the lack of technology, and the need for flashlights. It's the best way to gather everyone around a table to play cards. No one's distracted by anything, and you play by the candlelight, and you all watch the storm through the big back windows, but you stay away from the windows because you don't want to get electrocuted." I sigh, suddenly fighting off a wave of homesickness. The last time that actually happened, I was sixteen. The three of us were at Uncle Dan and Aunt Maria's for dinner.

Pilot eyes me thoughtfully.

"Your turn," I whisper.

"I've never met someone as outwardly passionate about their favorite things as you."

"Well, things inspire me and make me happy and feel more understood . . . if I can give that to someone else by recommending my things, I want to." The way he's watching me, I feel like I'm under a spotlight. I swallow.

"So, your turn now," I say quietly. "What things do you like?"

"I like mint chocolate chip ice cream," he says, trying not to smile. I wait.

"Because . . ." I goad.

He looks thoughtful again. "Because it's refreshing. Like when you walk out onto the street in the fall and the leaves are swirling around, and you get pummeled with the perfect amount of windchill." I nod appreciatively.

"Music, guitar, records. Troubadours in the wild. The idea of living day by day, making music, brightening someone's life with the things you make. The courage it takes to do something like that is admirable. They make me want to make things.

"Exploring places on foot with a real map, no GPS." He pauses. "My family. I can really get behind a good game of cards."

"So nothing too nerdy, then?" I ask.

"I like you." He grins.

I smile down at the bed, closing my eyes for a second. "What a line. I guess I set you up for that."

He continues, "I know you hate those chairs in the kitchen, but I can't help but hold a special place for them in my heart. Watching that ongoing struggle, Shane versus chair, has brought me so much joy."

I reach out my free hand and push his shoulder. He catches my elbow, slowly sliding his hand up to my mine and weaving our fingers together. I can feel the heat coming off him.

This has gone as far as I'd like it to in a room with two sleeping strangers. I sit up, twisting away to put my feet back on the floor in between our beds. I'm radiating dangerous levels of joy. The bed moves as Pilot sits up and scoots toward me.

"You okay?" he asks quietly. His concern fades when he finds me struggling to subdue the banana-sized smile spread across my cheeks. I bring my face close to his again, reveling in the electric feeling that sparkles over my skin. "I like you too," I whisper. "I've changed my answer: five-star Yelp rating for date number two."

He leans in to close a kiss, and I back out of reach.

"Good night." I chuckle, rising from the bed.

"Hey." He catches hold of my hand. I drop back down, grinning.

"Is this you officially surrendering to my whisper move?"

He scoffs. "Five-star Yelp rating, and no kiss at the end of the night? That just doesn't add up."

"Admit your surrender."

He holds my gaze. I shrug and push off the floor to stand. He tugs me back, and I twist around, landing happily back on the bed.

"You win," he concedes. His lips find mine, and they're charged full of fire. I'm floating when I pull away.

15. Don't, Don't Know What It Is

In the morning, Pilot and I meet Babe and Chad in the lobby before heading to the Louvre. We wander the museum as a foursome. Chad uses the word *bro* fifty times more frequently than necessary.

We all climb to the first tier of the Eiffel Tower. I'm bursting with blissful energy. I dance my way across the landings and skip up the steps. When it's time for tier two, Babe and Chad turn off toward the elevator.

Pilot meets my eyes with an impish grin. "So predictable."

I'm drunk on excitement. Happiness. I'm really happy. And it's intoxicating. I smile, turning my attention back to the first-tier view of Paris.

Pilot nudges me gently. "Ready to attempt to climb to the top and be turned away due to high winds?"

I snort. "Always." We round the corner and start the second leg, hiking side by side up another collection of metal steps.

Did I really just say *always*?

"Pies, would you agree that we're on a rom-com-esque date right now?" I start.

Pilot smiles at the steps, keeping his hands in his pockets. "Yeah."

"Well, I just said *always* a second ago when you asked me a question, and I hated it," I sass.

He scoffs, "Hated it? Like, hated the question?"

"Hated the word *always*."

"Because?" he asks, humoring me.

My smile spreads. "Well, I'm glad you asked. See, all the famous book-slash-movie couples have these, like, deep, meaningful moments where they say *always* in response to some deep, meaningful, cute, adorable question. And then all the fans of said book-slash-movie couple get *always* tattooed on them as a nod to that couple or that moment, and the word *always* is so completely overused that, like, how am I even supposed to know what couple or moment they're referring to in their meaningful tattoo, you know?" I drop my flailing hands back to my sides.

Pies pulls a goofy *eh* expression. "I guess," he concedes.

"And then there was *Okay, Okay* in *TFIOS*, where they finally broke the mold, and it was beautiful," I say, continuing my lecture as we circle around another landing and onto another flight of steps.

"What's *TFIOS*?"

"A great book."

"Okay," he agrees automatically.

"Okay, so the point is: Since we're in our own rom-com right now, we should have our own stupid, unique *always*, so people can make tattoos about us!"

He laughs. "What did you have in mind?"

"I don't know. We don't want to mess this up. We have to think it through, so we go down in history the right way."

Pilot snorts.

"What was that laugh?" I accuse, trying not to laugh myself.

"You're ridiculous."

"This is deep, meaningful stuff, Pies."

He smiles, hands still stuffed in his pockets. We climb in silence for a few moments, the metal reverberating under our feet.

"Any ideas?" I ask curiously.

He juts out his bottom lip. "*Leather?*"

"*Leather?* That sounds a little dirty."

Another snort.

"What about *lamppost*?" I propose. "It's innocent, catchy."

"*Lamppost?*"

"Yeah, as in, *lamppost* will be our *always*."

Pilot treats me to a deadpan glare.

"It's gonna be great. Here, let's test it out. Ask me a question."

Pilot's smiling at the air in front of us now. "What kind of question?"

"Anything! Just a tester question."

He stops on the landing between staircases for a moment, so I come to a halt in front of him.

He clears his throat and puts on a funny romantic voice. "Shane." He gazes into my eyes like a cartoon prince. "Are you Santa?"

I step up close to his face. "Lamppost."

He turns away with an eye-roll-smile combo.

"That sounded nice, right?" I goad. He pulls his hand from his pocket and takes mine as we continue up.

When we reach the second tier, I hurry over to the edge, pushing my hand up against the metal cage around us. Pilot shuffles up next to me.

"Still incredible," he says.

"Pies?" I ask, cheerily turning away from the view.

He turns to me abruptly. "Lamppost."

"No!" I whack him in the arm, compressed laughter buzzing out of me. "That's not how it works! I have to ask a question where the answer is—"

"Oh, that's not how it works?" he interrupts, smirking. "This isn't how it goes?" He closes the gap between us and catches my lips. I get lost in the glitter for a second.

I'm smiling and shaking my head as we break from the kiss. "I was setting up for the perfect lamppost question!" I protest.

"Ah, but it was time for me to clock in another move."

"Time for you 'to clock in another move'?" I mock him, crossing my arms. "Do you have a quota to hit or something?"

"Yeah," he responds matter-of-factly. "Gotta keep on top of things if I want to maintain my Trip Advisor rating, Shane."

I scoff.

We catch up with Babe and Chad back at the bottom. Pilot and I break physical contact as we come up behind them. The four of us walk along the Seine. As the sun's setting Babe stops short and spins to look back at the Eiffel Tower.

"Wait! What time is it?"

"Bro, you pumped?" Chad wheels around to Pilot as we stroll toward the sounds of music in the Bastille.

"Toe, I'm so pumped," Pilot replies enthusiastically.

"Bro, I bet it's hype up in that one down there." He points down the street to the bar we went to last time.

"So hype, Toe."

Next to me Babe's brow crinkles. "Are you saying *Toe*?" she asks loudly. I cackle.

Chad strides forward without comment. Pilot falls into step on my other side.

"You excited to hit this place again?" he asks quietly as the four of us come up to the black awning.

"Lamppost."

He smiles.

I raise my eyebrows. "How doth one top a live oldies-classic-rock-punk-rock-from-the-early-2000s cover band, Pilot? It doesn't get better than that."

The band is in full swing as we mosh our way to the bar. It's not long before our foursome is torn into pairs by the mass of people chomping at the bit for alcohol. Pilot and I both order a gin and tonic before heading out onto the floor.

We situate ourselves side by side, swaying and playfully singing along with the set. When they play "What's My Age Again," I jump around, baptizing everyone in the vicinity with my drink. We're mazing our way to the back of the room to set down our empty glasses when "Basket Case" starts to play.

"Oh shit!" I exclaim, lightly whacking Pilot in the arm. I hold his eyes, bobbing my head with the beat, and he laughs at me.

"Let's dance!" I talk-yell.

He holds his lips in a small smile. "I thought we were getting new drinks!"

"*I am one of those melodramatic fools, neurotic to the bone, no doubt about it!*" I yell-sing dramatically, shaking my shoulders in time with the bass.

"Remember how I don't really dance?"

I shake my head. "Nope, you are not pulling that crap after the Versailles stunt."

His smile stretches to full capacity as he rolls his eyes. I raise my eyebrows expectantly. We stare each other down for a beat. And then he abruptly joins in with the band, "*It all keeps adding up—*"

I grab his hand, leading him back onto the dance floor, hop-skipping to the music. This time we face each other, not the band. I let go of his hand and flail-dance, singing at the top of my lungs. It's a technique I use to scare people into moving out of the way, thus carving out some space to actually dance. He watches me, unmoving and stone-faced for a good twenty seconds. I stubbornly hold eye contact: *Dance with me.* And then he does— bobbing his head around a little more intensely than usual. I mirror his cool-guy head bob.

As the song comes to a close, I grab his hands, pull him toward me, and drag us to the right. I let my arms straighten out, dropping back, changing our momentum, and then I pull myself toward him again. We crash into each other. He lets go of one of my hands and manages to spin me out like he did at Versailles. I laugh like a madwoman, whipping away from him, hair covering my face. I slam into the nearest human who's crept his way into our dance space and spit a stream of apologies as I quickly whirl back to Pilot. My back slams up against his chest, and I'm cackling, and I can feel his chest vibrating behind me as the song fades out.

Our hands are still connected, and he twists me around in the sudden silence. My heart hammers as our foreheads fold together.

"I don't know if we should keep going. You're a hazard to everyone within a six-foot radius."

I bring my arms up around his neck as the band starts a new song. "I'm not the one who whipped out the ballroom dance moves in a mosh pit."

He raises his head, looking thoughtful for a moment. My brain takes note of the familiar song floating around us now, much calmer than the previous one. "Yellow Submarine." The room falls into a mellow side-to-side sway as they sing along. We join them.

"Hey."

"Hey," he replies.

"You almost kissed me during this song," I tease softly.

Pilot's eyebrows come down comically. "And you pulled away."

My heart jumps into my throat. *So I did. Affirmative.* My mouth dries up with my heart all in there. We rotate silently for a stretch of lyrics before I tell him, "I got scared."

Pilot's thoughtful as the song draws to a close.

"How's present Shane doing?" he asks. Another song from my middle-school years explodes through the room.

"She's great. How's Pilot?" I yell-talk over the now blasting music.

"Scared shitless, to be honest." He smiles.

I raise my eyebrows. I want to come back to that, but right now I need to dance. I let myself drift outward, letting go of his hands to dance more freely. *All the, small things, true care, truth brings.* He sings along and starts trying to mirror my random assortment of moves, looking absolutely ridiculous.

Watching. Waiting. At some point, I topple over to my right and smack into a girl with a sparkly-gold tank top, flailing for purchase. But before I get any closer to the ground, Pilot catches hold of my arm and yanks me back over to him. I fly upright, colliding into him, and then his arms are tight around my waist, and we're kissing and dancing, and my heart's having one of its out-of-body experiences. I feel it floundering around above my head like in The Sims. The music surges: *Nanananananananananananananana.*

I don't want to break apart when we break apart.

"Shit." His twinkling eyes search mine.

"Shit," I agree.

The band starts a new song. "Want to grab a drink?" he asks.

"I actually have to hit the BR. Go grab yourself a drink, and I'll meet you over there!" I assure him with a dopey smile.

I run into Chad at the mouth of the hallway into the dance/bar area on my way back from the restroom. He strolls right up to me.

"Hey, Chad," I say reluctantly.

"Hey." He comes closer.

I take a half step back. "What's up?"

"You have really great hair."

I widen my eyes sarcastically. "Thanks."

Over his shoulder, I spot Pilot making his way over with a beer. I refocus on Chad to find him already going for it. His eyes are closed, and his lips are coming at me. I pull back and smack my hand across his face. It makes a lovely *thwack*.

"Ahhh!" His hand comes up to cup his cheek. He glares with drunken, slow-motion shock.

"Step away, asshole. You've seen me with Pilot literally all weekend, and you're here with Babe. You don't get a douche-kabob pass because it's your birthday."

I step past him to where Pilot is watching wide-eyed and amused. He falls into step next to me as we walk away. I glance around for Babe.

"Damn, is that what happened last time? Because I can't believe I missed that!"

"No." I snort. "Last time, I slid down the wall, ducked out, and ran away. I thought maybe this time would be a little different since the weekend has been so different, but nope, still a douche canoe."

He shoots me a goofy smile. "Look at you, relapsing back into your old smack-happy ways."

"Ha. Ha."

He shakes his head. "Once a smack addict, lamppost a smack addict."

I snort. "Pilot! You're using *lamppost* all wrong! And you're making the word *smack* sound like slang for hard drugs."

He throws his head back, cackling. I spot Babe in the opposite corner of the room, leaning against the wall with her arms crossed.

"Babe's over there. We should go keep her company."

The band finishes up twenty minutes later, and the three of us funnel toward the stairs. "We have to find Chad," Babe sighs as we make our way down.

"Don't worry. We'll catch him at the coat check," Pilot reassures her. Behind Babe, Pilot takes my hand. His thumb draws light, sparkly circles on my wrist. It's distracting.

"Are you gonna be okay with him tonight?" I ask her.

"Yeah, he's a drama king, but he's harmless. I went in to make a move earlier because I thought . . . I mean, I know him trying to hook up with you was his super-mean way of driving home the point that he only wants to be friends."

"Well, that's pretty shitty," I point out.

"This is a pattern with him. He acts out like a five-year-old. We're in a room with two other people, so he won't be obnoxious."

"My phone's on if you need me," I assure her. "Also, just for reference, we've already missed the last Metro, so we have to head straight for the taxi stand."

As we come around the corner of the staircase, Chad is visible, standing near the door with his head down and his hands in his pockets. The three of us get our coats, and Chad joins us silently as we walk to the cab stand down the street. Babe takes up a brisk pace, speeding ahead, and Chad lags behind.

"Hey." Pilot nudges me softly as we stroll down the cobblestone street.

"Hey." I nudge him back with my shoulder.

"Remember how we were going to time travel back to that Beatles concert?" He beams.

"Of course."

His eyes are bright. "Should we finally make our way to Edinburgh next weekend?"

"Why? Are the Beatles playing?" I quip.

He releases a breathy laugh and looks down, smiling.

"What's this, no retort? Master of moves, five stars on Trip Advisor, Pilot Penn is flustered?" I grin at him triumphantly.

He rolls his eyes.

"To answer the Edinburgh question, I've been dying to hit the birth-place of my home skillet Harry ever since the first time we discussed this."

Pilot drops his gaze. When he raises his head a few moments later, his eyes are troubled. "I'm sorry we didn't get to go last time."

I sigh. "Me too, but we'll go this time." I squeeze his hand before letting it go as we come to a stop behind Babe in the taxi line.

16. I'm a Goner

Forty minutes later, Pilot and I step off the elevator onto the sixth floor. We make our way to the end of the hall, coming to a stop outside the door, in a classic end-of-date posture.

"And so date number three draws to a close." He smiles.

"We're pretty good at this date thing."

"I agree."

He takes my hands in his, I lean forward, and our lips find each other. This kiss is fire again. I welcome the blaze, get lost in it.

My arms twist around his neck, and his hands run down my sides, flames running rampant over my skin as they graze over my thighs. And then I'm no longer on the ground.

My back's against the wall, and my ankles lock around his waist. I run my hands up from the base of his neck and through his hair, and break away to catch my breath.

I glance down at the floor. "How did this happen?"

"Not sure. Something with time travel?" He bats his eyelashes. They're so nice and long.

My hands trail down his arms—they're all banded with muscle. Dang, he's stronger than I thought. Our lips meet again, slower and more deliberate. His hands run up my back. Down my legs. A full-blown inferno is raging in me now.

We're in a hallway.

I pull away again. He smiles.

"We should probably go in and sleep, being that we're in the hostel hallway."

"Okay." He nods without breaking eye contact.

"You know you have really pretty eyes," I tell him.

He closes them for a moment, smile broadening. "I was thinking that same thing."

I bite my tongue. "You were thinking about your eyes too?"

He takes a step away from the wall, pursing his lips. Yes, we should go inside, but my body wants to stay here with Pilot. The craving is captivating. It really likes him. This never happens . . . this always gets old pretty quickly. We kiss, it's nice, and I'm ready to say goodbye and go back to my own personal space.

Not now. No, thanks. I want less space. No space.

We've entered into a staring contest.

"So, I think for us to go in, you'll have to get down." He raises his eyebrows. I snort. *Oh yeah.*

Instead of getting down, I tilt forward so our foreheads meet. "I really like it up here."

"I like you up here," he breathes. He runs his hands down my jeans again and my leg death-grip tightens. Then I'm against the wall again, and his lips trail up my neck before reaching mine. I pry up the front of his shirt.

In a hallway. I drop the hem and break away. Suck in a breath. "We have to stop."

"Did we not stop?" He feigns confusion. I smile, and with a great sigh, unhinge my legs and come back to earth, ramming my hair back with my hand. The keys are on the ground. Our jackets are on the ground. Wow.

"Well, we should do that again," I add, casually turning the key in the lock.

"Agreed."

I swing the door open. The older man is sleeping in the far-right corner, and there's a younger dude two beds over. I drop my purse on the bed and look over at Pilot. He's still lingering by the door.

This could all disappear tomorrow.

He meets my eyes and raises his eyebrows. "What?"

I walk over and take his hand. Before I lose my nerve, I pull him toward the bathroom.

What am I doing?

I close the door behind us. Click in the locks on both sides. Pilot watches me carefully. I undo the top button of his plaid shirt. He doesn't move, so I continue, watching his face. I reach up and push the shirt off his shoulders. It falls. He's wearing a white T-shirt underneath. His hands take my waist and slide under my own shirt. They work their way up my stomach, sliding against my skin, pushing off the top as they go.

"Do you want to . . . ?" he breathes.

"Yeah, you?" I smile.

"I do, but." He laughs and hooks his fingers through my belt loops and draws me closer. "In this bathroom just seems so un-you."

He's right. I do hate this bathroom. His fingers trail around my lower back, tracing the waistband of my jeans. Fire. Fire. Fire.

"Right now, I don't see the bathroom," I answer honestly.

He exhales a breath, and his fingers move to unbutton my jeans. He lowers himself down to his knees and slowly guides them off. His fingers trace lines down my legs.

I'm trying to breathe normally. It's not happening.

I step out of the pants, still wearing my army boots because let's be real, this floor can't be trusted. As he rises off the ground, he picks me up again. It's the hottest thing that's ever happened in my romantic history. I wrap my arms around him. My legs relock over his waist. Our lips meet. More flames. We move. He settles me on the sink.

The hostel bathroom sink. I start to laugh through our kiss.

He pulls away an inch, smiling. "What's so funny?"

Another huffed laugh. "I don't know. I mean, you're right, we're in the hostel bathroom. Is this gross? Are we disgusting?" My smile is giant and toothy.

He beams. "I mean, there's a shower right there, Shane. Are you feeling disgusting?"

"No." I laugh against his forehead, and then his hands are around my thighs, and he's picking me up again. We're moving toward the shower. I squeal, unlocking my ankles and squirming.

"No!" I giggle, my head thrown back. "Not the shower! Anywhere but the shower!"

"What are you talking about? We love this shower!" he quips.

He steps into the tiny shower, fully clothed, with me wrapped around him, having a laughing fit. My legs press against the cold tile wall. We're taking up literally all the space in here just standing still. His smile widens. He lets go of one of my legs to slam his hand into the one giant silver button. I'm in straight-up hysterics as lukewarm water rains down, soaking us and our remaining clothes. Droplets hang from his eyelashes, and his white T-shirt clings to his skin. As our laugher dies, I release my legs and drop down with my boots. His mouth finds my ear and works its way back to my lips. My hands peel at his T-shirt, bringing it up and over his head. I throw it out onto the floor and take a second to study him. There are abs. His fingers play at my remaining undergarments, tickling my skin. And then, abruptly, the water stops.

Our gazes meet, and we both break into laughter. I drop my attention back down to the six-pack I unveiled.

I gesture to it, beaming. "What the hell is this? Does past you work out?"

He shakes his head with an embarrassed smile, and I run a hand over the chiseled-ness before slamming the water back on. He shivers and pulls me even closer. I'm so full of flames, I feel like my skin would glow in the dark.

"You should always be shirtless and in the rain," I tell him.

His mouth comes down on mine, and I fiddle with the belt on his jeans. "Only if you agree to the same dress code," he manages between kisses.

The water stops again. He slams it back on without breaking away and sweeps me off the ground again. He presses me against the cold wall, and slowly I start to slide down. He tries to steady me. I try to steady myself like a spy in a chimney. My boots squeak against the tile, the struggle.

"We can do this," I say between gasps.

"We can do this!" he echoes.

It's a very tiny three-walled shower. Everything's slick now, and we fumble like drunken sailors. Laughing, he takes a step back. We flail without the support of the wall. Mid-kiss, his back hits the tile behind him, and I yelp as we topple slowly downward, along the wall, tile squealing, until we're huddled in a clump on the floor. He hunches forward, snickering, and I'm convulsing silently, doing my best not to wake up the universe with the sound of my laughter.

The water stops again. I bite my lip to contain my giggles, and shiver in the absence of warmth.

"You know what?" He narrows his eyes.

"What?"

He pushes some hair out of my face. "We're getting a bed," he says.

I raise my eyebrows. "Where will we find this mystical bed?"

He takes my hands, helping me off the floor.

Five minutes later, we're running down the hallway, shivering, hand and hand, toward the lobby. My hair sprays water everywhere, the wetness of my bra soaks through my shirt. My boots squish against the floor. Pilot looks like he got pushed in the pool with his clothes on; his jeans are heavy and waterlogged.

We stop short in front of the teenager behind the front desk. Freezing, I press up against Pilot's side, still smiling like a moron. He wears his own goofy expression.

"Hi, we're going to need an empty room," he says.

The young girl looks up from her magazine, eyes sweeping over us in confusion. "Um . . . a private room is going to be more expensive—"

I shiver against Pilot. He runs his hand up and down my arm before pulling out his wallet. "We want the room."

I swing open the door to a room full of empty beds. Pilot pulls me inside, and I kick the door closed behind us.

17. Shining

I wake tangled with Pilot in one of our four beds, his breathing still soft and even next to me. I still feel like I'm sparkling inside and out. I'm tempted to make a *Twilight* reference, but I refrain. I've never had a night like that with Melvin. I never had dates like these with Melvin. I've never felt a shred of this with Melvin. Seriously, what was I doing with Melvin?

Our bags sit in the corner of the room. Pilot went back up to get them from our locker in the shared room last night. I slowly slip out of the bed and scurry off to the bathroom to get dressed and brush my teeth.

Pilot's eyes crack open as I return and sit on the edge of the bed. He lifts the thin, translucent sheet up in invitation. I slide in and snuggle up next to him.

"Good morning," he opens, voice thick with sleep.

"Morning," I say quietly.

"That was a really great three-date extravaganza."

I smile. "I'd concur."

One side of his mouth kicks up. "You'd concur?" he teases. "What's the Trip Advisor verdict? How many stars?"

I prop up my head on my hand. "Mmm, what do you think?"

He smiles lazily and holds up ten fingers. He blinks them in and out twice.

I cackle, dropping back down onto my back. "I concur."

Babe and Chad are on opposite sides of the waiting bench near the barren front desk.

"Hey," Pilot and I greet Babe. She raises her head, looking fabulous as usual with her red lipstick and white beret. Chad continues to stare at the floor like the charming chap he is.

"Hey, let's go grab a cab," is all Babe says before bolting for the door. I follow her, roller bag in tow. It takes the same long ten minutes I remember to find a cab. Babe loads in first while the driver chucks our luggage into the trunk. Before we left our room, Pilot and I had a heated debate about whether or not Chad would insist on a separate cab this morning, and whether or not he'd have a bruise on his left cheek.

"He's not going to have a bruise!" I laughed.

"He wailed a little too loud for there to be no bruise," Pilot snickered, as he slung his backpack up over his shoulders.

"Five pounds says he still whines about wanting his own taxi," I challenge excitedly.

"Ten pounds says he's definitely going to whine about wanting his own taxi."

"That's not how bets work!"

As the cab driver slams down the trunk, Pilot and I share a look.

I try not to outright smile when Chad barks, "I'm not getting in that taxi."

I cross my arms and glare at him from next to the taxi door. "There are four seats in this taxi. It took us ten minutes to find this one. You can come with us, or you can go alone."

"I don't want to go in the same taxi as her," he says in a quieter voice. He swings his eyes to Pilot, silently pleading like a four-year-old.

I duck into the car, taking the middle seat next to Babe. She's pointedly staring out the window at an empty metal gazebo across the street.

"Come on, dude, you can take the front," Pilot reasons calmly before ducking into the back. He scoots next to me, places his backpack near his feet, and closes us in. The two of us watch Chad through the window. He deflates, walks around to the passenger door, throws it open, and drops his ass into the front seat.

"Gare du Nord, please!" I tell the driver.

Pilot puts his hand on my knee and squeezes it, smirking at this little victory. He leans in until his lips are against my ear and whispers, "He's scared of you," sounding amused as hell.

Paris *whooshes* by our window as the Eurostar train pulls away from the station. I'm seated next to Babe. Pilot and Chad are a few rows up. Daily Babe lives and breathes somewhere around a nine on the happiness scale, but at the moment she's dipped to at least a four. We're silent for about ten minutes before I decide to try to draw her into conversation.

"Babe," I start hesitantly.

"Babe," I repeat a little louder because she's still staring out the window. I not sure what I'm going to say yet. The classic question is: *Are you okay?* But when someone asks me if I'm okay, and I'm clearly not, it busts apart my tear-duct dam.

"Babe!" I say one more time. She turns away from the blurry scenery to shoot me an exhausted look.

"What?" She sighs.

My forehead scrunches up as I try to find the right words. "Um . . . I . . . why is your name Babe?"

"Why is my name Babe?" she echoes, sounding disoriented.

"Yeah, it's a different name. I was wondering if there was a story behind it." I raise my eyebrows.

She sighs again, and to my relief, the corner of her lip flits up a tiny bit. "It's not actually my real name."

"*What?*" I say a little too loudly. I'm shocked that I don't already know this. I've known her for years now. How did I never ask this question?

"Yeah, it's Barbara." She smiles a little now. A really small one, but it counts.

"I can't believe all this time your name has been Barbara, and we didn't know. That's insane. Does everyone call you Babe?"

"Nope, I thought it'd be a cool nickname, so I changed it on Facebook and told you guys it was Babe when we first met."

"Wow. Kudos." I shake my head slowly, processing this. "I always wanted a nickname growing up, but there are no good nicknames for Shane."

"Shay?"

"Not a fan," I dismiss.

"Shaney?"

I stick out my tongue. "Shane is the only adequate form of Shane."

We fall silent. "Shall we play a game?" I suggest.

"You brought a game?"

"Only the best game, cards—or we can play the extremely annoying to those in our general vicinity, but fun for us, I'm Going on a Picnic!"

She laughs. "I've never played that! How does the annoying one go?"

"Okay, so we go back and forth, adding things to a list, that start with each letter of the alphabet . . . You know what'd be fun, let's make it so you can only bring things related to either Disney or Harry Potter. I'll start us off." I clear my throat. "I'm going on a picnic, and I'm going to bring . . . Albus Dumbledore."

She narrows her eyes with a smile. "I'm going on a picnic and I'm going to bring Albus Dumbledore . . . and Babboo?"

"There we go; we're doing it. Now, it's only a matter of time before the people in our car hatch a plot to smother us."

She giggles next to me, and I continue on, "I'm going on a picnic, and I'm going to bring Albus Dumbledore, Baboo, and Cedric Diggory."

"I'm going on a picnic and I'm going to bring Albus Dumbledore, Baboo, Cedric Diggory, and Donald Duck."

"I'm going on a picnic and I'm going to bring Albus Dumbledore, Baboo, Cedric Diggory, Donald Duck, and . . . umm . . . Extendable Ears!"

We entertain ourselves for ages playing a game for six-year-olds on a long car ride. It's numbing in a good way, like an elementary sort of meditation. It forces you to channel any wandering thoughts into remembering random words in alphabetical order. When we've finally finished, we lapse into silence. I can tell when Babe starts to fade back into her turmoil of upsetting Chad-related thoughts because her expression starts to droop.

"Hey!" I try to catch her before she falls too deep again. She turns to face me.

"Yeah?"

"Um." I swallow. "I just want to say, you're great, Babe, and smart, and organized, and fun, and you're going to find someone really, really great eventually. I know you are."

She rolls her eyes.

"Like really though. I'm not just saying that," I finish assertively.

She huffs a reluctant laugh. "Uh-huh. How do you know? You can see the future?" she retorts sarcastically.

"In a manner of speaking."

"Shane, you're something else," she answers, like she's aged fifty years and become my great aunt.

I smile at my hands. "Proud to be something else. Normal's overrated."

"Amen to that." She turns to look out the window. I reach over and wrap her in a quick, awkward side hug, and we fall back into silence.

18. Break Your Walls

January 24, 2011 (take two)

Mom and Dad,

When I write these, all I can think about is 2017.
I'm so confused about my life. When did I stop
manning the wheel? Was it here? Was it when I came
back home? Was it a gradual process or did I let go
all at once?

Last night, we Skyped before you went to dinner at
Aunt Marie and Uncle Dan's. When was the last time
we did that?

We don't even try anymore. When did you stop
trying? Why did you stop trying?

XO,
2017 Shane

After class, I knock on Pilot's door with my digital camera. It swings in after a few seconds. He openly smiles at me, and it's wonderful. His guitar lies on the blue bedspread.

"Hey!" He steps aside so I can come into the room.

"Hey, have you been guitar-ing?" I ask.

"Yeah, doing some light guitar-ing, working on some new stuff." I watch as he catches sight of the camera in my hand. "What's that?"

"This is my blender. I thought we could make smoothies."

He presses his lips together and takes a step back. "Did Shane Primaveri just make a dry, sarcastic remark?"

"I'll have you know, I make more than one dry, sarcastic remark per year now."

He drops back on the bed with a chuckle. I lean against the doorframe.

"So?" he asks with raised eyebrows.

"Oh yeah, so!" I do a little hop as I stand up off the wall I was leaning on. "I'm here to jumpstart your musical career."

"Oh yeah?"

"Yeah, I have an evil-genius foolproof plan. It worked for Justin Bieber, and it's going to work for the Swing Bearers."

He rolls his eyes, but humors me.

"We're gonna start your YouTube channel." I walk over and sit next to him.

"You know YouTube and all that stuff really isn't my thing."

"Is music your thing?"

"Yeah."

"Do you want people to hear your music?"

"Yes," he says with a small smile.

"Would you want to potentially make music for a living?"

He glares at me with a cynical grin and half-lidded eyes.

"This is just a platform to jump off. YouTube is huge. People can discover you there; you can build an audience there; it's a portfolio when you're trying to get a job. It can provide endless possibilities! I spend a lot of time on the internet. I've watched it with my own eyes!"

"And what exactly are you planning with the camera?" he asks, amused.

"We're going to record your first video!"

"Right now?"

"Why not?" I raise my eyebrows. His lips come together as he ponders this. After a moment, he picks up his guitar.

"I was thinking a duet." I scoot back so I can lean against the wall and sit crisscross applesauce.

He grins now, guitar in position. "You sing-sing?"

"You doubt me?"

"I would never," he says matter-of-factly.

We stare at each other for a moment before I clear my throat. "Okay! So, I think we should do a duet of 'Wrecking Ball.'"

He laughs, shaking his head. "Still set on that?"

"Just this one song. Come on. We'll call it a cover. We won't take credit. Humor me here," I ramble incessantly.

He smiles at the ceiling for five seconds before he turns to look at me again. "Give me half an hour to work out the chords."

I grin. "See you in half an hour."

When our slightly altered version of "Wrecking Ball" comes to an end, we smile at each other for a good long moment. I get up quietly and stop the recording before retreating to my spot next to him on the bed. During the half-hour break, I dressed up a little fancier and threw on some red lipstick for my YouTube debut. Now I feel a smidge overdressed.

"You have a nice voice." He carefully sets down his guitar by his desk.

"Thank you, O musical one," I say, crossing my legs. "Are you happy with that take?"

"I think that's going to be our most genuine take." We only did one take.

"I agree. It's 2011 YouTube; we can get away with that performance."

I hand him the memory card. He pops it into his computer and drops the file to his desktop before giving it back to me. I replace it as he lies down on the bed. He puts his hands behind his head and watches me. I stay seated on the edge, legs hanging off the side.

"That red lipstick is driving me crazy," he says after a few moments.

I laugh. "Did you want to use it?"

"Lamppost."

My heart ricochets. "Did you just use *lamppost* unprovoked in a real-life conversation?"

"I think I did."

I bring my face within centimeters of his. "You know cutesy, romantic callbacks to our shenanigans are my kryptonite."

He's silent for a beat before he says it again: "Lamppost."

I suck in a breath. "God, that's so hot."

He chuckles and tucks a batch of hair behind my ear. "You look gorgeous. We should go out."

I laugh. "Okay."

Paris was freezing but it's beautiful in London. The sun's out and the temperature's in the low sixties: it's *mild*, as I've heard the British call it. Pilot and I walk through the city hand in hand. I ride the London Eye at sunset with Pilot standing behind me, his arms draped around my waist, my head against his shoulder. We kiss on benches and on bridges. We get dinner and stop in at a pub for a drink. We walk through to Hyde Park. We find a perfect spot, not far from the Karlston, lie in the grass, and talk.

I learn more about his little sisters. He tells me about the day he taught the younger one, Holly, to ride a bike when his parents were on vacation. He seems really protective over them.

"Can I ask you something?" he says softly.

"Yeah."

"What's the deal with you and your family?"

I'm quiet for a moment. I don't know how to *really* talk to people about my family. Where do I start? You share surface details, and they don't understand why I needed to get away. But you dig too deep, and they only see the bad.

"It's hard to explain. I guess they always end up making me feel like I'm not welcome to be myself. That sounds dramatic." I sigh. "But they have this preconceived idea of what I should be, and if I don't lean in to it, I feel like I'm not up to par."

Pilot's thumb skates around on the back of my hand.

"I've been trying to lean in my entire life. I love them. I know they love me. I know they think they're helping me by setting these invisible rules. But I can't fit that mold, no matter how hard I lean, and it makes being around them"—I stare up into the cloudy night sky—"exhausting."

Pilot squeezes my hand. "Have you ever told them that?"

I shake my head against the hood of my jacket and heave in an uneven breath. "Topic change?"

Pilot releases my hand and rolls onto his stomach, leaning over me. He traces a finger down my jawline. Across my collarbone. "What's your favorite song, Primaveri?" His eyes sparkle.

"Like, what's my favorite to hear, or my favorite that makes me feel all the feelings?"

He settles on his side next to me, head propped up on his arm. "Both."

"Favorite to hear is 'Bohemian Rhapsody.' When it came on in the car, my dad always used to crank it, and the three of us would fall into the different parts as if we'd discussed it beforehand, belting out the lyrics." I grin, thinking of my mom headbanging to the guitar in the passenger seat.

He nods. "Solid."

"I feel like I'm going to be judged for my other favorite."

"Is it your BFF T-swizzle?"

I grin. "Yes." I gaze into the darkness. "It's called 'All Too Well.' And it's beautiful. I love the words and the pictures they paint and the way it always tears at my heart. Do you know it?"

"I do."

I whip my gaze back to his. "You do?"

"I do. I have *Red* in my iTunes library."

"Since when?" I demand.

"Since it came out in 2012," he says.

"You know the year? What, you like Taylor now too?" I ask incredulously. "But you're like that guy who thinks his indie record is so much cooler than hers!"

He laughs outright at that. "I am not." He drops back onto the ground.

I watch him suspiciously. "Sing something from 'All Too Well.'"

He raises his eyebrows, and sing-speaks, *"Time won't fly, it's like I'm paralyzed by it."*

"I can't believe this."

"*I'd like to be my old self again.*"

I fall next to him on my back. "I can't believe you've been holding out on me for, like, two weeks as a closet Taylor Swift fan!"

He laughs.

"What's your favorite song?"

"It's from one of my obscure artists."

"To be expected," I say, propping my arm up under my head again to look down at him. "What's it called?"

"'Holy Branches.'"

My forehead crinkles with unexpected recognition. "I know that song," I divulge happily. He smiles skeptically at me now. "No, I really do! The Radical Face?"

"What?" he yells, amused.

"What are the chances?" I say, feeling cocky.

He's giving me suspicious side-eye now. "How do you know them?"

"They're on my work playlist."

"How did you find them?"

"An author I love recommended one of their songs once. I have, like, six of their songs on my playlist."

"This is weird." He grins and pulls his hands up behind his head.

"Holy crap, it's two a.m." I drop my phone back in my purse and roll on top of Pilot, hovering on my forearms. "We should probably head back." I smile down at him. I've been smiling for hours. I lift a hand and trace his eyebrows.

"Then the night will end," he says. "And I don't think I'm ready for that." He watches me for a few moments. I feel like a googly-eyed teenager. We've been talking for hours.

"Remember that notebook you had, back in the day?" Pilot says softly.

My finger stops tracing. "Yeah."

He studies me thoughtfully. "I used to watch you scribbling in that all the time. You don't do that anymore."

My lips part. I scoot onto the ground again. Pilot shifts to catch my eyes.

"Your mouth would move like you were talking to the page. I imagined the sound of your voice being drawn out—going straight from your mind to the paper, like your arm was an audio cord."

I swallow, tamping down a sudden urge to cry. "Yeah, I guess I don't trust notebooks with my thoughts anymore."

Pilot frowns, dragging a finger delicately from my temple to my chin. "When did that happen?"

I watch the sky. "Sometime that year, someone got ahold of one of my notebooks and read it."

He squeezes my hand. "Shit, that's horrible. I'm sorry."

Pilot's wrapped around me, still asleep. Slowly, I extricate myself enough to look over the edge of my bunk. We got back so late, and snuck up here in the dark. I blow out a breath when I see the girls are both already gone. The blinds to the kitchen are open, but I don't see anyone in there. It must be late, usually someone's—

"Oh my god!" I bolt up in bed and hit my head on the ceiling with a bang. "Ah!" I fall forward and clamber over Pilot's legs to get to my phone sitting atop the closet against the bunk.

Pilot stirs as I snatch up the phone. "What? Are you okay? What's going on?" His voice is groggy.

Panic courses through me. Eleven o'clock. It's 11:00 a.m.! I turn to see Pilot propping himself on his elbows, hair poking every which way.

"Pilot, it's eleven and our internships started today!"

His eyelids fly back. *"Shit."*

19. Heavy as the Setting Sun

It's 12:16 p.m. when I step up to the door of *Packed!*. My hair is still wet, and I'm wearing minimal makeup. I've dressed in the first suitable thing I could find in my closet: dark blue jeans and a black T-shirt. I ran from the Covent Garden Tube stop, so I'm sweating. I fly up the stairs and bust through the office door as soon as Tracey buzzes me in. Tracy's sitting behind the desk, watching me.

"Tracey, hi!" I drop my hands to my hips, breathing heavily.

"Hi." She glances at her computer. "Are you okay? You're two hours and sixteen minutes late," she says quietly.

"Yeah, Tracey, I'm so sorry. My alarm didn't go off, and it won't happen again." I take a few more heaving breaths.

"Okay." She clicks a few things on her computer and turns back to me. "You can sit over there." She points to my old station. The aged white MacBook is already sitting on the table. "If you need any help, you can contact me via IM." I wring my hands in front of me, waiting for more, but she goes back to her work.

"Um, okay, great, thank you!" I stammer. I swipe my wet hair into a ponytail and sit in front of the laptop, still catching my breath as I power it up. I wonder if Pilot got to work okay.

I pull the British phone from my purse to find a text waiting.

Pilot: Hey, did you get to work okay?

314

Me: Yeah, I made it! I look like waterlogged newborn baby, but I'm here.

Pilot: Trust me, you do not look like a newborn baby. Waterlogged looks good on you. ;]

Me: Waterlogged looks great on you too

Pilot: Want to get waterlogged later?

Me: Lamppost down for waterlogged

Pilot: Waterlogged has lost meaning

I message Tracey three times throughout the day, asking if she has any tasks, and eventually she sends me to the grocery store for food and asks me to look up coatracks. Pilot and I text all afternoon. By the end of the work day, I'm itching to get back to him. When Tracey dismisses me at five, I practically leap out of my seat. I beam the entire way home—I think I left a trail of sunshine on the sidewalk.

Pilot sits against the far wall on the bed, and I sit perpendicular to him on the adjacent wall with my legs draped over his lap. My laptop is on my lap, and his laptop is balanced on my shins. Atticus is out at his internship, so we have the room to ourselves. We book train tickets to Edinburgh for Friday afternoon after class, and a bed-and-breakfast for the weekend.

"Oh, man, look at this. They have famous ghost tours!" Pilot exclaims.

"Ghost tours?"

"And famous cemeteries," he continues.

"I've always dreamed of visiting a city famous for its valleys full of corpses." I swoon.

He grins, continuing his scroll through *Packed! For Travel!*'s top ten list of Edinburgh activities. "It's going to be an interesting trip."

I go back to scrolling on my own computer. "Look at this. They have a thing we can climb! A real nature thing!" I scoot across the corner so we're against the same wall, to show him my computer screen. "Look, it's called a crag, and we hike it to Arthur's Seat!" The pictures look beautiful.

"Whoa." He leans in to see my screen. "We're hittin' Arthur's Seat, for sure."

"Fo sho," I tease in a Chad-like voice.

I dress to the business-casual nines the next morning and arrive to work ten minutes early in my best black pants and black blazer with my hair done up in a bun.

"Morning, Tracey! Anything you want me to start with today?" I ask. She hasn't showed me the tea station.

"I might have some mail to be sent out later."

"Okay, great . . . well, I'll be over there whenever you need me."

My phone buzzes as I sit at my table.

Pilot: You were a vision in business casual when you left this morning =]

Shane: LOL thanks . . . I didn't see you this morning??? =P

Pilot: If you're within sight, Shane, I see you.

Shane: When was I within sight?

Pilot: Saw you walking from the kitchen to the stairs on my way to breakfast.

Shane: You should have stopped me and said good morning!

Pilot: Figured you were trying to get there early.

Shane: I was, but I'd have time for you.

I put down the phone, my skin tingling. I've started to crave his touch in the same way I crave food or water. I look up to see Wendy switching up the office music at one of the editing bay computers. I haven't had a chance to say anything to her. My phone buzzes in my lap.

Pilot: Can I take you to dinner tonight at 6?

Shane: I already can't wait.

Pilot keeps me entertained until 4:30 when Tracey finally tells me she's ready with the mail. I head up to her desk.

"Okay, here's a bag of the mail. You can drop these off at the post office and head home, or you can come back and stay. We've got a potential sponsor coming in for a seven o'clock meeting today if you want to stick around."

"Thanks, Tracey! Um, I think I'm going to head home because I have plans, but thanks! I'll get these to the post office stat!"

20. Waves Come After Midnight

Thursday morning I get up early and stop to buy bagels for the office so I have an excuse to talk to Wendy. Since I was late that first day, I guess Tracey didn't have time to give me the tour, which is fine because I know the office, but I really should have talked to Wendy. I was just feeling so gross and unpresentable that day, I put it off.

Once I get to the office, I greet Tracey, and head straight for Wendy's door. It's open. I peek in—she's wearing a tight red business dress and a black blazer, typing on her computer. I knock carefully on the doorframe.

She looks up and smiles. "Hi."

"Hi, Wendy! Good morning!" I smile back. "I just wanted to introduce myself again—I'm Shane—and say how happy I am to be working here. Thanks for having me. This company's amazing, and I'm looking forward to learning more from you and everyone, and hopefully writing that study abroad piece for the site. I brought bagels for the office!" I hold up the bag enthusiastically.

"Shane, that's sweet of you. Thank you for the bagels! You can set them up in the kitchen. There's so much to learn in this office. I hope you really enjoy your time here." She pauses, pressing her lips together. "Just to be completely straightforward, as far as writing a piece, that was actually still up in the air. I've rethought it a little bit. It's a big responsibility, so I'm not sure it's on the table anymore."

It's as if she pulled the ground out from under my feet. I take a step back to steady myself.

"Oh, Wendy, um, I'm up for the responsibility . . ."

She folds her hands atop her sleek clear desk. "Do you have any travel-related writing pieces I can look at?"

"I . . ."

I think back to the rambly post I wrote up about take two of Rome. It doesn't have any focus. That's not good enough. I started another post, but never finished. I haven't posted anything since Rome. I never finished that first post about the initial differences I noticed between New York and London. *Oh god.*

"Um . . . no," I finish quietly. I startle as the phone on Wendy's desk rings.

"I'm sorry, sweetie, I have to take this. Have a good day! Thanks again for the bagels!"

I plod across the floor to the office kitchen and methodically arrange the bagels on a plate. My limbs feel heavy, like I'm wading through the ocean. *The article is off the table?*

I fall into my seat. *How . . . but why?* I need that article. How could she just take it away? Why don't I have posts ready to show her?

The table vibrates slightly. I glance at my cell.

Pilot: I just heard someone use the word ravish at work. Can I pull off the word ravish? Or is it like knackered? =P

I drop the phone in my purse and zip it away. Tracey doesn't give me a task until 2:30. She hands me a bag of mail to drop off and tells me I can leave for the day. I feel like a popped balloon as I trudge down the road to the Tube station. I check my texts.

Pilot: Is everything okay?

Pilot: I'm back early today, so find me when you get home!

Pilot: I hope everything's okay.

I drop it back into my purse.

On the train, I shove in earbuds and close my eyes. *Now I get to go home and pack for Edinburgh. We leave tomorrow at twelve. Pilot's out early today. We can go get shawarma when I get back.*

I walk home to the Karlston on autopilot. The conversation I had with

Wendy won't stop rewinding and playing back in excruciatingly slow motion across my brain. I'm tromping numbly down the basement steps when I catch sight of a dark-haired girl in a tan leather jacket, standing where my carry-on landed when I dropped it my first day here. She's fiddling with an iPhone, and there's a suitcase by her feet. Is she lost? I pull out my earbuds and take another step down. She spins to look up at me.

I freeze like a deer in the headlights, eight steps from the ground. My heart falls out of my chest and smashes right through the staircase under my feet.

The girl eyes me hesitantly. *She doesn't know me.* She's never even seen me because I've been neglecting Facebook altogether.

"Um," she starts in a quiet voice, "I'm sorry. I just got here, and I'm trying to visit someone. I can't get on the Wi-Fi to tell them I'm here, and I'm not sure where in the building he lives. I mean, I know it's in the basement . . . Do you think you could help me? I'm looking for my boyfriend, Pilot. Do you know him?"

I nod.

"Could you show me?" she asks.

I jog down the last eight steps and start down the corridor. At the end of the hall, I point to his door like the Ghost of Christmas Future.

Amy shoots me a funny look. "Thanks."

I step toward my own room and put the key in the lock. When Pilot's door opens, I twist to face them just as she yells, "Surprise!" and hurls herself at him. He quickly breaks from her lips and takes a step back. I watch as he catches sight of me over her shoulder.

I'm sinking. His face is a spattering of shock as he looks from me to her, and then back at me. I rip open my door and slam it shut behind me. That's not how someone greets you after you've broken up with them. That wasn't a broken-up-with girl.

No one's in the room. I pace back and forth across the carpeted floor. He either didn't break up with her or she flew across the Atlantic Ocean to try and mend their relationship after he broke up with her and still calls him her boyfriend.

I drop to the floor and push up into downward dog. My mind is spinning in a hundred different directions. I stand, throw open Sawyer, and try to distract myself with Twitter. That lasts about half a second before I abandon the computer on a chair. *Everything's falling apart.*

I pace until there's a knock at the door.

How much time has gone by? Half an hour? I whip it open so fast a breeze crashes into me. Pilot stands in front of me, looking frantic.

"Shane! Can we talk?" I step aside, so he can come in and let the door fall closed.

"Where'd she go?" I ask.

"She's in my room."

"In your room?" I yell in disbelief.

He runs his hands up over his head.

I explode. "How could you lie to me about breaking up with her?" I try to keep my voice level, but I'm so mad, it won't stay down. "*What the hell is going on?*" I ram my hands over my hair. "Holy crap, I want to throw things right now! Were you just using me? Was this all bullshit to you?"

His sad bay-water eyes pierce mine for a long moment before he says, "Shane, I swear to god, I broke up with her."

I swallow hard and grind out, "Then what is she doing here?"

"It's gonna sound ridiculous."

I cross my arms. "I'm listening."

He pulls a chair from the table and drops into it. "I haven't talked to Amy since the day I made the call to break up with her . . . I tried to get her on Skype, but she wasn't available, and then I called her cell using Skype, and I got her voicemail. I was so ready and so prepped with what I needed to say, and I needed to say it right then. I just needed to get the words out, and I left it all in a message."

My head swivels back and forth in disbelief. "Oh my god." I start to pace again. "You broke up with her via voicemail?" I sputter.

He pops up off the chair. "We had just gotten here and it felt surreal, like it didn't really matter! At the time it was like, this was all just a weird magical trip!"

I stop moving. "What about now? Is it all still just a weird magical trip for you?"

"No!"

"If you broke up with her, then why is she here?"

He exhales a breath and closes his eyes. "She never got the message." He looks at the floor. There's a beat of silence while I process this.

My next question is slow and deliberate: "Figuratively or literally?"

"Literally."

I bring my hands up near my face and shake them angrily. "Oh my god!"

"The message didn't go through or something! I just awkwardly asked her if she got my voicemail, and she didn't even know what I was talking about. She can't call me here, and I took her off my Skype . . . she emailed me a bunch of times . . . but I was just deleting them, and she sent me some Facebook messages . . . I never opened them because I'm not good with confrontation, and I didn't want to deal with it. She said she always planned to visit me, and when she wasn't hearing anything, she decided to just fly out and surprise me. Shane, I had no idea!"

Words scrape up my throat, "Did you tell her what was in the voicemail?"

He sighs. "No, not yet."

My head throbs. "Are you going to tell her now?"

"She just got here after traveling for the last ten hours," he says solemnly. I feel that one in my gut. I actually hunch forward a tiny bit.

"I'm going to tell her! I'm just going to get her settled into a hotel or something, and then I'll explain everything." He stands up and puts his hands on my arms. "Shane, I'm with you."

My skin pulses. I bring my fingers up and press them against the sides of my forehead before shrugging his hands away.

"What kind of person doesn't wait for confirmation that their significant other actually acknowledged that they've broken up with them . . . if they're serious about breaking up with them? You knew she would want to respond to that! You think you could just leave a message and never talk to her again? If you really wanted to break things off, you would have at least read her emails to see what she had to say! If you were having trouble dealing with this, why didn't you tell me? We could have talked about it!" My voice wavers.

Pilot steps toward me again.

"Please don't touch me right now."

Pain flashes in his eyes. He sits back down in one of the table chairs and runs his hands up from the back of his neck to his forehead.

"Shane, I'm sorry. I screwed up. What do you want me to do? Do you want me to go across the hall and dump her here and now?"

I close my eyes, shaking my head. Tears stream down my face now. I back up until I'm sitting on Babe's bed.

"No," I mumble almost incoherently.

"You don't?" he asks gently.

I wipe at the tears and stare at him. My chest aches. We watch each other in silence for four minutes. My heart pounds painfully against my ribcage. *How did we get here so fast?*

At minute five, I say, "Pilot, this isn't working for me anymore."

Pilot blinks and refocuses on me. "What's . . . not working?"

I shake my head and gesture to the general room. "This."

"This what?" he says slowly.

I heave in a few more steadying breaths and stand to pull my purse from the table.

"What are you doing?"

I open the little zipper compartment and pull out the silver object inside.

"Shane," he says cautiously. "What are you doing? Please don't do that. Help me understand what you're thinking."

His voice is full of patience. It breaks my heart. I grip the locket hard in my palm and let the bag fall across my chest.

His voice wavers. "Everything's been really great with us. This past week has been amazing."

"Pilot, I'm losing myself here."

"What, what do you mean?"

I mash my lips together. "I'm losing myself and I'm becoming *us*."

He shakes his head, bewildered.

I fall back onto the edge of Babe's bed. "Whatever this is—" I have to heave the words from my lungs. They come out saturated and heavy. "I can't handle it. All I've been thinking about—is you . . . Pilot. I'm starting to physically feel the loss of you when we're apart.

"You know, I've been so distracted that I haven't had a substantial conversation with my best friend in six days . . . She literally sleeps in the bunk underneath me. I'm not that girl." I swallow. "I'm so distracted that I was two hours late for my first day at the most promising shot at my dream job I've ever been given. I'm *not that girl*. I never want to be that girl."

I bring my palms to my cheeks and drag them down my face. "I've been texting you endlessly at work. How did I think that was okay? And I've barely posted on my blog. I haven't done anything substantial to work toward this huge life goal that I somehow miraculously got a second chance at. Today, Wendy told me getting a piece published in *Packed!* was no longer on the table." I throw my hands up and gesture wildly. "It's off the table, Pilot! Just like that! Because I've been acting like a distracted teenager at a summer job!"

Pilot's face crumples. "Shane. I'm so sorry b—"

"I . . . failed here, and I can't sit and endure this failure all over again. I've already lived it. I'm *not* going to stay and watch my family find out about this and disown me as their daughter a second time."

"Shane." Pilot's voice quakes. "I know you're upset right now, but please, let's just take a breath. We can figure this out. I am so sorry. I will leave you alone as long as you need. Please, just think this through, okay? Think on it for the next twenty-four hours. Please. Let's check in again in twenty-four hours. We have something really great. I mean, at least, I thought. I, I don't want to give up on us, on here." He swallows.

I sob-breathe. "Here is hurting me, Pilot . . . I can't choose us because *I need to choose me.* I'm not ready for this. Here, I'm still in school and I'm still dependent. I can't break from my shit path. But in 2017, maybe I can *do something.* I have some money saved, and I'll break up with Melvin and start over or something. I can figure something out there."

"Shane," he breathes.

"Pilot, I want to reset. I need to steer my own boat, and I can't do it with you in my head. Just go back to Amy. This was a mistake."

A tear rolls down Pilot's cheek. "How can you say that?" He scrunches his eyes closed and swipes his palm across his face.

My mouth quivers as he gets up and leaves. The door shuts quietly behind him. I cross the room and slam my back against it. Nausea fills my gut. I sob freely as I slide to the ground. The chair Pilot was sitting in looms in front of me. I rein in my legs and explode outward, kicking at it. It blows over sideways, right into the chair next to it. The second chair starts to fall as well, and I scream in surprise as both it and Sawyer crash to the ground.

"No, no, no, no, nonononononononono." I leap up, grasping at the metal legs and throwing the chairs away from my computer. I frantically drag my finger back and forth across the touchpad.

The screen flickers to life with a huge black crevasse stretching across its center. Even the lit-up parts fade and flicker as if in shock. I hold down the power button to restart.

"Please please please please please." The screen goes to black, and then half a buffering circle fades into view on the screen. The top half is blacked out by the same thick, dark crevasse. "Please just turn on," I beg.

It buffers and buffers and buffers, but never *whooshes* on.

All my half-finished stories. The detailed outline for my great American novel. The three thousand words I threw up onto the page my first day of take two. The cloud doesn't automatically back up my shit here. It's all gone. And I don't have the money to replace it. *Am I breathing? I feel like I can't breathe.* I stand and put Sawyer on the table. I think I'm suffocating. I run upstairs and barge out the front door of the Karlston.

My boots carry me down the sidewalk. The locket is slick in my palm. My insides are fissuring. *I can't be here anymore.* I only make it to the corner before I unclasp my hand, flip open the locket to reveal the obsidian-black heart-shaped button within it, squeeze my eyes shut, and bring down my thumb to detonate.

21. Ford Every Stream

One at a time, I unscrunch my eyelids. Tears are still sliding down my cheeks. I glance around. Everything looks the same? I'm still on King's Gate? I sprint down the block to the newspaper stand. It's still *2011*.

"You've got to be shitting me." I stare blankly down the street on the corner of Gloucester Road until someone rams into my shoulder from behind.

"Excuse me!" I bark, stumbling to the side as they stride on by. It's a woman in a suit.

"Not how it works," she sings out, red hair bouncing behind her. I stare for a moment before chasing after her.

"You said this was our way out!" I yell to her back, holding up the locket. I'm only a few feet behind her, but suddenly the sidewalk is congested and I'm weaving through tons of people in suits coming toward me, all chattering away on their phones. *What the—*

"Come back!" I stumble to a stop, and press down on the obsidian heart again.

Still nothing. There's a tap on my shoulder. I whirl, and she's right behind me.

"What the hell is going on?" I demand.

"It'll work when y'all are ready," she says simply before rejoining the tide of suited individuals in movement.

I gasp through tears, stumbling after her. "But I am ready! I'm ready!"

I press the button again and again, sidestepping and twisting through the crowded pavement.

"Please, I'm ready! Please! Stop! Everything's ruined!" I trip over my feet and crash to the ground, scraping my knees against the concrete. My chest caves in on itself as I stumble to my feet again.

Shoulders convulsing, I press my hands to cover my eyes. Trapped. I'm trapped. I'm trapped here.

When I lower my hands, the sidewalk is clear. She's gone.

Headphones are back in my ears. Nobody speaks to me, despite the tsunami spilling down my face. That's the way it is on the Tube. You can always trust people not to talk to you.

Shame snakes through me. *I made Pilot cry. Wendy doesn't like me. I killed Sawyer. I didn't stay late when there was a meeting I could have listened in on. I haven't made any tea at the office. I have no connection to the internet. I told Pilot to go back to Amy! All my files are gone. I can't reset.* I ride aimlessly, switching lines every once in a while, feeling perpetually nauseated.

The sky is streaked in darkness when I step outside again. I exited at a stop called Bethnal Green. My eyes are swollen and raw as I roam the sidewalks.

At some point, I come to a halt, blinking at the building across the street. It's . . . a bookstore? There's a bookstore.

I swipe my face dry and cross the street. Inside, the air smells of wooden shelves, fresh paper, and a hint of must. I inhale it gratefully. The place is narrow, but there are two floors, and every inch is packed with book-laden furniture.

I explore thoroughly, slowly winding through the shelves, reading every title, running my fingers over spines. I pick up and caress books I've already read. I examine all the different editions of the classics. I haven't picked up a book that wasn't medically relevant in so long. When did I stop reading fun books? Two years ago? Before that? How did I let that happen?

My lip curls up the slightest bit when I finally stumble across the Harry

Potter section. It's been years since I've reread them. I miss them. I slide out the British edition of my favorite, *Prisoner of Azkaban*, and hold it to my heart.

I stroll around the store with it, hunting for the perfect reading spot. When I've scoped out the least visible nook between shelves, I slide onto the floor. As soon as my butt hits the ground, I'm gasping for air again.

I am stuck six years in the past.

I drop my head between my knees. This means I'm redoing the last few months of London in an internship where they don't take me seriously, with no computer, and reliving the nightmare with my parents. *I can't do that. I can't handle it. I don't want to. I want out. I want to go home. I want to start over.* I've lost my one connection to the rest of the world. This phone I have is a piece of crap. I can't do any of my internet stuff without Sawyer. My body shakes.

I focus on the book in my hands. Breathe. My favorite book. I have my favorite book. An edition I don't own of my favorite book. Breathe. I run my fingers over the British cover art. These are the stories that made me want to write stories. These are the stories that shaped my heart. I slowly pull open the cover.

My breath catches at the sight of a handwritten note. There's a note in the book. I huff an airy laugh. I've heard of people doing this, leaving notes for strangers in Harry Potter books. I heave in more oxygen and dip closer to read the tiny, slanted handwriting.

> *Dearest Reader,*
> *Even in the darkest of times, one must only remember to turn on the light.*
> *Dreams live up in the highest of mountains; the pursuit is ominous, but without them, we're just asleep.*
> *When you need it, Hogwarts will always be here to welcome you home. x*

New tears slip down my cheeks. I read it again. And again. And again. And again. And again. And again. For fifteen minutes, I sit there and read it. Then I swallow hard, sniffle, close the book, and bring it to the register.

I have a fucking mountain to climb.

22. Going for the Knockout

When Professor Blackstairs dismisses us from Friday class, I walk down the block and set up camp at Café Nero. Horcrux Nine sits in front of me, practically empty now. I open to a blank page, sip my latte, and draft a Paris blog post. The train Pilot and I booked to Edinburgh leaves without me on it.

When I've got the writing all sorted the way I want, I walk back to the class building. Inside, they have a couple of old PCs in a tiny crammed room they call a library, down in the basement. The post goes live at three: "The Noob's Guide to Paris." I text Babe and Sahra, and we make plans to test out a dance club tonight and explore some new areas of England.

On Saturday, we do a trip to Bath, and on Sunday, we go to Stonehenge. I bring Horcrux Nine, jotting down thoughts and interesting facts I want to remember.

Sunday night, I sit on my bunk, scribbling away, until I have another new post drafted, "You Don't Need a Plane for a Day Trip: Making the Most of Your Weekends Abroad!" When it's ready, Babe lets me borrow her laptop to type it up and publish it. God bless her.

———

January 31, 2011 (take two)

Mom and Dad,

I'm not giving in this time. You'll be upset to hear Sawyer died prematurely. He was the best gift you've ever given me and I'm devastated, but I'm going to make do. I guess I'll be seeing you for our big falling out in about a month. Fingers crossed it'll be different this time.

XO,

2011 Shane

Tuesday morning, I stride into *Packed! For Travel!* with determination etched into every fiber of my being.

I eagerly step up to the front desk. "Morning, Tracey! I was wondering if you could give me a list of everyone's work emails, so I have them on file for any assistance I can offer?"

She studies me warily for a moment. "Er . . . okay. I'll email it to you," she answers slowly. I thank her, set my things down, and head to the kitchen tea station.

The first cup I fix is for Wendy. I carefully walk it to her office and knock on the doorframe. She's wearing a pretty, pink, off-the-shoulder sweater with a white skirt. "Yes, come in!" she greets.

I step forward. "Hi, Wendy! Good morning! I made you a cup of tea." I slowly set the cup and saucer down on her desk.

"Oh my goodness, thank you." She smiles.

"I know I did this on Thursday, but I wanted to reintroduce myself again. I think I started off on the wrong foot last week . . . I'm Shane. I'm so excited to be here and learn, and if there's anything you can use my assistance with, please ask me. If there are ever any opportunities to shadow you or watch you in action, I'd love to do so. I know I already mentioned this in our interview a couple weeks ago, but I have a blog myself and I've turned it into a travel blog. I just love what you guys do here. I'll send over an email with this info, so it resonates, and you have my email if you need it."

Her smile broadens. "Thank you, Shane. I'll keep all of that in mind."

I nod back, grinning. "I'll be over there if you need me." I gesture to my table.

I head back to the kitchen and make another cup: this one for Declan. I bring it over to the editing bay.

"Hi, Declan! I've made you a cup of tea. I just wanted to introduce myself. I'm Shane . . ."

Then Donna. I go on like that, making my rounds, talking to all of them: Declan, Donna, the middle-aged man named George I've never interacted with, Janet, and even Jamie, the posh, bleach-blond woman that I avoided the first time because she scared me. I end by taking a cup of tea to Tracey and reiterating my sentiments.

"Thanks . . . How did you know about our tea station?" Tracey asks.

"Um, I saw the chart while I was putting the bagels out on Thursday," I tell her.

Now everyone knows my name, my intentions, and that my blog exists. I send them all separate emails with this information. And in each one I sign off with:

PS: I know I already talked about my blog; here's a link to one of my pieces: frenchwatermelon19.com/NoobsGuideToParis. I'd love for you to check it out. Notes and constructive criticism are always appreciated.

At 3:00 p.m., I do a quick lap around the office, checking to see if anyone would like a second cup of tea. Declan asks me where I'm from. Donna jokes around, saying how impressed she is with her excellent cup of tea—she wouldn't expect that from an American.

When I come in the next day, everyone greets me by name. I bring them all their morning tea without being asked. Donna invites me to come sit with her while she plans out her next work trip: She's headed to Capri on Thursday. I sit next to her for most of the morning. She talks about traveling and asks me where I've been so far.

Before the end of the day, Wendy stops by my little station and tells me she read my "Noob's Guide to Paris" piece. My heart does a can-can. She tells me it was "hilarious and charming!"

Wendy leans forward on my table and says, "You know what? Maybe you *should* start putting together a piece about studying abroad in London for review. If all goes well, I might reconsider this piece. Maybe it could go live online mid-March and, who knows, maybe be printed in the April issue."

My feet dance over the floor under my desk. *I can do this.*

Wendy advises me to take another look at their various pieces covering travel to different cities and try to blend my style with theirs. I spend the rest of the day using the company MacBook to do just that.

Thursday, Wendy invites me out to drinks with the rest of the office. Apparently it's something they do every Thursday. I go. Wendy buys me a drink and talks about her college days, and when she took a gap year to travel. Declan asks me how old I am. When I tell him *almost twenty-one*, he's completely taken back—he thought I was in high school. He's a couple years out of college. Donna tells us a hilarious story about someone she went on a date with last week. Tracey talks to me without a hint of disdain about a singer she's going to see this weekend: Lily Allen. I know a couple of her songs. She asks me what kind of music I'm into, who I've seen live. I've only known her to begrudgingly tolerate me, and I'm overjoyed that we've connected over something. I start to get a feeling for who these people actually are. They're creative and outspoken and lighthearted. And I start to feel like I . . . belong among them.

Babe, Sahra, and I take a trip to Berlin together over the weekend. I bring my notebook. When we get back Sunday night, I write out a new post and borrow Babe's computer afterward to type it up and publish it. I'm loving crystalizing my experiences this way. I love anchoring my thoughts immediately on paper before they start to float away. I love the triumphant satisfaction that comes with reading it all back once the post goes live.

Little by little, I start to build a draft of the London study abroad piece for *Packed.* Every day I try to push myself to sample more of London: new lunch places, different supermarkets. When I have time, I ride different Tube lines. I get off at new stops and walk around to new areas. I keep notes. One day, while I'm on the train, I flip the notebook upside down, open the back cover, and start drafting the novel I had outlined in Sawyer. From then on, I flip it over at least once a day to keep working on it.

For the *Packed!* article, I'm trying to compile a list of my top twenty-five things to cram into your study abroad experience before you go bankrupt. If I want to travel more this go-round—which I've now resolved to do—the remainder of my college-student-summer-and-winter-break job savings will all be gone by (or probably before) the end of this semester. I put together a short blog post with the top five cities I'd like to get to.

> *FIVE PLACES I WANNA HIT BEFORE I HEAD BACK TO AMERICA:*
> *1) Every city I've yet to see in Italy (at least Florence)*
> *2) Dublin*
> *3) Prague*
> *4) Amsterdam*
> *5) Edinburgh*

To be safe, I mention that I'm running low on money for food in an email to my parents. They kindly transfer over a small cushion, and I set it all aside for meals. I've been avoiding Skype calls. Since the break, we've been communicating strictly over email, with very little detail, and I've been prompting them to read my blog to see what I'm up to.

———

Pilot and I have been mutually avoiding each other. I don't know what happened with Amy after that day; maybe he did go back to her. *Which is fine. I told him to.*

When spring break rolls around, I've already made plans way in advance with Babe to take on Florence, Pisa, and Venice. I did ask her if she'd rather go to Dublin alone. She said, "I can travel alone anytime. How often are we going to get to travel Italy together?" We have a grand ol' time, and I put together a post about our touristy adventures.

At work, Donna has completely taken me under her wing. This past week, she's been helping me work out how I want to format my piece, and we've talked about her personal life. I have her phone number now. I think we were on track to having a work friendship during London: Take One, but I most definitely was too intimidated by her success and coolness to talk to her casually about life when I was twenty. That instinct is still present to some extent, but it's easier to tamp it down and ignore it. It's weird how we have to get a little older to realize that people are just people. It should be obvious, but it's not.

23. I Have Confidence in Me

February 28, 2011 (take two)

Mom and Dad,
I'll see you two on Thursday. I'm nervous, but I'm
ready for you this time.
  XO,
  Shane

Somehow, it's March. I'm in the kitchen with Atticus and Babe. They're watching *Glee*, and I'm sitting next to them, staring blindly at the wall, clutching the leather armrest.

When the time comes, I stand up calmly.

"Are those your parents?" Atticus smiles.

"Yeah, they're visiting this weekend," I tell them. I suck in a deep breath before stepping out of the kitchen and closing the door behind me.

"Hi, sweetheart!" My dad sweeps me into a hug.

When he releases me, my mother swoops in. "Shane, surprise!"

"Take us into the kitchen. I want to meet your friends!" he exclaims.

"Can we just hang out the three of us tonight?" I ask immediately.

"We want to meet your friends and take them out! Then the three of us have all weekend," he says.

"Sweetie, we're so excited to get a taste of the world you're living in out here!" my mom gushes.

"Okay," I reason, "I'll introduce them now, and then we'll go out to dinner just the three of us, okay?"

"So all of you been traveling every weekend, huh?" my father asks as he drops his glass on the table.

We sit around a small circular table at Delia's. My feet vibrate against the floor. That's how fast they're moving.

"Oh my gosh, yeah. Shane, why haven't you been posting anything on Facebook?" Mom asks.

"I've been posting on my blog," I point out. My armpits are sweating.

"I don't know how to get to your blog. Can you send it to me in an email?" Dad commands.

I fiddle with my napkin. "I've put links to some of the posts on Facebook."

"Yes, I've been following the posts, honey, but the family wants to see pictures! You're taking pictures, right? This is such a dream come true, to be able to keep up with your studies and travel the world at the same time." Emotion coats her voice. Her smile wobbles with pride.

"Well, I've put some of the pictures in the blog posts."

"Yeah, but it's not the same as on Facebook!" Mom laughs.

"So where have you gone? Give us the rundown," my father says jovially.

I provide a rundown.

"Sounds like you're having the time of your life. Can we stay here with you for the rest of the trip?" Dad suggests jokingly.

I chuckle uncomfortably.

"Tell us about work!" my mom prompts. "I want to hear gory details!"

"We don't need the gory details," Dad shoos. "Just tell us about it. You learning a lot?"

Inhale. Exhale. Fiddle with a napkin. "Um, yeah . . ." My breaths are coming in big, swollen bursts. *You can do this.*

Mom puts a hand on my shoulder. "Are you all right, honey?"

Breathe. "Yeah. I'm fine, I. Okay."

"Okay?" my mom repeats.

"Drink some water or something!" Dad urges. I down a gulp of water. They watch me for a long moment.

"Are you okay?" Dad asks again.

"Yeah, I'm okay. I'm good."

"Good." Mom smiles.

"Okay, so how's the health clinic going?" he repeats.

"I have to tell you guys something."

"Do you have a boyfriend?" My mom smiles. "As long as you don't get pregnant—"

I cut her off. "No."

"Okay, no need to get crabby. What is it?" She laughs.

Her demeanor sobers quickly when my facial expression doesn't change. "Shane, what is it?"

I take one last breath and exhale the words, "I lied about this being a premed program."

Dad's face juts forward. "What?"

"What do you mean, you lied?" Mom says with confusion.

"I mean, there is no premed program out here."

They both speak at the same time.

"What do you mean? You signed up for it! *I read the damn brochure!*" my dad insists.

"How can there be no premed program? You're premed . . . yeah, the brochure!" Mom sounds disoriented.

I look over at Dad. "So, I made the brochure myself." I swallow. "There is no premed track out here."

There's a moment of silence as my father's face flushes neon, and then he explodes.

"You conned us? *You little shit*," he growls.

I push my chair away from the table, back straightening against the seat.

"Sal," my mother scolds.

"I'm sorry, it was wrong! I want to be a writer, and I saw an opportunity, and I did something stupid," I explain.

"A writer? Where the hell is this coming from!"

"I told you I wanted to write when I was applying to schools!" I screech. "You said I couldn't apply for any creative majors!"

Dad roars on like I haven't spoken. "Are you telling me you've lost an entire semester of required courses? You're supposed to take the MCATs when you get back!"

"You won't be ready for the MCATs," Mom echoes softly like she's drifting away.

"I don't want to take the MCATs," I breathe. I feel twenty pounds lighter as the words leave my mouth. I really, really don't. Why did I push myself through taking them?

"Shane!" gasps my mother. For Mom. That's why. But she'll understand. She has to understand.

"I can't believe what I'm hearing!" booms my father. "I'm over here shelling out thousands of dollars for *your* education, and you're out here completely disrespecting me? Lyin' to me!"

"I'm sorry! It's just not what I'm passionate about! I want to—"

"Stop. You're on the next fucking flight to New York!"

"I'm not going back yet. I'm seeing this through. I have a great internship." I struggle to keep my words coherent. "And I'm really doing well there."

Dad jerks up from the table. "What did you just say to me?"

"I said"—I heave a rattling breath—"I'm not going back yet."

"Give me your phone," he demands.

"I'm sorry, no," I answer.

His teeth grind. "You know, I do everything for you. You ungrateful little brat. I do what's *best* for you—"

"Forcing me into a life I don't want isn't what's best for me!" I scream.

I whip up my hand and cover my mouth.

The anger in his eyes sears a hole right through my chest. My voice drops. "Dad, I'm sorry I yelled. I'm sorry! But you're wasting your money pushing me into medical school. That's not what I want to do!"

"You throw this education away, and you're going to be living in a *fucking box* on the street! And don't think for a second you're going to be able to call me for help!" His words thunder around the dining room.

"Dad, why won't you believe in me? Why would you say that? What have I ever failed at to make you think that would happen? I'm working so hard! I always work so hard!"

I throw a desperate glance at my mother, who is staring into her plate. "Mom!" I yell.

She gives the tiniest shake of her head.

"Don't look at her, you look at me! I built this life for you. I work day in, day out for you to have this life! These opportunities. You know my dad had nothing, chasing cartoon dreams of being a fuckin' poet. I had nothin'. I handed you the tools for everything!" he bellows.

His eyes bore straight into mine as he growls, "I don't want to see you. I don't want to hear from you. Don't call me for money. Don't call me for anything." He charges away from the table.

"I'm sorry," I blubber after him. "I'm grateful, Dad. It's"—*sob*—"just not the right path for"—I inhale sharply as the restaurant door falls shut behind him—"me."

I look to my mother. "Mom, I'm sorry!" gurgles from my throat. She won't meet my eyes.

"Shane, how could you do this?" With another shake of the head, she follows him out. I try to quell the maelstrom of hurt raging in my chest.

You knew it wouldn't go over well.

I swallow, gulp down the rest of my water, head out onto the street, and walk. I walk and walk until I can think again. Until I can breathe normally. Until I can turn the light back on.

hey

Leo Primaveri <LeoBaseballPrimaveri@gmail.com>   . 3/6/11
to Shane

Heard you fucked up. Are you coming home? My mom won't go into detail.

I blow out a breath, staring at the email in the dank school library. Why did Leo send this? I remember getting it the first time I was here—I just dismissed it. But when I got back, Leo had dropped out of school. I gnaw at my lip for a few minutes before typing out a response.

I'll be home at the end of April. I lied and said I was here for a premed program, but I'm doing a writing internship. What's up with you?

Send.

Ten minutes later:

Oh shit, that's insane. Makes sense, though. You're always reading. I always thought you'd be an author or something. Your blog's been extra good lately. What'd he do to you when he found out?

Has Leo always . . . read my blog? We've never talked about it before.

He had a fit. Stormed off. Told me to never call him for anything ever again. You read my blog? What's up with you?

Send.

A minute later:

Could have been worse, I guess. Why wouldn't I read your blog? Meet me on Facebook Chat?

I pull up Facebook and log in.

Leo
I'm going through some
shit . . . It's fucking me up, and
I don't know what to do or who
to talk to about it.

Shane
Do you want to Skype?

Leo
No, typing is easier.

Shane
What's up?

Leo
I broke up with someone a
couple weeks ago.

339

Shane
You had a girlfriend? I thought
you just did hookups? For
how long? Why wasn't it on
Facebook?
Leo
I'm gay.

If I were holding the computer, I would have dropped it.

Shane
But you're always talking about
girls you've had sex with?!

Back in high school he hooked up with the cheerleading captain in
my year when he was still a junior! He's played along and laughed when
my other cousin Anthony has made cracks about me probably being a
lesbian.

Leo
I've been with the guy for
almost a year, but he got tired
of living in the fucking
shadows. But if my dad found
out, he would kick me out of
the house. I know just how the
conversation would go. I'd tell
him I'm gay and he'd say: "No,
you're not." There'd be an
awkward pause. I'd repeat
myself, and he'd tell me to get
out. And then, like, the guys . . .
Alfie, Anthony, Vincent,
Matt—I'd be exiled at every
family gathering.

My vision blurs because I can hear Uncle Dan saying exactly that. How many homophobic remarks has he had to endure from Uncle Dan over the years? How long has he been struggling with this alone? Was all that stuff he'd said about dating girls through high school a way to protect himself? I heave in a breath.

> **Shane**
> Aflie, Anthony, Vincent, Matt . . . they love you. Finding out you like dudes is not going to change that. Maybe it'll take a second to process, but you won't lose them. You're not going to lose me. Uncle Dan and everyone with an issue will have to evolve.

> **Leo**
> I can't bring myself to do shit right now. I stopped going to class. I'm going to lose my scholarship.

Jesus. My heart constricts. Is he out in 2017 to his friends? Was he dealing with depression? Did he ever talk to a counselor or something? Do Uncle Dan and Aunt Marie know now? Is that why 2017 Mom never talks about him? Did Uncle Dan exile him? Do they never talk about him? I wipe at my cheeks.

> **Shane**
> Leo, you should go talk to someone. You don't actually want to lose that scholarship, right?

> **Leo**
> I just want to be normal.

Shane
There is no normal.

He doesn't respond for a minute. Then:

Leo
Thanks for being here.

Shane
You're the closest thing I have
to a brother, Leo. Call me, beep
me, if you need to reach me =)

Leo
Sorry we don't talk anymore.

Shane
It's not too late to change that.
I'm here!

Leo
g2g

24. Through Accepting Limits

It's Tuesday, March 8, and I have the first draft of my study abroad guide typed up and saved on a thumb drive. When I get to *Packed!*, I boot up the white MacBook, plug in the drive, email it to Wendy, and wait. Nowadays I'm working side by side with Tracey, Declan, and Donna on a regular basis. Whenever they're doing something they can share with me, I'm shadowing them. Today, I'm shadowing Declan, who's working on a photo spread for their April issue. I end up periodically excusing myself throughout the afternoon to go refresh my email.

"Are you expecting something important that you keep running back to your desk?" Declan laughs when I return for the third time.

I sigh. "I'm sorry. Just an important email. Ignore me!"

At the end of the day when I'm packing up, Wendy emerges from her office and walks over to my table. My throat tightens. I'm pushing in my chair to leave when she stops in front of me.

"I read your draft," she opens.

I try to swallow. ". . . Thanks?"

A smile spreads across her face. "I love the direction you're taking with this. You're on for the article! I think we're going to use this to kick off a series, gathering pieces from people studying abroad all over the world. I'm going to put together some notes, and I'll call you in for a meeting to discuss everything soon."

My hands jump to my cheeks in astonishment. "Wendy, oh my goodness, I'm so excited. Thank you! This means so much to me!"

I blast Avril Lavigne's "new" album through my iPod and dance down the sidewalk on my way home.

Wendy pulls me into her office Wednesday afternoon, and we go through my piece together, point by point. She tells me what she likes and gives me notes on how I can improve it.

Wednesday night, I brainstorm Wendy's notes. Thursday morning, I type up a second draft on the white MacBook at work, and Thursday afternoon, Donna goes through it with me before I turn it in to Wendy again. Donna is great! She's really funny, easy to talk to, and endlessly generous with her time.

Thursday night, I check in with Leo.

> **Shane**
> Hey, how's it going?
> **Leo**
> Figuring it out.
> **Shane**
> . . .?

He doesn't say anything else.

Babe and I go to Dublin over the weekend, and while we're there, I open up to her about everything: Pilot, his girlfriend, the internship going wrong, my parents—everything but the time travel. She shares some of her own family issues in return. She has an older brother who's dealing with some alcohol issues, and it's taking a toll on her parents. I've heard bits and pieces about this over the years, but never in as much detail as she shared this weekend. I'm sad I was too caught up in my own drama during London: Take One to have been someone she could talk to about it.

It feels great to chat so candidly with her. It's almost like having 2017 Babe here with me.

When we get back Sunday night, I write up a post in Horcurx Ten (Nine overflowed) and borrow Babe's computer to type up and publish: "American Girls Do Dublin."

On Wednesday, March 16, I come into work and find the white MacBook already powered up at my station. When I get close enough, I see that Safari's open to an article on the *Packed!* site. I drop my purse when I read the headline.

The Top 25 Things to Cram into Your London Study Abroad Experience . . . Before You Go Bankrupt

by Shane Primaveri

"Tracey, this is my piece!" I yelp toward the front desk.

She smiles at me. "It is."

"It's up?" I squeak. "Wendy said . . . she didn't say when it would be—"

"It's up. Surprise! Congratulations!" she cheers.

"Congratulations, Shane!" Donna shouts from across the room.

"Congratulations!" Jamie, George, Declan, and Janet all echo after her. Wendy's door is open, and she emerges from her office to lean against the doorframe in a sleek, teal power suit.

I watch her, still frozen with delight, by my table.

"Good morning, Shane!" Wendy greets. "Congratulations on being our first intern to get a piece published in *Packed!*"

Donna whoops from her seat as Wendy strides over to me.

"Hey," she says more quietly, "I'm really proud of you. We're all taking you out to drinks later, so don't make other plans." She grins before walking back to her office.

I immediately email a link to Babe and Sahra. They both text me within minutes.

Sahra: Congratulations, Shane! This is so great! I know how hard you've been working on it.

Babe: YAYY!!!!!!! AHHHH!!!!! YOU DID IT!!!!!! [100 MORE EXCLAMA-TION POINTS] AHHHHHH!!!!! IT'S BEAUTIFUL! OH MYLANTA!

I can't stop smiling.

Wendy, Donna, and Tracey take me out to their usual pub down the street. We sit around a high table near the bar. They all tell me how appreciative they are of all the little things I've been doing around the office, and I start to cry right there at the table.

"Darling!" I look up at Wendy with a sad smile. Her brown skin is glowing in the low light. "What's wrong?" she asks.

"Nothing. I'm just really excited! And grateful." I laugh-cry. "And really sad that this is all going to be over in a few weeks."

"We're all going to be sad to see you leave us!" Donna smiles.

"Especially me!" Tracey laughs. "I'm going to have to go back to working alone. I have so much more time now."

"Who the hell's going to anticipate my daily 3:00 p.m. caffeine needs? It's been so long since I made my own tea, I barely remember how to use the kettle," Donna teases.

"Seriously, Shane, we've never had such a hardworking, efficient intern. You've been brilliant."

I huff a sad laugh. "I just hope I can find another job like this back in the US somewhere for the summer."

"Have you started looking?" Tracey asks. My stomach drops. Back in 2017 I have those eight other residency interviews lined up for internal medicine. I haven't been thinking long-term here.

"No, not yet," I reply. I make a mental note to buckle down and start researching tonight.

"Do we know anyone looking?" Wendy directs to Donna and Tracey.

Donna turns to me. "I have a friend who works at *Seventeen* in New York, and an ex-boyfriend at *NatGeo*. I'll send out some emails first thing tomorrow."

I raise a hand to my chest. "Thank you so much."

"Of course! I can't guarantee anything, but I'll ask my contacts."

"And I'll keep my ears open," Wendy adds. "We don't have an office in New York yet, but we're in the process of expanding to the States."

I gape at the three of them. "You have no idea how appreciative I am."

"You're going to land on your feet." Tracey squeezes my shoulder.

Wendy's phone sends a vibration through the table, and she picks it up excitedly.

"My husband's coming to join us!" she exclaims, before placing it back down with a brilliant smile. My mouth falls open. "He had a meeting that finished up a few blocks from here!"

"You have a husband?" I blurt in blatant disbelief. All three women laugh.

"Why are you so surprised?" Wendy asks, not without amusement.

"I'm sorry, um, I don't know," I fumble. "You're . . . so independent and successful and young, and I figured it's so hard to maintain a relationship and also be such a—badass."

She chuckles. "I mean, don't get me wrong, it's tough sometimes, but Spencer's my partner. He makes my life better, so I keep him around. It's really nice to have someone to share my success with." I nod absently, trying not to think about dessert foods.

When Wendy's husband joins us ten minutes later, I almost choke on my wine. I recognize him immediately because I've seen his headshot on the back of all the Broken Beaker books I have on my shelf back at home. Her husband is Spencer Matthews, the YA mystery novelist.

"You own your own successful magazine company and your husband writes one of the most popular YA series?" I start as Spencer leaves the table to get us a new round of drinks at the bar. "How do you guys find time to be a couple?"

Wendy snorts. "I mean, the series hasn't happened yet, but he's on that path. Book two's out soon. I guess you've read *Broken Beaker*?"

Oh lord, I almost just had a major time traveler slipup. I nod and she continues, "It's all about patience and support. I would have gotten here myself, but I'd like to think my journey was a little less rocky because I had him to lean on when things were really stressful, and vice versa with his books."

Thursday night, Babe and Sahra go out, but I decide to stay in. I want to use the time to write a blog post about my *Packed!* article and borrow Babe's computer while she's not using it. Babe, Sahra, and I are leaving for a trip to Prague tomorrow after class, so I won't have another chance to write before Sunday.

I set to work, delving into the process of putting the article together and of course what it means to me that it exists. The post goes live at 10:00 p.m. I link it on Facebook for people to see, and then head to Gmail.

Cara Primaveri, Sal Primaveri

Mom & Dad,

I love you and appreciate everything you've done for me. We didn't really get to discuss it, but I've been working for a magazine called *Packed! For Travel!* here in London. I've had so much fun there, and I've learned a ton. I've shown them the work I've been doing on my blog, and they liked my travel pieces! They offered me the opportunity to write something for their magazine. I wrote an article about study abroad in London and it's published on their site! Here's the link:

packedfortravel.com/london-studyabroadguide

I'm sorry I've disappointed you both, and I hope you can forgive me. I hated lying to you, but I needed to do this.

Love,
Shane

Right as I'm about to press send, there's a knock at the door. It's only 10:30 p.m., which is early for the girls to be back. The tiniest bit of hope sparks in my chest.

"Hello?" I call out from my perch on the bunk. No answer. I climb down and open the door.

No one's there. I scurry back up onto the bunk, press send, and research summer writing-related jobs in the tristate area. I apply for every one I can find.

Prague is beautiful. Sahra tells us it'll probably be her last trip for money reasons, but Babe and I convince her to join us for one more to Amsterdam the following weekend. Sunday night, when we get back, I blog about Prague and email the link to my parents.

Now that the article for *Packed!* is done, I focus more of my attention on the book I've been hand-writing about twins in college. I go to class, draft the book, go to the library, type more of it up, sleep, go to work, draft book, sleep, check for more job opportunities, go to work, write book, sleep, class, go to Amsterdam.

I blog about Amsterdam and send the link to my parents.

Babe gets free tickets to Disneyland Paris, so the following weekend, we go back to France and spend the day in the park.

I keep keeping busy. Busy at *Packed!* Busy traveling. Busy writing. Busy blogging. Busy sending out job applications. Busy. Busy. Busy.

The physical magazine edition of *Packed! For Travel!* with my article is released the second week of April. It was one thing seeing the article on their website, but it's a whole other rush to see it printed in the magazine on page nineteen of their spread! I take five copies from the office. Back at the flat, I use my digital camera to snap pictures of the article and attach them in an email to my parents.

25. Twice as Hard, Half as Liked

Re: Pictures of published piece!!

Sal Primaveri <Sal.Primaveri@yahoo.com>   4/13/11
to Shane

Shane,

I don't know what you think one article is going to lead to. You've betrayed our trust, and there will be consequences. Don't expect to come home and for all to be forgotten. You crossed a line when you flippantly misled us for months on end. We love you, but we cannot support this kind of behavior. I hope you can understand. You live under my roof, on my dime, and while that is the case, you will follow my rules.

Love,
Dad

I gulp another swig of my drink and set it down on the bar in front of me.

"Babe, that's amazing!" I exclaim. Babe's cowokers just connected her with the Disney college program in Florida that she's been itching to get involved with. Last time, I didn't get to celebrate with her when it happened.

"Thanks! I can't believe it! Ahh!" She throws her hands up near her face. "How's your job hunt going?"

I sigh. "I haven't heard back from any of the places I've applied to."

"There's still time!" she insists.

"Not really, we're done in a little over a week. If I don't find a job—" I stop short and take a breath. "If I don't find a job, things are going to be really bad when I get back to New York, and then I don't know what's going to happen with school," I ramble. If I don't get a job, and that button doesn't work, I don't know what comes next for me.

"Shane, stop working yourself up!" Babe interrupts. "You're going to figure this out! Come on, we should be celebrating. You have a published article in a real-life, physical, you-can-frame-it-and-hold-it magazine that people read all the time! That's huge!" She whips it out of her purse and waves around the copy I gave her.

"That's still in your purse?" I shoot her a small smile. "Still, it doesn't change the fact that I haven't found a job."

"A magical Harry Potter book spoke to you, Shane—" she chides, grinning over her glass of Guinness.

"I regret telling you about that—"

"Don't give up now!" She punches her fist to the sky with a laugh.

"I still haven't found anyone to go to Edinburgh with this weekend." Babe can't come because she's got a Disney DVD release party thing to go to with her coworkers.

"Well, you should go anyway," she says.

I shoot her an exasperated look.

"I'm serious! I think you should go yourself. It'll be a journey of self-discovery. Do a tour or something. It's good to travel alone. I've always wanted to do it. Heck, I'm going to after this!"

I snort at the déjà vu. "Go by myself?"

"Yeah."

"Travel alone in a foreign country?"

"Why not?" She grins.

I chuckle sardonically. "Because if I'm alone with my thoughts for too long, I'm going to end up dwelling on Pilot drama."

"Maybe you should." She shrugs. "It's part of the moving-on process. You have to deal with your feelings. What do you think I was doing all that time after Paris with the Disney movies in our room? *Dealing with feelings.*"

I drop my gaze to the table thoughtfully before yanking out Horcrux Ten. "Okay, but if I'm doing this, I'm uploading a pre-travel post to the blog so people know to call the authorities if I never return."

Babe giggles. "Feel free to use my computer!"

26. The Fear of Falling Apart

April 15, 2011 (take two)

Mom and Dad,

I know I've created a rift. Whether or not you've been aware, it's been forming for a while. I don't know what's going to happen when I get home, but this time, I won't stop trying to close it. There might be times where I need a break, and I retreat for a while, but I'll always try again. I need to live my own life, but that doesn't mean that I don't want you in it.

XO,

Shane

I catch the 3:40 p.m. train to Edinburgh.

The gray cityscape outside my window softens into an endless span of sheep and greenery. I pen down two new chapters of my work-in-progress as the sun falls away.

The moon hangs full and bright in the sky when I finally wander up to my bed-and-breakfast. It's 9:00 p.m. and I'm starving, so I drop my stuff in the room and meander down the road until I find a cozy old-fashioned-looking pub. I take a seat at the bar with my copy of *Prisoner of Azkaban* and order a burger. There's a handful of other people here chatting and enjoying a drink under the warm yellow lighting. It's nice. I open my book and fall in with Harry.

Halfway through the first chapter, I'm distracted by a young guy with longish dark hair and disarming gold-brown eyes who sits two stools away. I watch as he orders a Guinness with a Scottish accent. He turns and catches me watching. I quickly return to Harry Potter.

"Hey," he says. I glance back over. He's smiling at me now.

"Hi." I pull a half-assed, embarrassed smile.

"American?" he asks in surprise.

"Affirmative," I respond, raising my eyebrows and taking a sip of my drink. "Scottish?"

He laughs and propels us into conversation. He reminds me of a young Henry Ian Cusick (Desmond from *Lost*). His name is Greg; he's studying law at Edinburgh University. He does most of the talking, especially once my burger comes. Chatting with Greg makes me think about chatting with Pilot, and for the first time in weeks, I give in and let my thoughts wander in that direction. I would rather be here with Pilot, having stupid conversations about evil chairs or how likely it is that we run into J.K. Rowling on the street tomorrow, than be laughing and smiling politely with attractive Scottish Greg.

But I'm mad at Pilot, aren't I? Or am I mad at me? Have I forgiven myself? Did I make up for it? Can I be with Pilot and find the headspace and time to navigate a creative career? I don't know. I'm never late for things, but Pilot makes me forget about time. Or . . . I forget about time because of Pilot. I hate that Pilot didn't make sure Amy got his message.

I'm so confused.

Scottish Greg has a great accent and seems really smart, and wow, he has great hair, and he's keeping the conversation going, and it seems like he has a decent sense of humor. But the longer we talk, the more I want to excuse myself and head back to the B and B.

"Something wrong?" Greg asks. He's telling a story, and I've checked out.

"Oh, no," I answer. "Go on. I'm sorry!"

When he wraps up, I stand from my stool so Greg can see that I'm ready to head out.

The bill's been sitting untouched on my left, so I pull out my debit card. I do a double take when I glance at it to catch the price. There's a handwritten note across the top of it. I blink, my heart ramming uncomfortably against my ribs.

You're ready, if you're ready. x

Frantically, I glance around for the bartender. It was a man earlier—but there she is, red hair knotted up, serving someone ten feet down the counter.

"Hey!" I yell down to her. She looks up and meets my eyes.

"It'll work now?"

She nods. I pivot and leave the pub.

My pulse is still racing as I drop onto the bed at my B and B and extricate the locket from my purse . . . *I'm ready now? I don't feel ready.* I can't wrap my head around erasing the last four months. So much has happened that I don't want to forget.

In the morning, the B and B hostess gives me directions to the Elephant House. It's a bit of a walk, but I revel in the surprisingly warm weather and take in the city as I go. The architecture is all medieval-looking and walking through it is almost fantastical. When I spot the café, I skip up to it, jumping to a stop at the entrance. There's a little sign in the window pronouncing it THE BIRTHPLACE OF HARRY POTTER.

To the naked eye, it's just a café. There are four computers for use in the front left corner, there's a bar to order at, tables everywhere. It's full of windows with a beautiful view of Edinburgh Castle. But, a tingly feeling spreads over me as I step inside. This is where J. K. Rowling came to sit and birth the phenomenon that changed millions of lives. This is where she created a world that I could retreat to whenever things weren't so great in my own reality. I order a latte and sit down at a table near the window reading *Prisoner of Azkaban*. After a while, I pull out Horcrux Ten and pen another chapter of my own book.

Down the road, I stumble onto one of Edinburgh's famous graveyards.

I take my time there, roaming lazily from one elaborate gravestone to the next. I stop short when I spot one in particular that reads: *In loving memory of Thomas Riddell.*

"What?" I yell in disbelief. I whip out my camera and snap a selfie.

When my stomach starts to rumble, I wander back onto the streets to find a pub where I can grab lunch and regroup. I settle in alone at a small table along the wall and pull out my British phone.

There's a text from Babe.

Babe: How goes the finding yourself?

I smile and type back.

Me: This just in: I hate dealing with feelings, but Harry Potter is helping numb the pain.

Babe: Harry Potter heals all! :]

Me: True story! I'm headed to go climb a crag-mountain-hill thing soon!

Babe: Take a hoard of pictures for the blog!

Me: OBVIOUSLY! =]

It takes twenty-five minutes to find the crag, but I make it there with just the waiter's verbal instructions to work off. At the base of it is a park of sorts. Children and dogs splash around in big contemporary fountains, and a bright sidewalk runs among big flat stretches of green grass. The crag looming ahead is rocky, green, and gorgeous. I'm going to climb the crap out if it.

I unzip my purse and check for texts again. There's one new one from Babe.

Babe: Excited to hear about it!

Shane: About to start the hike. Cross your fingers I don't slip on a pile of rocks, trip over the edge, and die.

Babe: PLEASE DON'T DIE.

I stare at my phone for a few more seconds before I pull up the text thread with Pilot. The last messages are from February.

Pilot: I just heard someone use the word ravish at work. Can I pull off the word ravish? Or is it like knackered? =P

Pilot: Is everything okay?
Pilot: I'm back early today, so find me when you get home!
Pilot: I hope everything's okay.

My chest tightens. I want to text him something stupid like *I miss you . . .* but instead I chuck the phone into my bag and trek toward the foot of the trail.

The path curves gently up and around the hill before narrowing out and getting steeper. Thirty minutes in, I take a seat off to the side of the trail on a giant rock. There's been a group of four dudes maybe three hundred feet behind me throughout the trek. I make a deal with myself that once they pass, I'll get up and keep going.

The view from my perch is gorgeous: fantastic rock formations, endless green hills, and medieval-looking architecture. This must be such an interesting place to live. I glance down the trail, catching sight of the guys on their way around the corner before bringing my gaze back to the horizon. My heart stutters. I think I just saw Pilot in that group? I slowly turn my head to look again.

My eyebrows pull together. No, just four college-aged dudes with hair in varying shades of brown. *Great, I'm Bella Swan-ing circa* New Moon. They pass me, chatting easily about sports in American accents. I push up off the rock and continue.

Forty minutes later, I stumble around a giant rock into a vast green valley. At its edge, the ground cuts off with an abrupt drop. To my right, the land bulges upward toward Arthur's Seat. I'm so close to the tippy top! A scattering of people are climbing up to the peak where the Seat is, but no one's wandering the valley.

I pull my frizzy curls free of my ponytail and run out onto the green. My hair flies out behind me as I throw myself into a cartwheel, my crossbody flying around and knocking into me. The land is surprisingly springy and soft. It feels a little like those fake turf football fields, but with more give. I leap around like a five-year-old, scout out a good spot, and collapse onto the ground to gaze up at the wispy clouds overhead.

A gust of wind tickles my nose as I fish my phone and the silver locket from my purse. I flip the locket over, running the pads of my fingers over the inscription. Angst sidles around inside me. *What's the right decision?*

I applied to so many jobs. I stepped up my blog game. I got my piece published. I had the people I work with looking out for me . . . and nothing has panned out. If my parents throw me out, what will I do? What if they won't pay for me to go back to school? What am I going to do? Maybe I won't get a degree or I'll go to community college?

I don't know what happens now. I don't want to live in this world where I've proved them right: *I'm not good enough.* I do know I can be a successful gastroenterologist. I've got eight more interviews lined up for residency. My grades kicked ass. And with Pilot—maybe Babe's right. She doesn't know the whole story, but maybe the healthy thing to do is *move on*. It'll be easier to move on if I don't remember this.

Disappointment swells in my chest. I blow out breath after breath trying to dispel it.

Palming the locket, I type up a draft to Pilot: `I miss you.` I stare at the words for a minute before backspacing them into oblivion. I type: `Depends how you use it, could be creepy.` I press send and wait.

My brain counts the seconds as they pass. Two minutes. Three minutes.

Four.

Five.

Six.

Seven.

Eight.

My fingers twitch. I drop the phone into my purse and stare at the sky.

I played everything out. I tried with Pilot. I finished the internship. I blink at the emotion gathering in my eyes as my fingers find the locket's edge. The silver top flips back like a pocket watch. Inside, the image of a clock is etched delicately into the silver. I didn't notice that before. On the opposite side sits the obsidian heart. I close my eyes and let my thumb graze back and forth across the cold surface, trying to feel out a decision. *Do I hear music?* I listen harder.

There's music in the wind. I think I know the song; my heart warms with the familiarity of it. Is someone listening to music up here? *Don't they know I'm trying to enjoy nature and make maybe the most important decision of my life?*

It's getting louder. My brain clicks the song into place. I snap the locket shut in surprise and open my eyes to the bright afternoon sky, ears perked. It sounds like it's just a guitar—and then Pilot's face swings into view, hovering over me.

"Ahhh!" I scream, flipping onto my stomach and scrambling into a sitting position. *"What the fudge?"*

27. Marching On

Pilot laughs and continues playing the guitar slung over his shoulder. *Am I hallucinating?* I blink in confusion as he settles onto a single, random, boxy black rock ten feet away.

Then he starts to sing, *"And I neverrrrrrrr, saw you coming-ing, ayayayay-ayayay."*

I inch closer, like a spooked kitten. "What are you doing?" I shout.

"And I'll neverrrrrrr be the say-yah-yay-aye-yay-ahh-mme." He raises his eyebrows with impish amusement.

Did he get my text? How is he in front of me on a mountain playing Taylor's . . . "State of Grace"?

"You come around and the armor falls . . . pierce the room like a wrecking ball, now all I know is don't let go."

I hug my legs to my chest. He keeps singing. He's changed the song a bit, morphing certain lyrics and parts together. "Pilot," I interrupt.

He breaks song for a second and smiles bashfully. That's an expression I've never seen on him before. I melt a tiny bit.

"Hold on," he says. "I have a three-song concert prepared. Let me do this."

A three-song concert? The melody changes to one of my favorites. A happy-go-lucky song that Taylor plays on the ukulele.

He sings, "*I'm pretty sure we kinda broke up back in February . . . I was an idiot, a how you say? Douche. Canoe.*" I snort.

"*We made things all dramatic and I let you walk away. And I, I, I, I, I, I, I, I'm sorry.*"

I try to scoff. "That really doesn't rhyme at all."

He shakes his head, smiling. "*Stay, Stay, Stay. I've been loving you for quite some time, time, time. I think that's it's funny when you're mad, mad, mad, and I think that's it's best if we both stay . . . Stay. Stay. Stay, Stay.*"

I open my mouth to speak again.

"Wait just one more," he protests, holding up his hand and smiling at the ground. He starts the last song. I snort-sob.

"*And you got a smile that could light up this whole town, I see it right now and it'll always blow me down . . . I hope that means we can go forward from here?*"

"Okay, stop!" I wipe at my cheeks. Pilot lowers the guitar into a black case he must have brought with him. He sits next to me on the ground.

"Hey," he opens.

I stare for a second and shake my head. "What . . . what the hell are you doing here?"

He shrugs. "I needed to make a move."

"How did you even know I was here?"

Pilot grins. "Are you kidding? I never miss a post from French Watermelon Nineteen. You said you were headed to Edinburgh . . . and I gathered more exact intel from Babe."

"Babe?"

Babe endorsed this? I blink some more, unsure of what to say. He glances nervously at the ground. I fiddle with my hands. "Um, what happened to Amy?"

"I broke up with Amy."

I meet his eyes. "And she knows it?"

"Yes." He nods and closes his eyes like it's an immense relief to speak this aloud.

I smile the tiniest bit. "Oh."

A frown tugs at his lips. "I've wanted to come talk for a while now, but you were doing really well without me, like you said you would, so"—he presses his lips together—"I started to think you were right. I mean, maybe I was getting in the way of why you were really here. You've been kicking ass." His eyes meet mine, sincere and olive green.

I swallow, looking at his cheek rather than holding direct eye contact.

"I was going to come talk to you the night your piece went up on *Packed!* I was so pumped; it was so good too." He bites his lip. "But I chickened out because after the way we left things, I wanted to—I mean, I needed a move."

Pilot shifts to meet my averted eyes. "Listen, I know this is scary, the pull between us or whatever, but it's also really rare. And great, and I'd really love to try and make it work. I know you're worried about losing yourself. Let's have dates where we just read so you don't fall behind on that, and we'll have ones where you can write whatever you're working on, and I can work on music. We can work on a balance. Shane, I want you to choose you too . . . I just"—he exhales shakily—"lamppost."

My chin wobbles. I bring a hand to my forehead, and watch him sideways. "I really like those ideas . . . I've missed you," I say quietly. I drop down on my back again.

He comes down next to me. "I missed you."

I blow out a shaky breath. "That was a big move," I tell the sky. I turn my head to find his eyes. He's already watching me. "I tried to make a move like this once."

He smiles. "For who?"

A wispy tear trickles down my cheek and into the grass. "For you."

His brow furrows. "In Paris?"

I shake my head. "No, the first time we were here."

"When?"

"I wanted to tell you, that I"—I pause to take in a breath—"that I really, really liked you. And I didn't get my shit together to do it until I was at Heathrow. I turned around at the bag drop, and took a taxi back to the Karlston. I ran down to your door and knocked on it incessantly.

"But no one answered because you had already left. The door wasn't locked . . . I opened it and all your stuff was gone. I hadn't thought to ask what hotel you were moving to.

"It was stupid. I spent too long looking for you there and I missed my flight."

His eyes pierce mine. "Shane . . ."

My cheeks redden. "Yeah . . . Lamppost back atcha."

He reaches out, takes my hand. "I followed you up a mountain today, so . . ."

A gurgled laugh bubbles out of me.

He smirks. "I had to keep a group between us so you wouldn't see me, or else it would spoil the moment, you know."

I study him in silence for a minute. My lips purse. "Did you mean what you and Taylor said in those songs, literally?"

"Yeah, I think I really, really like you a lot, Shane Primaveri. Like, even more than the kitchen chairs."

I inhale sharply. "I might like you more than the shawarma."

"Damn. Shawarma was basically why you wanted to come back and study abroad again in the first place."

"I mean, yeah, basically."

"I'm honored." He shifts closer, but I pull back and suck in a breath.

"Pies, I was about to push the reset button. Like, my finger was on it." His expression falls.

I sit up and bring my clenched left hand forward to reveal the silver arti-fact. "I'm pretty sure my parents aren't going to let me live with them unless I revert back to their life plan. I might not be able to go back to school. I'll have no place to live. I didn't find a writing job. I have no com-puter. I have no money! I used it all traveling . . . I don't know—"

"Hey." He sits up next to me. "Wait, what, no computer?"

"It broke," I mumble sadly.

Pilot tucks my hair behind my ear; his touch sparks through me. He smiles ever so slightly. "Is that why you've been using notebooks again?"

I reach up and catch his fingers in my hand. "How the hell do you know that?"

"I told you, Primaveri, if you're in sight, I see you.

"I know how much Sawyer meant to you, I can't imagine how hard these past two months have been without a laptop. But . . . whatever happens, you'll get through it. Future Shane is going to be an amazingly successful author."

"Pies, I'm serious." I roll my eyes and shake my head, sending tears running down my face. "Becoming a doctor? It's so solid. There's a blueprint; there's a set path to follow." I swallow. "Becoming a writer is like . . . being lost and just having to hope to god you stumble to your destination."

He coaxes my face back toward his and looks me right in the eyes. "I am an avid French Watermelon fan. I believe in you, one thousand percent, and everything else . . . I'd like to be there to help you figure it out."

A close-mouthed grin wobbles onto my face. "Seriously, you really want to do this? 2011 and onward all over again? With me?"

"I'm in if you're in."

I fidget, nerves flickering in my gut. "But it's going to be really hard, Pilot. We've changed the timeline . . . so many things can go wrong."

He guides my fingers closed around the locket. "But think how many things could go right."

I suck in a breath and gaze out at Edinburgh. What would life be like if things went right? If I mended things with Leo? Kept working things through with my parents? Changed my major? Never went to med school? Never moved to California? Kept working on my book? Dated Pilot?

I scoot over until I'm right in front of him on my knees, and study his eyes. "You're sure?"

His smiles at 100 percent. It sends my heart sprinting. "I'm scarily sure."

A grin creeps up my cheeks. "Like, forty-two percent sure?"

"Like, a hundred and eight percent sure."

I pull him into a hug. His arms wrap tight around me.

"I'm scared shitless," I whisper over his ear.

"It's all part of the vulnerable idiot experience."

I pull back. "What about you? What about the divorce? You're going to have to deal with that all over again."

"I'm better equipped to deal with it now."

"How are your sisters?"

"They're working through it. We've been talking once a week. You can meet them on the next Skype call if you want."

"I'd like that."

"I uploaded our video yesterday."

My face lights up. "What? 'Wrecking Ball'? Really?"

He moves to stand and helps me to my feet. "Really."

"Oh, man, I am so proud." I squeeze his hands. "I hope Usher's waiting to sign you on Monday."

He scoffs, leaning forward so our foreheads meet. Our noses brush. I watch his eyelashes flutter.

"I think I love you," he says softly.

My mouth goes slack, a rush of glitter hurtling into my chest. I pull back a few inches and give in to the goofy smile itching at my lips. "Well . . . I love shawarma so, like, by definition . . ."

His eyes light up, but he doesn't smile. He bites his lip. "It's so hot when you compare me to shawarma."

"I love you too." I grab a fistful of his shirt and close the gap between us.

We're trekking down the crag, hand in hand, when my purse pulses against my hip.

I raise my eyebrows. "Did you finally text me back?"

"You texted me?"

"Yeah, before." I let go of his hand to dig the phone from my purse. It's a text, but not from Pilot.

Donna: Finally heard back from my friend at Seventeen. You have an interview on Monday. xx

Epilogue

www.abowlofbookishness.com/authorinterviews?1french-watermelon

AUTHOR INTERVIEW WEDNESDAY
with FrenchWatermelon19

Posted January 24, 2017 by Dani aka A Bowl of Bookishness

ABOUT THE AUTHOR:
Sixteen-year-old Dani is president of her high school's creative writing club and an aspiring author.

Who's FrenchWatermelon19, you ask? The alias of bestselling author of *Flailing Through the Freefall*, Shane Primaveri. The sequel hit stores this week (thank god because I was dying to read it), and I had the opportunity to interview her after her signing event here in New York! (I couldn't make it before the event started when she was doing longer interviews because school . . . uuugh.)

367

If you don't already know, Shane started out as a blogger! She worked for *Seventeen* magazine for three years, and then she worked as an editor at the *Packed! For Travel!* NYC headquarters for three more years while she worked on her duology.

The bookstore was packed yesterday. It was an especially special event for her because she's from New York. I got to meet her boyfriend afterward (heart-eyes, more on this later), and her parents were there, and, like, ten cousins that look kinda like her. I only recognized Leo because he's always on her Instagram. Her mom and dad actually went to the front of the room halfway through the event and used her microphone to give a little speech about how proud they were. Shane cried. She was wearing a black blazer over a pretty red dress that poofs out at the waist with that same silver locket she always has around her neck.

After a fun round of Q&A and a signing, she was nice enough to stay after and talk to me! I was given fifteen minutes. Enjoy!

So how does it feel to be done with this duology?

Amazing! Scary! I never thought this would really happen and . . . I'm so grateful and excited for everyone to finish the story. It's so close to my heart.

You seemed really emotional earlier. Did you know your parents were coming tonight?

(She laughs.) Yes! I invited them, but I wasn't expecting a speech. We've gone through some stuff, and we're closer now because of it.

At this point she politely asked if she could run to the bathroom (she hadn't been able to go for hours). Her boyfriend came over as she stood, kissed her, and reminded her that he made reservations somewhere. She smiled and whispered something in his ear. He was dressed all nice in a red button-up shirt to match her. He's got ruffled light-brownish hair. Shane slipped off to the bathroom, and he sat in her seat and smiled at me.

Him: Hi!

Me: Hi?

Him: I'm here to entertain you while Shane's in the bathroom. So, you're a blogger?

Me: Yeah, Shane's my favorite author! I already finished book two. I stayed up all night the day it came out.

Him: That's amazing. I did too when she finally let me read it.

Me: (giggles) Are you a writer too? Did you work with her at *Packed!*?

Him: No, I make music, produce it, and write stuff with new artists.

Me: Oh! That's cool. Does that mean, are you—? Are you obsessed with the Beatles like Ian in the book?

Him: I mean—

(He shrugs and pulls a weird, fat, wooden-doll version of John Lennon from his pocket, grinning like a little kid with a toy, and shakes it. It rattles like there is something inside it.)

369

Him: Oh, she's coming.

(He grins again and stuffs the doll back in his pocket before he hops up. Shane shoots him a bemused look before sitting back in the chair. He leans against the wall, watching. I put my interview face back on.)

Do you have any advice for aspiring writers?

Keep going no matter how dark things seem. You'll get there!

click to continue reading

"Are we there yet?" I ask again.

"Relax, Primaveri. I've got you."

I laugh, squeezing Pilot's arm excitedly. "Okay, I'm relaxed! Can you give me a hint ... ? Have you finally managed to meet Taylor Swift at work? Are we doubling with her tonight?"

"Yep, you caught me. It's eleven p.m. on a Wednesday night, and we're headed to Taylor's apartment."

I snort, tripping over my feet a bit. "Which reminds me, we're having dinner with Leo and Jared next Friday."

"Sounds good! We have a Taboo score to settle. We shouldn't have left things all tied up last time. Is Jared cooking again?"

"He is. I am freaking pumped."

"Amazing."

I stumble and Pilot's arm tightens around me. "Careful. We're coming up on steps." I step up. "Keep stepping," he prompts. "Okay, stop. Now just walk."

A door opens, and the air warms as we step inside. Pilot lets go of me, and I tense up for a few moments.

"Can't see here, Pies," I remind him.

I feel him return to my side. "Okay," he breathes. He loosens the blindfold, and it slides down, settling around my neck.

I blink a few times, my eyes adjusting to the light. Lots of lights. Fairy lights, an endless array of them, are strung up everywhere. It takes me a second to see anything else. "Whoa," I breathe.

There's a round table at the center of the room, with things on it. Not a room—we're in a lobby. There are silver elevators all along the left wall and a receptionist desk on the right, with someone—

"Ah!" I yelp, stumbling backward over my heels. Pilot steadies me from behind.

"Shane," he starts calmly.

"What is she doing here? What are you doing here? Where are—?" I spin around, gaping. "This is—why are we here? What are we doing here? *We're done with you, spirit guide!*" I point at her accusingly.

She raises her hands in surrender. "Darling, you're fine."

"Shane." Pilot takes my elbows and turns me carefully to face him.

I crane my neck, trying to keep her in view. "You don't want to—What are we doing, Pilot?" I can't form full sentences. I grasp at the locket around my neck.

"Shane," Pilot says again. I turn back to him. "Breathe, we're okay. She's cool." He drops his forehand against mine. *She's cool?*

"I'm sorry. I'm really confused." I try to keep my voice level. My heart's pounding a mile a minute.

"She asked me if we wanted to hold on to this"—he taps the locket—"anymore, or if she could have it back."

I blink. My voice drops to a whisper. "I, I don't need, do you, do you want to keep it around?"

Pilot smiles and shakes head. He carefully moves my hair, unclasps the necklace, and places it in my palm.

I look from him to our spirit guide, still disoriented. She holds out her hand. I shuffle over slowly and drop the locket into it. "Um, thank you," I whisper.

She nods and turns away, exiting swiftly through a door behind the front desk. I pivot around to shoot Pilot a wide-eyed look.

"Pies, what, when, what's—"

He comes forward and takes my hand. He leads me toward the table I saw at the center of the room. A number of items are lined up around the edge of the small circular surface. There's a gym lock? A picture of us kissing, a key, a ceramic piece of apple pie—I shake my head and look up at him again, confused.

He takes both of my hands in his, searching my eyes. "This is where you changed my life," he says.

He gestures to the pie on the table. "On our walk home that first day in London, you called me *Pies* and rambled something about me being . . . warm?" His eyes twinkle under the lights. "That's when I first felt something shift."

He looks back at the table. "That lock is from the first time we spent the night together in Paris."

I look down at it, breathing hard now. The picture is next. Looking at it now, I see it's the one we took on our way down the crag in Edinburgh. Pilot looks from it to me. "From the day we decided to stay."

I bite at my lip. "You did all this?" My voice wavers as I gesture to the lights around us.

He points to the key sitting next to the picture. "That's the key to our shitty studio apartment." A tear escapes my eye. I loved our shitty studio apartment. I loved working near the window and being able to look over at him, a few feet away, playing on our bed. We moved to a bigger place last year, after my second book sold and Pilot got hired as a full-time producer at Stone Glass Records.

I follow the curve of the table all the way around, past a small streetlight figurine, to the last item—the John Lennon Beatles nesting doll. It's set right in front of me.

"Oh my god, where did you find that?" I blurt, pointing to it.

Pilot picks it up with a small smile. "I got it when I went back to the store the second time around."

"When you got the cards? I still can't believe you went without me," I scold.

His smile slips into a smirk.

"You've had this since then?" I ask in disbelief. He glances down at it before meeting my eyes again.

"Shane, I love you. I wanted to stop in here one more time to pay my respects to the moments that brought us to where we are."

I huff a small laugh. "I love you."

He offers John Lennon to me. My brows pull together, but I reach out slowly and take it from him.

"Open it." He smiles. I narrow my eyes before looking down at the doll.

I open John Lennon. Inside him, I open Paul. And then George. And then Ringo. Inside Ringo is a tiny wooden bowling pin–shaped guitar and . . . a ring.

It knocks the wind out of me. I look back up at Pilot, but he's not standing in front of me anymore.

He's on his knee. My jaw drops.

"I have no regrets. I have no interest in ever going back to before. I only want to move forward with you."

I shake my head in disbelief, sporting the toothiest smile of all time.

"I, I'm just." I carefully get down on my knees and take his chin in my hand. "Pilot Penn," I start softly. "Screw you, I'm never going to be able to top this move."

Acknowledgments

I can't believe I've reached this stage of my *Again, but Better* book journey. I'm writing the acknowledgments for my first novel? This is surreal. I have so many people to thank. The first two have to be my parents. Thank you for letting me study abroad. Those four months forever changed me, and the paths I would choose to take.

To my agent, JL, and my editor, Eileen, thank you for believing in this long, rambly contemporary book and continuously challenging me through the revision process. Thank you to the entire team at New Leaf and Wednesday Books.

Thank you to my best friend, Dr. Katie McCormick-Huhn, for sitting on the phone with me, brainstorming titles and names, and helping me work through any scene at all hours of the night. Thank you for being the first person to read this story, back when it was in its most primal state. Thank you for always cheering me on. Your enthusiasm and kind words were so integral to this book.

Thank you, Julia Friley. You've been reading my crap, and helping me make it better, since 2011. Thank you for constantly pushing me to cut shit out of this book, helping me with emails, and tolerating my insecure calls and texts. Thank you for picking up the phone and brainstorming major plot drama whenever I found myself in a bind. Thank you for reading Part One three separate times. This book wouldn't be the same without you.

Acknowledgments

Thank you, Kat O'Keeffe, for agreeing to be critique partners with me, even though I was such a noob. Your feedback and support are always spot-on.

Thank you, Natasha Polis, for reading Draft Three and being there to discuss these characters with me whenever I needed to. Also, thanks for that time we sat around during a thunderstorm reading the chapters aloud in the dark.

Thank you to my other best friend, Dr. Jenna Presto, for reading a huge chunk of the first draft and being my official go-to source of knowledge for all things med school.

Thanks to Tiernan Bertrand-Essington and Christina Marie for providing me with thoughtful, valuable feedback when I needed it most.

Thank you to my cousin Holly Springhorn for being the first person under twenty to read a chunk of the draft. Thank you for sending me so much love.

Jesse George, Kat O'Keeffe, Larry Lane, Sasha Alsberg, Kristina Marjieh, and Allison Gottlieb, thank you for your endless support throughout this process.

To my siblings, Olivia and Paul: If you made it to the end of this book, thank you for reading it—it means a lot. Olivia, I'm honored to have written the second book you've ever voluntarily read. I hope you're not reading this before you actually finish the book.

Thank you, Juan, for the endless encouragement in the final stages of the publishing process.

To my whole Booktube, Bookternet family, ALL OF YOU: Thank you for being the best, kindest, most welcoming, most understanding, most supportive, gorgeous friends a girl could ask for.

To my subscribers/viewers: Thank you. Thank you. Thank you. You are a perpetual source of happiness for me. You have enriched my life in every way. I hope you enjoyed my first book. I hope it made you happy in some way or another. I hope you laughed. I hope it made you want to face your fears. *AGGRESSIVELY HUGS YOU* *APOLOGIZES*

Nana, thank you for blessing me with your passion for reading. Mrs. Gearing, thank you for reading aloud to us in class and enforcing DEAR time in fourth grade. J. K. Rowling and Stephenie Meyer, thank you for the stories that made me fall in love with books.

Acknowledgments

Dearest reader, thank you for picking this up and supporting my writing endeavors. I hope *Again, but Better* brought you joy! If you're not a big reader, I hope this made you want to read more! If it didn't, please hit me up on YouTube at youtube.com/polandbananasBOOKS so I can try to turn you via video.

xoxo 2018

Behind the Scenes
with Christine Riccio

An Exclusive Q&A with Christine

In *Again, but Better*, Shane and Pilot get the opportunity to redo their year abroad in London. If given the chance, is there anything you would do over? Or do you think things happen the way they do for a reason?

There isn't! When I really start to spiral into the black hole of *what would I do over*, I can't help but panic about who I would be if everything I've been through didn't happen exactly how I've already been through it. I've day-dreamed over the years about going back to the year I studied abroad because it was such a pivotal, life-changing era for me, but the more I delved into that line of thinking the less attractive the idea became.

What was your favorite thing about writing *Again, but Better*?

My favorite thing was basically getting to study abroad again through Shane's experience. I'm past the days when I could just jump to a new country for four months and start anew, but I got to relive that excitement through writing, which was a hoot.

You have a series of videos on your YouTube account, polandbananas-BOOKS, about the process of writing Shane's story. For the readers

who haven't seen them, what was it like writing this novel of second chances?

SPOILERS AHEAD: Don't read this answer if you haven't finished the book. It was so much fun. Second chances are something we so often crave, but are very rarely given, and they're a vital part of growth! We have to give ourselves second chances all the time, to learn and move forward as smarter, more adaptive humans. What's fun about *Again, but Better* is that not only is Shane given a second chance, she's given the opportunity redo her first time in London differently. She gets to live out that reset fantasy we always think about.

What was the inspiration for *Again, but Better*?

As I've mentioned, I studied abroad, and it was the most life-changing, amazing, pivotal experience for me—and it has been that way for everyone I know who has done it. For ages afterward I raved about studying abroad in my IRL community of people—especially my siblings. But no one was moved to actually do it. My sister just didn't get it; she was too jarred by the idea of living in a different country. There's still hope for my brother, who is a sophomore in college, but he isn't completely convinced. And I came so close to not doing study abroad myself—I was petrified of leaving my environment. But *I'm so glad I did.* I want to give more people the courage to take the leap and do something new. To step outside their comfort zone. To make a change. Of course there were a bunch of other inspirations pushing me forward alongside that, but this answer is long already and I don't have the space for an essay.

What did you study when you went abroad?

I studied film and television when I was in London. That was my university major, with a concentration in screenwriting. For a long time I didn't believe in my ability to write an entire novel, and instead set my focus on writing scripts—which I also loved. My favorite part of writing any scene is the dialogue, and that's where the focus really lies in a script.

Is there a specific moment you can share when you had a breakthrough while you were writing?

SPOILERS AHEAD: Don't read this if you haven't finished the book. I'll always remember this one huge breakthrough I had during the first draft that changed the entire dynamic of the novel. I was trying to write the break into the second half of the book, and I couldn't find the right back-and-forth with Take Two Shane and Pilot. I kept rewriting the first scene. I put the laptop down one night, got in the shower, and stared at the wall for a good ten minutes with the water running down my face. Amid the steam and dribble, it hit me that I needed to take Pilot back in time as well. My initial idea was that Shane gets to do study abroad again, but bringing Pilot into the mix changed everything for the better in so many ways. I couldn't move forward until I sorted that out. As soon as I got out of the shower I sat down and wrote the scene in 2017 where Shane goes to visit Pilot and ask him to grab a cup of coffee. It was *the best breakthrough feeling*. I stayed up till three o'clock that night writing.

Can you talk about your chapter titles?

Writing the chapter titles was such a highlight of my *Again, but Better* journey! If you haven't picked up on it, or just blew past the titles like I sometimes do when reading, they're all references to songs. Like a lot of authors, music is an integral part of my writing process. I tend to categorize my scenes via song lyric. When it came time to divide the book into chapters, I'd assess each chapter, a song would rise to the forefront of my brain, and I'd pick out the lyric from that song that sounded most appropriate as the title! As I got further in the editing process I started playing each song as I was rereading the chapter named for it, and it made revision way more fun. If you have any interest in reading to music, I've created an entire playlist on Spotify called "Again, but Better."

Music plays a big part in the story. If you were to study abroad right now what would your top six playlist songs be?

It does! I tend to associate my own time studying abroad with the slew of songs that I had in my ears 24/7; I did a lot of walking and I had my iPod in at all times! The top six would be:

1) "Price Tag"—Jessie J feat. B.o.B
2) "A Hard Day's Night"—The Beatles
3) "Hold It Against Me"—Britney Spears
4) "Hello"—Martin Solveig feat. Dragonette
5) "Everybody Hurts"—Avril Lavigne
6) "Smile"—Avril Lavigne

Deleted Scenes

1. The Letter

January 16, 2011

Dear Melvin,

This is so hard to write. My name's Shane. You don't know me yet. But, if we ever do meet, I'm breaking up with you.

Gah, that sounded abrupt. I'm sorry! I don't mean to be abrupt, but there's really no easy way to say I'm breaking up with you!

We start dating in late 2012, but I need to make it clear now that we're not dating. And we won't be dating in the future either, because this is me breaking up with you infinitely and forever.

I've recently been involved in a time-travel situation and we were dating in my original timeline, so the lines are weirdly blurred. I'm going to start seeing someone else, and I can't date you. I'm really sorry!

To be clear, I was going to break up with you even if I didn't start dating this new guy. I don't mean to be harsh! I just finally realized we're really wrong for each other.

Also, to be fully transparent, this guy isn't completely new. We studied abroad together back in college and we kind of reconnected in this time-travel situation.

To continue with the transparency—this guy and I kissed the other night, but it was unexpected and I'm now here writing to you. I'm sorry to have betrayed the trust of our relationship! I honestly didn't realize I was doing anything wrong because 2011-you doesn't know about our relationship yet, but now I don't know! I don't know! I'm really sorry.

I don't like eggs, Melvin. I know you hate asparagus and olives. Why can't you remember I hate eggs? Like, I've said it at least ten times over the last few years, Melvin. Why? Why!

Sorry. I didn't mean to get angry, but I wanted to give you a little context about our relationship so maybe you can grow from this experience. Also, you always think it's okay to use my towel when you shower. Melvin, that's not okay. There are clean ones in the closet; use your big brain and get one before you go into the bathroom.

So, in conclusion, we're no longer dating and never will be from this point onward. We are broken up. Sorry! Please don't ask me out if you see me.

I would attach a picture for reference, but I don't have access to a color printer right now. I'm average height, with poofy blond hair and gray eyes. Avoid Shanes.

You asked me to marry you the last time we spoke, and I'm sorry but the answer is no.

Bleh, this is so awkward. Bye!

xoxo
Shane

(To clarify, I don't mean those xo's as actual kisses and hugs, because we've broken up. I'm going to start dating someone else.)

2. The Video

An Energizer bunny drums in my chest as I brush my hair and teeth while simultaneously brainstorming new lyrics for our cover. Pilot agreed to Hot Tub Time Machine for YouTube and I can't quite shake the thrills of victory and mischief running through me. I keep bouncing on my toes like I'm prepping to leap into double-Dutch ropes.

I dig out my old red Revlon lipstick and smile nostalgically as I smack my lips together. It tastes like watermelon. I pull on my old favorite black high-waisted skirt and sleeveless white top. This wardrobe is severely lacking in the nice-clothes department. Once dressed, I use my remaining ten minutes to scribble out lyrics on the back of a class syllabus.

Precisely on time I'm outside Pilot's door, armed with a camera, lyrics, and an enormous amount of enthusiasm. I rap the wood.

"It's open," he calls.

I twist the knob and quickly step inside, closing the door behind me. His guitar's in his lap, and he's still sporting one of his plaid long-sleeved shirts. He smiles up at me. "Look at you all fancy."

I plop down next to him, grinning. "Look at you in classic Pilot garb. I figured I'd snazz it up a bit for my YouTube debut."

He bobs his head. "I like it. So what now, Internet Guru?"

"Now we film!" I hop back up and pull his desk chair out. I position it in front of the bed then assess the rest of the room. Atticus has a ton of books on his side. I snatch a stack of them. "How long do you think we've got till Atticus comes back?"

"Are you planning to rob him?" His words brim with amusement.

I drop the books on the desk chair and reach over to grab a couple more. "Yep, you caught me. This relationship has been a ploy to acquire Atticus's book collection." I shoot Pilot a wry look.

He smirks back at me. "Two dry, sarcastic remarks within the span of an hour, Primaveri. Look at you go."

"Can it, Penn, I'm working." I smile to myself, studiously placing my little Casio camera atop the newly formed book tower. I scoot to the other side of the chair and take a second to frame the shot.

When I look up, Pilot's looking at me like I'm the most desirable being that exists. The magnetic pull I feel around him rumbles through me as I meet his gaze. We study each other for a moment.

"Are you going to come back over here now?"

"I am." I nod, take the few steps back to his bed, and sit next to him, suddenly feeling the need to tell him things. "You know, there's something I've kind of wanted to say since you told me something on our way to Paris."

Pilot's smirk deflates into concern, and he lowers Lucy carefully. "Tell me."

I shake my head, grinning. "It's nothing bad, it's just that you said those things on the tube about knowing me.

"I've wanted to say, I know you too. I know you own about twenty different plaid shirts. I know you don't like it when people touch your guitar. You tolerate Twitter and Facebook, but social media makes you uncomfortable. You put up a super-cool front, but you're a closet nerd. You care about things more than you like to let on. Your eyes are kind of like if you were to shine a flashlight through a jar of pickles. I knew enough to know you back then, and I want to keep . . . knowing more."

He blinks, coming closer, lips curling up at the edges. "I'd really like to kiss you right now—"

I pull back, tamping down the urge to scoot closer. "But yo[u] because we're about to film and I'm wearing lipstick. Also, maybe d[o] anything else. I shouldn't have gotten gushy, I gotta direct this sho[ot] pickle eyes are distracting me."

Pilot's head falls back with a "Pfft." He beams down at the be[d] low. "Not fair, Primaveri."

I want to touch his face. I clear my throat. "So I wrote down o[ur] on here nice and bold so we can see them." I pull my legs up crissc[ross] plesauce and offer him my scrap paper. He unfolds it gingerly and [reads] my notes.

After a moment he meets my eyes over the top of the page. "T[he] grand plan to kick off my music career?"

I snatch the paper back. "I had to change some of the words f[or] right reasons."

He bites back a smile. "These new ones are so . . . artsy."

"Don't worry, it's gonna be great."

"Okay."

We take a few minutes to discuss which parts each of us will s[ing] 1, verse 2, the chorus, when he'll come in, and when we'll sing [together] While we do this his hand sits on my knee. It occasionally mov[es] down, giving me a reassuring squeeze. All the while waves of glit[ter shim] mer through me. It slows my progress, but I eventually get all [of it] scribbled down along the edges of the paper. When we're good a[nd ready] I get up and hit the record button. Pilot positions his guitar, wa[iting] as I make my way back to the edge of the bed.

"Okay." I swallow and place the lyrics precariously against [the] tower tripod in front of us. Pilot leans forward to get a better v[iew of the] words. I look at the camera, feeling slightly feverish with exciter[ment.]

"Okay." He smiles to himself.

He starts to play. I close my eyes for a moment, sinking int[o the flow] ing notes. When my cue comes, I suck in a deep breath and go[:] *tweeted, we waved, our hearts, in vain, we krumped, never asking [why,]* to Pilot. *"We hugged, I fell, onto your belt. It hurt, no one can deny.[. . ."]*

Pilot stops playing and deadpans to camera, "What is *krum[ping?]*

391

I exhale an amused huff. "*Don't you ever say—*"

Pilot joins me. "*I just walked away, I will make you beef stew.*" Goose bumps run over my arms. His singing voice is huskier, deeper than his speaking voice.

I sing, "*I can't eat a pie.*"

He sings, "*Running for my life.*"

I look to him dramatically. "*That would wear down my shoes.*"

He stops playing again. "You know stew is not a pie."

I narrow my eyes at him, and together we turn to belt toward the camera: "*I came into the dining hall! I never sat so hard in gum. You just looked at me and I said yum.*" Pilot snort-laughs mid-lyric, but I continue and he joins back in. "*What you never did was, te-eh-ext me. Why not teh-eh-ext me?*"

Pilot starts the next verse. "*I put Wi-Fi up in the sky, you said, you would be on AIM. I felt misled, you broke my bed, and now we're apples on the ground.*"

Together we sing, "*Don't you ever say, I just walked away, I would make you beef stew.*"

He sings, "*I can't eat a pie.*"

I sing, "*Running for my life.*"

Pilot struggles not to break composure. "*That would wear down my shoes.*"

We both heave in a breath. "*I CAME INTO THE DINING HALL! I NEVER SAT SO HARD IN GUM. YOU JUST LOOKED AT ME AND I SAID YUM, WHAT YOU NEVER DID WAS TE-EH-EXT ME!*"

I'm breathless. "*I came into the dining hall! Yeah, I just closed my eyes and krumped.*"

He sings, "*I am sorry that I said mean stuff!*"

We sing to each other again, "*What you never did was te-eh-ext me, when will you, te-eh-ext me?*"

Pilot stops playing.

I hesitate.

He picks up his phone. "Sorry, just checking for texts."

I snort and turn my attention back to the camera. "*I never meant to be a chore. I just wanted you to let me in. You had already knocked on the door. I guess I should have opened it.*"

Pilot shifts with his guitar to look straight at me, the mirthful glint in his expression fading. "*I never meant to start a war. I just wanted you to let me in. I guess I should have let you in.*"

Wrong lyrics. He holds my eyes and I join him. "*Don't you ever say I just walked away, I will always want you.*"

My heart swells like in *How the Grinch Stole Christmas.*

2013 | Marissa, High School Sophomore

"Marissa!" Caroline's voice is frantic through the phone.

"Yeah," Marisa answers calmly from her couch.

"You know that song we used to belt everywhere in middle school?"

"What song?"

"The YouTube one! Plaid shirt guy's channel."

"'I Came into the Dining Hall'?"

"Yeah! *I never sat so hard in gum!*"

"Yeah."

"GO LISTEN TO MILEY'S NEW SONG."

"Why?"

"Pull it up on your laptop."

Marisa reluctantly opens Spotify. "'Wrecking Ball'?"

"That one."

Marisa presses play and listens for thirty seconds. "What the?" She hits pause and her cursor races to open a new tab. She pulls up YouTube. Opens the video she and Caroline watched religiously for weeks after stumbling across it on Tumblr. "I Came into the Dining Hall": 8,423 views.

"What the hell!"

"I have no words," Caroline blurts.

"I can't—'wreck me'? ALL YOU NEVER DID WAS TEXT ME. IT'S TEXT ME!"

"Yeah, her lyrics are way less nuanced."